"A gifted storyteller."

—*Kirkus Reviews*

"Rebecca Yarros writes words that are pure, sweet, sizzling poetry."
—Tessa Bailey, *New York Times* and *USA Today* bestselling author

"Readers will be *wowed*."

—*Publishers Weekly* (starred review), on
The Things We Leave Unfinished

"A haunting, heartbreaking, and ultimately inspirational love story."
—*In Touch Weekly*, on *The Last Letter*

"Thanks to Yarros's beautiful, immersive writing, readers will feel every deep heartbreak and each moment of uplifting love."
—*Publishers Weekly* (starred review), on *The Last Letter*

"Rebecca never disappoints—she's an automatic one-click for me!"
—Jen McLaughlin, *New York Times* bestselling author

VARIATION

Flight & Glory

Full Measures

Eyes Turned Skyward

Beyond What Is Given

Hallowed Ground

The Reality of Everything

Legacy

Point of Origin

Ignite

Reason to Believe

The Renegades

Wilder

Nova

Rebel

VARIATION

A novel

REBECCA
YARROS

Text copyright © 2024 by Rebecca Yarros
All rights reserved.

Published by Montlake, Seattle

www.apub.com

Amazon, the Amazon logo, and Montlake are trademarks of Amazon.com, Inc., or its affiliates.

ISBN-13: 9781662514708 (paperback)
ISBN-13: 9781662514692 (digital)

Cover design by Caroline Teagle Johnson
Cover image: © Rebecca King / Arcangel

Printed in the United States of America

CHAPTER ONE

Hudson

Eleven years ago

On days like this, I understood why seventy-three percent of candidates for rescue swimmer school didn't make it through training. I had two summers left to make sure I'd be in the twenty-seven percent who would.

The afternoon weather off the southern coast of Cape Cod served up six-foot seas, complete with whitecaps and a side of hypothermia for Memorial Day. It might have been miserable and challenging, but it was the perfect weather for practice.

Tired had hit twenty minutes ago, exhaustion followed ten minutes later, and I was quickly approaching full-out ruin, but I needed five more minutes. Another hundred yards would put me past my personal best in these kinds of swells, and I wasn't quitting until I hit that mark.

Three hundred seconds was nothing in the scheme of things.

I concentrated on my breath work, kept my head down, and swam forward, counting each of those seconds. At two hundred and eleven, I sucked in a breath of pure salt water and came up coughing, ripping out my mouthpiece as soon as I was free of the swell that had overtaken the tube of the snorkel.

"Hudson!" Gavin shouted from my left, killing the motor of the twenty-three-foot fishing boat our father lovingly referred to as his fourth child, though she'd qualify as his first, given her age. "Enough for the day."

"I need another thirty yards for a personal best," I called back, treading water through the next swell.

"You need to get your ass in the boat before the swells get any higher," he countered, looking over his sunglasses from the dashboard despite the overcast sky. "You're wrecked. Thirty yards isn't going to happen."

"Go to hell." I popped my mouthpiece in and prepared to go again just to prove I could.

"This hangover is kicking my ass, and unless you want Caroline at the helm for your next practice session, you'll get in here before I have to circle back in this current." He walked toward the stern as the boat drifted, then leaned over and unfastened the swinging top of the ladder before pushing it into the water.

Shit. He wasn't kidding.

Our older sister was a clucking mother hen who would never remotely consider bringing me out in seas like this, which meant the personal best was going to have to wait. Frustration kept me warm for the next handful of strokes as I made my way toward the boat. Then I timed the stern's rise and fall with the swells before heaving myself up the three-rung ladder.

"I've missed you and I'm glad you're home, but you suck. I almost had it." I climbed over the narrow swimming deck and onto the towel-covered seat, then pulled up the ladder. Dad would murder us if we didn't protect the faded leather. The boat pitched again as I ripped off my face mask, then the hood of my wet suit, and tossed them into the black canvas duffel near Gavin's feet.

"You wound me, little brother." He touched his chest sarcastically and held on to the back of the driver's seat with the next swell. "Let's get home so I can listen to the lecture Dad's been working on all day.

I'd hate for him to go to all that work and have no one to deliver his speech to."

"He's just . . ." Words failed me, just like they had since he'd announced his decision in the middle of our parents' café this morning.

"Disappointed that I'm dropping out of college," Gavin supplied. "Unlike Caroline, who managed to get her degree while married and holding down *two* jobs."

"Don't compare yourself to our sister, and give Dad a break. He's just stunned." I peeled off the rest of my suit, leaving me in a pair of his old Hawaiian-print trunks once I ditched the diving socks too.

"I changed my major four times in two years," Gavin said, reaching above the wheel for my Bruins cap. "Trust me, Dad isn't shocked."

Good point. Gavin was known for a good time, not for sticking things out.

"You could spend the night at Caroline and Sean's while Mom smooths it over." I made my way over the salt-and-sun-worn deck carpet toward him.

"I'm not leaving Mom with my mess. Subject change." A smile curved Gavin's mouth. "You're barely seventeen and here you are dumping your savings into a new wet suit. It's like you're trying to actually swim your way to Alaska. Don't think I didn't notice that map above your bed."

"Some dreams don't change." I'd stumbled onto a documentary three years ago and wanted to be a rescue swimmer stationed in Sitka ever since. Helping people? Check. Adrenaline? Check. Moving to the other side of the country from the only place I'd ever lived? Check. I grabbed the towel from the back seat, then ran it over my head and chest before dragging a T-shirt on. "And thank you for bringing me out. Dad gets busy."

"I'll bring you every day if it helps." Gavin shoved my hat at my chest, keeping perfect balance as the boat heaved.

"Thanks." I knew better than to take him at his word. He had the best of intentions, but follow-through wasn't his strong suit. "The practice is probably a little overkill, but it gives me something to work for." Goose bumps rose along my arms with the breeze as I set my hat on backward. Sixty-four degrees was a high for this time of year, but it was still fucking freezing right out of the water.

"Which I respect." He turned the key, starting the engine but keeping it in idle as he looked past me. "Is that a *rowboat*?"

"Out here? No way." My head whipped to follow his line of sight, and I quickly spotted the small vessel about a hundred meters west, with what looked to be a small outboard motor and two people . . . ducking?

"What the hell are they doing?" Gavin asked as the boaters blinked in and out between the swells, repeatedly leaned down in what had to be their seats. "Bobbing?"

My stomach sank like a boulder thrown overboard, and I grabbed the binoculars from the glove box and peered through the lenses at the other boat.

Damn it. Two girls about my age sat in the middle of what looked to be a fourteen-footer with a tiny outbound motor that had seen better days, scooping out water with their bare hands. "They aren't bobbing, they're bailing." And neither of the brunettes was wearing a life jacket. I handed Gavin the binoculars, and he lifted them to his eyes. "We have to help."

"Well, shit." Gavin threw the binoculars into the glove box and slammed it shut. "Hold on."

I braced one hand on the edge of the windshield and the other on the dashboard's handrailing as Gavin punched the throttle.

The front of our boat kissed the sky before Gavin adjusted the trim, and we nearly planed as the boat came level, but there was no softening the swells' blows against the hull. After the third bone-jarring hit nearly threw us sideways, Gavin swore and adjusted our approach.

"We'll have to come at them—" he started.

"With the current," I finished. Spray drenched the windshield with every wave. I kept my eyes locked on the vessel, and fear shot through me, quickly chased by adrenaline as the little boat tipped downward with the next swell and water rushed over the bow.

If they'd been in trouble before, they were in imminent danger now.

I moved to starboard behind Gavin and flipped up the back passenger seat as he pulled back on the throttle and slowed our approach. Boats didn't exactly have brakes. You had to be *kidding* me. "There are only two life jackets?"

"Only two of us on board," Gavin called back as we slowed to idle about twenty meters off the vessel's port side.

I yanked on one of the bright-yellow vests and fastened the three clips across my torso, then reached for the second and did the same, yanking on the tabs to expand the size to fit over the first. "Can you get us closer?"

"Not without drifting right into them or past them," he answered, taking off his sunglasses. "Fuck, I think they're—"

"Help!" the girl in the pink shirt shouted, standing at the bow of the violently rocking boat and waving her hands frantically as if there was some chance we *hadn't* seen them.

My eyes widened. "Sit down!" What the hell was she thinking?

"Give me a jacket." Gavin stuck out his hand.

The girl sitting in the back lunged for the other one, but the damage was done, and the next swell came over the side of the already destabilized boat and capsized it.

The girls disappeared into the water, and my heart lurched.

"I'm going." I climbed onto the passenger seat. There was no time to wait.

"Like hell you are. I'm not letting you—"

I dove.

With a wet suit, the water had been barely tolerable. Without it, the temperature hit like a punch to the gut, and I fought to keep the air in my lungs. The life jackets tugged me upward, and I drew in a full breath as soon as I broke the surface, salt stinging my eyes.

"Damn it, Hudson!" Gavin shouted from somewhere behind me, but I was too focused on swimming to answer.

Please, God, let them both be alive.

I moved faster than ever, even encumbered by the jackets, fueled by adrenaline and terror at what was waiting for me.

My heart pounded as I approached the bow of the capsized boat and found the two women clinging to the side. Their hands gripped the ridge along the bottom of the shallow hull, and relief stole my words. They were fine. In a precarious but deteriorating situation, but alive and . . . arguing?

"I didn't *know* it had a hole!" the one in the pink shirt shrieked at the girl in green, who had her back turned toward me. "Or that it was low on gas, and I certainly didn't ask you to jump in as I left the boathouse!"

"Of course I jumped in," the one in the green replied, her voice surprisingly calm despite the distinct sound of chattering teeth. "I thought I could stop you. Dad told us to *never* take this boat."

"I just wanted a few minutes away from *her*!" the girl in pink wailed. "And now she's going to kill us both when she finds out we sank the boat!"

"Feel like getting out of here?" I asked, my chest heaving beneath the jackets as I swam around the side of the vessel.

Both women snapped their heads my direction, soaked ponytails flinging water as they looked over their shoulders at me.

It was the streak of red down the closest girl's temple that caught my attention, but it was her eyes that kept it. They were almost too big for her heart-shaped face, the color of straight-up whiskey, and bordered by thick, water-spiked lashes that lowered as her focus swept over me and lingered on the buckles at the top of my chest.

The second her gaze lifted to lock with mine, I forgot how to fucking *breathe*, let alone think. I'd never been hit by lightning, but I bet this was what it felt like. And she was bleeding. Right. *Get ahold of yourself.*

"You're hurt—" I started, my chest tightening with a completely irrational amount of worry.

"Oh thank God!" The girl in pink pushed off the boat and flung herself my direction.

I caught her on pure instinct.

"I'm only fourteen, and that's entirely too young to die just because I didn't check the gas . . . or the boat," the girl in pink declared dramatically, clutching my shoulders as she looked up at me with frightened brown eyes. "And I don't swim very well."

And she'd come out on an ancient rowboat without a life jacket? "Give me a second and we'll get you sorted." I kicked toward the boat. "Hold on like your life depends on it."

The girl drew back her head in indignation, her jaw practically unhinging.

"He's wearing two life jackets, Eva," the girl with the whiskey eyes said quietly. "You need to get one of them on before he can take you back to his boat."

"Oh. Of course." Eva grabbed hold of the hull as another swell lifted, then dropped us but didn't submerge the vessel. "You'll come back for Allie, right?"

"I'll be fine, Eva—" the other started to argue.

"Actually, I think I need to take you back first," I said to the girl in green—who I assumed was Allie—as the cold seeped into my very bones.

"She's sixteen, and she swims way better than I do." Eva's voice rose.

"That's absolutely true." Allie's teeth chattered. "Please take Eva. I'll wait."

"You're *bleeding*, and we don't have time to argue." I kicked to stay between them as the current dragged us along.

"It's just my scalp, not my legs. I'll be fine." Her worried gaze darted toward Eva.

"I'm sorry?" In what world was a head wound better than one to an extremity?

"She really doesn't swim well. Please get her out of here," Allie pleaded, pink water dripping off her jaw. "What's your name?"

"Hudson Ellis." This was taking too long. I undid the top set of buckles, and Eva snatched the jacket as soon as it cleared my shoulders. "Hey—"

"Hudson." Allie's teeth chattered. "I'm Alessandra. I don't know if you have siblings, but there's nothing more important to me than my sisters."

Sisters. That explained her refusal.

"Except dancing," Eva muttered, shoving her arms into the life jacket one by one as another swell rocked us.

"*Nothing*," Alessandra repeated, holding my gaze hostage. "You have to take my little sister first. Please. I can't leave her here." Fear streaked through her eyes, knitting her brow and pursing her lips, but she raised her pointed chin. "I won't go until she does."

Shit. Just like I could never leave Caroline or Gavin. I understood that need on a cellular, primal level. We might give each other shit, but we showed up for each other come hell or high water, and Alessandra felt just as vehemently about her siblings as I did. Something inside my chest cracked open, and every ounce of my common sense must have spilled out into the water, because that one simple demand made me feel like I *knew* her.

"I have siblings," I said, reaching for the next set of buckles. "I get it."

Her eyes quickly narrowed in confusion. "What are you doing?"

I shrugged my right arm out of the jacket, then reached up to hold on to the boat between them before sliding the rest of the yellow neoprene-covered flotation device off my left arm and offering it to her. "Put it on."

"No." She glanced down at the jacket and back to me. "You need that. The waves are too high."

"I don't. I'm a great swimmer, and this is the only compromise I can think of." I gave her what I hoped was a reassuring smile. "It will take us less than five minutes to get you both in the boat."

"Five minutes?" Eva panicked.

"Less than," I repeated, keeping my eyes on Alessandra. "Anything is doable for five minutes. I'll stay with you both the entire time. Take the jacket." It went against everything I'd ever read about performing rescues, but I couldn't bring myself to give a shit.

"I can't do that to you." She shook her head.

"I'm a stranger," I reminded her.

"No. You're Hudson Ellis." Her arms trembled.

"Then we're at an impasse, because you won't leave your sister and I won't leave you." I pushed the life jacket toward her. "I'm pretty stubborn, so all waiting does is prolong the time you're both in the water."

"Come on, Allie, I'm *freezing*!" Eva cajoled.

Alessandra took the jacket, and once she had it on, all three of us swam toward Gavin.

By the time I got the girls into the boat, both their lips carried a bluish tinge, and the waves had devoured whatever was left of their rowboat.

"What the fuck were you thinking?" Gavin snapped at me.

"They're alive." I gave my black Rip Curl hoodie to Alessandra despite her initial protest, then handed almost every towel we had to Eva before sitting them both down. "We should get you to a doctor."

Alessandra shook her head, zipping up my sweatshirt. "Our mother will realize we're gone."

Seriously? My eyebrows hit my hairline.

"If you need a doctor, then we have to go," Eva whispered.

"I don't," Alessandra assured, her tone sharpening toward her sister. "Can you imagine what she'll do to us?"

The fuck? Even when Gav and I were caught doing something we weren't supposed to, Mom's first reaction was always relief that our idiocy hadn't killed us.

"We could just call Dad. Wait. You're not going to tell her that I—" Eva started, her eyes filling with panic.

"I *never* tell her, do I?" Alessandra retorted, her hands disappearing into the sleeves of my hoodie. The damned thing was practically a dress on her.

"Can I look at your head?" Gavin asked, brushing past me as the boat rocked. Our hull was deeper than the little rowboat, but we shouldn't be out here much longer with this storm coming in.

Alessandra nodded, and Gavin leaned over her, examining the wound.

"It's small and has already stopped bleeding. Probably doesn't need stitches," he announced, then shot me a look that said we'd talk about my choices later.

"Can you please take us home?" Alessandra's shoulders straightened, and she composed herself with a speed that was both impressive and a little jarring, but her eyes were a dead giveaway that she wasn't as calm as she wanted us to think. *Almost like she's performing.* "We live—"

"I know where you live," Gavin interrupted with a grimace. "We'll take you."

He did? My gaze jumped his way.

"Thank you." Alessandra tucked her knees up into my sweatshirt, and her gaze flickered toward mine. "Really. Thank you, Hudson."

"No problem." Damn, I liked the way she said my name.

"We're about fifteen minutes out." Gavin looked over at me, then motioned toward the console, and I followed him to the seats behind the dashboard. "That was fucking reckless." He shook his head at me, and I barely had time to grab ahold of the handrail as he put the throttle down, heading toward the cliffs at the west side of town, past the local beaches. "And watch the way you're looking at her. You know who they are, right?" Gavin asked, just loud enough for me to hear, but not them.

"No, but obviously you do," I replied, rubbing my towel over my arms to get the blood moving. Fuck, it was cold. "And I'm not *looking* at her." It wasn't exactly a lie since I was faced forward.

"I watched that whole thing go down. You're looking." He scoffed. "And it's just going to get you in trouble. They're the youngest Rousseau girls. Alessandra and Eva, if I'm remembering correctly. Forget asking her out, if that's what you're thinking. Their parents don't let them interact with anyone outside their social circle, let alone locals."

Rousseau. One of the families with summerhouses on the cliffside. Old money.

My chest went all wonky. "The ballerinas." No wonder I didn't recognize them. They trained here every summer, but mostly under lock and key until their mother trotted them out in August for the competition that brought an onslaught of dancing tourists and their rich families every year. "There's four of them, right?" Pretty sure I'd seen a couple of them in the café once or twice when I dropped in, but I usually spent my summers lifeguarding at the beach.

"Yep," he confirmed. "And you've got your eye on who Lina calls the *quiet* one, so just don't."

"Who's Lina?" It was hard to think of Alessandra as quiet after the way she'd just argued on Eva's behalf.

He flinched. "The oldest. Nineteen, incredibly talented, and gorgeous, and so *fucking* frustrating. She's got walls ten feet thick, and unfortunately for you, I think they run in the family."

"Clearly they interact with *some* locals." I shot him a knowing look.

"Alessandra isn't Lina. She's not going to break rules," Gavin said as we cut across the current. "And this little rescue stays between us, because Caroline fucking *hates* them. Something about a milkshake incident and them being entitled."

Shit. The last thing I wanted was to hurt Caroline's feelings. "Doubt it was Alessandra." Maybe I'd only spent five minutes with her, but she hardly seemed entitled.

"So much for not looking at her. And seriously, they're not allowed to date, and I don't want to watch you get all angsty over there." Gavin rolled his eyes, then mercifully stopped digging.

I looked over my shoulder and found Alessandra watching me in a way that made me think noticing the two life jackets wasn't an anomaly for her. I'd bet she was always that aware, that attuned to detail.

Observant could easily be mistaken for quiet, especially with that many siblings around.

She tilted her head, and I was struck straight in the ribs with the illogical need for more time with her. Not romantically, of course—she was entirely out of my league. I wanted to know what kind of music she listened to, what books she liked, which movies were her favorite. I wanted to know if she minded the way she was kept sequestered, and what made her smile. And the closer we came to the cliffs, the more my chest tightened.

Whatever I said or did in the next five minutes would determine if I ever got the chance to actually know her, or if this would be a one-time encounter that always left me wondering.

She hugged her knees to her chest with one hand and held on to the handrail with the other, then looked away when her sister said something I couldn't hear.

When we finally made it to a massive ocean-side pier and boathouse at the base of the cliffs on which most of the summer mansions sat, there were two brunettes waiting, one worried and one furious.

"She's pissed," Gavin muttered, staring up at the angry one as we approached on the port side of the pier. "How's it going, Lina?" he called up, idling the engine when we reached drifting distance. The next couple of waves would put us at the ladder, and if Gav misjudged the distance, Dad was going to murder us.

"You have my sisters in your boat, so that about explains it." Lina put her hands on her hips. "Though I'll admit it's nice to see you, Gavin."

"Noted." Holy shit—was my brother *blushing*?

"How do you know them?" Eva shouted up as I moved to starboard and threw out the buoys so we didn't crush the hull against the pier, then leaned over the hull, preparing to catch the ladder and hold on.

"None of your business," Lina retorted. "Now, thank the Ellis boys and get up this ladder—oh shit, Allie, are you hurt?" She dropped to her knees above us, looking over the edge of the pier as we rocked in toward the ladder.

"She's hurt?" The other sister immediately joined Lina. "How badly? Can you make it up the ladder?"

"It's nothing to worry about, Anne," Alessandra answered. "I promise."

I grabbed hold of the thick ladder, and the wood groaned as I caught the weight of the boat, quickly looping a rope around the entirety and tying us off at the middle cleat so the next wave didn't carry us away or take out the structure.

"She knows them? Lina sneaks out?" Eva hissed at Alessandra, and Gavin cut the engine.

"Sounds like it," Allie replied, biting back a smile as she and Eva made their way toward me. "Good for her."

A spark of hope lit off in my chest like a firecracker. Maybe Gavin was right and she wasn't a rule breaker, but I bet she just might be a rule *bender*.

Eva dumped her wet towels on the floor of the boat, then muttered her thanks and scrambled onto the ladder between waves. The next swell splashed water over the swimming deck and onto the seats.

"You should get up there before the next one hits," Gavin said to Alessandra, and I seriously debated punching my brother in the face.

"Right. Thank you for coming after us." She offered me a quick smile.

"You're welcome." I offered my hand to help her, but she was already climbing over the seat, making it to the ladder effortlessly.

She cleared a few rungs before the next wave came along, then looked down with a grimace as a smaller wave rocked us. "Crap. I'm still wearing your hoodie."

"Two choices." I grinned up at her. "Keep it or bring it for the next time I take you boating."

"Fucking bold," Gavin muttered under his breath.

It was, but I had maybe ten seconds before the next wave.

"I . . ." Her mouth opened and shut twice. "I'm not allowed to date, and I'm only here for the summer."

"I figured." My grin widened. "Can you have friends for the summer?"

Her brow knit. "Debatable. I'm not really good with people."

"Just drop a note by the Ellis—the café—if you decide it's worth debating, Alessandra." I reached for the cleat and untied us, keeping my eyes on her.

"All right." She smiled, and I had to remind my heartbeat that we were only ever going to be friends, if that. "A friend would call me Allie."

Hell yes.

"Allie it is." I slipped the rope free of the ladder as Gavin started the engine.

She shook her head like she couldn't believe she'd just admitted to *thinking* about bending the rules, and climbed the ladder toward her sisters.

By the end of that summer, she was my best friend.

By the end of the next, she hated me.

And I didn't blame her.

CHAPTER TWO

Allie

Fifteen months later

My vision wobbled and my ears rang. What had just happened?

"You're okay," Lina promised, holding something against my head as liquid dripped down the side of my face. "You're going to be okay, Allie. You just have to hold on. I'm so sorry. I never should have taken the curve that fast."

Flames danced in the corner of my eye as I looked up at my sister, but I couldn't find words. The acrid scent of smoke and melted rubber singed my lungs with every breath.

Lina smiled down at me. "I love you, Allie. I'm so sorry."

I opened my mouth to tell her that I loved her, too, but all that came out was a whimper as pain rushed over me, blaring from my head and radiating up my leg. I tried to move, but while my left foot caught the grassy edge of the embankment just enough to jar the rest of my body, my right foot wouldn't respond. Where were we? The edge of a road? Why was I so cold?

"Listen to me," Lina ordered, her tone sharpening, and everything spun for a second before she came back into focus, but some of her words disappeared into the incessant ringing that split my head. She put more pressure above my temple. "Follow your heart, and take care of what I'm leaving behind."

Leaving? Why would she leave us? How was I supposed to take care of Anne and Eva? They needed her, not me. Lina was the one we all looked to.

"You have to live." Lina slipped her ring—Mom's ring—off her hand, and stuck it in the pocket of my white skirt.

At least it had been white. Now it was brown and gray in places, and red in others.

Lina lifted my hands to the bundle of fabric pressed against my head. "I love you. Don't move. Help is coming, just wait right here." She stood and brushed off the hem of her blue dress, then ran down the edge of the embankment, her long brown hair flying behind her as she broke into a sprint.

Stay. The word was clear as day in my head, but my lips didn't move.

Flames rose into the night sky, licking up the limbs of the gnarled tree Lina ran toward.

Not just a tree . . . Lina's car. It was crumpled against the base of the trunk, passenger door wide open, and fire rose from the sides of the mangled hood.

An accident. We'd been in an accident. What the hell was she doing?

No. I tried to scream, but nothing came out as Lina raced to the driver's side. Didn't she see the flames?

What could possibly be so important in the car?

Oh *God*, were Anne and Eva with—

Boom. Heat rushed against my face and lit up the night.

The car exploded.

CHAPTER THREE

Allie

ReeseOnToe: OMG, she's the best. I'm watching her dance Giselle tonight and I can't wait!

Ten years later

My finger hesitated over my favorite playlist. Tonight wasn't the night to take chances, so I tapped the routine selection below it before setting my phone beside me on the blanket. Picking up the needle and thread, I got to work.

Stab. Push. Pull. Stab. Push. Pull.

Adolphe Adam's *Giselle* played in my earbuds, the familiar music drowning out every thought besides the performance to come. I'd been a second late on the diagonal hops during the first act's variation last night, and that couldn't happen again. Muscle memory guided my hands as I stitched the bottom of my tights to one of the pointe shoes I'd prepared for opening night.

It should have been Lina here, not me. She'd been perfect for this role, as our mother had no trouble reminding me over the last three months of rehearsal.

Stab. Push. Pull. I stitched as if the thread could hold closed the decade-old wound of grief that never quite healed.

Bad ankle be damned, everything tonight had to be perfect.

Mom was coming, and the flaws would be all she remembered from the performance. My hand trembled, and the needle poked through the fabric and bit the tip of my finger. I swore at the sharp sting, whipped the digit to my mouth on instinct, then checked for damage. Thankfully, the skin was insulted but not broken.

Everything in my life had led up to this moment. Every hour at the barre. Every broken toenail—and toe, every month of rehab after the accident, even the tendinitis that never seemed to actually heal. For *this* role on *this* stage with *this* company, I'd sacrificed my body, my time, my mental health, and any semblance of a normal relationship with the very woman I was desperate to make proud tonight.

I'd sacrificed *him*. A familiar ache pulsed in time with my heartbeat, far more painful than the needle's bite. Or had he sacrificed me? My hand paused.

"You all right over there?"

The music muffled Eva's question, so I popped out an earbud and looked over my shoulder at where she sat perched on the only chair in my dressing room. My little sister's sharp brown eyes locked with mine in the vanity mirror as she lifted her lip liner mid-application.

"Allie?" She arched a painted eyebrow. Eva may have looked like the sweetest of us with her heart-shaped face, dainty features, and round eyes that could feign innocence with startling plausibility, but she was the quickest of the Rousseau sisters to strike when wounded . . . or just inconvenienced.

It was only fitting that she looked the most like our mother, seeing as Mom had a talent for drawing first blood.

"I'm fine." I presented a polished smile. Fixating on Mom right now wasn't an option. If I did, my heart would race, my breathing would falter, and my throat would close up like . . .

Crap. Arching my neck, I swallowed the growing knot in my throat. *Like that.* I breathed in through my nose and out through my mouth to dispel the knot and quell the rising tide of nausea that always gripped my stomach before performances. It felt like a tsunami tonight.

Eva's eyes narrowed slightly in the mirror. "Why don't I believe you?"

Like hell was I giving her any reason to worry about me, not during her first performance as a company dancer. I knew of at least four other pairs of sisters who danced in the same companies across the United States, but we were definitely the only ones in the Metropolitan Ballet Company.

But there should have been three of us.

"Nothing to stress about." I turned my attention back to my shoe, leaving the left earbud beside me on the soft gray blanket as the orchestra moved into the variation in the right. *Push. Pull.* Focusing on the methodical movement of needle and thread, I went over the variation's choreography in my head. It was one of my all-time favorites—not that favoritism made it any easier to perform.

There. That was the instant adrenaline had stopped masking the pain in my ankle last night during dress rehearsal, causing me to hesitate and lose rhythm. I was pushing too hard, but the role demanded it.

"How's the Achilles?" Eva asked like she could read my mind.

"Fine." Any other answer would have Eva running to Vasily within seconds, in the name of sisterly concern.

"Liar," she muttered, rustling through her makeup bag, her movements becoming increasingly agitated. "Where is it?"

Pull. With one ear open, I could hear the music blending with the soft click of Eva's makeup brushes on the counter, the rustle of my warm-up pants as I shifted positions slightly, and the hum of the space heater in the corner of my dressing room, which warded off the late-January chill that had taken up residence backstage at the Metropolitan Opera House.

"Where the hell is my lucky lipstick?" Eva's voice pitched toward the roof.

"Check my bag."

"You don't wear Ruthless Red!" That bordered on shrill.

"No, but you do." I glanced back at her. "And I love you."

Her shoulders dipped. "And you knew I'd lose mine." She let go of her makeup bag and reached for mine, a corner of her mouth rising.

"And I knew you'd lose yours." I nodded.

"Thank you." Her relief was almost palpable.

Lacey knocked gently on the doorframe, clutching her favorite clipboard, and I took out my other earbud, losing the music entirely.

"Thirty minutes to places," Lacey informed us. "Oh, and your sister is—"

"Right here," Anne interrupted, leaning into the open doorway with the wide, easy smile she'd inherited from our dad, along with his hazel eyes and the golden brown curls she'd pinned into a sophisticated updo. Eva and I favored our mother in the hair department, with strands darker than any espresso I'd ever seen brewed, and while Eva's were pin straight, my waves could only be tamed by a bagful of products and regular maintenance at the salon. Anne's curls always seemed so effortlessly perfect.

The pressure in my chest immediately eased, and my mouth curved to mirror hers, widening into a grin. In our ocean-loving family, Anne was the palm tree—she swayed in the hurricane, but never broke.

"Anne!" Eva jolted out of the chair and threw her arms around our older sister.

"Whoa!" Anne laughed and wrapped her arms around Eva, the diamonds in her wedding band glittering in the bright lights.

"Thank you, Lacey. We've got her," I said, and the stage manager nodded in return before moving on.

"You look great!" Anne pulled back from Eva and gave her a quick once-over, her eyes softening. "Costume fits perfectly. I can't wait to see you up there."

"I'm just in the corps." Eva shrugged and stepped aside. "It's Alessandra who's the real star. Right, Allie?"

"Only for tonight." I tied off the row of stitches, then flexed my foot a few times to make sure it held.

"Every night, in my book." Anne knelt beside me despite her stylish black dress and hugged me gently, careful not to smudge my stage makeup.

I leaned into the embrace, closing my arms around her tightly, needle grasped between thumb and forefinger so I wouldn't prick her. "I'm so glad you're here."

Anne had a way of making everything all right. Dad away on business? No problem, Anne knew the schedule. Mom lighting into one of us about our turnout? Anne stepped in to distract. She was the living embodiment of a warm hug. Lina may have been the firstborn of the four of us, but Anne had always been the one with the oldest-sister vibe.

"Me too," she whispered before withdrawing just enough to give me the same appraisal she had given Eva. "Beautiful as always. You're going to do great."

"I just want it to be perfect for her," I replied as she swept her knees to the side and sat on the blanket.

"As if you have any other setting but *perfect*," Eva muttered.

Anne shot her a reproachful look, and I brought my right foot into my lap, wincing slightly at the tenacious burn along my Achilles. "Are you hurting?"

Leave it to Anne to miss *nothing*.

"I'm—" I started.

"If you so much as say the word *fine* . . . ," she warned, her astute gaze locking on my ankle.

"She had a cortisone shot yesterday," Eva said, leaning in toward the mirror to check her eyeliner.

Anne's eyebrows jumped. "Does Kenna know?"

"As my best friend or as the Company's doctor? Because the answer is yes to both," I countered. "And you're twenty-five years old, Eva." I gathered my tights to my other shoe and started stitching. "At some point you have to stop tattling on me, right?"

"At some point *you* have to learn when to take it easy," Anne chastised.

"Tomorrow," I replied, sewing quickly.

Tomorrow, the set would be changed from *Giselle* to *Romeo and Juliet*, and while Eva would be dancing in the corps for that show as well, I would officially be off for the next couple of weeks, at least for performances. I'd give myself a day or two to rest the ankle, like Kenna suggested, and then test it out with Isaac.

"It's always tomorrow with you." Anne sighed. "If Mom knew you were dancing injured . . ."

"Who do you think we learned it from?" Eva quipped.

A corner of my mouth tugged upward. She wasn't wrong. Performing through pain was the first lesson Mom taught us, both on and off the stage. Sadly, that made us a family of not just professional dancers, but professional liars too. "I'm fine. It's just been a hard couple of weeks, between rehearsals, performances, and working with Isaac."

"Isaac?" Anne looked up at Eva as my fingers ghosted across the silver scar along my Achilles tendon.

The sound of breaking glass skittered through my mind, but I cut off the memory before it could take hold. *Not tonight.* Tonight I would dance for Mom, because Lina had never gotten the chance.

"Isaac Burdan," Eva answered.

"Ah, the next Balanchine," Anne said, rising to her feet and dusting off her knees. "Don't look at me like that, Eva. Just because I don't dance anymore doesn't mean I'm not up on what's happening in the scene. I do read."

Anne did more than read. She organized most of the Company's events, including the entire Haven Cove Classic—which, thanks to our mother, had become one of the foremost summer competitions in the under-twenty division.

"Never said you didn't." Eva put her hands up like she was being arrested. "Just surprised you're reading about Isaac being the next Balanchine."

"Don't say that in front of him." I grinned, finishing the last few stitches before tying them off. "His ego won't fit in the building." Flexing, then pointing, I tested out the stitches, only standing once I trusted my handiwork.

"Did you read that Allie choreographed a ballet with him?" Eva's tone pitched mischievously.

"Really?" Anne's head swiveled my direction, her eyebrows jolting upward.

"It's nothing. Maybe. He was the artist in residence before *Nutcracker* season, and it was more like he choreographed and I just showed him what would and wouldn't work." Thinking of late nights in the studio and early mornings in his bed made me grin. He wasn't Mr. Right—that ship had long since sailed. But he was certainly Mr. For-Right-Now, and that was quite perfect.

"That's huge!" Anne's smile could have powered the building. "A ballet of your own—"

"We'll see." I kept my smile small, just like my expectations when it came to Isaac, and reached for my costume for act one.

I ran my fingers over the amethyst ring in my right pocket, then unzipped the worn, faded black hoodie with its fraying wrist cuffs and hung it on the back of the chair. Then I shucked off my warm-up pants and stepped into the costume.

"Must be nice to have a zipper," Eva muttered as Anne reached for mine. "Corps still has hook closures for multiple wearers."

I pulled my act-one hair out of the way when Anne reached for my zipper, and somehow managed to curb my tongue regarding Eva's sulking.

"I'm sure you'll have a zipper next year," Anne assured her, patting my back once she'd finished with my costume. "Mom was thrilled to hear both of you will be onstage tonight."

Cue another wave of nausea. The vegetable soup I'd choked down an hour ago threatened to make a reappearance.

"She's in the family box?" No doubt with Anne's husband. I scooped the blanket off the floor and tossed it on top of my bag.

"With Finn and Eloise." Anne watched like a hawk as I rose en pointe a few times, testing my shoes and my arches.

"I thought Eloise was teaching at Vaganova." I schooled my features as pain shot up my Achilles in protest.

"She just retired. And you have an understudy for a reason," Anne finished in a whisper, her brow furrowing. "You put too much strain on that Achilles of yours and—"

"I just need the music to start," I interrupted just as softly, my gaze darting to Eva's back as she walked toward the hallway. "Any other role, and maybe I'd consider it, but Giselle . . ."

Anne's eyes met mine, the light catching on a sheen she quickly blinked away before pressing her lips between her teeth and nodding.

"Shall we?" Eva asked over her shoulder as dancers walked by the open doorway, headed for the wings.

"Absolutely." I plastered on a fake smile and nodded.

Anne hooked her arm through mine and kept her voice down. "You let her get dressed with you? Shouldn't she be with the corps? Building camaraderie and all that?"

"For all her bluster, she gets nervous. She's still the new girl to everyone but me." I'd started dancing with the Company at eighteen, moving from apprentice to principal dancer by the time I blew out twenty-five candles, but Eva hadn't been invited to try out for MBC until she'd spent several years in Boston, then Houston, working up the ranks. "Just trying to make things a little easier on her."

"You got her the tryout and agreed to that ridiculous Seconds app account she loves so much," Anne responded, squeezing my arm gently. "I think you've more than helped."

We stepped into the hallway and found Eva waiting for us with Vasily Koslov, the Metropolitan Ballet Company's artistic director. My chest tightened. Vasily had the power to make or break us. His silver hair was trimmed neatly as always, his three-piece suit pressed to perfection. It was hard to believe the tall man with the dancing blue eyes had seen the same sixty-four years as my mother.

They'd been in this very company at my age, but Vasily had eventually moved into choreography and marriage to our executive director, while Mom had reluctantly retired in her prime, to motherhood and eventual teaching.

"There she is." Vasily smiled, reaching for my hand, and I gave it. He brushed a perfunctory kiss over my knuckles, as he'd done before every performance since I'd been promoted to principal. "Ready to dazzle us, Alessandra?"

"I'll do my best to make you proud." My stomach rolled.

Hold it together. You're not going to puke in front of Vasily. He was the closest thing I had to a father since mine had passed.

"She'll be dancing for our mother tonight," Eva added.

"Sophie is here?" His gaze jumped to Anne, two lines deepening between his brows as though trying to place her. "She never leaves that exclusive little school of hers except for the Classic. Will she be—"

"I'll be sure to give her your best," Anne interrupted, before he could ask to see her and we were forced to make excuses.

"Ah." His brow furrowed. "Annelli, isn't it? The daughter who doesn't dance?"

"She also runs Company events, including the Classic." My hackles rose in immediate defense of Anne, even though I knew Vasily didn't mean any harm by it. He had a bad habit of only truly seeing people in his orbit.

"That's me," Anne answered with a practiced smile, then glanced at Eva and me. "I'll meet up with you two afterwards. We have to talk about summer plans for the beach house."

"I can't—" Eva started.

"You can and you *will.*" Anne leveled a look on our little sister that meant business. "We're not losing the house just because you won't take a vacation." She whipped those hazel eyes at me. "And that goes for you too. See you after."

She left without another word, disappearing into an ocean of costumed dancers in the hallway.

"The house in Haven Cove?" Vasily asked me as we started toward the stage, dancers moving from his path like rushing creek water around a boulder.

"Mom put the house in a trust last summer and made a ridiculous condition that we have to sell it if all three of us don't provide proof that we spend time there together every year," Eva answered before I had the chance to.

"Doesn't sound like Sophie." Vasily blinked. "She hated that house, and the fact that your father made her take you girls there in the summer. So many missed opportunities for trainings at summer intensives, but at least the Classic came of it." He glanced at his Rolex. "Oh, Alessandra, I spoke with Isaac. He wants to meet next week about including the new ballet he's choreographed in the fall schedule."

My heart leapt. "*Equinox?*"

"Is that what you're calling it?" His mouth quirked into a bemused smile. "Lovely." He clucked his tongue at a young corps de ballet member who'd scurried into the hallway, and the dancer immediately slowed at the rebuke.

"I'll make myself available if you need to see any of it performed," I promised, struggling to keep the excitement out of my voice. Vasily admired comportment above all else.

"I'd appreciate that." He nodded as the hallway split into two, each path leading to a different side of the stage. "Make me proud, Alessandra. You, too, Eve. Ah, Maxim, there you are." He headed down the other hallway toward his pain-in-the-ass choreographer of a son who looked like every picture I'd ever seen of Vasily at thirty years old.

"It's *Eva*," Eva hissed once he was out of earshot. "He's completely oblivious to me. But I'm excited for you." She wrapped her arm around my waist.

"Thank you." I leaned the side of my head against my sister's. "And he'll know your name by next season. You shine brighter than any other corps dancer, and he'll see that." Years of discipline were all that kept me from shouting in absolute glee. If we put *Equinox* on the fall program, I'd have a role created just for me.

We walked into the welcoming dark of the wings for our preperformance ritual, and I felt the years evaporate with every step as we passed a dozen other dancers and a few stagehands. By the time we reached the very edge of the curtain, where a few precious inches of light separated us from the crowd, I was six again, peeking to see if Mom and Dad were in the audience.

Except there were two of us where there had been four.

"I see her," Eva whispered, using her extra inches to look over the top of my five-foot-five frame.

"Me too." Heat stung my palms and my heart started to race as I looked up at the family seats—right mezzanine, box seven—spotting Mom and her best friend, Eloise, immediately.

Damn it. She was already in a mood.

To the outside world, the legendary Sophie Langevin-Rousseau was Metropolitan Ballet Company royalty, the height of sophistication and elegance, but I saw a powder keg with a lit fuse. She sat with her shoulders straight, her chin lifted, her silver-streaked dark hair pinned into a flawless french twist, but it was her manicured fingertips drumming impatiently on the railing that gave her away as she peered down at the orchestra. She wasn't watching, she was hunting imperfections. Sure enough, her perfectly painted lips pursed in disapproval as a flute player scurried in, obviously running late.

Anne reached the box, taking her seat beside her pinstripe-suited husband, and I could have sworn she shot a look our direction before opening her program.

"Eloise looks good," Eva whispered. "So do the men she's brought with her."

"Eloise has always had impeccable taste," I agreed, a cool breeze lifting the hair on the back of my neck as Eva backed away, leaving me alone at the curtain's edge.

I fought the impulse, but it won—it always did—and I glanced back at the very last row of the floor section. The seat in the center remained unoccupied, as my contract stipulated. That ache erupted in my chest again, just like it had every night this week.

The only time I'd ever truly nailed the variation, he'd been—

Stop it.

I did it once—danced the routine perfectly—and I would do it again tonight. Ripping my gaze from the empty seat, I headed back into the wings for my place.

A handful of minutes later, the curtain went up, the music started, and I watched Everett take the stage as Hilarion, then Daniel as Albrecht, both exuding the perfection expected at our level.

Adrenaline flooded my system the second I made my entrance to the applause of the audience, quickly conquering any protest my ankle thought about making. The lights and music consumed every thought, stealing the pain, the worry, even the lead weight of Mom's gaze, until I wasn't just dancing Giselle, I *was* Giselle.

Twenty minutes in, adrenaline waned, pain shimmering up the back of my leg every time I rose en pointe, and I noticed Eva slip for a heartbeat in the corps when she glanced up at the family box. It was the most minuscule of mistakes, but no doubt our mother would berate her for the rest of the night for it. I gave her a reassuring smile when my back was turned to the audience, but it didn't lessen the pink flooding her cheeks beneath layers of stage makeup.

The music shifted into my variation, and I breathed deeply, lifting my arm in gesture to the only mother who mattered in this moment— the one onstage—and then to my would-be lover, Albrecht.

And then I danced.

I rose into the first arabesque en pointe, and pain exploded in my right ankle. *Shit.* My smile never slipped as I gritted my teeth.

The hurt was momentary, but that arabesque had been flawless, and that was all that mattered. As I moved across the floor, the ache lessened until I repeated the arabesque. Then it flared like a flame doused in lighter fluid. Again and again it rose and ebbed, higher and more painful as the variation continued, each movement testing the limits of my smile, my pain tolerance.

Anne was right. I had an understudy. But I wasn't just dancing for myself. Tonight, I danced for Lina. I danced for Mom.

Just tonight, I promised my Achilles. I could rest tomorrow, turn the role over to my understudy for the next performance if it would get me through tonight. I couldn't falter, not in front of her.

After a series of turns, my smile slipped into a grimace, and Eva's eyes widened slightly from where she sat with the other peasant girls. I ripped my gaze from hers and turned my attention back to the audience, moving into a series of hops on my left foot diagonally across the stage, giving my right ankle enough of a reprieve for the pain to recede to a grating, nauseating, but manageable level.

I just had to make it through the piqué turns.

The music shifted, and I headed into the series of eighteen turns that would circumnavigate the stage.

Anything is doable for five minutes. His voice slipped through my mind, uninvited.

This was only fifteen seconds. I could do it.

Faces blurred as I spun en pointe, and I whipped my head to my chosen spotting points to keep balance, as flames of pain licked up my leg, burning through me in an agony so acute that I bit into my lip . . . and kept going. I reached stage left on turn eleven, glancing to the empty chair in the back row, the only place in the theater that anchored me.

Twelve. My arms faltered and my breath caught as I spotted the man occupying that seat. *Impossible.* Only one name could retrieve those tickets, and he hadn't done so in ten years.

Thirteen. My head whipped around with the turn. The seat was vacant. Pain must have addled my brain.

Fourteen. Or was that a glimpse of sandy-brown hair, wind mussed and sun kissed?

Fifteen. The fire rose from my ankle, up through my chest at the memory of sea green eyes and the dimple in his left cheek when he smiled. Was he here?

Sixteen. That chair was *empty*. It had been for a decade, and it would be for as long as I made the Company hold it so, just like the cavernous pit in my chest where my heart had been, since the night the glass shattered, steel crumpled, and my ankle—*Focus!*

Seventeen. I became pain itself. My ankle screamed as I moved into the last two turns, straining the tendon beyond its limits.

In the silence between the last staccato beats from the orchestra, I heard it, like the snap of fingers underwater.

I fell to my right knee, the last position of the variation, and extended my arm to my onstage mother.

I did it, Lina. I did it.

Rousing applause sounded from the audience as I tried to stand, but gravity yanked me forward. My palms smacked into the polished surface of the stage, and I heard Eva gasp somewhere to my right.

It took a heartbeat, then another, to understand.

My foot.

It wasn't responding, almost like it belonged on someone else's body.

A nuclear blast of bone-rattling anguish washed through me, pushing into my veins like acid, burning away my very being, until it erupted from my mouth in a scream that silenced everyone in the theater.

My career was over.

CHAPTER FOUR

Hudson

NYFouette92: Has anyone even seen Alessandra Rousseau since that break? And I don't mean reused content. I bet she's hurt worse than they're letting on. RousseauSisters4

Four months later
Off the coast of Cape Cod, Massachusetts

"Knock it off!" I shouted over the roar of the angry ocean and the incessant, high-pitched screaming of the midforties man whose life I was trying to save.

His screaming I didn't mind so much.

The way he was trying to drown me—that was getting on my last fucking nerve.

I got another face full of the Atlantic as the guy pushed down on my shoulders, trying to use me as his personal flotation device.

That's enough. Shoving his hands off my shoulders, I broke free and kicked upward, sucking in a full breath of air before manhandling the flailing guy so his back faced my chest.

"Stop it, or you'll drown us both!"

"I don't want to die!" he shrieked.

"No shit, me either!" I locked his arms with mine and kept an eye on his dog—a golden retriever struggling to paddle near the capsized vessel we were dangerously close to. From the timeline of the distress call, they'd been in the water over forty-five minutes, and the dog was barely keeping her head over the waves. "Hold still and let me get you to the basket. Then I'll get your dog."

"Fuck the dog!" He clawed at my arm, fighting to break free.

For a heartbeat, I debated the order in which I wanted to rescue these two. Clearly, the dog would be a better choice.

"You're getting mighty close to the wreck, and we're running on fumes," Ortiz said through my coms, but it wasn't like I could free up a hand to push the button to respond to the pilot hovering to my left.

Instead, I kicked us away from the sinking vessel—what looked to be a twenty-one-foot ski boat—and into the downwash from the helicopter. Water smacked us in the face, which only made the guy flail harder. He wrenched an arm free and elbowed up, catching me in the jaw.

The pain barely registered, but I knew it would later. "Get in the fucking basket!"

He damn near scrambled over me to get there. I kicked free of the line and signaled up to Beachman that the basket was ready to be hoisted.

"Roger," Beachman answered through coms from his position on the hoist. "Reeling him in now."

The basket rose from the waves, and I turned back for the boat.

"Just where in the hell do you think you're going, Ellis?" Ortiz lectured through my earpiece, no doubt glaring down at me from the cockpit.

"Grabbing the dog." I hit the button to reply, then swam headfirst toward the capsized vessel. The morning light reflected off the show-room-shiny hull—it was obviously a new purchase.

Pretty sure I heard Ortiz grumble "Of course you are" through the radio.

"You honestly going to tell me *not* to save the dog?" I let go of the button and continued swimming.

"Make it quick. We have maybe ten minutes of fuel." We'd been out on patrol when the call came in. Otherwise we'd have been able to hover out here another few hours.

I battled the swells to where the dog tried fruitlessly to climb back aboard, and muttered a swear word. She was too close to the boat. Pursing my lips, I forced through a whistle. The dog perked her ears before a swell rose up and swallowed her.

Fuck.

"Don't even—" Ortiz warned, but I already had my mouthpiece in.

I ducked beneath the surface and swam dangerously near the careening craft, grabbing ahold of the dog's collar and yanking her surprisingly small frame against mine before swimming back to daylight. I was either wrong about the breed, or she was a puppy.

Lucky for me, the dog took a breath the second we hit air, because I wasn't exactly certified in canine CPR. I dragged her to my chest, then spit out my mouthpiece and swam backward, away from the ill-fated ski boat that shouldn't have been taken out of the damned bay. "You did a good job," I told her.

"Passenger secured," Beachman announced through the coms. "Sending the basket back for you, Ellis."

"Roger." The dog didn't so much as flinch when we entered the rotor wash, and her breathing was eerily slow. Hypothermia. May wasn't exactly hospitable to swimmers around here. "Almost there. Good girl." I ran a gloved hand over the dog's head.

Once the basket was lowered, I put her in first, then climbed in as gracefully as a guy in flippers could. After I had her in my lap, and a good grip, I hit the coms. "Passenger secured. Ready for extraction."

"Roger that. Raising the basket," Beachman replied. A second later, we had a front-row seat to the sinking of the ski boat as the ocean claimed her. I'd seen at least a hundred similar scenes in the last ten years.

"Glad you weren't on that," I said, not that the pup could hear me over the noise of the helicopter.

Beachman brought us in, pausing his constant gum chewing to smile wide under his helmet when he saw the dog. "All passengers are aboard."

"Roger that. We're headed back to base," Ortiz responded from the pilot's seat.

"Heavy one canine," Shadrick added from the cockpit, looking back over her shoulder and flashing a grin.

"Heavy one canine." I nodded, then got myself into a seat and more practical footwear—my boots—while Beachman wrapped a blanket around the puppy. Now that we were out of the water, it was easy to see the size of her paws. She looked about seven, maybe eight months old. He quickly handed me the sodden bundle so he could see to her keeper, who stared out the window with a glazed look I'd seen too many times throughout my career.

"Cape Cod station, this is echo six-eight," Ortiz said over the wide channel. "Incoming with one passenger in need of medical attention. Hypothermia suspected."

Dispatch responded as I held the puppy against my chest. She struggled to keep her eyes open, even when I rubbed her down to keep her circulation moving.

It was a twenty-minute flight back to the Cape Cod air station, and to my relief, she was still breathing when we got there. Beachman and I got the guy out and headed off the tarmac toward the waiting ambulance, while the pilots ran the aircraft down. "She looks to be about seven months old?" I shouted over the decreasing noise of the slowing rotors once we were far enough from the bird.

"Something like that," the guy responded, clutching the corners of the blanket around his neon-green polo. "Can't remember."

"What's her name?" I adjusted her in my arms as we approached the medical team—and our commanding officer. Captain Hewitt usually carried an air of annoyance, but today he looked *pissed*.

"Sadie," the guy muttered. "Ex-girlfriend named her." He lifted his gaze to mine. "Any chance we can salvage the boat?"

Was this guy fucking serious?

"No. She's long gone," Beachman answered for me before giving the paramedics the rundown on the patient. "There's a reason this place is called the graveyard of the Atlantic."

"You risked an aircrew over a dog?" Captain Hewitt asked me, furrowing his bushy silver brows and crossing his arms across his perfectly pressed uniform.

No doubt I was in for yet another lecture on my recklessness, but I'd learned long ago that it was far better to risk myself and come back with a survivor than not.

"Zero risk to the crew. We made it in five minutes shy of Ortiz's deadline," I replied before handing Sadie off to the paramedic. Anger reared its ugly head when the patient completely ignored the pup. "She needs a vet."

The paramedic nodded.

"You outran your fate, little girl," Beachman said, scratching her head as he walked by. "Or outswam it, I suppose."

Captain Hewitt's sigh gave the rotor wash a run for its money. "Any particular reason it's always your name on my desk, Petty Officer Ellis?"

"Always seem to be in the right place at the right time." I shrugged. It was my biggest blessing, and sometimes a curse.

"Luckiest bastard I've ever met." Beachman knocked on my helmet. Eric and I had transferred to Air Station Cape Cod around the same time three years ago, and the Californian was my closest nonlocal friend.

Captain Hewitt rolled his eyes. "Get dried off. See you both back in twenty-four."

Hell yes. A whole day off before we were due back for another shift. "Yes, sir."

"You coming out tonight?" Beachman asked as we walked back toward the hangar, tucking his helmet beneath his arm and running his hand over his short brown curls. "In case you need the reminder, Jessica's sister is dying to meet you."

"I'll think about it." And I did, until I opened my locker and saw the text message from Caroline.

Two hours and a change of clothes later, I carried two bags of groceries into my parents'—scratch that—*Caroline's* kitchen, coming in through the unlocked side door. My older sister had bought the place off our mom and dad five years ago when they left her the café and moved inland, but I couldn't seem to stop thinking of it as theirs.

"I'm here!" I called out over the classical music blaring from upstairs and set the bags on the linoleum counter of the island, along with my keys.

The kitchen hadn't changed since my junior year in high school, when Mom had a serious thing for apples. Apple wallpaper. Apple curtains. Little red-apple drawer pulls. Caroline always talked about changing it, but never did. This place was frozen in time, and I'd felt like an anachronism since coming back three years ago. Nothing fit quite right anymore.

"Thank you!" Caroline hurried into the kitchen, shoving pins into her blond hair to keep it behind her ears. "You're an absolute godsend, Hudson." She smashed a kiss on the side of my cheek and tucked in her white button-down embroidered with **THE ELLIS** above her heart.

"Any clue where he is?" I curved the brim of my Bruins hat and tried to keep the annoyance out of my voice. Saturdays were money days for Caroline, and Gavin fucking knew it. Not showing up was a dick move.

"Probably sleeping off his night." She shrugged and reached for the purse hanging by the door. "You know how Gavin is."

"Right." Unfortunately, I did, which was exactly why her text this morning hadn't surprised me. He was about as dependable as one-ply toilet paper. Someone was usually getting shit on because he flaked, and it wasn't funny anymore.

"If he shows up, just let me know. I'm off at five." She glanced at the clock, where both the hands were nearly upright. "Can you handle five hours? She's . . . in a mood."

"She's ten." The three-bulb light fixture above the island rattled, and then the music cut.

"Says the only person my daughter likes. Bet she just saw your car in the driveway, because she's been blaring that music at me for two hours straight." Caroline slung her purse over her shoulder. "I swear, she thinks I'm public enemy number one."

"It might help if you'd just sign her up at Madeline's." Given the selection of the tunes, they'd no doubt had yet another argument about dance class.

"And watch my kid turn into one of those spoiled prima donnas?" she scoffed as light footsteps sounded on the stairs behind me, then paused. "No way. It's bad enough those insipid Rousseau girls turn this place into a circus with that competition every August, but the way the local girls get their hopes up like they have any chance of beating those trained brats who steal all their chances to get a scholarship at that stupid school is just . . ." Her spine stiffened. "Just, no."

Here we go again.

"Juniper could be really good. You won't know if you don't give her a chance." I ignored her jab at our little town's most famous vacationers just like I always did, but pressure settled in my chest as I shoved my hands into the front pockets of my jeans. Only one of the Rousseau girls came back every August—Anne. Never Eva or . . . Allie, which was definitely for the best. A step creaked behind me, no doubt the third one that had always given me away as a kid. "And you've never complained about all the money those ballerinas bring into Haven Cove with that competition."

The pressure transformed into an ache. How the fuck was it possible to still miss her like this after ten years? Her whiskey-colored eyes, the way her nose scrunched when she laughed, her smile—the real one, not the polished, fake shit she gave everyone else—the way she'd had the rare ability to really listen . . .

"Their *parents'* money. And just be on my side here." Caroline jabbed her finger at me and lifted her brows. "Between you and Gavin giving June everything she wants . . ." Her shoulders dipped and she sighed, the light hitting her face in a way that highlighted the deep-purple circles beneath her eyes. "I need someone on my side."

"It's our job as her uncles. You want someone on your side, call Mom and Dad." I shrugged unapologetically. Had we both been overindulgent since Sean died and left Caroline a single mother? Sure. But did I regret it? Not one bit. I'd promised Sean on his deathbed I'd try to be the balance to Caroline's anxiety about everything regarding Juniper so the kid would get to have a little fun, and I was keeping that vow, period.

"What's in those?" Her head cocked to the side as she spied the grocery bags.

I reached into one and pulled out a bunch of bananas. "You'd better get going."

"Five hours," Caroline promised. "And thank you. Really, Hudson, I couldn't do it without you." She could, but refused the help Mom and Dad offered over and over. I kept my opinions on that to myself.

"I've got this." I motioned to the door with my head, and Caroline walked out of it, the screen slamming closed behind her. Once I heard her car pull out of the gravel driveway, I turned toward the doorway to the living room. "You can come out now."

"Uncle Hudson!" Juniper whipped around the post at the end of the staircase's banister and ran into the kitchen, then threw herself at me in a tangle of gangly limbs and long brown hair.

"Hey, June-Bug." I caught her easily and hugged her tight for a second before leveling what I hoped was a serious expression on her and setting her on her feet. "You fighting with your mom again?"

"She's limiting my creative expression." She shoved her hair out of her face. "What happened to your jaw?"

I gingerly touched the area she pointed to. "Someone hit me while I was rescuing them."

"What kind of person does that?" She crinkled her freckled nose.

"Fear does strange things to people. What kind of ten-year-old weaponizes Bach on a Saturday morning?"

"It was Stravinsky." She lifted her brows and gave me the same look Caroline just had. June may have been adopted, but she'd definitely inherited my sister's no-fucks-given attitude. "From *The Rite of Spring*. Just because I'm not allowed to take class doesn't mean I'm not allowed to *watch* ballet." She folded her arms across her chest. "It's a stupid rule, anyway."

"It's still her rule." Juniper was right. My sister's no-ballet rule made about as much sense as my parents grounding Gavin and me as teens when we had a perfectly good ladder outside our shared room, but I wasn't the parent here. "Did you text Uncle Gavin?" I changed the subject as June took a seat on one of the two barstools at the island.

"No. I'm not supposed to have a phone." She bit back a smile and feigned innocence.

"Like Gavin doesn't know?" I moved the bananas and then unloaded the contraband from the bags. With Caroline working her ass off at the café, the phone seemed the responsible choice to make when it came to Juniper. Not to mention that Gavin would usually pick up for our niece, even if he was ducking Caroline or me.

Juniper's brown eyes lit up. "Pop-Tarts!" She reached for the variety pack, then clutched it to her chest. "You're my favorite."

"Uh-huh." I ruffled her hair and put the rest of the snack food in the cabinet behind the mixer Caroline never used. Maybe it made me a shit brother to be my niece's sugar dealer, but I was a hell of an uncle, and I was okay with that.

She ripped open the foil and stuffed half a strawberry pastry into her mouth. "Uncle Hudson?"

"Hmm?" I threw the reusable bags onto the stack on top of the refrigerator and braced for impact, leaning back against the honey-oak cabinetry.

"If there was a way to change Mom's mind about taking ballet, would you help?" She broke off a small, measured piece of the second pastry, a clear giveaway that she was up to something.

"There isn't." I shook my head.

She scrunched her forehead. "But if there was, you'd help me, wouldn't you? The new session starts in less than two weeks."

"In the interest of us not going round and round about this, sure. If there was a way to change your mom's mind, I'd help." Easy promise, knowing there was zero chance. Juniper had a better chance of talking her mom into a tattoo than stepping foot in a studio.

"Pinkie promise." She stuck out her hand, curling every digit but her pinkie.

I reached forward and hooked my pinkie with hers in our sacred ritual. "Pinkie promise."

She grinned, her dimple popping on her left upper cheek, and the hairs on the back of my neck lifted. "See"—she popped a small piece of Pop-Tart into her mouth and chewed—"I think she hates ballet because she hates the *ballerinas*."

"I think that's a logical assessment." I nodded.

"Because she grew up waiting on all the rich tourists at the café." She devoured another frosting-laden piece.

"Something like that." I swiveled toward the fridge and pulled out the jug of orange juice. "Have you thought about taking tap? Or jazz?"

"But you don't hate ballerinas," she interrupted, ignoring my attempt to change the subject as I poured us two glasses of juice and put the jug away.

"Correct." That ache in my chest constricted. There had to be a way out of this conversation. I gulped down half the glass of juice like it would wash away the memories that had nipped at my heels relentlessly since I'd come back to Haven Cove.

"Because you loved one," June whispered.

My stomach heaved and I nearly spat out the juice, barely managing to swallow it before painting the kitchen orange. "I'm sorry?" The glass clinked on the linoleum as I set it down.

"You loved Alessandra Rousseau," June declared, throwing around the words I'd never dared to voice as a teenager like they were as common as the seashells around here. "Or at least you really liked her."

What the hell? Speechless. My ten-year-old niece had rendered me completely fucking *speechless*. How did she . . . ? Caroline didn't know—she would have raised hell. Not even Mom and Dad caught on. Only Gavin knew about those two summers.

I was going to fucking *kill* him.

"And that means she can't be spoiled or entitled," June continued, her nostrils flaring like she could smell her victory.

Allie was both of those things, and somehow neither. She was the ultimate oxymoron, self-centered yet selfless for her sisters, spoiled yet kind, driven yet reluctant, an open book of emotion on the stage and an impossible puzzle when off it.

At least she had been at seventeen.

"And if you were even just friends with her, she couldn't be mean." June put her hands in her lap. "Which means if Mom met her, talked to her, then she'd see that I could be just like her." She sighed wistfully, turning those big brown eyes on me like the little weapons they were. "Have you ever seen her dance? She's so beautiful, and graceful, and is one of the youngest principal dancers in her company's history. She's . . . flawless."

She was all that and more. Allie was born for the stage. Hell, she'd been bred for it.

I had to get a grip on this conversation and nip it in the bud. "Look, June. I don't know what Uncle Gavin told you, but—"

"Don't deny it!" She slid off the stool, reached into the back pocket of her jeans, and slapped her hand on the counter, leaving behind a picture.

I glanced at the Polaroid, and the knife in my chest sliced me clean open. It had been years since I'd laid eyes on the picture of Allie and me outside the Haven Cove Classic, my arm around her shoulders, her arms holding the grocery-store bouquet of roses I'd bought on the way to the competition. Ten years later I could recall every single detail of the moment we'd stolen while Lina distracted Mrs. Rousseau so Gavin could snap the picture.

It was the false high in our story, the moment I truly thought anything was possible between us, only for the entire world to crumble beneath our feet a few short hours later.

"You went through my boxes in the attic." It wasn't a question.

She pushed the picture toward me. "They were just sitting there. I mean, you've been back for years and it's not like you took them to your house." Her voice trailed off, and her eyes lowered. "I went through your boxes," she whispered.

"That would be like me reading your journal. It's a violation of privacy." What else had she found?

"I know." She took what appeared to be a fortifying breath and looked up. "And I'm sorry. Kind of."

"Kind of?" My eyebrows flew.

"Come on, Uncle Hudson!" She pushed the picture to the edge of the counter, but I didn't touch the damned thing. "You obviously dated one of the most famous dancers in the world! We can go over to her house and get her to talk to Mom—"

I put my finger up. "One, I did *not* date her." She'd been my best friend, and that had made my actions even more unforgivable. "Two, just because the Rousseaus have a summerhouse here doesn't mean she's actually in town. And three—trust me when I say this—I am the last person in the world she would ever want to see." The usual weight of guilt I carried when it came to Allie swelled until I was certain it would crush my lungs.

"She's been here for a whole week already!" June hopped off the barstool and snatched my keys from the counter. "She was injured in January and came here to recover."

My eyes widened. She'd been here for a week? "And how would you know that?" Wait, from *January*?

"Seconds." Juniper stared at me like I was an idiot. "She has an account with her sister."

"You have Seconds?" My voice lowered and my eyes narrowed. "I thought there was an age restriction for that!"

"Oh, please." She rolled her eyes. "I had to scroll a whopping three more years to create a log-in."

I blinked. This moment right here was why I was nowhere near equipped to be a parent. Fuck, as soon as Caroline found out about any of this, I was going to have my uncle privileges revoked.

"Let's go," June urged. "It's what? A five-minute drive?"

"Four," I muttered. There was zero chance I was showing up on Allie's doorstep.

"Even better!" Juniper thrust my keys at me.

I shook my head and said the word I'd sworn I never would after Sean died. "No."

"You pinkie promised!" She shook the keys and stared up at me with a determined purse of her lips and a plea in her eyes. "You said you'd never break a pinkie promise."

Fuck my life.

Pinkie promises outweighed my own discomfort.

I held up my finger. "On one condition. If she isn't there, you put that picture back where you found it and we *never* speak of this again." *Please God, don't let her be there.*

"Deal." She grabbed her backpack off the hook and nodded.

Shit. What about—"Did Seconds happen to tell you exactly which of the Rousseaus are here?" If it was her mom . . .

"Just Anne and Alessandra." She swung her backpack over her shoulders. "Why?"

If she knew Anne's name, she'd done her research.

Was I really about to throw away ten years of self-control? Face down the biggest regret I had in my entire life? Juniper looked up at me with all the expectation and trust she had in her little body. Yeah. For June, I would. "Let's get this over with."

Six minutes later, I pulled my truck off the coastal road that ran alongside the body of water the town was named after, and into the long gravel driveway I'd avoided since I'd moved back. The Rousseau house. *House* was a quaint term for an estate with seven bedrooms, a carriage house, two acres of prime real estate along the beach, and that coveted pier that had somehow withstood the last two nor'easters to rip through here.

And damn, it looked exactly the same as it had the last time I'd sneaked over and climbed the rose-covered trellis to Allie's room on the second floor. Same grayish-blue paint job with white trim, same pattern on the cushions of the porch swing. Nostalgia hit with a wicked right hook.

Every muscle in my body clenched when I put the car in park in front of the wraparound porch, forsaking the drive on the right hand that led back to the carriage house. If I didn't love Juniper so much, if I didn't treasure her unwavering certainty that I would keep my promises—that *someone* would—I would have driven my ass straight off the property.

As it was, Juniper was already out of the car and walking up the steps to the covered porch, her purple backpack bouncing with every step. What was with the backpack, anyway? Did she think she was moving in or something?

I shut off the ignition, pocketed the key, and got out of the truck, half expecting Mrs. Rousseau to appear in the doorway to shoo me away from her daughter with threats and poignant insults.

Juniper rang the bell as I walked up the four steps to the porch, uncaring if the wood creaked beneath my feet for the first time. Then she knocked as I moved to stand beside her. Shit, my palms were sweaty, my pulse was pretty much tachycardic, and my stomach seriously considered emptying its contents.

I was seventeen all over again, trying to do the right thing by walking her to the front door, and yet I was simultaneously eighteen, losing her all over again. Darkening her doorstep again had never been in my plans, which left me horrifyingly . . . unprepared. And I was *always* prepared.

This was officially the most reckless thing I'd ever done.

I counted to thirty, and relief beat out the sting of disappointment. "She's not here."

"She has to be!" June jabbed the bell again.

"Maybe Seconds is wrong. She hasn't been back in years, June-Bug," I said softly.

Juniper shot me a look that was half dejection and half panic, then spun on her heel. "She has to be here!" she called back over her shoulder, then jumped the steps and took off running around the side of the house.

She had to be *kidding* me.

"June!" I caught up to her in a matter of seconds, right at the cursed rose-covered trellis that had earned me two of the scars on my hands. "We can't trespass."

"She could be in the backyard." She marched forward. "Let's just look, please? I have to meet her. I just have to," she downright begged, using those kryptonite eyes on me.

Fuck, if this day wasn't one problem after another. I wavered. It wouldn't be the first time I'd sneaked into the backyard. Besides, at this time of day, Allie would have been in the studio, and given that it was right next to the front door, she would have heard the bell, which meant there was zero chance she was actually here, no matter what the damned clock app said.

"Fine," I agreed. At least it would put an end to this insanity.

Juniper grinned. "How did you meet her, anyway?" she asked as we passed the corner of the back porch, where I'd sat on the roof for countless hours, stargazing with Allie. "It's not like you run in the same circles."

"I was in the right place at the right time," I said for the second time that day.

"And why aren't you friends anymore?" June blinked and covered her eyes with her hand as we stepped out of the shade and into the sun of the backyard. The manicured lawn dropped off sharply at the cliff, and a wooden bridge covered the distance down to the beach and pier.

"That part's . . . complicated," I answered quietly, scanning the yard with its pool and lush landscaping in full spring bloom, finding it empty.

"Did you do something stupid?" She narrowed her eyes at me, taking Allie's side in an argument she didn't even know existed, and she walked toward the cliff steps, leaving me to follow after. "Mom says Uncle Gavin is prone to stupidity, but you're supposed to be the one who does the right thing."

Ouch.

"The curse of being in the right place at the right time is that sometimes there isn't a *right* thing to do." We reached the steps, and I turned my Bruins hat forward to block the sun as we looked down at the beach. My gaze followed the line of the pier and caught on the shape bobbing off to the side of it.

"That doesn't make any sense," Juniper argued.

"Tell me about it." I leaned forward, my senses blocking everything out but that bobbing figure in the ocean below us. It sank beneath the waves, and I began counting in my head as June lectured me on the finer points of maintaining a friendship with a girl.

When I reached forty-nine, the figure popped up again, only to sink once more.

Every fiber in my being screamed with inexplicable certainty that figure was Allie.

And she was drowning.

CHAPTER FIVE

Allie

Dancegrl6701: Must be nice to get into every intensive you want.

Ryandnzx: Work harder.

Thirty-three.

I counted in my head as I sat on the ocean floor, my eyes closed behind the goggles, holding tight to the kettlebell weight I'd thrown in twenty minutes earlier so I wouldn't float to the surface.

Thirty-four. The ocean roared deliciously around me, rising in a crescendo with each wave that threatened to push me to shore before ebbing again. It was the noise that finally allowed me to think, to simply exist beyond the incessant demands of everyone around me, asking when I'd be back, asking how the rehab was going, asking if I was back at the barre yet.

Thirty-five. Rather than lie, I'd simply left.

Thirty-six. The water drowned out everything but the feel of my own heartbeat and the beautiful aching need for air that reminded me I was still alive. Each time the pressure drove me to the surface for oxygen, it not only reminded me that my lung capacity was shit after going months without training, but also drove home the inescapable truth that I still wanted to live.

Thirty-seven. For a couple of terrifying months, I hadn't been entirely sure.

Thirty-eight. Damn, it's cold. I really should have gone with the wet suit. The water was still freezing this time of year, and my skin had progressed from prickling to numb.

Thirty-nine. My lungs burned. I was out of shape. I should be able to hang for at least a minute, if not two, even against the driving waves.

Forty—

Something grabbed hold of my waist and pulled, wrenching my hand from the kettlebell, and flooding my veins with terror. My breath expelled in a scream of bubbles and my eyes shot open, looking for a shark—

Water rushed by as I was yanked upward through the ten feet of water that separated the sand from the sun. I fought the strength—holy shit, those were *arms* around me—hauling my back against someone's chest. My lungs shrieked for the air I'd so recklessly let escape, but the arms wouldn't budge.

We broke the surface, and I gasped for air, then quickly shoved my feet into the stranger's stomach and kicked, propelling myself out of his viselike arms and into the open water beside the pier. "What the actual hell are you doing?" I shouted, turning around to face my attacker once I was a few feet away.

"Saving you!" the man shouted, sea green eyes locking with mine as we rose with a swell and dipped back down again.

My heart faltered.

Hudson? Had I gone hypoxic and started seeing things?

Gravity wavered. That was the only explanation as to why my stomach pitched against the waves, why I suddenly couldn't tell if the sky was above or below me, why my heart couldn't pick a rhythm, why I ceased swimming . . . and promptly sank.

Water rushed over my head.

I startled, then kicked back to the surface as Hudson reached for me. Sputtering at the first breath of air, I batted away his hand. Like hell was I ever going to let Hudson fucking Ellis think I needed rescuing. "I'm not drowning, you asshole!"

Those annoyingly gorgeous eyes of his flared. "Are you sure about that?"

Holy shit, it's really him. His sandy-brown hair was cropped short at the sides and only slightly longer on top instead of falling into his eyes, but his voice, the way his brow knit, even the fact that he'd jumped in the ocean fully clothed all screamed that I wasn't hallucinating.

"Sure about you being an asshole? Absolutely. And I'm quite certain I wasn't drowning." The years had carved away the traces of the cute boy I'd known in his face and left the angles of a fully grown man who'd become a stranger. A *beautiful* man with a strong square chin, full lips I'd never had the chance to kiss, and eyes that had haunted my dreams for nearly a decade. And damn whatever was left of the broken little pieces, but my foolish heart leapt straight into my throat.

"Then what would you call whatever that was?" He motioned toward the water with his head, his arms busy treading water just like mine were. "Because it didn't look like swimming."

"Working on my lung capacity!" How was this even happening right now? "Unbelievable." That's exactly what this was. Of all the times I'd practiced what I'd say if I ever ran into him, this was one scenario I hadn't envisioned.

Every emotion I kept locked tight in a little steel box when it came to Hudson flared to life, flooding me with disbelief, and yearning, and anger . . . so much anger. That's what I held on to as I swam past him for the ladder mounted on the third pylon.

It had been so long that I'd felt anything but numb that the anger was a blessing.

"Wait, you were working out?" He swam my direction while I found the familiar wood and began climbing out of the water and onto the pier.

"*Was* being the key word there," I said over my shoulder, continuing the ascent. The sun did little to combat the breeze on my ocean-chilled skin, and my teeth chattered as I made it to the top of the ladder, then quickly scrambled for the towel I'd wedged between boards so it wouldn't blow away.

"The water is still in the fifties!" The wood groaned under his weight as he climbed the ladder.

"And I have three more months to rehab an injury that should take another six." I wrapped the towel and tucked it under my arms, more than a little conscious that I wore a completely unsexy black one-piece that was better suited for a swim meet than a chance encounter with . . . well, whatever Hudson had been to me. "And who are you to lecture me about water temperature? About *anything*? Let alone scare the shit out of me—"

"I thought you were *drowning*," Hudson repeated as his head crested the edge of the pier.

"So you said." I tugged the towel closer. So much for that one revenge fantasy where—oh my *God*.

Hudson made it onto the pier, and he was *huge*. He'd been a little over six feet when we'd met, but he'd gained at least a few inches and a good forty pounds of what looked to be pure muscle with the way his white Bruins T-shirt clung to his chest and abs as he stood.

"I was trying to save you, Allie!" He had the nerve to look all wounded, like I was the one in the wrong here. "I thought you needed help."

Save me? After all this time? Anger flushed up my neck, stinging my cheeks with much-needed heat. "Yeah, well you're a little late for that. And you don't get to call me Allie. Not anymore."

Crap, that came out a little more aggressively than I'd intended.

His eyes slid shut like he was in pain, and he breathed deeply before opening them again, his gaze momentarily pinning me in place. "Been holding on to that one for a while, have you?"

A heartbeat passed, then a few more as I stumbled down all the possible avenues this conversation could take. I was too damn tired to fight with him—with anyone, really.

"About ten years," I finally admitted.

"Sounds about right, give or take a few months." The dip of his wide shoulders almost made me feel bad.

Almost. Then I remembered the hospital stay, and the rehab . . . and the funeral, and the anger overpowered the guilt with glee.

"What are you doing here, anyway?" I shifted my weight to take it off my aching ankle. The Achilles repair had been done by the best orthopedic surgeon in the country, but that didn't mean I was happy with how long it was taking to heal, or the rather grim prognosis. I was lucky to already be walking unaided, not that I'd ever admit that out loud—especially not to Hudson.

"I live here." He ruffled his hand through his wet hair, sending water droplets flying, then looked over the edge of the pier, into the water. "And there goes another hat."

"Still making a habit of jumping into the ocean to rescue perfectly safe swimmers?" I ran a hand down my low ponytail, squeezing the cold salt water out of my hair.

"One, you weren't perfectly safe the first time I jumped in after you—" He looked away from the water, obviously giving up on the hat the cove had swallowed.

"That was eleven years ago—" I argued.

"—and two, yeah, it's my job to jump in and rescue people, but I thought I'd learned not to take my favorite hat." He dropped his arms to his sides.

"—and I'm perfectly capable of swimming!" I finished, then blinked. His job? Silence hung between us as his words settled on me. "You're a rescue swimmer, aren't you? You made it." The sixteen-year-old girl inside me stood up and cheered for him, but she was quickly hushed by the misanthrope I'd become.

"Yeah." His lips quirked upward for a second, and he dripped water onto the pier. I probably owed him a towel or something, given that his intentions had been pure. "And you're a world-famous ballerina." He cocked his head to the side and searched my eyes. "Or do you prefer Seconds star?"

I huffed. "That's all Eva. I just lend her my name and do some of the videos to help her out." Now we were talking about Seconds? This was officially the most surreal conversation of my life.

"I figured. You usually sought the praise of one person, not multiple millions." He twisted the bottom of his T-shirt in his hands, wringing out more water.

He did not just say that. Pretty sure my therapist heard that all the way from New York City.

"It's only one point one million," I said. "And you don't know me well enough anymore to say what type I am." Pulling my towel tighter, I walked past him on the aging pier, grateful Dad had it built twelve feet wide so I had plenty of room. "You didn't answer the question, Hudson. Why are you at my house?"

To say I'm sorry. To explain why I never called. That was the dream, wasn't it?

He followed me down the pier and across the wide platform that had served as the foundation of the boathouse until a storm took it out. "I'm keeping a pinkie promise."

"What?" My eyebrows shot up in disbelief as I glanced back at him.

"I was banking on my niece being wrong, and you not being here, and now I'm scrambling for a game plan, honestly." He ruffled the water out of his hair.

"Well, I'd certainly hate for this to be hard on *you*." The sarcasm I shot his direction was strong enough to withstand the waves breaking on the beach as I started up the wooden steps that led to the house, Hudson only a step or two behind me. About halfway up, the ache in my ankle became a throb, and I gave in to the urge to limp. Just a little, though.

"I wouldn't have bothered you except . . ." He drifted off. "Are you all right? Juniper—that's my niece—mentioned you were here recovering." Was that worry in his tone?

No, thank you.

"I remember her name. Caroline and Sean adopted her that last summer I was here." Not that Hudson's sister had known we were friends, and even if she had, she never would have let me near her baby. I glanced back to see him staring down at my ankle, where two pink scars flanked the silvery one, then continued up the stairs. "I'm fine."

"Your Achilles? Again?"

"Again?" I whipped my head around, my wet ponytail smacking me in the shoulder as I halted the climb to stare down at him. "So you knew?" A whole other kind of scar split open inside of me, leaching scalding, fresh pain from a wound that had never completely healed. "You knew it had been torn in the crash? You knew there *was* a crash?" Every worst fear and ugly thought resurfaced. He'd known. He'd freaking *known*, and still hadn't reached out. "All this time, part of me wondered if you were mad at me for not showing up that night, and that's why you left for basic without saying a word. But you *knew* what happened to me?" His mouth closed in a damning admission of guilt. I reached past the pain for any emotion besides anger, but only found a drowned, watery sense of betrayal that I didn't have energy for. "I think I preferred not knowing for certain."

"Allie . . ." He winced. "I mean, Alessandra—shit, that doesn't sound right either." How did he have the right to look genuinely devastated?

"Don't give me that look." I gestured at his stupidly beautiful face, nearly losing my towel. Of course he'd gotten better looking with age while my body had all but given out on me. I wasn't even thirty yet and I was falling apart. "You don't get the honor of looking . . . ruined. Not when you apparently straight-up abandoned me. Do you know how many times I texted you? Called you from my hospital bed?"

The blood drained from his face. "There aren't enough words in the English language to convey how sorry I am, how sorry I have been, and I know that's not enough."

There were the words I'd craved for so long, and now they didn't matter.

"You're right. It's not enough. I don't want an apology." My fingernails scraped against the grain of the banister. "I want an explanation as to why my best friend couldn't be bothered to show up when I needed him most. You had *days* before you had to report to basic."

He opened his mouth, then shut it and looked away.

"If we'd been dating, I would have chalked it up to a really bad breakup—which is shitty enough—but losing your best friend without so much as a word?" My voice broke. There was no comparable pain. I never let *anyone* all the way in, but he'd been the closest.

"I was a stupid eighteen-year-old kid." He white-knuckled the railing, and his jaw ticked. "And I made what I thought was the only choice I had, and it was the wrong one. By the time I figured out just how wrong, I was at basic and knew you'd never forgive me."

My chest threatened to cave in.

"You were a kid? That's the best you've got?" *Fuck this.* Hudson Ellis didn't get to know the depth of how he'd wounded me. I forced the hurt, the sour taste of betrayal, and the dying hope that he'd had some forgivable reason for ghosting me into a mental box and locked it away just like I did the physical pain during rehearsals. I refused to let it touch me. Then I plastered a practiced public smile on my face.

"Shit," he muttered.

"Doesn't matter." I shrugged, then continued up the last few steps. "Maybe it's hyperbolic to call us best friends when we were really just a summer thing. That particular summer was over. No need to drag up the past." The words sounded hollow, but I choked them out. I'd convinced myself to believe far bigger lies than this.

"You have every right to an explanation."

Hold up, was that *anger* in his tone? I wasn't turning around to look. The faster I got away from him, the better. "I don't think I want one, anymore. Nothing you could ever say would make it right. So, let's just let it go. Obviously, you were too immature to handle what happened to me. Shit happens, right? I'm only here for the summer. You should keep busy . . . rescuing people. It will be easy to avoid each other." The breeze picked up as we reached the top of the steps and walked onto the perfectly maintained grass.

I startled.

A young girl waited for us, her hands gripping a cell phone in front of her petite frame, her brown eyes widening to the size of saucers as her gaze found mine. There was something familiar about the tilt of her button nose, the hints of copper in her eyes, but I couldn't put my finger on it. Had I met her before? At a performance? An intensive?

And what was she doing standing in the middle of my backyard?

I blinked in confusion as Hudson walked past me to stand behind the girl, putting his hands on her shoulders before turning those green eyes on me in an uncharacteristic plea. Hudson Ellis wasn't a guy who pleaded for *anything*. "I'm here because Juniper wanted to meet you."

Oh. This was his niece. No wonder she looked familiar. Of course, he'd shown me pictures when she was a baby. She'd been a cute one, from what I remembered.

Juniper stared at me and handed him the cell phone. "Did you save her?" She risked a peek up at Hudson.

He kept that beseeching look aimed at me. What? Like I was going to be a jerk to a little kid? Maybe I'd earned my reputation for being quiet, maybe even a little standoffish, but never mean. Only Hudson brought that out in me.

"I wasn't drowning," I answered the girl, then retucked my towel and held out my hand. Her uncle might be an ass, but that wasn't her fault. "Hi, Juniper." The corners of my mouth tugged upward as her face lit up. She pushed her windblown hair out of her eyes before taking my hand silently. "I'm—"

"Alessandra Rousseau, I know," she answered with a toothy grin. "You're the youngest principal dancer in the history of the Metropolitan Ballet Company, including your mother, who was a legend in her own right before she retired," she gushed, her words running into each other as her grip tightened. "Your performance of Juliet was perfection, and your fouettés during *Swan Lake* last season were epic, and all I want to be when I grow up is you."

Hudson winced.

What? Like I was a bad role model? I bristled, but didn't let it show. "Well, I'm not much of a dancer right now, but thank you." Pretty sure she was cutting off circulation to my fingers.

She shook her head with confidence, sending her locks flying again. "You're just injured. You'll be back by next season." Letting go of my hand, she waged war with the wind on behalf of her hair and lost.

"You're very kind to say so." Crap, did Hudson's niece have to be the sweetest kid ever? "I'm guessing you're a dancer? Is Mrs. Madeline your teacher?"

"Not exactly." Her teeth bit into a chapped lower lip.

I glanced up at Hudson and immediately regretted it. That face, the way he looked at me like he knew *me* underneath the years of layers I'd worn for everyone else, cut right through my defenses like that kettlebell through the water, and I hated it. Whatever string had tied us together all those years ago—friendship or something that could have been more—it had been unraveled to a thread, but was still there, as annoying and certain as physics. *Time to snip and get it over with. Closure and all.*

"This is where it gets awkward." His focus bounced over my features like he needed to memorize everything in detail in case this was the last time he ever saw me.

"Oh, we're just now entering awkward territory?" I arched a brow.

"Point taken." The asshole bit back a smile. "Go ahead and ask." Hudson tapped Juniper's shoulders. "I did my part and got you here, but she can't say yes if you don't ask."

Juniper looked up at him with the kind of trust I'd once given him, and I couldn't help but melt a little and worry a lot. I knew what Hudson did with trust.

"So, Juniper," I said, clutching my towel and crouching to her eye level, "what is it you'd like to ask me?"

Her gaze swung to mine, little flecks of copper catching the sunlight, and she took a big breath. "I want you to convince my mom that ballerinas aren't all horrible people."

Okay, then. "I'm sorry?"

"She thinks they're all spoiled rotten, and vicious, and mean"—her head bobbed with every accusation—"and that if I do ballet, I'll become a stuck-up snot with body issues just like the tourists," she blurted, her cheeks turning pink. "Not that *I* think you're snotty! I know you aren't."

"Umm. Thanks?" I stood slowly, my heart sinking at the thought of breaking this little girl's. "Look, Juniper, I'd love to help you convince your mom, I really would. But as great as she is and as much as she obviously loves you, unless something drastic has changed in the last decade, I have the wrong last name for the job. She's not . . . overly fond of Rousseaus."

Caroline had loathed us all, especially my mother.

"No, it's just your little sister she hates," Juniper rushed. "Eva, not you."

Hudson groaned, his eyes sliding shut momentarily.

"Well, that's comforting to know." I pressed my lips in a line and fought the irrational urge to laugh, something I hadn't done in months. "Eva can be an acquired taste. Either way, I'm afraid that I'm the wrong person to ask. You'd have far better luck picking a dancer from a local family to help you convince her. And you probably need a towel." I aimed that last part at Hudson, backing up a step and preparing to turn toward the house. Anne was due back from her appointment any minute, and she'd freak if she knew I'd been in the ocean alone without a wet suit.

"I'm used to—" he started.

"No, it has to be you!" Juniper shouted at me, panic pitching her voice higher as she broke away from Hudson. "You're the only one she'll listen to! Not just because you're the best, or the nicest, but because if you tell her I should dance, she'll let me! She'll have to!" Each word grew more frantic until she was practically shouting.

"I don't have that kind of power," I said gently.

"Just listen to me!" she begged. "Someone has to listen to *me*!"

An ache bloomed in my chest, pressing tight against my ribs. How many times had I wanted to scream the very same thing?

"Juniper," Hudson lectured softly, but the girl lifted her chin in the air and marched toward me.

"I'm listening," I assured her. "Why are you so certain your mom cares what I think?"

Juniper swallowed and glanced back at Hudson, who looked as confused as I felt, then locked her big brown eyes on me. "Because"— she straightened her shoulders—"you're my biological mother."

CHAPTER SIX

Allie

Bright2Lit: The genes in this family are phenomenal. RousseauSisters4 are you born in
pointe shoes, or what?

Biological *what*?

I stared at Juniper, then leaned in a little, certain I'd misheard her.
"I don't understand."

"I've watched all your tapes," she blurted, her words tripping over
each other. "We move the same. We look alike. We have the same color
hair and eyes, and the same birthmark!" Juniper spun, turning her back
to me and lifting her hair to reveal a stork bite at the nape of her neck.

Just like mine.

Strangling my towel, I looked up at Hudson, who was busy staring at
his niece like she'd grown another head. Guess this was news to him too.

"Juniper—" I started.

"Don't deny it!" she begged, her lower lip quivering before she bit
into it again. "You're my mother. I know you are. It's why I love ballet
so much. It's in my—our genes." Her eyes watered.

Oh God, she was going to cry. How the hell was I supposed to let her down easily? "It's just that I—"

"We have the same smile, and the same hands," she interrupted, wiggling her hands my direction. "And I know you're probably surprised to see me, and I shouldn't have ambushed you, but you're my last chance."

"But I've never—" I tried again.

"Look, I can prove it!" She shook off her backpack, dropping it to the lawn. "I took a DNA test, and all you have to do is take the same one—"

"You *what*?" Hudson moved to my side and glared down at his niece.

"I took a DNA test, naturally." Her forehead crinkled like we were the illogical ones here, impervious to the look her uncle unleashed on her.

"Does your mom know?" he demanded. "And how?"

"I ordered it online, and—" she started.

"Let me guess, scrolled a few years past your actual birthday?" he interjected, folding his arms across his chest. "This isn't Seconds, Juniper."

"If companies didn't want kids to break the rules, they'd make them a lot harder to get past," she countered, folding her arms in his mirror image. "I just stuck a cotton swab in my mouth and shipped it back." She slid her phone out of her back pocket and opened an app, then showed it to Hudson. "See? And of course Mom doesn't know. She'd *lose* it. She says I have to wait until I'm eighteen to find my birth family, which is totally unfair."

"I never should have gotten you this phone," Hudson muttered, taking the device and looking through the app.

"Like I wouldn't have figured out another way? It's not like the school library doesn't have computers, and Uncle Gavin gave me a prepaid Visa card for Christmas." She threw a glance my way every few words.

"Smart girl," I admitted despite our current circumstances.

"I'm *your* girl." Juniper stared up at me with complete and total certainty. "It makes sense. You gave me to your friend's sister. Occam's razor and all that."

"Occam's razor. They teach fourteenth-century philosophy in elementary school out here?" I asked Hudson.

He opened his mouth, but Juniper ran him right over.

"I'm in the gifted and talented program." She enunciated every word, clearly insulted. "And it's a *really* good school district, which is why Mom didn't move inland with Grandma and Grandpa."

"Noted." I swiped my hand across my forehead to keep salt water from dripping from my hair into my eyes.

"Look, one of my friends was adopted too. We talk about it all the time, and obviously I know how to use the internet. Point is, I'm not mad at you for placing me for adoption—though I do have some questions that are statistically proven to help minimize the time I'll need to spend in therapy." She nodded. "And really, I love my mom; she's pretty great other than not wanting me to dance, but if you tell her that I should, then she'll listen to you." The hope was back in her eyes.

My shoulders sagged, and I did the one thing I swore I'd never do again, and looked to Hudson for help.

His brow furrowed in the second our gazes locked, and then he sank to his knees in the grass and braced his hands on Juniper's upper arms. "June-Bug, you know I'd never lie to you, right?"

"Right." She glanced between us.

"Allie—Alessandra—isn't your biological mother." He delivered the blow gently, and a part of me that could have thrown him off the cliff a few minutes ago softened. "It would be impossible."

"You don't know that." Her voice broke.

"I do." He nodded. "Your birthday is May fourteenth, just a few days ago, and I saw her a couple of months before you were born. She was here for spring break, and she wasn't pregnant."

"Maybe you didn't notice," she argued, then looked up to me like I would correct him.

"I've never had a baby." I shook my head slowly. "I'm so sorry, but I'm not who you're looking for."

"I don't believe you." Her brow knit, and red crept up her cheeks. "We have the same birthmark!"

"Stork bites are common—"

"And they can be genetic! I looked it up online!" She twisted out of Hudson's hands and grabbed her backpack, yanking on the zipper. A few seconds later, she retrieved a softball-size white box wrapped in plastic. "Just take the test, and then I'll believe you." She held out the box to me. "It's the fastest on the market. I checked."

"I'm sure you did."

"You can't ask her to do that." Hudson stood and swiped a hand through his hair.

Some nervous tells never changed. If he had his hat on, he'd be shaping the brim.

"She can't say yes if I don't ask. Isn't that what you said?" She glared up at him.

Gravel crunched in the driveway, and we all turned in time to see Anne pull her blue Mercedes sedan into the carriage house.

I was so busted.

"So will you do it?" Juniper asked, undeterred by my sister's arrival.

"How long have you been planning this?" Hudson asked her.

"Four months," she replied, staring at me. "Will you do it?"

"I'm not your mother," I said softly.

"Prove it." She shook the box and I took it because it seemed like the only polite thing to do. Victory flared in her eyes, and I blinked, struck again by the weirdest sense of déjà vu. I had to have met this girl somewhere else.

"Absolutely not." Hudson grabbed the box before I had a firm grip on it. "We're done. Go get in the truck."

"Uncle Hud—"

"Now, Juniper." I knew that tone well. It left zero room for any argument, and from the immediate sag in her posture, she knew it.

62

She sent an imploring look my way, then snatched her backpack with both hands, ignored the zipper entirely, and strode the opposite direction from Anne, heading back toward the northeast side of the house.

"I am so sorry." Hudson watched Juniper retreat around the corner of the porch.

"Please tell me you didn't know . . ." I turned my head slowly to look up at him.

"I had no fucking clue." Stunned was an expression I wasn't used to seeing on him.

I reached for the box, and to my surprise, he gave it to me. "She actually ordered DNA tests."

"I never even knew she was looking for her mother." He wrung out the bottom of his T-shirt, and I averted my gaze at the first hint of skin.

"I can get you a towel." I did a double take when I caught him staring at me in disbelief. "What? I can simultaneously ignore that you destroyed me as a teenager while having manners. It's called adulthood."

We locked eyes, and I fought to summon the anger back, to feel something that would give me a chance at escaping this encounter unscathed, but all I found was the exhaustion that had been my companion since January.

"I have one in my car. A towel, that is." He ripped his gaze from mine and motioned to the box. "Do me a favor and throw that away for me? God knows who she'd sic it on next."

"I can do that."

"Thank you."

Anne cleared her throat from the back porch, and we both pivoted to face her across the pool. She drummed her fingertips on the railing, took one look at Hudson, and shook her head. "Did we turn our clocks back ten years or something?"

"Nice to see you, too, Anne." Hudson offered a mock salute.

"And what are you doing—" Her eyes flared and she pointed a finger at me. "You went swimming alone at the beach again, didn't you?"

"Maybe?" I gave her a cringing smile. "But I was safe the whole time. And Hudson here is now a rescue diver, so there was nothing to worry about."

She glanced between us like we were teenagers again and she had to cover so Mom didn't find us sneaking out. "Which is why he's all wet, I'm guessing. Fully clothed, at that."

"That one's on me," Hudson admitted.

"Great." She nodded sarcastically. "I'll . . . leave you to whatever it is you're doing." Her heels clicked on the porch as she headed inside. "Hudson, do me a favor and at least say goodbye to her this time before you go, would you? It would be a shame for me to go to jail for acting on a decade's worth of intrusive thoughts when it comes to your demise." The screen door slammed behind her.

"And that's my cue." Gripping the box, I walked through the grass and around the pool, letting every question I'd silently gathered over the years die on my tongue.

"Allie," he called out. "Alessandra."

I paused but didn't look back. That was the only way I'd survived the last ten years, keeping my eyes forward.

"I'm truly, genuinely sorry. For everything."

My eyes slid shut, and I waited for the words to hit, to soothe the festering wound that refused to heal, but they fell into me like a coin tossed down a wishing well, too small to effect any change—shiny, but pointless. "Get her home safely."

I headed inside without another word, slipping up the carpeted back steps and down the long hallway past Eva's room and the shrine that had been Lina's, to mine, which sat across from Anne's.

Then I showered off the salt and shock and tried like hell to scrub any thought of Hudson off me. My skin was more than wrinkled by the time I finished and dressed in simple leggings and a lightweight sweater, ignoring all the trendy items Anne had packed for me. It wasn't like I had to impress anyone here.

The sound of a knife meeting the cutting board repeatedly greeted me as I walked into the professional-grade kitchen.

Anne had ditched the matching jacket to her navy blue sheath dress and was chopping the hell out of a bag of carrots. Something at her meeting had gone very wrong.

Barefoot, I padded across the hardwood floor to the refrigerator, then pulled out two bottles of Smartwater and slid into the middle of eight high-backed barstools that sat along the white marble island. I twisted open a bottle, then waited for her to pause her vegetable massacre before sliding it across the expanse.

She caught it with her left hand and put down the knife with her right. "Thanks."

"How was your meeting?" I asked, cracking open my own bottle.

"Finn wants the brownstone and said I could have everything else." She glanced away a second too late to hide the shimmer of tears in her eyes. "So my attorney thinks it went swimmingly well. I'll leave the marriage financially better off than I came into it, which is a win for some people, I guess."

Sorrow settled around us, thick and bitter. "I'm so sorry, Anne."

She threw back the water like it was tequila. Maybe it should have been. Then she picked up the knife. "When you can't give your husband the only thing he's ever asked for in an eight-year marriage, he divorces you. Nothing to be sorry about."

"There's more to life than having kids." I took a drink.

"Not to Finn." She assaulted the next carrot. "They mean the world to him."

"You deserve someone who thinks *you're* the world." I picked at the label, wishing it was one of Finn's eyes.

She paused. "He said I failed him." The knife fell from her hand onto the cutting board, and she braced her palms flat on the gray marble. "How screwed up is that? I'm the one who went through the miscarriages, the IVF, the hormones, the—" Her head drooped. "But *he's* the one who feels let down. Like I'm not heartbroken too?"

I slipped out of my chair, rounded the island, and hugged her from behind. "You're not a failure. You're a freaking lawyer."

"Who quit practicing after a year because Finn thought it would help relieve stress and make getting pregnant easier." She scoffed.

"You're beautiful, and kind, and smart, and a thousand other wonderful things. You're definitely the best of us." I dipped my chin to rest on her shoulder.

She hooked her hand over my arm and squeezed, then let her head rest against the side of mine for a moment. "I'm certainly the only one capable of decent cooking, so why don't you sit down and let me finish making you some chicken soup? You might need it after risking hypothermia." She gave my face a pat with her left hand, and I retreated back to my side of the island.

"It was only for a few minutes. The pool doesn't have the same resistance that waves give." I finished the bottle of water and reached for the bag of celery.

"Nope." Anne grabbed it and pulled it into her murderous clutches. "I've seen the havoc you wreak in a kitchen. Besides, you're supposed to be letting me take care of you, remember? That's why we're here."

"We're here because of Mom's draconian occupation requirements." I drew a knee to my chest and watched Anne lay into the celery.

"True."

Naturally we'd procrastinated the deadline Mom had imposed, laying down the law that once every three years, the house had to be used the entirety of a summer by at least one of us, and occupied by all three of us for one of those weeks. Guess it was her little way of ensuring we'd still spend time together, but I kind of wondered if it was a little revenge dig at Dad, setting us up for failure so we'd lose the house he'd loved.

Until now, Anne had been busy with her job and husband, only popping into the beach house for the annual Haven Cove Classic in August, while Eva and I had been too busy at the Company to make it work. Maybe if I'd come in the last couple of years, I would have seen Hudson sooner. How long had he been back?

Doesn't matter. Let it go.

"Has Eva told you when she's coming?" I asked.

"I think she's planning on staying the full week of the Classic, but I hope she comes for the Fourth of July," Anne answered, transferring the vegetables to the pot. "She'd better show up, because I love this house and I'm not losing it."

"You know, you could always just live here year round if you wanted. Neither of us would care, if it made you happy."

"And leave you two in New York unsupervised? I'll pass. Want to tell me what Hudson Ellis was doing here?" The gentle tone and concerned gaze reminded me of Dad.

"His niece wanted to meet me." The rest of it was too ridiculous to bother her with after the day she'd had. "Guess she follows Eva on Seconds."

"It's half your account too." She grabbed a fully cooked chicken from the refrigerator and kicked the door shut. "And did he happen to explain if the earth swallowed him whole while you were in the hospital? Or maybe aliens abducted him?"

"No." I rested my chin on my knee. "But he did apologize."

"Well, that makes up for everything." The chicken hit the cutting board with a thud. "Did you tell him to get fucked?"

A corner of my mouth rose. She never swore. "I told him we'd be best off ignoring each other while I'm here. It's been years. I'm over it."

"Hmm." She started in on the chicken with deft strokes of the knife.

"What's that supposed to mean?" I watched every slice, mesmerized by her efficiency.

"It means I can't remember a time where you and Hudson were in the same town and capable of ignoring each other." She tilted her head. "You guys were glued at the hip more than Gavin and Lina, and they actually dated."

"When Mom wasn't looking." Being in this house brought it all back with startling clarity, as though this place was a honing stone for the memories. If I wasn't careful, they'd sharpen themselves into knives. I stretched my arms as the typical midday lethargy stole over me.

"When Mom wasn't looking," she agreed. "Man, she and Gavin snuck around for months that summer before she got bored and dumped him." Her head cocked to the side. "Was that the summer before she joined San Francisco? Or MBC?"

"A little of both, but mostly MBC," I answered, since neither of us was going to say *the summer before she died*. My jaw practically unhinged as I fought the yawn and lost. "Swimming must have tired me out."

"Hmm." She set the knife down. "You call Kenna back? She's tried you at least three times this week."

"I'll call her later," I lied. Did I feel guilty about dodging her calls? Yes. Was I going to remedy that by speaking to her? No.

"She's your closest friend, Allie," Anne lectured, but it was the note of worry in her tone that kept me from sniping back.

"And the Company's orthopedic specialist," I reminded her, grabbing the empty water bottle and starting toward the recycling bin inside the pantry. "And we both know I'm not making the progress she'll want, and she'll have to report that to Vasily. He'll scrap my ballet with Isaac for the fall, and I can't risk it. I'm not slacking. I'm doing it all. The Pilates, the strength training, the resistance bands—but I'm not strong enough to get on demi-pointe."

"Did it occur to you that maybe she just wants to talk to her friend?" Anne countered as I leaned against the doorframe to her left, taking some weight off my ankle. "No one thinks you're slacking. I don't think you comprehend *how* to slack. Everyone at the Company knows you're working yourself to the bone to get back in the studio. It's the *only* thing you're doing. I thought being out here might help you relax or maybe at least smile—"

"You stop and see Mom on your way back?"

"Don't change the subject." She stared at me.

I stared back.

If there had been a contest in our house for who could hold an awkward silence the longest, I would have a crown and we both knew it.

"Yes, I stopped in at the school and saw Mom." Her sigh was a white flag.

"Not sure I'd call it a school." It was more like an institution.

"Do you want to take a walk once I have this put together?"

"Smooth segue, but I think I'll take a nap." Fatigue won. *Seems like it always does.* "Sleep equals healing and all that."

"How about we go out for a movie after dinner? They're running a Brat Pack marathon, and nothing perks you up like John Hughes." She offered a soft smile.

Just the idea of putting on real clothes, of putting forth enough energy to play the role of Alessandra Rousseau in public, had me stifling another yawn. "Maybe tomorrow."

"Maybe tomorrow," Anne agreed, her smile slipping. "Get some rest. I'll make sure you don't sleep through dinner."

"Thanks." I walked out of the kitchen and up the front stairs, glancing at the gallery of candid photos along the wall and pausing at the last one. Dad had captured the four of us sitting side by side at the end of the pier, our backs to him in a rare moment where even Eva was still.

She lounged farthest to the right, her hands braced behind her, her fifteen-year-old head thrown back to embrace the sun. Lina and Anne held the center, nineteen and eighteen respectively, their faces turned toward each other in laughter, no doubt over some private joke, while seventeen-year-old me sat with Lina's arm wrapped around my shoulders, my head resting on hers as I stared off into the water.

God, I missed that feeling, that comforting peace and certainty of the future. We'd been as steady as the pylons of the pier as long as we were together, weathering the storm that was our mother, leaning on each other to balance the load when the waves of her expectations threatened to pull any one of us under.

The brief sensation of peace faded quickly as I remembered that Lina had died only a couple weeks after Dad framed the shot. Life was so fucking unfair. She should've been here, or on a stage in New York dancing *Giselle*, or wherever she wanted to be.

She should've been alive.

She would have known how to make Anne feel better, and whether to push or rest my ankle. She would have known how to guide Eva and deal with Mom. She would have shown us all how it was done—this business of being an adult.

I walked into my room and crashed onto the bed, then crawled beneath the familiar, comforting weight of the rose-blush quilt. At some point maybe my body would catch up on all the rest I'd denied it over the years. Until then, I'd give it the sleep it seemed hell bent on taking with or without my consent.

Rolling toward my white wicker nightstand to deposit my phone, I checked to make sure Lina's amethyst ring was tucked away safely in my drawer and spotted the DNA test Juniper had demanded I take. A pang of sympathy rang through me. She just wanted to know where she fit in the world.

For the briefest of seconds, I felt bad for Hudson. The little girl had seemed wrecked.

"I'm truly, genuinely sorry. For everything."

At least he'd apologized. There was a time I would have forgiven him, no questions asked, would have known that whatever kept him from my side was out of his control. I'd trusted him more than my own sisters. And just like I'd never understand why Lina had been taken so young, why I'd survived the crash and she hadn't, I had to make peace with never understanding why Hudson had walked out of my life without a goodbye.

You were both kids. Let it go.

I picked up the box and read the back. Seemed easy enough. All I had to do was download the app, swab my cheek, and send it back.

Considering I'd never had a child, it wasn't like I was scared of the results. Hell, I'd been a virgin until almost twenty, long after Juniper was born.

Maybe I wouldn't get the answers I needed from life, but I could help her by proving I wasn't the answer to her question.

Six days later, the app sent me a notification.

My jaw dropped.

CHAPTER SEVEN

Hudson

OnPointe34: Not you guys correcting a professional dancer in the comments. Dead. The only person better than RousseauSisters4 at this is the missing half of that duo. Hey, Eva, cough your sister up before we send out a manhunt.

I rolled the warm glass of Yuengling between my palms, scraping the knobbed edges of the bottle against the table as Kurt Cobain sang about a heart-shaped box from the archaic jukebox in the corner of the bar, on which Gavin only allowed his selection of grunge or the rare punk song to play.

Six days.

Somehow, I'd made it six fucking days without driving my ass over to Allie's and begging her forgiveness. Our past demanded more than a simple apology or a bullshit excuse. A lot more. What I'd done to her required blood, full-knees groveling, and probably a piece of my soul, and even then I wasn't sure it would be enough.

A swift shin kick jarred me, and across the ill-lit booth, Eric Beachman's eyes rose in expectation. "Isn't that right, Ellis?" he prompted, glancing at the woman sitting next to me.

Right. Shit. I was supposed to be on a double date. It was the first time in a week my schedule had matched Eric's to get out for a drink, and he'd brought his girlfriend's sister. What the hell was her name? And what had Beachman asked?

"He doesn't have to answer," the brunette said with a quick, bright smile.

Jessica—Eric's girlfriend—narrowed her eyes at me.

"Every swimmer likes to brag about the number of rescues they've had." Eric helped me out, but simultaneously sent me the are-you-fucking-kidding-me look.

I cleared my throat. "Actually, I don't keep count." There, that was easy, even if I'd blanked on the last ten minutes of the conversation, which had been my MO all week. I'd be in the middle of something, and I'd think of Allie. Ordering new gear for the shop? Allie. Taking Juniper's phone? Allie. Working out in the pool? Allie.

She usually lived in the back of my mind, but now she was up front and *everywhere.*

"I think that's humble." Beth—that was her name—said, her fingers drumming on the side of her empty glass as her smile widened. "I like that in a guy."

Allie knew I was anything but humble. She'd known I was impetuous, and cocky, and *so* fucking arrogant, and liked me anyway.

"I'm sure he likes that you like that." Eric took a drink.

Not sure I did. Beth was beautiful, with wide blue eyes and soft brown hair that leaned more toward chestnut than the dark coffee of Allie's—

Stop comparing them.

It was all I'd done all night, put my funny, outgoing date up against the woman who had set my standard a dozen years ago, and that wasn't fair. I was being a dick, and she didn't even know it.

"How about I grab you another drink?" I offered, already sliding out of the booth as Beachman protested that we had a waitress.

I pushed my way through the Friday-night crowd, nodding to a few guys I'd gone to high school with at the dartboard and who were not perks of me being stationed in my hometown, and made my way toward my brother—who wasn't always in the perks column either. Gavin was serving at the far end of the twelve-seat bar, so I snagged one of the two empty barstools along the narrow end and sat.

"What the hell is wrong with you tonight?" Eric took the seat beside me.

"Distracted." I curved the brim of my ball cap.

"You've been spaced out all week," he accused, then shot a glance over his shoulder at a group of boardroom types who were all yelling for Gavin from the corner of the bar. "Is there any reason to be in a dive bar in a two-thousand-dollar suit?" he muttered.

"'Tis the season." I watched my brother make his way down the line of customers. He was a couple inches taller than my six-two frame, which gave him an advantage behind the bar, and perspective to see over the crowd, but I still had twenty pounds of muscle on him, giving me the advantage whenever I needed to kick his ass. "It'll be thick in here next week." Memorial Day weekend was always the unofficial start of the influx, and the Grizzly Bear Bar was a good indicator of the current tourist population. Come Fourth of July, this place would be packed to fire code.

"You worried about your test score?" Eric mirrored my posture, bracing his elbows on the edge of the bar.

"Nope." The results of the exams we'd taken last week to qualify us for promotion wouldn't be out for another couple weeks, but I knew I'd nailed it.

"Worried that even if you get picked up on the list, and promoted, there's nowhere for you to advance here at Cape Cod with eleven other swimmers so you'll have to pick another air station and leave your family?" He leveled a knowing look at me.

"Strangely detailed and usually accurate, but also, no." But *now* I was worrying about it.

"I mean, you could go for Port Angeles and soak up the Pacific Northwest, or San Francisco and find out why I love California so much, or even up to Sitka. You know, like you've always wanted." His head tilted slightly, waiting for me to react. That was Eric's primary skill—finding out what got under someone's skin and protecting them if he considered them a friend, or digging at it until they bled if he didn't.

"I'm good here." It had taken me two other East Coast duty stations before I secured Cape Cod, and I wasn't leaving anytime soon. Not as long as Caroline needed me.

"Is it the date?" Eric tried again as Gavin took the orders next to us, my brother's eyebrows knitting as he shot a perplexed look my direction.

"It's not the date." I watched Gavin methodically pull a couple beers from the tap a few feet away, his head inclined our direction at an angle that told me he was listening. "Beth is . . . fine."

"Fine?" Eric's eyebrows shot up. "She's a fucking ten, and that's without my practically-in-laws bias. She's a teacher, which means she's smart—you've heard how funny she is. Plus she seems to like you—not that you have an issue in that department—so what's the problem?"

I shifted on my seat.

"She's not Allie Rousseau," Gavin answered for me, sliding two beers to the boardroom crew on our left.

"Shut the fuck up." I glared at my brother and second-guessed my escape plan. He was clearly in the mood to screw with me.

"She's not." Gavin shrugged and reached for the liquor on the top shelf. "Brown hair, nice smile, petite. Totally his type, but she's not Allie." He poured four shots from the bottle of tequila. "You see, Bachman—"

"Beachman," Eric corrected.

"Whatever." Gavin pushed the shots at the suits, then picked up the tablet to record the drinks on their tab. "You brought him in a nice year-rounder—"

"He means local," I interjected.

"—but little brother here has been hung up on Allie since he was seventeen, and there's nothing you, or I, or Teacher back there in the booth can do about it." He set the tablet down on the back bar and faced us, flipping his Grizzly Bear ball cap backward. "Hence the reason he's sitting at my bar instead of ordering a refill back there." He gestured toward the booths. "Hudson might be the baddest motherfucker alive to the US Coast Guard, but you put Allie Rousseau in a room with him and he'll trip over his own feet."

"Who is Allie Rousseau?" Eric's face scrunched as he glanced between my brother and me.

"You just had to, didn't you?" I narrowed my eyes at my brother.

"It is the sacred privilege of an older sibling to embarrass the younger one at their discretion." He smiled shamelessly and reached for a lager glass beneath the bar.

"Who is Allie Rousseau?" Eric repeated.

"Sometimes I can't decide if I love or despise you." The harder I glared, the wider Gavin grinned.

"Both, little brother." He jostled the brim on my cap like I was twelve again, then poured a Yuengling. "I'm not doing my job if it's not both."

"Who the fuck is Allie Rousseau?" Eric raised his voice.

Gavin lifted his eyebrows at me in challenge and slid the lager my way.

"You're an asshole." I took the offered beer.

"Alessandra Rousseau? The ballerina?" the suit closest to us interrupted.

All three of us turned our heads in surprise.

"What?" The guy loosened his silk tie. "I live in New York and my wife likes ballet."

"Wasn't talking to you," I all but snapped.

"I was." Beachman turned his full body. "Tell me more."

I took a long pull of the beer while Boardroom showed Eric something on his phone.

"Hooooooooly shit." Beachman whipped the phone my direction. "This is who you're talking about?"

A Google image search brought up half a dozen pictures of Allie, mostly on the stage, the long lines of her body contorted flawlessly into impossible positions. He pointed to her formal headshot for the Company, which was—of course—a fucking showstopper. The photographer had caught her without a smile, wide eyed as though waiting for his next direction.

"That's the one," Gavin remarked, starting on another drink and blatantly ignoring the customers at the far end who looked like they wanted another round.

Eric returned the phone and thanked the suit before swiveling his seat back toward me. "And you've never told me about her because . . . ?"

My mouth opened, then shut. This right here was definitely in the drawback column of being stationed in my hometown.

"Because he's still in love with her." Gavin set a drink down in front of me that looked suspiciously like the one Beth had been drinking, rum and Coke. For all his issues in the reliability department, he had a memory like an elephant.

"No, I'm not." Even another swig couldn't wash the taste of a lie out of my mouth.

"Yeah, you are. He is," he repeated to Eric with a nod. "Which is why he doesn't talk about her."

"For fuck's sake, will you stop?" I pushed away from the bar.

"He's either your closest friend or he's not." Gavin scoffed.

"I am." Eric leaned forward like an old man at a barbershop, hungry for gossip disguised as news.

"She was my best friend," I said just to shut up Gavin. "Her parents have a place here, and we met when we were teenagers. We were close for two summers and . . ." Words failed me, just like always. Everything that happened that night had been and still was unspeakable.

"And he was in love with her," Gavin whispered loudly before pouring a Coors Light from the tap.

"Don't you have customers?" I gestured down the bar.

"Don't you have a date you're avoiding?" he countered, sliding the beer to Eric.

"Truth." Eric winced, taking the draft and glancing over his shoulder toward the booths.

"Point is, Bateman—" Gavin started as he mixed a vodka and cranberry juice.

"Beachman," Eric corrected yet again.

"That's what I said." Gavin stuck a cocktail straw in and swirled. "That woman you so kindly brought to meet my brother doesn't stand a chance. Never did. The nicest thing you can do for her is put her out of her misery before he does something truly stupid, like date her."

"Not true." I stood and reached for the beer.

"It is." Gavin glanced my way and pushed the cocktail toward Eric, giving him his full attention and ignoring me. "You see, Barman, I've been there, hung up on a Rousseau girl, and it's an infatuation like no other." He glanced away, then cleared his throat.

My grip tightened on the lager despite the condensation quickly gathering on the glass. I wasn't the only Ellis who didn't talk about those summers.

"But the Rousseau sisters always had the look-but-don't-touch vibe, and a touch-them-and-I'll-ruin-you mother, and while I let that torch burn bright and hot before letting it go, Hudson here still carries his, and now that she's been back in town a couple of weeks?" He flared his hands and made a sound like a bomb. "Hudson is the Death Star, and that woman is Luke, about to blow his ass up."

"That's a shitty analogy." I took another drink and contemplated the mileage between here and Allie's. I'd had maybe a third of a beer all night. I was safe to drive.

"Is it, though?" Gavin cocked his head to the side. "We could go with you're the *Titanic* and she's the iceberg, or she's Oppenheimer and you're the test site in New Mexico—"

"Point taken." I reached for my wallet.

"Wait, did you say *you* had a thing for Allie too?" Eric stepped off his stool.

"God no. Her older sister. Never Allie." Gavin glanced at me, years of history flickering over his gaze in that millisecond before the corner of his mouth rose in a smirk. "Allie was way too young for me. Too tightly wound. Pretty little thing—"

My spine stiffened.

"—but too prim, way too proper, too quiet, way too mousy—"

"Too fucking *mine*," I snapped, flinging a twenty onto the bar top. "And she was none of those things. You never really knew her." Heat flushed up the back of my neck.

"There he is!" Gavin raised his arms in victory. "I've been wondering when you'd wake the fuck up."

Shit, I'd given him *exactly* what he was after, a reaction.

Eric's attention flickered between us like we were opponents in a tennis match.

"Now go have the balls to tell that nice brunette that she's auditioning for a role that was filled over a decade ago." He shoved the twenty back at me. "And you know your money's no good here."

"How did you know she was back in town?" I picked up the rum and Coke in my free hand, leaving the twenty where it was.

"Word travels fast." Gavin shrugged and backed away. "And our niece is a gossip. You know she's going to hound that woman for an autograph."

Juniper. Of course. What else had she told him? "You're watching her tomorrow morning so Caroline can open, right?"

"Are you on a twenty-four-hour shift?" Gavin countered as the voices behind him rose to get his attention.

"Yes." I only pulled them four to six times a month.

"Then looks like I don't have a choice." He saluted me with two fingers and headed toward the other end of the bar, a towel hanging out of the back pocket of his cargo pants.

Eric and I started back toward the booth.

"What happened between you and the ballerina, anyway?" he asked as we made our way through the growing crowd.

This was why I never wanted him to know. Beachman was a fixer, and now I was a problem with what he thought was a solution. "We fell out when I was eighteen, just before I went to basic."

"Let me guess, she didn't return the feelings?"

My stomach twisted. "She . . . it was just complicated. End of story."

"But it's not the end if she just happens to be here while you are. You really are the luckiest bastard I've ever met."

"Trust me. It's over. Allie isn't the type to give second chances." Or let anyone all the way in. I spotted Jessica and Beth and lowered my voice. "There are some fates even I can't outrun, my friend. Do me a favor and let it go."

We quieted as we approached the booth, and I gave Beth my most apologetic smile as I slid in beside her, drinks in hand. "Here you go."

"Thanks." She took the drink, then tucked her hair behind her ear. "So, you grew up here, right? We didn't move here until I was a junior. I think you'd already graduated."

I started to nod, since those dates lined up from what she'd told me earlier, but paused. Gavin was right. I could date this woman and even have a few laughs along the way, but it would eventually end because I'd never give her a full chance, especially not while Allie was a thirteen-minute drive from here.

"Right," I said slowly, noting the tension winding in my chest as my thoughts spun. "I'm so sorry, Beth, but—"

"Hudson?"

The rest of my sentence died, slayed instantly by the sound of her voice. I turned and looked over a pair of jeans that made my palms itch to feel the curves under them, past the lightweight green sweater that fell off one delicate shoulder—exposing a pale-pink bra strap—and up into my favorite pair of whiskey-colored eyes. That tension in my chest cranked to a breaking point, and every thought besides carrying her out of here so I could beg her forgiveness privately fled the mush I called a brain.

"Holy shit, you're the ballerina," Eric announced.

Fucking kill me now.

Allie's eyes widened, and she ripped her gaze from mine. "I . . . am."

"Nice." Beachman grinned and stuck out his hand. "I'm Eric Beachman, Hudson's best friend."

"Alessandra Rousseau. Nice to meet you." Allie shook it but didn't smile. Not even her public, polished, bullshit one.

"Or, I guess I should say, his *new* best friend." He winced, and she retreated to hold the strap of her purse with both hands. "Not that I'm saying that he talks about you being his old best friend, or that you're replaceable or . . . You know what? I'm going to stop talking."

"That would be preferable." I shot him a death look.

Asshole smiled back.

"Okay." Allie glanced between the four of us, finally settling on me, and my ribs ached. God, had it always been like this around her? Hard to breathe from just a look? *You're not eighteen anymore—get a grip and formulate a plan.* "I'm so sorry to interrupt, but I was hoping I could have a word with you? In private?"

Hell yes. Fuck yes. Absolutely yes. Screw a plan. Whatever she wanted, she could have.

"Sure." *Great vocabulary, jackass.* I abandoned my beer and slid out of the booth as she backed up a few steps to make space. "Back room?"

She nodded, then turned toward the bar and started walking. I kept my eyes off her ass and used every second to strategize my possible responses to what she might say. Forget logic and the very real reasons I'd ghosted her; every single scenario I pictured began and ended with the one thing I'd never done for any woman—groveling.

She opened the door near the corner of the bar like it hadn't been ten years since the last time she'd turned the handle, and damn if it didn't feel like I was eighteen again, hiding out with her while Gavin was on a shift, studying for the entrance test and laughing and talking about nothing yet everything at the same time.

I walked in after her, noting the scent of air freshener and stale beer, and closed the door behind me. For as bad as it smelled, it was neat and organized, from the file cabinet in the corner to the desk to my left. That's where I put my ass, leaned it right on the edge of the surprisingly sturdy furniture so she'd have a clear line to the door and wouldn't feel trapped.

"This place looks exactly the same." She turned slowly in the flickering fluorescent light, taking in the details of the space in that quiet, observant way she had. I'd always thought she'd survived in that house because she was acutely perceptive, able to predict when a storm was headed her way. "But you . . ." She folded her arms across her chest and studied me with eyes that had lost the angry fire I'd faced back at the house. Given the cursory, almost empty way she looked at me, the fire would have been a blessing. "You take up more of it than you used to."

"A couple inches of growth and rescue swimmer school will do that." A corner of my mouth lifted. "And you look good too." Better than good. She was a knockout, with big eyes, bow-shaped lips, and the cutest freckles across her cheeks. The girl I'd always thought was beautiful had grown far past that word as a woman.

She scoffed. "I look like I haven't taken class in four months or slept since childhood." It came out as flat as her gaze.

"Never could take a compliment."

A spark of that fire flared in her eyes, and I barely leashed a cheer. She was still in there. "Not the point." She shook her head, and her hair fell around her face in a soft deep-brown curtain as she dug into her purse. The wavy mass was a little longer now, falling a few inches past her collarbone. "I came because Anne mentioned that Gavin still worked here, and I thought he could tell me where to find you."

"You came looking for me?" A full-on smile spread across my face. So much for strategy—I was going on instinct and hoping it didn't fail me for the first time.

"Well, yeah." With one hand she swept her hair from her face while the other tugged her phone free. "I didn't know who else to go to. Or who to tell. Or who you'd told."

"About?" I leaned forward.

"You need to talk to Caroline. I'm not Juniper's mother." Her fingers worked the screen.

"Of course you're not." Hadn't given it a second thought.

She held up the same app Juniper used. "Turns out I'm her aunt."

CHAPTER EIGHT

Allie

PointePrincess50363: That Ballanchine technique hurts to watch. Bring back your sister to show you how to do it right RousseauSisters4

Two days later, I tucked my knees under me in the oversize chair, and stared across the formal living room at Hudson, the ticking of the grandfather clock filling the miles of silence between us as it counted away the late-morning hours.

After Gavin burst in about thirty seconds into our conversation at the bar, we'd agreed to meet somewhere we wouldn't be disturbed. I'd thought delaying the conversation would give us time to compose ourselves, or at least make it less awkward. I was wrong.

"Five minutes." Hudson broke the silence.

"I'm sorry?"

"This might go a little easier if you pretend for the next five minutes that you don't hate me." He leaned forward on the blue-and-cream-striped couch, and braced his elbows on his knees, ignoring the hot cup of coffee on the coffee table between us. At least one thing hadn't changed in the last ten years; he was wearing a Bruins cap.

"Five minutes isn't going to do it, and I doubt that would make this any less awkward."

"Let's give it a shot." He pulled his phone out and showed me the timer. "Take it five minutes at a time."

"Five minutes. Fine. I kind of thought you'd be in uniform after getting off a twenty-four-hour shift." I tugged the sleeves of my sweater down over the heels of my palms. Soon, it would be too hot for my favorites. June was breathing down our necks.

"If you want to see me in uniform, all you have to do is ask." A playful smile tugged at his lips.

Warmth stung my cheeks and I quickly looked away. Flirting had been something he'd saved for other girls. "Is Caroline coming?"

"I haven't told her." His smile vanished.

My spine stiffened.

"First"—he held up a pointer finger—"I haven't seen her, and this is the kind of thing you need to say in person. Secondly, she's been adamantly opposed to Juniper looking for her birth family before she turns eighteen, but I also feel that Juniper has a right to know things like her medical history, so my loyalties are kind of torn right now. Caroline gets one hint that Juniper's been hunting—let alone actually found you—and she'll lock that girl down so tight supermax would look like a breeze."

"Because our family is evil incarnate?" I tilted my head at him and tried not to let the insinuation ruffle my feathers.

"Because she's been terrified someone would come and take Juniper from the time the adoption agency called to place her."

I bristled. "We would never—"

"I know that. You know that. But it's hard to overrule anxiety with logic." He curved the bill of his hat and glanced down at the designer rug Mom had paid too much money for. "I figured we'd piece together as many facts as possible, then come up with a plan before going to Caroline."

My phone buzzed on the arm of the chair, and Kenna's name flashed on the screen. I swallowed my guilt and hit the Decline button. It was the second time today she'd reached out, and as much as I wanted her to stop, I'd probably wallow even deeper into my little nest of misery if she did.

"And then we let her decide if she wants to tell Juniper." And in the meantime, that little girl would just keep wondering. What a shitstorm. I shifted my weight and grabbed the bottle of Smartwater from the end table on my right like Kenna was in my actual ear, lecturing me about hydration. My ankle was sore from the early-morning workout—I'd pushed hard on the Peloton this morning, then pushed a little *too* hard by escalating my calf raises to not-quite-demi-pointe.

"Have you told Anne?" He lifted his brows.

"She's . . . delicate." I ran my finger over the bottle's label and debated how much to tell him, how far to let him in. How much did someone change in a decade? Had to admit, there was something ironically poetic to be said about how we were forcing ourselves full circle—from confidants, to strangers, and back to whatever this was. "She's in the middle of a divorce, and her feelings about children and motherhood . . ." I spoke toward the picture of Anne holding Eva as a baby. "It's complicated for her right now." Which was why I'd scheduled this meeting knowing she'd be out of the house.

Hudson nodded, looking at the collection of black-and-white photographs in their silver frames on the built-in bookshelves. "You want to say it, or should I?"

I tracked his gaze to a photo of the four of us in tutus in our early childhood. For the last two days, my mind had scrambled over every prospect and come up with the same conclusion every time.

Juniper couldn't be Eva's. She'd never been out of my sight longer than a week in those years. Neither had Anne. She'd left for college the same month I'd joined the Company as an apprentice—a full year before I graduated from high school.

"She has to be Lina's." As inescapable as the truth was, I still couldn't wrap my mind around it, couldn't fathom that I didn't know my older sister as well as I'd thought I had. I ripped my focus from the pictures and found Hudson watching me, waiting for me to finish the thought.

It had always been one of my favorite parts about him. He was decisive, reckless even, when taking action, but he'd always listened to me first, something I hadn't realized I'd been missing in a house of four kids and busy parents.

"If Juniper was born in May, then Lina had to have gotten pregnant in September," I said softly, voicing the thoughts that had spiraled through my mind the last thirty-six hours. "Which is when she'd joined the San Francisco Ballet Theater."

"The one you wanted, right?" he asked softly, rising from the couch and walking toward the bookshelves.

I pressed my lips between my teeth to keep from denying it.

"You did." He glanced over his shoulder, picking up a silver frame that held a photo of Eva and me from the Haven Cove Classic when I was sixteen. "You told me once that you didn't want to dance in someone else's shadow, and since your mother had danced in Paris and London, San Francisco was your number one choice."

"I was there. I remember," I finally forced out as I stood, putting down my water and walking around the coffee table to stand at his side.

"What changed?"

My gaze darted over the professional pictures, ninety percent of which were taken with us in costume, as though the only moments worth recording for public consumption occurred when we performed. "You know what changed."

"Lina died." He slipped his hands into his front pockets. "So you turned down all the offers you got that day and went with the Metropolitan Ballet Company, like your mother wanted."

Was that a hint of disappointment I heard in his voice?

"I don't exactly see you in Sitka," I fired back. That had been our little joke of a dream. Him living in the middle of nowhere, rescue swimming, me in San Francisco, visiting when I could.

"Sean died too. Cancer. I *chose* to come back to help Caroline with Juniper. Did you *choose*, or was that all your mother, living out her dreams with whichever daughter fit the shoe at the moment?" He folded his arms across his chest.

"She'd just lost her firstborn. I *chose* to honor her wishes." *And that came out too defensive.* We were still within our first five minutes. "Anyway, I saw Lina at Christmas, but she didn't say anything, or look different. The next time we were together was that summer. She'd declined an offer to renew her contract in San Francisco and came home to train with us in June to prep for auditioning for MBC again. She was determined and focused, but she acted normal . . . happy, especially after August auditions. She got the invite to join the Company, and that was what? Two weeks before the Classic?" I shook my head. "I know the proof is in Juniper, but I can't believe Lina would have a baby and not tell any of us. Not even Anne. They were close, way closer than I am with Eva. But unless I have another sibling I don't know about, Juniper has to be Lina's."

"Is there a chance Anne knows and never told you?" He rocked back on his heels and glanced out the window, then muttered a curse.

"Sure, there's always that chance," I admitted. "But why would she keep it a secret this long after Lina died? None of it makes any sense."

"You have to be kidding me." Hudson strode toward the entry hall.

"What's wrong?" I hurried after him, my socked feet skidding in the foyer.

He practically consumed the entrance as he threw open the door, but I ducked under his arm to see Juniper drop her scooter in front of the porch steps.

Something in my chest sparked, then flamed slowly, like a campfire started with damp kindling, as Juniper unbuckled her purple helmet and tossed it on the ground next to the abandoned scooter.

"You're supposed to be at school," Hudson lectured. "Mrs. Ashbury is going to lose it when she realizes you snuck off."

Her button nose lifted when she raised her chin at Hudson, and the morning sun caught the copper in her narrowed eyes as she stared him down while climbing the steps. She was fearless and determined and looked more than a little indignant. The flame in my chest spread, and my skin prickled. It wasn't déjà vu. They were all elements of Lina that I'd recognized as familiar without truly *seeing*.

Holy shit, I'd been blind. Juniper looked just like her.

"I sent her an email from Mom's account last night saying you were taking me to an appointment this morning." She reached the porch and glared at Hudson. "She has her hands full with the Gibbons twins, so we both know she isn't mourning one less kid in the class."

"You have your mom's password?" Hudson lifted his brows at his niece.

Our niece. I stared at her wind-snarled brown hair, the lines of her cheeks and chin, noting the similarities to my sister.

"Juniper0514 isn't exactly hard to crack," she drawled.

I leaned back, my head brushing against Hudson's arm. The contact steadied my feet, but nothing calmed the speed of my heart. Juniper wasn't just a notification on an app, or a discussion to be had, a question to ponder. She was Lina's very real daughter.

"You can't excuse yourself from school and run amok!" Hudson's tone sharpened. "It's not safe!"

"Right." Juniper folded her arms across her chest. "Because I was in *sooooo* much danger riding my scooter all six blocks from where Mom dropped me off at school. Mr. Lobos says hi, by the way. He was gardening in his front yard when I rode past. Super scary."

Even the way she rolled her eyes was just like Lina. How had I missed it? I wobbled, and Hudson braced his arm around my waist before I could make an ass out of myself and fall.

Breathe. You have to breathe.

"Not the point. How did you know I'd be here? I still have your phone." His stern voice was at complete odds with the gentle pressure he used to keep me steady.

"I didn't know *you* were here until I saw the truck." Juniper motioned to the royal blue late-model pickup in the driveway. "I came to see *her*." That hand swung around, gesturing at me. "Just because you took my phone doesn't mean I can't log on to the website when Mom isn't using her computer. It notifies both people when it finds a connection, you know." She looked at me, her entire expression shifting from fearless to apprehensive as she swallowed, her hands falling to her sides. "You weren't lying. You're not my mother. But it says we're related. How?"

So much for waiting for Caroline.

I took a deep breath and prepared for the world to change. "I'm your aunt."

"So you really have a ballet studio here?" Juniper asked ten minutes later, staring at the double doors off the foyer that kept the studio private.

"We do." I handed her a glass of lemonade as Hudson followed me out of the kitchen post-emergency-game-plan-session with his, not that either of us had a clue what to do. I sipped mine, hoping the quick burst of sugar would kill the knee-wobbling feeling of being way over my head. "My father inherited this house. It was his favorite place to be. But the only way my mother would agree to let us spend summers out here was if he turned what had been a ballroom into a studio so we wouldn't miss the crucial summer months of training." Reaching past her, I turned the handle and pushed the door open to reveal the L-shaped studio.

Juniper gasped and her eyes brightened in a way mine never had for the space.

"It looks smaller from this angle than it is, because it runs down the side of the house." I walked around her and into the studio, flicking the switch on the right as I passed. The lights came on, not that they were necessary this time of day. The twenty-by-thirty-foot space was perfectly lit by the wall of windows that made up the front and southeast faces of the house, and the line of continuous mirrors on the other side didn't hurt either.

The floor shone. The mirrors didn't hold a single fingerprint. There were no water bottles scattered around the windows, or ballet bags tossed against the wall. The speakers built into the ceiling were silent, and yet I was struck with the overwhelming urge to hurry to the barre before my mother caught me slacking.

"It's beautiful," Juniper whispered reverently, stepping inside.

"No shoes." I shook my head.

"Oh, right." Lemonade kissed the edge of the glass but didn't overflow as she kicked off her sneakers and hurried in, like I might retract the invitation if she waited too long.

"That means you too," I said to Hudson as he followed her in.

"I remember the rules." He motioned toward his shoeless feet with his empty hand. "Though it's been a few years."

I sucked in a breath. The last time we'd been in this room together, he'd watched me practice the variation from *Giselle* for hours in preparation for the Classic. He'd been my number one supporter and, little did he know, my biggest distraction. After all, who could concentrate when Hudson Ellis was in the room?

You can, because you're not a teenager anymore.

Juniper walked past me and looked around the corner, where the true space began. "And you have a gym too?"

"The last ten feet," I confirmed, watching her expressions shift from wonder to curiosity as I caught up. "What we do back there makes it possible to do what we can up here."

"This is how you're training away from the Company," Juniper noted, setting her lemonade on the windowsill and climbing over the Pilates machine at the edge of the mat. "Eva made it sound like you were quitting by coming out here."

I blinked, and my steps faltered.

"She watches Seconds," Hudson reminded me in a whisper, reaching my side.

Oh. Right.

"I mean, most ballerinas rehab at their company." She shot me a knowing look and walked by the free weights stacked along the mirror. It was an accusation and question all in one.

"I'm not quitting." My spine stiffened at the implication. "I recover better on my own, without"—*competitors salivating over my demise*—"eyes on me." I took another sip of the tart lemonade and composed myself. "Besides, Eva knows how the algorithm works. Anything controversial or negative is going to get engagement." And what she really wanted was followers.

"So you'll be back for the fall season?" Juniper trailed her fingers along the barre.

"That's the plan." In time to debut *Equinox* in the fall season, as long as Vasily liked what he saw on the recording and gave us the go-ahead.

"Pushing it, don't you think?" Juniper crossed in front of Hudson and me, walking to the pictures that hung on the walls in the spaces between the windows. "It took Michaela DePrince a year to recover, and you think you can do it in nine months?"

"I had a newer procedure, and eight, since you're counting." I followed her to the wall. "I'll have to rehearse at full strength the month prior. And I know the odds. Our family beats them."

"Our family," Juniper whispered, looking up at the earliest photograph in the room. All four of us were in tights and leotards at the barre, our hair pinned into buns. Eva couldn't have been more than two. "You're all named after prima ballerinas, right?"

"Yes. Mom likes to set expectations early."

"Alina is my mother, isn't she?" Her gaze slid to my oldest sister.

That comment hit me like a punch to the stomach. "What makes you think that?" I felt Hudson behind us, watching, but he stayed quiet as Juniper's gaze shifted to the picture below, where the four of us wore matching leotards and skirts. I was seven, making Lina nine—one year younger than Juniper was right now.

Glancing between the two, my chest constricted. The resemblance was uncanny. I should have noticed the second I laid eyes on her.

"I thought for a second it might have been Eva," Juniper said, moving down the line of windows, studying each photograph. "The shape of our eyes is the same, and she doesn't seem the motherly type."

Grandma's eyes.

"The shape of your eyes probably comes from my dad's mom, your great-grandmother, and just because you follow someone online doesn't mean you know them." Though I couldn't exactly argue with her observation.

Juniper glanced my way and paused as though weighing my comment, before turning back to the pictures. "But you would have known if she'd had a baby, right? And you looked pretty shocked to meet me."

"True." I followed her line of sight to the next picture, where only three of us wore costumes, holding bouquets after a performance. Anne stood at our side, smiling for the camera, her arms empty. She'd quit at fourteen, when Mom told her she'd never reach the level needed to be hired by a company.

My pity had rivaled my envy of her freedom.

"Anne doesn't dance, so she can't be my mother." Juniper sighed at the photo and moved to the next wall.

"That's not how it works," I countered, following her path. "And she can dance. She's an amazing dancer." My defenses bristled at Juniper's skepticism. "It's hard to grow up in a house like this. Hard to be great when . . ." My words trailed off before I could disparage my sister.

"When you're surrounded by phenomenal," Juniper noted, pausing at the next picture. All four of us stood outside the very first Classic, but again, only three of us were costumed. She crossed the final window and stared up at the last picture.

Eva and I were dressed for the barre, teaching a summer intensive, and Anne beamed beside us in a black dress and an engagement ring.

"How old are you here?" Juniper asked, picking up her glass from the nearby windowsill.

"Twenty." I couldn't help but notice that my smile didn't reach my eyes, and wondered if I'd even manage that smile if someone snapped a picture right now. "I'd just come back from the first time my Achilles ruptured." The last few words slipped into a whisper.

Juniper's shoulders dipped and she looked up at me, both hands on her lemonade. "My mother is Alina." The statement was as decisive as it was laced with sadness.

"I think so," I answered gently. "We called her Lina. She was the oldest, and had the brightest smile, and the loudest laugh, and gave the best hugs—the kind where you feel like love moves through osmosis, like she could infuse you with her joy." My throat tightened.

Juniper glanced beyond me toward where I knew Hudson was standing. I'd always been able to pinpoint him in a room without much effort. He was a magnet, drawing everything and everyone toward him—including me. Always had been. He and Lina were similar that way. "And she's dead."

I nodded, my stomach twisting, knowing I was probably doing this all wrong. There should be therapists here, and Caroline, and a host of other support, and people who knew the right thing to say, like Anne. Instead, Juniper was stuck with me.

And I never knew what or how much to say, which was why I'd always preferred staying quiet.

"How did it happen?" she asked.

I swallowed, and the twisting tied my stomach into knots.

"Juniper." Hudson's tone was a warning, and I heard the distinct sound of a phone vibrating.

"She has the right to know," I said over my shoulder as he reached into his back pocket and pulled out his phone.

He tapped a button and put it away. Our five minutes had turned into thirty.

"How did it happen?" Juniper repeated.

"It was a car accident." I pushed the words through my dry throat.

"That part was in the articles." Her hands twisted on the sweating glass. "But how did it happen? You were with her, right? That's what the news said."

"I don't remember." I lifted my glass, but it was empty, which wasn't exactly helping the throat-closing feeling that always took hold when I tried to recall that night. "I know that we were coming back from celebrating after the Classic. I was told she lost control around a curve, and we hit a tree, and I . . ." It was nothing I hadn't been through in therapy dozens of times to help me move past it, but the words clogged my airway and my heart started to race. "I lived, and she didn't."

You left her there to die. Mom's voice screamed in my head.

Tires squealed in my memory. Glass shattered. Metal crunched. No matter how much was missing from that evening, the moment of impact stayed with me. And parts of what memory I did have didn't match the official report, which made me question the rest of it.

"Allie," Hudson muttered, suddenly filling my vision. He traded my lemonade for his. "Here, take mine."

I gulped his down and concentrated on breathing deep and even. It was another reason for keeping lemonade in the house—the sour burst of flavor was supposed to help distract from anxiety attacks . . . or so my therapist told me.

"You have every right to know," he said to Juniper. "But for now, you have to change the subject."

"I'm fine," I managed to say, and handed his glass back. "Thank you." I pushed the memories away like they belonged to someone else's story and faced Juniper. Her lips were pressed flat, and worry puckered her brow. "You have nothing to feel bad about," I promised. "If I could remember more with any certainty, I'd tell you."

"How can you not remember?" Juniper asked.

Hudson stiffened and his pocket started vibrating again.

"I hit my head so hard that I lost most of my memory from the hours before the crash, and then I didn't wake up for a couple of days."

Good job. I lifted my hair and tilted my head so she could see the scar that ran down my hairline.

"Oh. I'm sorry." Juniper glanced between Hudson and me as he declined another call. "Do you . . . do you know who my father is?"

"I wish I did, but I don't." She must have been seeing someone in San Francisco.

Juniper absorbed the news with a slow nod. "Will you tell me about her—my birth mother?"

I nodded. "If that's what you want. We should probably talk to your mom—"

"No!" Juniper shouted, and Hudson somehow managed to pluck her glass out of her hands before it spilled. "You can't!"

Hudson's phone vibrated again, and I snatched all three glasses out of his hands, pinning one between my forearm and stomach. "Just answer it already."

He shot me an apologetic look, then swiped the device to answer as he walked a few feet away. "What? I'm not on today. He did *what* with the dog?" Hudson snapped, and we both pivoted as he twisted his hat backward.

Oh, that's exactly what I needed, Hudson Ellis to look even hotter than usual. What the hell was it about a backward baseball cap that made me feel seventeen again?

"Absolutely not." He sighed. "I'm in the middle of something, but I'll be there as soon as I can." He hung up and shoved the phone back into his pocket as he came our way. "Sorry about that. Juniper, we have to tell your mother." He relieved me of two of the lemonade glasses. "Thank you."

I almost asked if everything was okay, but entwining my life with Hudson's more than necessary was a bad idea given our current situation. "He's right, we have to tell her."

"No." She shook her head vehemently. "She would have felt like she had to listen to you if you were my mom, but she won't let me see you if she knows you're my aunt!" Panic filled her eyes. "She's made it crystal clear that I'm not allowed to find my family until I'm eighteen."

Guess Hudson wasn't exaggerating about Caroline's position. Heaviness settled in my chest. Finding out that Juniper existed only to be denied the opportunity to know her felt like losing Lina all over again. *And if that night had gone differently, it would be Lina standing here, not me.*

"But you already found your family," I said softly. "So, if we aren't allowed to know you, then what's left?" I looked up at Hudson. "Where do we go from here?"

Hudson's jaw ticked. "Caroline deserves to know."

"What about what *I* deserve?" Juniper interrupted, her eyes watering. "My mom wanted to adopt me. Alina wanted to give me up. They both got what *they* wanted. Why doesn't it matter what *I* want? Why do I only matter when I turn eighteen?"

"You matter," I whispered, my grip tightened on the glass. This was unfair on every possible level.

"Of course what you want matters," Hudson assured her, palming the bases of both glasses in one hand and stroking his other over her hair.

"Good." She swiped at her eyes with the back of her forearm. "Because I want to know my biological family."

"I don't see how that's possible without telling your mother," I said gently.

"We'll tell her," Juniper promised, her gaze darting between us. "Just not yet. She has to get to like you first."

That was *never* going to happen.

"Which would also convince your mother that not all ballerinas are stuck up?" Hudson lifted an eyebrow, clearly on to her plan.

"Two birds with one stone," Juniper admitted, lifting her chin.

"I think you greatly underestimate how your mother feels about my"—I winced at the slip—"our family."

"You can change her mind." Two little lines appeared between her eyebrows, and her gaze shifted quickly, like she was thinking. The smile that spread across her face was pure mischief. "Uncle Hudson can bring you to my birthday party."

Wait. What? My stomach hit the floor.

"That's usually classmates and family only," Hudson reminded her.

"Your birthday already passed." Sweat broke out on my palms at the idea of being anywhere near Caroline, carrying a secret like this.

"We always celebrate my birthday Memorial Day weekend so the whole family can be here." She turned a full-on grin at Hudson, bouncing on her toes. "And that's why it's perfect! Bring her as your girlfriend. Mom let Uncle Gavin bring his girlfriend last year."

My stomach abandoned my body. His *girlfriend*?

"Absolutely not." Hudson lifted his eyebrows. "No."

"Just pretend." Juniper tilted her head at me . . . exactly like Lina. "You'll get to know my family. I'll get to know you, and once Mom knows how great you are, we'll tell her."

I blinked. The scheming, the sneaking out, the general disrespect for authority—that was all Lina, too, though I didn't doubt Hudson's influence. But faking it so Caroline would like me was preposterous . . . and wrong.

"Juniper—" Hudson started.

Something rustled in the doorway behind us.

"I thought I heard someone in here!" The excitement in Anne's voice was palpable, and I turned toward her without thinking, Hudson doing the same. She peeked around what appeared to be a sample centerpiece in her arms, a tall vase overflowing with pink-and-green flowers. "Interesting company to . . ." Blood drained from her face, turning her pale as the paint on the doors as she looked directly between us. "Lina?"

The vase slipped from her hands and shattered.

CHAPTER NINE

Hudson

WestCoastPointe: Nepotism isn't going to help that technique, RousseauSisters4

"You will do this!" Anne shouted as I walked up Allie's porch steps for the second time that day.

Surprise jolted my eyebrows upward. In the years I'd known the Rousseaus, I'd never heard Anne raise her voice. Eva? Absolutely. Lina? Once or twice. But Anne? Never.

She had to be yelling at Allie, convincing her to go along with Juniper's plan. My hackles rose, and Sadie whined at my side as I rung the bell. The little golden hadn't quit shaking since I'd picked her up at the vet's office a half hour ago. "It's all right," I promised her, reaching over her leash to give her a pat.

The door flew open, and Anne's frantic gaze jumped from me to Sadie. "Where is she?"

"Not a fan of that tone, Anne," I warned. "I told you I was taking her back to school." I said it slowly, as though we hadn't all participated in the same conversation an hour ago and agreed that we needed an adults-only meeting. Anne had been overruled two to one, but she'd still participated.

"Let him by," Allie ordered from inside the house, her tone flat, just like it had been when I'd arrived earlier. The tone made me wish she'd yell or scream, anything to prove she was in there.

"He has a dog." Anne stepped aside, giving me a clear view of Allie, who sat on the second-to-bottom step of the main staircase, her arms wrapped around her middle. "Dogs aren't allowed in the house."

"By all means, let's talk on the porch," I offered.

Allie's head tilted as she stared at Sadie. "Mom's not here, so we make the rules. Let them in."

Her mother not being here was the only reason I was allowed through the front door.

Anne sighed, then motioned us inside the house with a jerk of her hand. "If she makes a mess, you're cleaning it up."

"Of course." I walked by Anne into the foyer and took a seat next to Allie on the steps like it was the most natural thing in the world to position myself at her side.

"You brought your dog?" Allie reached over my knees and stroked Sadie's head.

I'd never been so happy to see a tail wag in my life. "Not mine. I rescued her from a boat accident a little over a week ago. Her owner told the vet he has no intention of picking her up, so here she is. Her name is Sadie."

"Hi, Sadie," Allie whispered, and just like that, the puppy stopped trembling. She scooted her butt right on over to Allie, wedged herself between our knees, and set her head on Allie's lap. "Forward, aren't you?" A faint but real curve pulled at the edges of Allie's mouth, and my own mirrored in response.

Come to think of it, it was the first hint of genuine amusement I'd seen on her face since dragging her out of the water last week. Worry stirred in my gut.

"Now that we know the dog's name"—Anne shut the door—"do you want to tell me how the hell your family ended up with our niece?"

"Stop it," Allie chastised gently. "It's not like he had any say in what Lina did."

"You sure about that?" She leaned back against the door and folded her arms. "Are you Juniper's father?"

Allie's hand froze, and I tensed. "That would be physically impossible seeing as I never touched Lina." My eyes narrowed on Anne. It had only ever been Allie for me.

"So *our* sister just happened to have a baby no one knew about and give that child to *your* sister?" Anne narrowed her eyes right back.

"I was just as surprised as you are when Allie told me about the results."

"I just found out the day before—" Allie blurted, and I immediately regretted my words, realizing what I'd let slip.

"You told *him* first?" Anne shouted, her voice breaking at the end. "He didn't just bring her over this morning?"

"I told him first," Allie answered, her hand still on Sadie's head. "And maybe I shouldn't have, but he already knew—"

"You should have told *me*!" Anne shoved her fingers into her curls.

"I know—" Allie whispered.

"How could you keep it from me? Our Lina has a daughter out there!" Anne's voice rose.

"Maybe if you let her finish a sentence, she'd be a bit more open with you." I let Sadie's leash drop.

"Don't talk to her like that." Allie bristled, her spine stiffening, and both sisters glared at me.

Shit, I stumbled right into that one. I should have known better than to intercede during a Rousseau-sisters fight.

"Take me to see her," Anne ordered before I could even utter an apology. "I barely got five words in before you ushered her out of here like I was the enemy."

"No way." Allie shook her head. "It's bad enough that she came here behind Caroline's back. We're not going to steamroll this girl's life, which is exactly what—"

"Is she healthy? Happy? What are her grades like? Are the kids nice to her at school?" Anne fired off question after question.

"—will happen if you step in," Allie finished, scratching under Sadie's chin.

"Yes," I answered. "When she gets her way. Decent. And yes, she's well liked, from what I hear. And Allie's right. You go barging in there and Caroline will slap you with a restraining order. She'll see you as a threat, and she's terrified of losing Juniper."

"I have every right to know my niece," Anne argued.

"No, Caroline has every right to protect her *daughter*," Allie countered. "We don't have a single right when it comes to Juniper. Not legally. Whether or not we like it, Lina didn't leave her with us, and there had to be a reason Lina never even told us she existed."

"I just want to talk to her." Anne slumped against the door, and Allie's shoulders dipped.

This whole situation was a clusterfuck. "Caroline is an excellent mother and would die for that girl," I added. "She's in good hands."

"And we're supposed to trust *you*?" Anne snapped at me.

"Don't," Allie warned her sister. "You want to fight, come at me."

"I'm more than capable—" I started, only to shut my mouth when Allie lifted a single hand.

"You'll do this." Anne repeated her earlier demand with a softer tone, but no less determination. "Please do this, Allie. Just pretend to be Hudson's *anything* if it keeps you close to Juniper."

Allie focused on Sadie as if Anne wasn't even speaking.

This was *so* unfair to ask of Allie, but I respected her wishes and kept my mouth shut.

"She really doesn't have a home?" Allie asked, glancing my way with somber eyes. "The dog?"

My brow knit at the quick change of subject. "No. Not yet, at least. My landlord has a no-pet policy, and twenty-four-hour shifts aren't kind to pets, but I'll find someone for her."

"You can't take her to a shelter." Her tone sharpened.

"I wouldn't." My gaze raked over Allie in quick assessment. She seemed exhausted. I had no idea what she usually looked like, so I couldn't tell if she was eating normally, or if the circles under her eyes were typical, but I'd bet she was training herself into the ground.

Her family had never let her take her foot off the fucking gas pedal.

"You'll do this for *me*, Alessandra," Anne reiterated, jarring me back to the conversation.

Holy fucking guilt trip.

Allie sighed. "Do you really think Caroline will ban us from seeing Juniper if we just tell her?" she asked me, rubbing Sadie behind her ears.

I curved the brim of my hat and thought it through. "I honestly don't know. She's been more than a little overprotective since Sean died, and I don't see that changing. I hate to admit that Juniper is right in one regard. You have a better chance of Caroline accepting you if she gets to know you first." If we survived when it blew up in our faces.

"So you think this is a good idea?" Allie asked. "You want me to slip into your family under false pretenses so I can worm my way into your sister's good graces?"

"It's pretty horrendous when you put it that way." I slipped my hat backward. "I'm torn. If it was anybody but you, I'd say to get fucked. But it *is* you." I swallowed the big-ass knot forming in my throat. "I think Juniper has a right to know where she comes from, and if Caroline realizes her biological family isn't something to fear, it will take a massive weight off her shoulders. But I hate the thought of lying to my sister, and if your mother finds out . . ." My stomach pitched like I was still that eighteen-year-old kid.

"Mom's too busy teaching to bother with us," Anne interrupted, and Allie looked away. "She won't interfere." Anne's voice quieted as she walked toward Allie. "Juniper's the last—the only—piece we have of Lina, and this is our chance to know her."

"Then you do it." Allie stroked her hands down Sadie's neck.

"No." The word slipped out before I could stop it.

"Won't work," Anne agreed. "He doesn't look at me the way he looks at you. It's the only reason I think this rather . . . childish plan might work. He could carry the whole ruse just glancing your direction."

Was I that transparent?

"And it's foolish," Anne continued, "but it's all we've got, and Juniper isn't wrong in thinking you can win Caroline over. You win *everyone* over with that heart of yours. And what's the worst that happens? Caroline finds out and we're right back where we started, barred from seeing Juniper. There's nothing to lose and everything to gain. Go to the party, Allie. Please."

"I'm not going to change her mind in a single day." Allie didn't bother even glancing up when Anne fell to her knees on the foyer floor before her.

"True." I nodded. "Knowing my sister, it will take weeks, if not months."

"Then you'll do it for as long as it takes to convince her." Anne set her hands on Allie's feet, and her words started to tumble quickly. "We have to be sure Juniper is okay. We owe that to Lina. And if I can't be the one asking the questions, making sure Lina's little girl is thriving, then you'll do it for me. You have to, Allie. Juniper asked you, and saying no would be like denying Lina—"

"That's a low blow," I interrupted when Allie drew in a sharp breath. "I'm not doing anything she's not a hundred percent enthusiastic about."

Anne bristled.

"What day is the party?" Allie asked, glancing my way.

"You don't have to do this. I'm not even sure we should." I searched her eyes for a hint of the fire I'd seen when I pulled her from the water, or when I'd prodded her at the bar, but found only grim determination. "Or if we can."

"We can." She tilted her pointed chin. "I'm here and Lina isn't. This is the least of what I owe her. Will you help me or not?"

My jaw flexed once. Twice. I would have told her anything she wanted to bring the fire back into her eyes. God only knew what I would have done to see an actual smile, to know she was happy after everything she'd been through. Maybe getting out of this pressure cooker of a house, spending some time away from the studio with my weird but smotheringly close-knit family would provoke a little laughter. We'd be good for her, Juniper especially.

But faking a relationship with Allie? My chest tightened as she waited for my response. How the hell was I supposed to be that close to her without losing myself? Maybe I had to. Maybe that was my penance. There was no hope for any kind of actual future between us—she'd never forgive me for what I'd done if she knew the full truth—but maybe this was my chance to make even a small portion of it up to her. I could help her find that fire, even if she aimed it at me. "Saturday at noon. My parents' place. It's Caroline's place now. Alessandra, we'll have to be flawlessly convincing to pull it off. My family is disturbingly perceptive."

"Okay." She stood, and Sadie rose with her. "Five minutes at a time, right? Isn't that what you used to tell me? As long as you hold up your end, I can pretend to be in a relationship with you. I'm great at playing a role." She bent at the knees and picked up the end of Sadie's leash. "Juniper has to understand that I'll be back in New York mid-August, so we can't drag this on indefinitely. If Caroline doesn't like me by then, it's a lost cause." Allie shrugged. "But we've always been good for a summer, right?"

Ouch. That hit somewhere in the vicinity of my rib cage.

"Okay. Summer it is." Guess we were doing this. I nodded, fully committing myself. If this was what she wanted, I would do it for her, for all of them, even Caroline. And it wasn't like I had to pretend to want Allie. Apparently, I was shit at hiding it, anyway. "I'll more than hold up my end."

"Good, then I'll be there Saturday. Now, Sadie and I are going to take a nap. No need to find her a home. I'm hers now." Allie started up the steps with Sadie. Her voice, her motions, they were all so flat that my ribs constricted as I twisted to watch her walk away. "Oh, and Hudson?" she said from the top of the stairs, turning to look at me. "To be *flawlessly convincing*, you should unblock my number so you can get ahold of me, assuming that's why you never picked up any of the times I tried to call you."

"Yeah." My gut hollowed, because that's exactly what the eighteen-year-old fool I'd been had done. "I can do that."

She walked into her bedroom and shut the door.

"I think she just stole your dog." Anne rose to her feet and dusted off her knees.

"She was never mine. I just rescued her." And I couldn't think of any better place for her to be. I stood, then walked down the last two steps to the foyer. "Now, what's going on with Allie, and why aren't you doing anything about it?"

CHAPTER TEN

Hudson

User936221: This is satire, right? Your turn-out is all wrong, and don't get me started on your arms.

Anne wrapped the edges of her cardigan around herself defensively. "Nothing is *going on* with her. And I am helping. She refuses to rehab at the Company, so I'm here with her, making sure she doesn't . . ."

"Fall further into depression?" I waged a full-on battle against my instincts to keep from trailing after Allie. "That's what it is, right?"

"What's Juniper's favorite food?" She tucked a curl behind her ear and stared when I didn't reply. "One for one, Ellis."

I weighed my options, and Allie won. "Pizza. She's ten."

"Pizza." She echoed my response with a sad smile. "You're right about Allie. But she's medicated and sees a therapist. It's not uncommon for athletes when they're injured and can't do what they love. She'll pull out of it once she's back on the stage, just like she did before."

Before. She'd gone through this after the accident too. My shoulders ached under the weight of well-deserved guilt. I should have been there for her then, but I was here now.

"What's her favorite movie?" Anne asked.

Seemed safe enough. "*Star Wars.* Marathon if she's sick. Episode five if there's only time for one. Is Allie seeing anyone?" My eyes squeezed shut with immediate regret. "Never mind. Forget I asked that." When I opened my eyes, Anne arched a brow.

"No," she replied slowly. "She's not. No one lasts longer than a casual fling and they're always other dancers. She'll say it's because she's focused on her career or gets bored easily. Personally, I think someone gave her some pretty unconquerable trust issues."

That landed like a punch to the stomach. "Someone being me."

"That would be my guess. What is Juniper afraid of?"

Too far. "Try again. You're not getting the details of what she puts in her diary." I headed for the door. Funny, I'd walked out of it more often today than I had in my entire life.

"That's not fair," Anne sputtered. "I told you about the depression."

"Yeah." I reached for the door handle. "And I'm way more protective of Juniper's secrets than you are of Allie's, apparently. Ask something else." The door creaked as I opened it.

"What does she want to be when she grows up?"

I scoffed. "A fucking ballerina. She's part Rousseau, isn't she?" Every cell in my body abhorred leaving Allie to sleep off today's events, but the longer I stayed, the more Anne was going to question me about Juniper.

"Not every Rousseau is a dancer," Anne argued, catching the door as my shoes hit the porch. "What do you get out of doing this?"

I hesitated, reaching the steps. "Juniper's happiness, Caroline's eventual peace of mind, and a shot at earning Allie's forgiveness."

"How uncharacteristically selfless. You know I saw you, right?"

That had me turning to look at Anne over my shoulder.

"That morning before the Classic." Her knuckles whitened on the door handle. "Tucked away with Lina in the back hallway. Whatever you were doing, it wasn't something you wanted anyone else to see."

A muscle in my jaw ticked. "Nothing went on between Lina and me."

"And yet your family ended up with her daughter." Anne's shoulders straightened.

Looking up at the sky, I muttered a quick prayer for patience, then walked down the porch steps. "You know, Allie's walls were about six feet high as a teenager, just short enough for me to peek over. I was never foolish enough to think she let me all the way in, not with the way you Rousseau girls keep secrets for each other." Allie had only let me into the places she felt safe enough to share. I turned at the base of the steps to face Anne. "But now, those walls are thick as hell and easily twenty feet tall, if not more, which is fine—I know how to climb—but we both know those bricks aren't *all* because of me."

Anne paled and looked away. "I don't know what you're talking about."

"Almost forgot how good you guys are at lying too. What did your mother do? Did she wait a day, or was it a month before she expected Allie to fill Lina's shoes? Was she even allowed to recover? Is that why she's training herself into exhaustion now?" I took a stab with the last one.

The way Anne drew back told me I'd hit the mark. "Asks the man who left for basic without so much as stopping by the hospital."

"Yeah." I nodded, accepting the pain of the truth she hurled my way. "I fucked up. But have you admitted the same? I *should* have been there, but you *were*." My teeth ground.

"I was . . . in college." Anne tugged the cardigan so hard I expected it to rip. "And I'm keeping an eye on her training—on *her*—now. Thank you for doing this, Hudson, but make no mistake. I want to know my niece, but not at the expense of ruining Allie. If you so much as think about hurting my sister again, I won't keep my mouth shut this time around. I'll tell her I saw you with Lina."

"Go ahead and tell her." I headed toward my truck. Guess Anne didn't need the pointe shoes to learn a few things from her mother. I looked back over my shoulder and reached for the keys in my pocket. "We're on the same team, Anne. I want what's best for Juniper and Allie. The only place our interests diverge is Caroline, who I will choose over you every time, just like you'd choose your own sister." I gestured between us as I rounded the hood. "Same team. Stop trying to draw my blood. Leaving Allie the first time bled me dry already."

"You sure she's coming?" Juniper whispered that Saturday as she hopped out of my truck.

"She said she was." I reached into the bed and pulled out two of the biggest bags 7-Eleven kept in stock, which were hopefully enough for Caroline. "And I've never known Alessandra to lie."

Juniper chewed on her bottom lip but eventually nodded. "And you think you can fool Mom?"

"Worrying about the viability of your plan?"

"No." She kept one step ahead of me as we walked down the crowded driveway to her kitchen door. "Worried you won't do your part, therefore ruining my plan? Yes."

"Your faith in me is comforting." I switched my grip on the bags as they started to slip. The temperature was a balmy seventy-seven today, not bad for the end of May, and the ice had already started melting on the drive back. "Any advice for improving my performance?" Gavin walked out of the kitchen, carrying a tray of cupcakes to the backyard, but I wasn't worried about him hearing since he was all too aware of Juniper's ballet-dancing goal for the deception.

He just didn't know about the familial relations.

"Girls like it when you get them drinks or ask if they're hungry," she lectured, her hair whipping in the breeze. The wind had kicked up today, just ahead of the storm we were expecting for tomorrow. "At least Mom liked when Dad did things like that."

"I'll keep that in mind." I shifted my grip on the slipping bags.

"And you should touch her. Couples are always touching each other on the back or holding hands." She turned, her pointer finger raised. "But only if she says it's okay."

"Duly noted." I motioned toward the house. "Grab the door, would you please?"

"Happy to help." She held open the kitchen door, and I walked into mayhem.

"Those are the tablecloths," Caroline told our cousin. "The park tables are gross this time of year, and—yep, those are the clips. Thank you." She turned to our uncle. "Would you see if Gavin has his station up and if it's age appropriate?"

"We've got the ice." The two hurried past as I sat the ice in the empty side of the sink.

"Hudson, honey!" Mom put up her hands as soon as I turned, and I leaned down so she could cup my cheeks for her usual examination. She was five-three on a good day, with shoulder-length blond hair that only seemed to show the silver in the sun, laugh lines at the corners of her green eyes, and cat-eye, red-polka-dot glasses. "Oh, you look good. Getting enough to eat?"

"Always." Her smile was infectious, and I bent for a hug as Dad clapped my back.

"There he is." Dad pulled me in next, a short but tight squeeze before he let go. "Any daring rescues lately?"

"Stop it, George." Mom playfully swatted his arm with the back of her hand. "He does not exist to give you stories to tell at poker night."

Dad's eyes lit up when he saw Juniper. "The girl of the hour!" He swept her into a hug, hoisting her off her feet like she was still in kindergarten. "Did you see my shirt?"

"Hi, Grandpa!" She grinned and shoved her hair out of her eyes to read the absolute eyesore of sequins bedazzling his CARNIVAL DIRECTOR shirt with a laugh. "It's great!"

My smile deepened. This was exactly what Allie needed. Noise and laughter.

"Juniper, honey, get upstairs and get dressed so we have time to tie your hair back. I'm pretty sure I saw your uncle unpacking Silly String, and I am *not* untangling that from your hair." Caroline gestured toward the stairs and lifted her eyebrows.

"On it!" Juniper ran for the steps as soon as Dad set her down.

"Cupcakes are on the table," Gavin announced from the doorway, sidestepping to avoid our aunt and two of our cousins as they scurried out, their arms full of balloons.

"Thank you." Caroline picked up her clipboard and ran her pen down the paper, which no doubt had perfectly spaced boxes to check off. "Okay, if we can get the stations set up in the next half hour, then we'll be good. Kids start arriving at noon."

"How many are we expecting this year?" Dad asked, his arm around Mom's waist.

"Forty-two. Pretty much the entire incoming fifth grade." Caroline stuck the pencil in her hair, just above her high ponytail. "With family, that's fifty-nine people. Dad, do you have enough for the grill?"

"And leftovers," he assured her.

"Actually, it's sixty." I leaned back against the counter by the sink.

Caroline's gaze snapped from me to Gavin. "Another one? Didn't you just break up with the last one?"

"Not me." He pointed my direction with a shit-eating grin on his face.

"You?" Caroline dropped the clipboard on the island. "You have a girlfriend?"

"I do." *Here it goes.* As much as I valued my honor, it wasn't like this would be the first time I lied to my family in order to spend time with Allie. She was the exception to every rule I ever set for myself.

"Is it Beth Pierre?" Caroline smiled at me with so much hope that I inwardly flinched. "I know you were out with her last weekend."

"No. It's not." I shook my head and mentally cursed. *Plot hole.*

"That wasn't a date." Gavin reached into an open bag of potato chips and pulled out a handful. "Trust me, I was there. Beth and Jessica must have gotten their wires crossed, because Beth was pretty crushed to find out Hudson was already in a relationship."

He lied smoother than butter.

"Oh." Caroline's shoulders fell slightly. "Well, who is it?"

"Alessandra Rousseau." I drummed my fingers on the edge of the counter to fill the enormity of the silence as Caroline and my parents openly stared at me.

"As in Sophie and Thatcher Rousseau's daughter?" Mom's eyebrows rose above her glasses.

"Yes." I nodded.

"As in the Rousseau sisters?" Caroline's mouth hung open.

"I'm only dating one of them, but yes. Everyone stop acting as if there's more than one Alessandra Rousseau in this tiny-ass town. You know exactly who I mean." I looked each of them in the eye, pausing on Caroline. "And she's nervous as hell to be coming today, so you will *all* be nice to her. She means a lot to me." Damn if that didn't feel good to get off my chest. I'd only been holding that in for eleven years or so.

Caroline blanched. "She means a lot to you? She's been back in town a handful of weeks and she already means a lot to you? Hudson, she's going to be gone at the end of the summer. What are you thinking? A *Rousseau?*"

"So understanding," Gavin quipped sarcastically, grabbing another handful of chips. "With support like that, you wonder why we don't bring more girls around."

"Oh no." Mom shook her head, reached over, and squeezed my arm twice. "Of course we'll be nice." She pushed her glasses up her nose and turned to Caroline. "And we can't help who raises us, Caroline."

The door burst open, and Uncle Jared—Dad's brother—rushed in. "We're ready for the ice in the cool . . . What's going on?" Couldn't help but notice he had a similarly bedazzled shirt that read CARNIVAL OPERATOR. God help me if they had one around here with my name on it.

"Hudson here was just telling us that his girlfriend, one Alessandra Rousseau, will be joining us," Gavin answered, clearly enjoying himself.

Uncle Jared blinked, then laughed boisterously as he crossed the room. "Good one, Hudson. And here I was thinking Gavin was the prankster."

Knock. Knock.

Everyone turned at the faint sound on the screen door, and Gavin pivoted quickly to open it. "Speak of the devil. Welcome to our private little hell."

Allie walked through the door, and my pulse skyrocketed.

Her long, incredible legs were on full display in a pair of thigh-length khaki shorts that held my attention for a heartbeat too long to be considered platonic. She'd rolled the sleeves of her white button-up shirt, and her hair fell in soft waves to just above her breasts. What would it look like finally spread out on my pillow, tangled in my hands?

I blinked those thoughts straight out of my head.

Yeah, there was nothing fake about how much I wanted her. I'd never stopped thinking about her, missing her, wishing we'd had our shot at something beyond the friendship we'd both hidden our feelings behind. But I remembered . . . and she didn't, which was both a curse and a blessing.

She lifted her oversize sunglasses to the top of her head and offered my family a tentative smile that didn't reach her eyes as she clutched a gift bag at her side. Her shoulders relaxed when her gaze landed on me. "Hey."

"Hey." This was how it should have been back then, me introducing her to my family, us walking together in broad daylight instead of sneaking around in the cover of darkness.

This was what we could have had if I'd been strong enough to hold on to her.

You're strong enough now.

But I was ten years and one enormous mistake too late.

She gave me that fake-ass show smile as I crossed the kitchen to her, and I shook my head. That wasn't going to fly. My family needed to see *her*, not whatever mask she thought they'd expect. I hooked my arm around her waist and hauled her against my chest.

Her pretend smile vanished, and a very real but faint gasp escaped her lips as her eyes flared. There she was. Right there in that little spark of surprise that swiftly ignited to indignation and was immediately stoked by . . . Was that *interest?*

I wasn't the only one who wasn't going to have to fake attraction.

"There you are." I grinned. "Glad you could make it." Forget climbing her walls, I'd tear them down brick by brick. This arrangement might be fake for her, but my intentions were very real. Allie had given me the summer, and I was going to use it to bring her back to life.

"You can't seriously be dating my brother."

Unless Caroline ruined it.

CHAPTER ELEVEN

Allie

Bway11te: Your control is breathtaking. Stunning. Better than your sister, to be honest.

For a second, I forgot how to breathe. Forget the nerves of walking into hostile territory—who cared about his family staring when Hudson had me pinned against his hard chest.

Friends. You're just friends. Ex-friends at that. And this was just pretend, but damn did he feel *real*.

Maybe it was the pep talk I'd given myself on the way over about committing to this part, or the fact that I'd gotten up this morning and forced myself to put thought and care into my appearance for the first time in months. It could have been that I hadn't taken anyone to bed since before *Giselle*—or even wanted to—but my entire body woke up and took notice of Hudson like someone had flipped a switch on my sex drive.

He was wearing a different Bruins cap, black board shorts, and a white monotone athletic shirt with the letters **SAR** emblazoned across his massive chest. A chest I *really* wanted to see without the shirt.

"There you are." He grinned, and my brain ceased all function as that dimple popped in his cheek. "Glad you could make it."

No, no, no, I lectured my stupid, inconvenient hormones. He was the last person on earth I should be attracted to, but the truth was he'd been the first. First real friend, first crush, first unrequited . . . whatever, followed by a real and lasting first heartbreak. I needed to *play* the besotted girlfriend, not actually get besotted.

"You can't seriously be dating my brother." Caroline glowered at me.

The spell broke, and I remembered we were anything but alone as Hudson moved to my side and shot a glare at his sister. I recognized the members of his family from pictures and the quick moments I'd bumped into them as a teenager, and my grip tightened on the gift bag containing the present I'd brought for Juniper as I plastered a smile on my face. This was just a part, and I was an expert at acting. No big deal.

It wouldn't be the first time I'd had chemistry with the other lead.

"If you're Caroline, then yes, I am," I replied as Hudson's hand slid across my back to splay over my hip. Heat danced up my spine from the casual contact. "I'm Alessandra, by the way." I waved at his family instead of shaking their hands, since he had me anchored to his side. They all stared back in what appeared to be a fair amount of shock. "Allie for short," I added, hoping that would help.

Hudson stiffened slightly when it didn't.

"Fucking say something," Gavin said from my left, holding a bag of potato chips. "You guys are making this as awkward as a middle school dance. Hey, Allie." He offered the charming smile that had won Lina over one summer.

"Gavin." My smile stayed glued in place.

"And you knew?" Caroline turned an accusatory look on her brother.

"Of course I knew. Who do you think encouraged him to make a move?" He shook his head.

Wait . . . we were going with the story that Hudson made a move? Shit. We hadn't gone into specifics about what our *story* was. It was day one of this ruse and we were already screwing up.

"Well, it's lovely to meet you, Allie." Hudson's mother smiled warmly, then picked up a clipboard from the island and all but shoved it at Caroline's chest without even looking at her. "We're all so delighted that Hudson's finally brought someone home." She glanced at her daughter. "Close your mouth, dear. We have a party to host."

I glanced over his family, and heat stung my cheeks. They were all in variations of T-shirts and casual shorts. I should have asked for the dress code.

"Let's take this to the gift table," Hudson suggested. "We have a half hour before everyone gets here, Caroline?"

"Twenty-three minutes," she replied, watching me like I was a venomous spider who'd crawled a little too close for comfort.

"Twenty-three minutes," Hudson responded, taking the gift. Hand on my hip, he guided me out of the house and into a driveway that rather resembled a parking lot. "How's Sadie?"

"She's lovely even if she snores. I'm overdressed." It would take too long to go home and get something more casual, but I didn't want to stick out like a sore thumb either.

"You look beautiful." He sounded so sincere I almost believed him.

"You don't have to do that." I spoke only loud enough for him to hear. "Compliment me."

"It's just the truth, *Alessandra*." His hand flexed on my hip.

"You don't have to touch me right now either. No one can see us." The gravel driveway crunched under my favorite pink Vans as we wove our way between cars on the way to the backyard.

"Does it bother you?" We slipped into the narrow path between the house and the garage.

"No. Yes. I don't know." It bothered me how much I liked it, considering it had been months since I'd felt *anything* close to desire. "Maybe we need ground rules." I wasn't going to survive if he was actually going to flirt with me.

"Okay. Set them." His smile was hot enough to set an iceberg on fire.

"From what I remember, rule-following isn't one of your strong suits."

"Normally I'd argue that I've matured into an actual adult since the last time we spent any real time together, but since my commanding officer would agree with you, I'll let it slide. Set your rules." His smile faded as he stopped us halfway down the garage, and I glanced both ways to make sure no one was close enough to hear before I faced him. As a teenager, Hudson had always been dangerous when smiling, but giving me the intensity of his full attention? He was lethal as a fully grown man.

Rules. Right. Crap, now I had to think of them. "You can touch me in public for the purpose of authenticity, but that's it." I lifted my chin like I had a prayer of making up for our height difference.

"Noted." His hand fell away, and I hated that I immediately missed it. "Next?"

My mind raced, searching for the holes in our plan. "You can't actually date anyone while we're doing this or it would ruin the whole thing." Crap, was he dating someone? That girl at the bar? My instincts said no, that he never would have agreed to this if he was.

"Not a problem. I'm not seeing anyone, and even if I had been, it's hard to focus on anyone else once you walk into a room," he said, like it was a simple fact.

What the hell? My eyebrows rose.

"No saying things like that." I stepped backward, bumping into the garage.

"You'd rather I lie?" The heat in his eyes made me swallow. Hard.

"Isn't that what we're doing?"

"Just to everyone else. Not each other. That's *my* rule." He leaned into my space but didn't touch me. "Everything we say to each other has to be the truth."

"Because you're so very good at that?" Ah, there the anger was, and so much safer than the desire. I grabbed hold of it with both hands.

"Like you're an open book?" He retreated with a heavy sigh. "I fucked up when I left without saying goodbye. I have regretted it every day of my life. That's the truth. Can you accept that just enough to put it aside for the next few months?"

A little piece of that gaping wound yanked itself together as if his words were stitches. It was foolish to believe him, and yet I did. "I can."

"You sure you're up for playing this particular role? I know it's tough, but our main goal today should be convincing them we're together." His eyes lit up like he was purposely poking me for a reaction.

Game on.

I scoffed. "Please. Once you master faking an orgasm, any role is easy. This is cake."

His eyes bulged for a heartbeat before he schooled his expression. "Okay. Then let's do this."

I definitely won that point.

We walked into the backyard, and my jaw dropped.

The house backed up to Founder's Park, and the entire two acres of space had been taken over for Juniper's party. Little stations were set up around the perimeter, leading to the picnic tables that were covered in bright colors.

"It's a little much, but we have a good time," Hudson said, leading me into the park, which had been transformed into a carnival. "Juniper, Mason, and Melody—those are my cousin's twins—are the only kids in the family, so we all get together for their birthdays. Juniper chose the carnival theme, so everyone brought something to add."

We walked past a giant bounce house with an obstacle-course slide.

"Caroline's responsible for that one, and you should have seen her panic when we thought the extension cord wasn't going to reach." A corner of his mouth tilted upward and he gestured to the station on the right. "Aunt Jo and Uncle Mark are running a balloon dart booth." They both waved in between blowing up balloons. "And their teenagers are in charge of face painting."

I gave the teens a wave as we passed by.

"Over there"—Hudson pointed to the stations lining the other side—"we have a three-legged-race track, Gavin's bottle-toss station, and the Nerf-dart target—something which I've already been banned from playing because everyone knows I'll smoke them." He set Juniper's gift next to a few others on one of the picnic tables as I tried to take it all in. "The twins are bringing out folding chairs for the middle. Something about musical chairs."

"Your family just . . . does this?" My breath caught. Our family didn't even do dinner.

"I mean, it's no tea party at the Plaza—" He shaped the brim of his hat.

"It's better." I watched his family scurry about, setting up their stations.

"You'd better make sure you're set," Hudson's dad lectured as he carried out a net-covered tray of food, passing by to get to the grill next to a table covered with dishes. While Gavin took after their mother, just like Caroline, Hudson was entirely his father. "If those kids get here and you're not ready to go, Caroline will never let you hear the end of it."

"Good point. You set on the grill?" Hudson's hand skimmed my lower back, and the nerve endings fired, sending a shiver up my spine.

"You know it." He lifted two silvery eyebrows at me and pointed to an empty camping chair beside the smoking grill. "If he gives you any trouble, you just come over and sit with me."

"Yes, sir." I couldn't help but nod as Hudson led me away, to the unoccupied station a little way off from the picnic tables. The ground was covered in a thick foam mat in what looked to be a twelve-by-twelve square.

"I may have borrowed it from the gym at the station." Hudson crouched next to an assortment of beige and brown . . . somethings.

"What is this?"

"We're the T-Rex battle station." He stood, dragging the head of a costume up so it unfolded in front of him.

"The T-Rex battle station?" I asked, certain I'd heard incorrectly. There were at least eight more on this side of the mat.

"I may have gone a little overboard, but I wanted to make sure we had one in every size." He grinned, and the dimple popped in his cheek, completely eviscerating my train of thought. That dimple had always been my kryptonite. "This one is yours."

I opened and shut my mouth a couple of times, searching for the correct response.

"You heard me," Hudson whispered, his eyes sparkling like they used to when he'd talk me into doing something I wasn't supposed to. "Let's knock a few blocks out of those mile-thick walls you've got around you."

"Is that your goal?" My eyebrows shot up.

"Absolutely." He grinned. "I promised I wouldn't lie to you. You're not allergic to fun, *Alessandra*."

I scoffed. "Good luck with that. And I'm not sure I trust your idea of fun, considering you jump out of helicopters, but kicking the shit out of you with impunity has some merit." I tugged my lower lip between my teeth, because he was right, they looked . . . oddly fun. "Not worth explaining that I reinjured my ankle in a blow-up dinosaur, though." Vasily would kill me.

"I won't let anything happen to you," he promised, his dimple deepening. "Come on, Rousseau. My girlfriend would put it on and kick the shit out of me. You know you want to."

Strangely enough, I kind of did.

Five minutes later, I found myself ensconced by the scent of vinyl, looking out a clear square from inside a dinosaur costume as the fan puffed it out around me, elastic tight at my wrists and ankles to keep the air in. "This is ridiculous." What the hell was I doing?

"And yet here we are." Hudson circled me on the mat in his own costume, looking out of the window beneath the T-Rex's mouth. "Make it good. I think Caroline is watching."

"You can't seriously expect me to charge at you." I whipped around to follow him, the tail throwing me slightly off balance. My ankle wavered with a whisper of protest, but no pain.

"I have nothing against you losing." He ran for me, and I side-stepped, but our costumes collided, bouncing us both sideways.

I scoffed, catching my balance, but Hudson was already on me, bouncing me backward. Damn, he was quick. I stumbled, and gravity claimed its prize as I fell. This is what I got for putting on a freaking blow-up costume like a ten-year-old.

The costume crinkled, and an arm wrapped around my back, tugging me into a spin so I fell forward—onto Hudson's chest as he took the brunt of our impact. The air gushed out of our costumes faster than the fan could replenish it, and I felt another arm hooked under my right thigh, keeping my knee bent, my ankle safe.

"I win." He grinned up at me.

"I'm on top." I fumbled with my hands to get some form of leverage on him.

"I'd still call that a win for me." His smile told me I might have met my match in the acting department.

"Fool around later, you two!" Hudson's mom called out. "The kids are arriving!"

"She thinks we're fooling around." His eyes lit with pure mischief. "See? It's working."

I rolled my eyes and got the heck off him.

For the next hour and twenty minutes, I helped kids—and a couple of adults—in and out of the T-Rex costumes, watching in absolute fascination as they sent each other bouncing across the mat. I did my best to soak in the happiness of the people around me, and didn't think of ballet once, not even for a second, until Hudson's mother declared a break for lunch.

"I'll get you a plate," Hudson offered.

"You don't have to." I shook my head.

"Taking care of you is the least I can do in the circumstances, and it's what my parents would expect. I'll be right back." He pointed to the only picnic table not entirely consumed with children, then waded into the melee surrounding the grill.

I stepped over the bench of the picnic table, taking a seat in the middle.

"Alessandra!" Juniper bounded over to me in a pair of hot-pink shorts and a rainbow tank top, with a turquoise-and-pink butterfly painted on her cheek and her hair woven into a french braid. "You came!"

"I promised you I would." My lips quirked at the flush in her cheeks, the excitement in her eyes. She was the whole reason I was here, but I couldn't act like it. "Happy birthday-party day."

"Thanks!" She slid in next to me, putting down a soda and a paper plate loaded with barbecue and sweets in front of her. "I'm sitting with you."

"You know my daughter?" Caroline sat down in front of me, quickly followed by Hudson's mom on the left and, to my relief, Gavin on her right, each setting their lunch on the table.

"No need to take that tone," Hudson's mom rebuked over her glasses, but it lacked the cutting sting my own mother would have put into the words.

"I think I should know who my brother introduces my kid to," Caroline argued as Hudson sat on my left and his dad took the last spot on our side.

"Hey, Caroline"—Hudson slid a plate my way—"when I keep an eye on Juniper on the weekends so you can work, sometimes we see my girlfriend. Now you know." He took two bottles of water out of his pockets, putting one in front of me and taking the other for himself.

"Thank you." I picked up the fork and knife he'd put on my plate next to a piece of grilled barbecue chicken, a large portion of salad, fresh vegetables with a little ranch, and a *brownie*. Another little section of that gaping wound inside my chest pulled tight and closed. He remembered far more than I would have expected him to.

"June-Bug, you sure you don't want to sit with your friends?" Caroline offered in a tone that wasn't suggestive.

"Nope. I'm good here." Juniper flashed me a smile. "Mom, did you know that Alessandra is a famous dancer?"

Real subtle, Juniper. Guess it was time to hold up my end of the bargain. I cut into my chicken and waited for Caroline's response.

"Is she?" Caroline jabbed a piece of potato salad with her fork, and I silently chewed my chicken.

"She's like . . . *world* famous." Juniper nodded and grasped her cheeseburger with both hands. "Some say she'll be the next prima. There's only a handful in the world, you know." An impossible amount of that burger disappeared into her mouth.

"So, what is she doing in Haven Cove?" Caroline aimed that question at me. "Shouldn't she be off in New York City, living the life of a world-famous ballerina?"

"I'm recovering from an injury." I pushed my fork into my salad. "Snapped my Achilles tendon in a performance in January."

Was it me, or did her posture soften just a little?

"So once you're recovered, you'll go back?" She shot a glance at Hudson.

"That's the plan," he answered, completely unbothered.

I shoved food in just so my mouth would be full if she asked another question. Anne would have been so much better at this. She always put people at ease.

Her eyes narrowed. "I still can't believe you're dating." She waved her fork at us. "There's something weird about it."

"It's only weird that she finds him attractive," Gavin teased.

"Please excuse our daughter." Hudson's mom shot Caroline a look that didn't need translation. "The sun must have addled her manners."

"How did you two meet?" Caroline pushed ahead, and Gavin watched as he ate like he was sitting front row at a show.

Shit. My stomach plunged.

"I rescued her," Hudson answered between bites.

"Did you fall off daddy's yacht?" Caroline lifted her brows at me.

"No." I shrugged. "We actually keep that in the Med."

Gavin choked and quickly took a sip of his soda.

Hudson bit back a grin. "She was out past the cove in a boat with a hole in it."

When I was sixteen.

"Only because Eva was going to go by herself if I didn't climb in, and she was my responsibility." I shook my head at the memory. *"You won't leave your sister and I won't leave you."* I'd fully, instantly, trusted him with my life in that second.

"That's your little sister, right?" Caroline asked. "The one who knocked over her entire milkshake in the café because she hadn't liked how I made it? Then left me to clean it up while she and her little friends laughed their way back to your in-home studio?"

Yep, that sounded like Eva.

"Caroline," Hudson snapped.

My fork hovered above the salad as heat stung my cheeks in a wave of simultaneous embarrassment and protective anger. "You have my apology," I said slowly. "She was a difficult teenager."

"But Alessandra's really nice," Juniper interjected. "Oh, there's Maia! Be right back!" She hopped off the bench and ran to see her friend.

Traitor.

"What is it you like about my brother?" Caroline asked, studying my face.

Hudson tensed and I took a drink, wishing it was alcohol. "He's decisive."

"You like that he's . . . decisive?" Her brow furrowed.

"Because I'm not," I admitted. "It takes me a really long time to make decisions, usually, and then I second-guess them. It's one of my worst qualities. But Hudson . . ." I looked his way and let myself remember him—really remember him beyond the haze of anger I'd kept him veiled behind. "He makes the choice, makes the save, has this aura of certainty that I'm not sure I ever will."

He reached up and tucked my hair behind my ear.

"Still don't buy it." Caroline shook her head. "What's her favorite color?"

"Blue." Hudson's hand fell away.

"What's his birthday?" Caroline jabbed at her plate.

"April twenty-fifth," I answered, my temper pricking. Knowing Caroline disliked our family was one thing, but swimming in her contempt was quite another. "Next?"

"Caroline, you'll stop it this instant," Mrs. Ellis chided.

"You expect me to accept this tourist into our family for the next few months until she tires of Hudson and dumps him?" Caroline countered. "What, is she coming camping with us too? Is she going to join the family trip and risk breaking a nail?"

"Invite accepted." Hudson shrugged.

Wait. What?

"She won't last the first night," Caroline fired back.

Damn. I'd never been camping, but it certainly couldn't be that torturous if people went willingly.

"Dial it back, Caroline," Hudson warned. "Alessandra's family doesn't joke around like we do."

"I'm not joking." She lifted her brows.

"You want to help me out here?" Hudson asked Gavin.

"Nope." He reached for what was left of his hot dog. "You're holding your own better than I'd anticipated."

"You're acting like children," Mr. Ellis chided, and the table fell silent as Juniper ran back over, sliding into her seat. "I'm going to finish up what's left to grill. Juniper, are you ready to do cake and ice cream? I'll get it all prepped if you are."

"Yes, please." Juniper nodded, and Mr. Ellis headed back to the grill. She turned to me excitedly. "My grandma made cupcakes, but my mom makes the best strawberry shortcake you've ever tasted. You have to try it."

I winced. "Oh, I can't—"

"Ballerinas don't eat strawberry shortcake, honey," Caroline said. "Or ice cream, or cupcakes, or anything that might put an extra ounce on their perfect little bodies."

I sent up a silent prayer of forgiveness to Lina, because I was *so* fucking done.

"She doesn't eat strawberry shortcake because she's allergic to strawberries," Hudson snapped. "Hence why I got her a brownie. She loves chocolate. And before you start in on any more of your bullshit, let's just get this over with. Her birthday is March seventh. Her favorite movie is *Titanic*, which I've never really understood, but fine, I'll sit through it again. She prefers Bloch over Capezio for pointe shoes. She'd rather watch sunsets than sunrises, can annoyingly taste the difference between different types of bottled water, and puts sugar in her coffee and milk in her tea. Oh, and she's only indecisive because too many people tell her what they think she *should* want, and she likes to make everyone happy at her own expense. Is that enough for you, Caroline?"

I stared at him and struggled to find a breath. He remembered all of that? Word by word, he'd somehow stitched the wound closed that his unexplained departure had left. Not healing it, not even scabbing it over, but stanching the blood loss.

"You could have made that all up." Caroline shook her head. "And you've been together for what? Two, three weeks? No one knows all of that about someone else."

My blood *boiled*.

"Stop it!" Juniper shouted, slamming her hands on the top of the picnic table. The drinks rattled. "Just stop it, Mom! They haven't known each other for three weeks, they've known each other for *years*." She reached into her back pocket and threw a picture on the table.

I gasped at the photo. We were outside the Haven Cove Classic the day I'd won. Hudson's arm was around my shoulders while I cradled the beautiful bouquet of flowers he'd brought me. Our smiles were bright and happy, and we looked so full of hope that my heart hurt. Those two had no idea what was coming for them in just a few short hours.

"They were best friends, and he never brought her around because he knew that *you'd* be like this to her, and now you are. And you're ruining my birthday!" She stormed off toward a group of her friends, and our table fell into awkward silence.

Caroline deflated as she stared at the picture. Then she glanced up at Hudson with wordless apology before taking off after Juniper.

"Parties are so much more entertaining when you're around, Allie." Gavin winked.

Hudson snatched the picture off the table and shoved it into his pocket. "Juniper went through a box of my things."

"Alessandra, I'm so very sorry." Hudson's mom's voice sounded far away as I focused on the way Caroline dropped to her knees in front of Juniper.

Juniper nodded a few times to whatever Caroline said, and then hugged her mom tightly. Holy shit, Juniper had a mother who *apologized*. What a novelty.

This was a fucking disaster. All of it. Caroline didn't just hate my family, she hated *me*. She was going to make life miserable for as long as I pretended to date Hudson, and drag everyone else down with me. And what was worse was that she was right. There was something *off* about us.

All our little scheme had succeeded in doing today was upsetting Juniper, when our intention had been the opposite.

"I think I'm going to go." I stood up from the table, taking my plate and water with me.

"Allie—*Alessandra*." Hudson followed as I threw my trash away and thanked his father for cooking. "You don't have to go."

"I do." I nodded, then took my keys out of my pocket and started walking across the park toward Caroline's house.

"Don't give up on her." Hudson kept up with me.

"I'm not." I paused just before the entrance to Caroline's backyard. "But today isn't the day to force my presence on Caroline. You saw what it just did to Juniper."

"Hudson! It's time to do the cake!" Caroline called out, and I looked back to see her standing in the middle of the park.

"You should go." I forced a smile.

"Don't do that fake-smile shit with me." It was practically a growl.

"Go." I let the smile fall, leaving my face blank. "This is apparently a marathon, not a sprint. When Juniper opens her present—it's a jewelry box—do me a favor and don't let Caroline throw it away just because it has a little ballerina inside of it. It was Lina's."

"Alessandra," he whispered, and I stepped out of his reach, retreating as quickly as my feet would take me.

An hour later, Anne walked into the house and found me curled up on the couch with Sadie stretched out across my lap.

"How did it go?" She dropped her purse on the end table and sat down on my right.

"She's kind of horrible." I dragged my fingers through Sadie's fur. "Caroline, not Juniper."

"I'm sorry." Anne's face fell. "I shouldn't have forced you. I wasn't thinking, just reacting." She stroked Sadie's head. "What do you want to do? I'll support whatever choice you make."

"Today? Quit." Every cell in my body felt drained, like the life had been sucked out of me. "Ask me tomorrow." My phone buzzed on the coffee table, and Anne reached for it. "If it's Kenna, hit Decline."

"You can't keep avoiding her." She picked up the device and handed it to me.

"Watch me." I took it, and my chest clenched at Hudson's name above the text message.

> HUDSON: I know this is probably the last thing you want to hear, but my mom is inviting you to a family beach day to make up for today's shit show.

I showed it to Anne, then let my head fall back against the couch. "Yes, please, sign me up as Caroline's dartboard again."

Anne sighed, leaning her shoulder against mine. "Are we wrong? Do you think Lina would want us to leave her alone?"

The thought cut into my heart like the tip of a dagger. "I'd give anything to be able to ask her."

"Me too." Anne kicked off her shoes and stretched her legs out, resting her feet on the coffee table. "Why didn't she tell us? Before this, I would have sworn we didn't have any secrets from each other." She paused. "Should we tell Eva?"

"God no." I shook my head. "Not yet. She's not exactly known for her discretion." Plus, if there was anyone Caroline loathed most in our family, it was Eva.

"Good point." She scratched Sadie behind the ear, and I stared at the text from Hudson, debating exactly how much torture I could take. "Who else knows? Lina had to have told someone, don't you think? Juniper's father?"

Juniper would want me to go to the beach. Hell, she was counting on me.

"No clue," I said quietly, grasping my phone with both hands. "All I know for certain is Lina loved to dance, and if her daughter wants to dance, then we owe it to her to help, even if it means I have to wear Kevlar over my swimsuit."

ALLIE: I'll be there.

CHAPTER TWELVE

Allie

Mtn2Creek: Man, I'm glad I never did ballet.
That looks like torture, not training.

The sun peeked over the horizon, changing the white walls of my bedroom to delicate hues of pink and orange as I opened my eyes. My room had the best view of the sunrise.

But Hudson was right. I preferred sunset, preferred the anticipation of those hours when I'd been able to sneak out to see him, or sneak him in here. The irony wasn't lost on me that we'd gone from completely concealing our friendship to faking a romance.

I groaned in frustration, realizing I wanted to see him, that my eyes had been open exactly fifteen seconds and I was thinking about him.

Sadie huffed in my ear and wiggled closer.

Right, she was why I'd woken up. "Another half hour. Come on, you know you can hold it." I threw my arm over her back and snuggled into my pillow.

She. Licked. My. Face.

"Another fifteen minutes?" I begged. Sleep had become my greatest friend, and maybe, if I was being honest, a coping mechanism that was quickly turning into addiction. In unconsciousness, there were no ankle injuries, no rehabs, no decisions to be made about how hard to push myself and when. There were endless possibilities and zero consequences.

The mattress jostled me as Sadie jumped down, shaking her head and jingling the newly minted tags—one for her vaccinations and the other with her name and my number—on her new pink collar at a decibel my head immediately disliked.

"Five minutes?" Was I seriously negotiating with a puppy?

She whined from the door, warning me to get out of bed now or clean up the mess she was going to bless me with.

"Okay, okay." I forced myself out of bed and shucked off my pj's, then slipped quickly into my usual morning workout gear, sliding my phone into the side pocket of my leggings. *An object in motion stays in motion.* That's what my mother always preached, and the Rousseau girls were never allowed to *stop* moving.

Sadie pranced, and I opened my door as quietly as possible so I wouldn't wake Anne. She'd been up late with the planning committee for the Company gala. The Fourth of July was only a month away, and she was in crunch mode.

There was no point tiptoeing down the hall when Sadie took off at a run, her nails clicking against the hardwood as she bounded down the front stairs. I detoured only long enough to snag a bottle of water from the refrigerator, then walked Sadie down the long central hallway, past the dining room, office, and family room to the back door, groggily remembering to put in the alarm code before opening the door.

Sadie leapt across the porch and raced for the grass.

I closed the screen door quietly, then settled onto the outdoor love seat and twisted the bottle open. Hydrate, that was always the first order of the morning. I chugged half the bottle down despite the morning chill and checked on Sadie, who was happily sniffing around the bushes.

She hadn't run yet, and always came back when I called her, but our relationship was only a week old, so I wasn't exactly counting on her to be a paragon of puppyhood.

It was beautiful out here, the clouds reflecting the pink of sunrise from the storm that had passed yesterday. Only when I'd nearly finished the water did I open my phone and take it off Do Not Disturb. Three text messages popped up: two from Eva and one from Kenna.

KENNA: If you don't call me back I'm going to send out a search party.

It was too early for the guilt that came along with that one, so I opened the next.

EVA: You should def shoot some rehab content tomorrow. People need to see you're still alive.

EVA: Might be good to correct some misinformation too.

I sighed and clicked on the Seconds video she'd sent accompanying the message. The app opened on my phone, and a video from a popular dancer started playing.

"So let's talk about the four reasons dancers are injured. First, physique." The video transitioned to a dancer I was mildly acquainted with falling after he'd come back too soon after his third knee replacement. "Second, technique." I winced as a dancer inappropriately distributed her weight in an arabesque and rolled her ankle. "Third, mishap." A pas de deux went incredibly wrong and the man dropped his partner. "And fourth, overuse."

My stomach dropped to the porch as I appeared on the screen, going into the eighteen turns in the Giselle variation. *Turn it off. Scroll. Now.* It didn't matter that my brain threw out every warning—I couldn't look away, my gaze locked on the train wreck that ended my season . . .

and maybe my career. There it was, the second I'd faltered, lost my focus when I'd thought I'd seen him in the empty seat. The video didn't catch the sound of my tendon popping, but my brain filled in the audio just fine as I screamed and my castmates rushed to carry me offstage.

"Principal dancer Alessandra Rousseau had already had one Achilles repair, and rumor around the Company is she knew she was injured and went on anyway. That decision may have cost her a dream career." The video transitioned back to the original poster. "So what do you think? Was this mishap? Technique? Physique? Or overuse? Let me know in the comments."

The little witch *tagged* us.

Like a masochist, I opened the comments.

Ballet4Life97: Definitely overuse. So stupid of her.

Ryandnzx: Could be physique. She looks a little out of shape.

    Ballet4Life97: Good point, those costume seams are screaming

Dancegrl6701: A second achilles tear? May as well fill her spot. She's not coming back.

    OnPointe34: No shit right? Get out of the way for a corps member

CassidyFairchilde1: She could make it back.

Dancegrl6701: Sure, if she wants to teach. But dance? No way. Not as principal.

NYFouette92: From what I hear, they're already replacing her.

Bway11te: how do you throw a career away like that?

ReeseOnToe: Shame. She's ballet royalty. Hope she heals

Tutucutex20: Fucking idi*t Play stupid games and all that.

Bright2Lit: Even if she comes back, she'll never be 100

WestCoastPointe: Met her once. Pretentious and arrogant

OnPointe34: Really? Figures. Most nepo babies are

WestCoastPointe: Company's better off without her. Trust me. Diva.

I closed out the app and fought to breathe through the crushing, sharp pain blooming in my chest. Formal reviews in the *Times* had nothing on the casual viciousness of the internet.

Sadie plodded up the steps and climbed into the chair, her paw barely missing my thigh as she completely consumed my personal space and made herself at home, turning in the tight space and collapsing across my lap.

I sank my fingers into her fur and drew one breath, then another.

May as well fill her spot. She's not coming back. As hard as I tried to let the comments go, that one stuck an ice pick in my soul and left a mark. Why would Eva send me something like that? Didn't she realize I was already well aware of what people were saying?

"I can't even escape myself out here," I muttered as my heart rate slowed. Wouldn't matter where I went, the internet could follow. It was one of the reasons I hadn't wanted a damn Seconds account.

May as well fill her spot. She's not coming back.

Yes, I was. It was as simple and as impossible as that. "Let's get some breakfast."

I took Sadie inside and fed us both, then hit the gym. The only person telling me what I could and couldn't do was *me.*

"Hey, are you—" Anne peeked in through the open studio door, fully dressed for the day in white linen shorts and a blue polo, holding a small silver picture frame. "What are you doing?" She kicked off her sandals and walked in.

I swept my right foot forward back into first position, keeping my left hand on the barre. "Rond de jambe. What does it look like?" I repeated the move, tendu to the front, pointing my foot, then drawing it out to the side, then back before bringing it back to first again.

"It's seven a.m." She studied the movement of my foot. "How long have you been in here?"

"Started my workout at six." I repeated the move, testing my Achilles with each flex and point of my foot. The pain was minimal, whatever that meant. "Cardio on the bike, Pilates machine, everything the doc prescribed." No demi-pointe.

"Turnout looks good." She walked over slowly, eyeing me like I was a wild animal poised for flight. "What else have you been doing?"

"I warmed up with the fouettés from *Swan Lake*." Forward. Side. Back. First. The motions were muscle memory after decades in the studio, but my ankle wasn't quite getting with the program.

"Ha ha. Very funny." She folded her arms. "Do you do this every morning?"

I nodded. "While you're asleep so I avoid the lectures."

"Alone?" There was a definite purse to her lips.

"Sadie keeps me company now."

The golden lifted her head in the corner in response to her name, then went back to chewing on her toy.

"I thought you only worked out once a day, not twice." A hint of disapproval slid into Anne's tone. "You have to take it easy on your ankle or you'll . . ." She sighed. "Train yourself into the ground."

"This *is* easy. I'm used to being in the studio ten hours a day." I wasn't taking baby steps; I was barely crawling from where I wanted—needed—to be.

"If you tear that tendon again—"

"I know!" I dropped my hand and yanked off my split-sole slippers. "I'm well aware that if I push and it snaps again, I'm done." One. Two. I tossed them at my canvas ballet bag beneath the windowsill as I crossed the studio floor. "But if I don't push, don't fight to heal, I'm done too. They'll replace me, Anne. There's always someone waiting in the wings. Charlotte danced my part all of five minutes after they carried me off the stage that night." I snagged my Hydro Flask and my phone off the windowsill, then opened it to Eva's text message and handed it to Anne.

"You are irreplaceable," Anne said gently. "There is no one capable of taking your spot, Allie. You're a once-in-a-decade talent." She glanced down at the phone. "What is this?"

"Watch." I sat on the floor and stretched my warm muscles between drinks of water, cringing when I heard the content creator's voice.

"This is bullshit." Anne crouched in front of me. "Allie, tell me you know this is bullshit." Her eyes searched mine, and when I didn't respond, she scrolled down. "And *please* tell me you didn't read through these heinous comments." She closed the app and put my phone on the floor. "Why would Eva send something like that to you?"

"I'm sure she thought it would motivate me to hit the workouts harder. Which it did." I put my feet into a butterfly stretch, sole to sole, then tugged my ankles toward my torso. "After it cut me into bite-size pieces."

"People say stupid shit when there's no accountability for running their mouths," she muttered.

"It was both physique and overuse." I released the stretch. "My Achilles never fully healed after the accident, and I refused to slow down even when it became apparent I needed to. I had every intention of rehabbing post-*Nutcracker* season, but then Vasily offered me Giselle, and all I could think was . . ." My shoulders dipped.

"You wanted to make Mom proud. I get it."

"Yeah." But she didn't. Once Anne quit, the pressure evaporated off her shoulders, only to be redistributed between Lina, Eva, and me.

Now there were only two of us to carry it, and if I broke, it would leave only Eva.

"Speaking of Mom." She sat in front of me. "I looked through the pictures in their room last night."

"Feeling nostalgic?"

She handed me the five-by-seven frame. "Something wasn't sitting right about Lina."

"You mean the part where she hid an entire pregnancy from us? Or the part where she never mentioned she'd had a baby and given it up for adoption?" I glanced at the photo, noting Mom's and Lina's bright smiles, their heads leaned together in front of the lit-up poster advertising *Don Quixote*. "What am I missing, here? Mom went to San Francisco to see Lina perform. We all knew that."

"They're in full winter coats." Anne sat up on her knees and tapped the glass at the top of the frame, where the poster read **MARCH 3-13**.

"Oh." I looked over the picture again, searching for any sign of Lina's pregnancy under the thick puffer jacket and finding none. "She would have been seven months pregnant."

"Right." She took out her phone, pulling up the internet. "And I remembered that I'd been on spring break from NYU that week and Mom wouldn't let me go with her. Said she needed the one-on-one time to get Lina's head on straight because she was only in the studio company. She was disappointed that she wasn't an apprentice yet, let alone corps." She turned the phone around to show me the cast for that season. "Lina isn't on it." She flipped back a few programs to the fall. "She's here." Flip. "And here." *Nutcracker*. "Even there—'Lina Rousseau, Studio Company.' Then she disappears. Mom brought that picture home, but Lina isn't listed in the program."

"They staged the picture." My heart started to pound. "Mom knew about Juniper."

Anne nodded. "Get dressed."

CHAPTER THIRTEEN

Allie

> **User45018:** Of course they got in. Look who their mother is.

> **CassidyFairchilde1:** Maybe she opened doors but they kept themselves in the room.

"Annelli Myers and Alessandra Rousseau to see Sophie Rousseau," Anne said to the guard stationed outside the Brookesfield Institute.

His pinched face disappeared beneath a black ball cap as he looked at his tablet, then reappeared. "Go on ahead."

"Thank you," Anne replied, then rolled up the window on the Mercedes as the gate ahead of us opened. The lawn was thick and green inside the circular drive, the hedges trimmed to perfection along the right side of the driveway as we drove the quarter mile up to the sprawling estate my mother had determined would be her home. It was a Gilded Age mansion, built by some oil tycoon over a hundred years ago and renovated in the last few decades.

Anne parked in the small lot beside the north wing, and we climbed out, both taking a second to stretch. It wasn't a bad drive, only about an hour and a half from Haven Cove down the coast, but I had a suspicion Anne had clenched the whole way here, just like me.

"You ready?" she asked, clenching the strap of her purse.

"Ready enough. Let's go." I slung my small bag over my head to hang cross-body, and we walked along the winding sidewalk, up the wide stone steps, and through the pillars onto the porch.

My phone vibrated while we were waiting to be buzzed in, and I quickly checked the text message.

HUDSON: Still on for the beach tomorrow?

Right, that was tomorrow. Just thinking about it made me tired.

"Everything all right?" Anne asked, lifting her sunglasses to the top of her head.

"Hudson wants to know if I'm still up for family fun at the beach tomorrow." My thumbs hovered over the keyboard.

"Are you?" Her brow knit with worry.

It was hard to explain how the thought of making myself present-able two days in a row, of the effort it took to appear like I was enjoying myself because that's what everyone expected, was daunting as hell. It was one of the reasons I'd left New York for the beach house. "Yeah. It will be good to see Juniper."

And Hudson.

The door buzzed twice, and Anne opened it. We walked into the marble foyer, complete with Roman statuary, and handed over our IDs to sign in. There were only four people Mom would allow to disturb her.

Then we waited.

ALLIE: Will there be verbal fisticuffs involved?

HUDSON: Only you would use the word fisticuffs.

ALLIE: Not an answer.

HUDSON: Caroline will be on her best behavior.

Best behavior meaning maybe she'd stick to just glaring at me.

ALLIE: I'll be there.

HUDSON: Pick you up at noon.

Like a date, because we were supposed to be dating.

ALLIE: Ok.

I slipped my phone into my back pocket.

"It's quiet," Anne noted, glancing down the empty hallway to the right, then left. "Classes must be in session."

"When's the last time you were here?" I smoothed the lines of my black blouse, but there was nothing to be done about the wrinkles in my shorts from sitting on the drive.

"Last weekend." Anne smiled as a woman with a flawless bun and clipboard hurried by. "You?"

"A little over a month." I splayed my hands, checking that I'd scrubbed all the dirt from under my nails. "She let me stay long enough to express her disappointment, then kicked me out. Said she was late to teach."

"Sounds about right," Anne muttered as Rachel—the newest of Mom's minions—came down the wide carpeted staircase in front of us. "She's going to be angry that we're here on a weekday."

"It's so good to see you girls!" Rachel exclaimed, her smile crinkling the edges of her eyes and mouth. Her light-blue sweater matched her eyes, and her red hair was pulled into a neat bun. "She has some time before her next session. Why don't you come on up?" She led us up the carpeted steps, curving at the landing, then continuing to the second floor.

"Anyone else come by?" Anne asked, her knuckles doing their best impression of Casper along her purse strap.

"Miss Eloise stopped up a couple of weeks ago, but if you're asking if your sister has been here . . ." Rachel shook her head.

"Of course she hasn't," Anne muttered.

We turned left into the north wing, passing a few rooms with closed doors, classical music streaming through each of them.

"And how is her mood today?" I asked, my stomach twisting. On her worst days, I was mostly limited to yes or no answers when she deigned to speak with me, especially after I'd *embarrassed* her when I fell in January, but she was usually in a good mood for Anne.

"So far it's a good day," Rachel said with a thoughtful nod. "She did yell at one of the new staff members, but they were late."

"Understandable." Anne paled as Rachel opened the six-paneled double doors into Mom's suite.

It was decorated in pastels, every piece hand selected by Mom, from the tasteful seating arrangement with its tufted love seat and matching chairs to the similarly upholstered headboard on the heavily pillowed bed. The walls were covered in black-and-white photographs of both us and Mom at the different stages of our career. The lone photo of Dad sat on her nightstand, the glass smudged with fingerprints.

And Mom stood at the far end of the suite by the enormous windows, her profile to us, painting yet another picture of yet another ballerina. Her hair was pinned neatly in place, and those tailored black pants and pink blouse didn't have a speck of paint on them, from what I could see.

"Sophie," Rachel called out gently. "Your daughters are here, and you have about twenty minutes before your next class." She gave us both a pat on our backs, then slipped out the door, leaving us alone with our mother.

Anne and I looked at each other, and when I lifted my hands, so did she.

One. Two. Three. I mouthed silently, then threw my hand flat.

Anne had two fingers pointed out.

Scissors beat paper. Crap.

"Mom?" I walked forward across the gleaming hardwood floor, passing by the conversation area on my right and the door to her bathroom on my left, stopping when I was about ten feet away. "Anne and I need to talk to you."

Her head turned my way, and her withering gaze swept over me, lingering on my Vans. She opened, then shut her mouth, like she couldn't believe what I was wearing. "Fifth."

Ugh. I let loose a sigh and shot Anne a look.

"Fifth!" Mom shouted.

I placed my feet closely together in opposite directions, right before left.

"Sloppy feet." She went back to applying the delicate lines of the ballerina's skirt.

At least the critique was quick and succinct. "We wanted to ask you about Lina."

Her brush paused for a heartbeat before continuing on as if I hadn't spoken.

Foolishly, I charged ahead. She might not ever want to talk about her, but we needed answers. "Anne and I have been at the beach house, just like you wanted," I told her, hoping the fulfilled request might put her in a more amiable mood. "The one in Haven Cove."

"Studio needs waxing." She continued painting. "It's dull. Lifeless."

"We'll have it done," I promised.

"Like your dancing. Dull. Lifeless." She picked up the water cup and rinsed the brush. "No fixing that."

Ah, and we've moved on to the insult portion of the visit. Excellent. I looked over my shoulder at Anne, blatantly begging for help.

"And Allie's been seeing Hudson Ellis," Anne said, coming my direction, opening her purse as she walked.

Mom's brush paused in the pink paint, and I flinched even though I'd known the plan. If Mom knew about Juniper, there was a chance she'd know who was raising her. "River boy?" Disdain dripped from her words.

"That's the one." I managed not to sigh. The first time Mom had caught me with Hudson on the beach, she'd told me, *"That boy is like the river. Pretty to look at, but we don't swim there."*

The second time she'd caught me, I'd been grounded to the house for two weeks and sentenced to extra hours in the studio.

"It's good to see you, Mom," Anne said, and I could only hope she'd have better luck.

Mom gave her the same appraising examination, then smiled. "Anne."

That flare of hope behind my ribs shone a little green.

"Hi, Mom." Anne walked between us, then leaned in and kissed Mom on the cheek. "Doesn't Allie look great? She's already back in the studio. She'll be back on the stage in no time."

"By fall," I said, stepping out of fifth. "Vasily might showcase the ballet Isaac Burdan choreographed for me."

"Second," she barked.

Seriously?

Anne shot me a pleading look, and I arranged my feet into second position.

"Vasily chooses *his* interests," she told Anne, her brow furrowing as she glanced back at me. "Sloppy."

For fuck's sake, I was in perfect alignment.

"He likes Allie," Anne said gently. "Always has."

"He liked Lina." Her hand clenched the brush. "Allie is no prima."

Awesome. Neither was Lina, and considering that Lina had driven into New York and begged him to reconsider after the first year he hadn't offered her a contract, I would have argued that I had higher standing, if it would do me any good with Mom. But now I was simply the daughter who'd fallen in front of all New York City.

I made the mistake of sighing.

"Third!" Mom snapped.

I angled my feet and expectations accordingly. I could be the youngest principal dancer in the history of the Company, have dance roles that were created for me, earn critical acclaim, but until I had that scarce, extraordinary title bestowed upon me, none of it mattered in her eyes.

"Sloppy lines. Sloppy feet." She moved her own into position. "Third."

I readjusted my stance even though it was perfect. "Third."

Her stare prickled the hair on the back of my neck before she turned back to the painting.

"Mom, we know you have to get to class soon." Anne took the framed picture out of her bag and showed it to Mom. "We just wanted to ask you about this picture."

Mom stared at the picture. "Lina." A smile ghosted her face.

"Did you know she was pregnant?" Anne asked.

Mom froze and so did my heartbeat. She blinked once, then pivoted toward the painting, stepping out of position. She'd shut us out. We weren't going to get anywhere with her.

"In this picture of you two, Lina is seven months pregnant. Did you know?" Anne tried again.

"Mom, talk to us," I begged quietly.

"Fourth!"

I moved accordingly.

Anne took a deep breath. "Did Lina have a baby?"

Mom shook her head, and the brush slipped, pink streaking across what had been a red curtain on the stage. "Now it's ruined." She threw the brush into the water glass. "Get out. I have class."

My heart thundered in my ears. She *fucking* knew. "Lina had a baby." I stepped out of position. "Her name is Juniper."

"Do. Not. Ask. Again." Mom bit out the words.

"We have to! Did you help give the baby up?" Anne pushed forward. "Why didn't you tell us?"

"Who is her father?" I added, quickly falling silent as the door opened behind us.

"Hey, girls," Rachel said from the doorway. "Sophie, Elle Gibbons is hoping you'd have a few minutes to look at her Aurora variation before class."

"No." Mom picked up her paintbrush and dipped it in red, then started to cover the pink mistake. "Fifth."

Defeated, I moved my feet into position, and Anne stuffed the picture into her purse. We both trusted Rachel, but this secret was bigger than us.

"Elle's father is a large donor," Rachel reminded Mom. "It will only take a minute."

"We're not done discussing this," Anne said quietly to Mom.

"We are," Mom countered. "Tendu."

I complied, shoes and all. "We have to know," I whispered.

"Relevé!" she demanded, grabbing hold of the water cup in one hand and dunking the brush with the other to rinse it.

"I can't." I shook my head. Going up on the balls of my feet wasn't an option yet.

"Maybe you could give us a second?" Anne asked, walking past me toward Rachel.

"It will throw off the whole schedule," Rachel replied apologetically.

"Relevé!" Mom glared my direction.

"I can't, Mom. My ankle isn't ready." I relaxed my posture.

She threw the cup at me, water and all. The plastic hit the hardwood a couple feet away with a thwack, and water splashed up, splattering the bottom of my legs. I waited for the embarrassment to hit, the sorrow that I'd disappointed her yet again, but there was nothing.

She was the water, and I was now a sieve. Being numb had some perks.

"Mom!" Anne shouted.

"Oh, Allie." Rachel raced past me into the bathroom, then came out and handed me a fluffy pink towel.

"Thank you." I wiped down my legs, mourning the loss of my pink Vans, which were now splattered with paint and water.

"I'm so very sorry." Rachel glanced over her shoulder at Mom. "Sophie, how could you?"

Straightening my posture, I looked right at my mother. "Easily. Though not usually in public."

Rachel gasped, and Mom's hands curled.

Shit, I shouldn't have said that.

"It should—" Mom's face blotched red, and she snapped her mouth shut as her gaze flickered to the photo of Lina at my left.

"Go ahead and say it." I lifted my chin. "It wouldn't be the first time, and it might make you feel better." At least one of us would.

"Mom," Anne warned.

"Should. Have." She jabbed her finger my direction, biting out every syllable. "Been. You."

"Mom!" Anne shouted. "Take that back!"

"Yeah." I blew out a slow breath as the words crushed my heart in a sharp-nailed fist, cutting into the areas I could have sworn were too thick with scar tissue to feel, but even numbness had its limit, and this pain was acute. Raw. Devastating. "Most days I wish it had been," I answered truthfully, anger getting the best of me. She *knew* about Juniper and hadn't told us. Wouldn't tell us.

"Allie, no," Anne whispered, reaching for my hand, holding tight. "Never that."

"But I can't help but wonder what you would have done when Lina didn't measure up to your impossible standards either. Who would you blame then?" I held on to that towel like a lifeline with one hand, and Anne's with the other.

"Leave *now*." Mom dismissed me without another word, striding out of her suite while Rachel scurried after her.

"Even now, she'll protect Lina over everyone else," Anne muttered.

Mom wasn't going to help us. We were on our own.

CHAPTER FOURTEEN

Hudson

Ballet4Life97: You look like a piece of art.
That fouetté? Gorgeous.

Allie Rousseau looked good as hell riding shotgun in my truck, looking out the window like she'd done it a thousand times, her hand
wrapped around the oh-shit handle as we pulled onto the bumpy
beach-access road.

And I struggled to concentrate on both the road and what
Beachman was saying from the back seat. He was my backup plan, a
second set of eyes and ears to look out for Allie just in case Caroline
decided to go back on her promise to back off.

"So we pull up on this vessel, right? And we're talking thirty-foot
seas—" Beachman continued.

Allie turned her entire body to look into the back seat, her oversize
sunglasses making it impossible to get a hint of what she was thinking.

"They were more like twenty," I corrected.

"Still, the waves are fucking huge." Beachman leaned forward. "And
this fishing vessel is bobbing like a cork, taking on water from all sides,

and Ellis here is somehow dodging the crow's nest as he brings up the crew."

"That's more the pilot than it is me." I drove past the hot spots teeming with tourists, and the road got rough with sand.

"Whatever." Beachman waved me off. "So he starts down for the last guy as this swell comes up over the bow, and the captain fucking *jumps*."

Allie's lips parted, and I fought to keep my eyes on the road.

"Right? So Rafferty's got the controls, and he's telling Hudson that we gotta reel him in and reassess because it's dark as shit and we think the captain's been dragged under the hull."

"He's exaggerating. I had a visual." The new comfort station came into view, and I spotted Mom and Dad's SUV parked nearby. Despite the remodeled showers and bathrooms that would normally draw the tourists, this section of beach was still the best-kept secret in Haven Cove.

"The fuck you did," Beachman countered. "Anyway, so Ellis starts arguing that he can get to him, but I started the hoist because, you know, orders."

"You're a swimmer too?" Allie asked.

"Hell no. I have respect for my life and am therefore a flight mechanic. Swimmers are fucking crazy. No offense intended." He slapped his hand on my shoulder as we approached the coned-off area designated as a parking lot.

"None taken."

"So, the second Ellis is clear of the vessel, the asshole disconnects from the cable, and falls like twenty-five feet into the water."

Allie's eyebrows rose above her sunglasses.

"Exactly." Beachman threw up his hands. "So now I'm scrambling to get the basket ready, and Ellis is down there in thirty-foot swells—"

"Twenty," I corrected.

"And get this—he *finds* the captain. The boat starts to pitch, and the whole fucking thing goes over on its side, and the crow's nest had to have been two or three feet away from Ellis when it came crashing down."

"Oh my God," Allie whispered.

"It was more than ten feet." I shot a look over my shoulder at him. "Stop exaggerating."

"Are you telling the story? Or am I?" Beachman threw his hand over his heart. "So the swell yanks the boat back up again, and Ellis starts hauling this giant fucker through the water like he's no bigger than a toddler, trying to get some distance between them and the hull, and the whole vessel bobs right back like it's a game of Whac-A-Mole. I think that thing came for him at least three times before we got the captain hoisted, then once more before Ellis was back on board. Rafferty was *pissed*."

I pulled into a spot and put the truck in park.

"When was this?" Allie asked me, unclicking her seat belt.

"Last night, off the coast of Maine," Beachman answered, already moving for the door. "I'm telling you, Ellis here is the luckiest bastard I've ever met in my life."

"Last night?" Allie leaned on the console between us. "We could have canceled today."

"Everybody lived and I'm perfectly fine," I promised, undoing my belt. "Just another day at the office."

"Potential death is just . . . commonplace for you."

"Pretty much." I nodded.

She stared at me a few seconds longer, but the damn glasses hid whatever was going on in her eyes. Something about her was off today.

"Let's go, lovebirds," Beachman called into the truck before shutting the doors.

"He . . . umm . . . he knows, right?" Allie asked.

"About us pulling off the fake date for the sake of getting Juniper into ballet? Absolutely. He's all for it." Beachman was more than ecstatic to facilitate what he saw as the fix for the problem I represented. "I left the rest out."

"Good. The less people we have to lie to, the better." She plopped on a floppy sun hat, and we stepped into the midday sun. Seventy-seven degrees was hot for this time of year, but I wasn't complaining about the warmth or the cloudless blue sky.

"You all right?" I tilted my head. "You're more quiet than usual."

"Yeah. I'm fine. Had a shit day yesterday, and just really don't want to think about it." She hefted her beach bag, about half her size, onto her shoulder.

"Or talk about it," I guessed.

"Definitely not." She shook her head, which didn't surprise me. Allie was harder to crack than a Rubik's Cube.

"Then allow me to distract you with sand, water, and what I hope might even be a little bit of fun." I motioned toward the beach.

"A distraction sounds perfect, actually." She did me the honor of not faking a smile.

Beachman and I divvied up what needed to be carried, and a few minutes later, we trekked through the sand past the tiled comfort station with its wraparound deck, and onto the beach where my parents and Caroline waited.

Dad had outdone himself as usual, planting four giant beach umbrellas—their scalloped edges fluttering with every gust of wind—with two camping chairs under each in the sand about twenty feet from the waves.

"Let the games begin," Allie muttered, her hand holding her hat in place.

"I've got your back," I promised as we approached. Her back, her front, I'd cover whatever she needed.

There were only a few other families on this section of the beach, and I savored the quiet. In a few weeks, there wouldn't be an empty place to sit as we hit peak season.

"Hudson!" Mom stood up from her chair as I sat the cooler next to Dad's, then leaned into a quick hug. "Allie!" She pivoted without warning and threw her arms around Allie.

Allie froze for a noticeable second, then hugged her back awkwardly. "Mrs. Ellis."

"Call me Gwen, dear." Mom pulled back and squeezed Caroline's shoulders, then grinned at Beachman. "Eric! It's been too long!"

"Mrs. E." He all but swallowed Mom in a hug.

"Her parents weren't huggers, I'm guessing," Dad said quietly from beside me.

"She's affectionate." My tone sharpened. "Especially with her sisters."

"Didn't say she wasn't." Dad clapped my back. "She's tough, I'll give her that."

"Because she grew up with Thatcher and Sophie?" I asked, noting that Caroline hadn't looked up from her book under the third umbrella.

"Thatcher wasn't terrible," Dad mused. "Came into the café every morning to read the paper and ordered a strong black coffee. Always said lovely things about his girls. Yours, in particular, though he doted a little too much on the youngest. I was saying Allie's tough because she came back after Caroline dug her claws into her. She must care about you."

"She's incredible," I said, watching Allie fearlessly settle into the chair next to Caroline, putting her bag between them.

"She has to be, if you felt the need to hide her away from us when you were kids." He leveled *the* look on me, the one where he was disappointed but wasn't going to say it.

"You were never the problem." I opened the cooler and snagged two Smartwaters. "Well, maybe Caroline was part of it."

"She hated that family ever since the day Sophie Rousseau had Madeline cut her best friend from the advanced class to make room for the oldest daughter. What was her name?" Dad scratched his clean-shaven chin.

"Lina." My brow furrowed. "I don't remember that."

"Oh, it was years and years ago. You were little. There had to be seven or eight years between the girls, which started a whole thing. Sophie had their studio built the next year and started bringing in all those professionals to teach, and the Classic was born. Great for the economy, tough on the year-rounders." Dad adjusted the first umbrella to better cover Mom as she sat down.

I walked over to Allie and handed her the water, glancing between her and Caroline to see if there'd been any bloodshed yet. I wasn't above chucking my sister into the water after the way she'd treated Allie at the party.

"Thank you." Allie took the bottle, and I sat beside her. Beachman had already sprawled over the chair to my left. "I can't believe you remember which water I like."

"I remember everything." I turned my hat backward to keep it on, and Allie set hers down, pinning the edge with her beach bag. Staring while she tied her hair up in a loose knot wasn't an option, so I looked past her to Caroline. "Where's Juniper?"

"On her way." Caroline turned a page of her book. "She's been spending Sunday mornings with Gavin for the last few months, which has been a huge help so I can get errands done or the house clean without that little tornado throwing everything into upheaval as I go. Gives them some good bonding time, though I had to make sure he wasn't teaching her keg stands or anything. He hasn't been late *one* time for a Sunday morning."

Damn, that was impressive for Gavin.

"She could come over to our house every single Sunday if you lived near us," Mom called out from her seat. "Or I could come help you with laundry, or cooking. You're not alone, you know."

It wasn't the first, or the hundredth, time they'd made the offer.

"I have Hudson and Gavin," Caroline replied. "I'm not alone."

Which was why I had to put Cape Cod as my first-choice duty station when they asked me for my list next month. I pushed away the irrational flare of impatience that I'd have to wait at least another three years before asking for Sitka. Maybe by then, Juniper and Caroline would function on their own, and I could be the fun uncle instead of the necessary one.

"Juniper's great. I've never met a smarter ten-year-old." Allie kicked off her sandals and dug her toes into the sand.

Caroline fought a smile and lost. "She's something else. Did you give her the phone back yet, Hudson?"

My stomach pitched. "The phone?"

Allie leaned back, clearly taking herself out of the line of fire.

Caroline looked up over her sunglasses at me. "Come on. I'm busy, but I'm not completely oblivious. I just let you think you have one up on me."

"How long have you known?"

"Since the first time she connected it to the Wi-Fi," Caroline answered. "What did she do to get it taken away?"

"I think that falls under *uncle privilege*." I settled back in my seat.

"Hmmm." She looked past us and grinned. "Hi, honey!"

Juniper raced across the sand, sandals in hand, and hugged her mom. "Hi, Mom!"

Gavin followed and dropped Juniper's backpack on the next empty seat.

Pulling back, Caroline stroked her hand over Juniper's head and down her hair. "What is in your hair? It's all sticky." She shot an accusing glance at Gavin.

"I just pulled the uncle-privilege card, if that helps," I told him.

"Uncle privilege," Gavin declared, throwing a hand in the air. "Good to see you, Allie."

"Hey, Gavin." Allie waved.

"Allie!" Juniper grabbed her hand. "Want to help me build a sandcastle?"

"That sounds fun." Her mouth curved into the start of a smile.

"Mom, you too," Juniper declared.

Oh fuck. *Here we go.*

Ten minutes later, the four of us were on our knees with a bag of sand toys, constructing a castle while Beachman and Gavin tossed a Frisbee nearby. Allie had shucked off her usual button-up, revealing a black tank top that I was trying like hell not to stare at.

"That's good." Juniper supervised as I pulled the bucket off the dampened sand that would serve as the center tower. "You, too, Allie."

"Thanks." A smirk played across her mouth as she did the same with a smaller bucket.

I immediately started filling mine again, struggling to keep my eyes off Allie, like she'd disappear if I looked away for too long.

"Did you make a lot of sandcastles in the summer?" Juniper asked. "With your sisters?"

"Not really." Allie sat back on her heels, holding the little green bucket in her lap. "We didn't get a lot of playtime in the summers, and when we did, we liked to hunt for shells or read on the pier."

"Or sneak out and stargaze," I said.

"Or sneak out and stargaze," Allie agreed, her eyes hidden behind those damned glasses.

"Because you danced all the time?" Juniper dug into the sand, continuing the moat, and Caroline paused in the middle of packing sand into another bucket.

"Yes." Allie pushed her sunglasses up her nose. "It took up more time as we got older, and eventually we were at it about ten hours a day between the gym, taking class with whomever Mom had brought in for that session, then rehearsing in the afternoon."

She'd been miserable and euphoric all in the same breath during those summers, and I hadn't understood it until my first few close calls out on the water. Loving something that actively worked to destroy your body was a bitch.

"Sounds like you didn't get to be a kid," Caroline noted, resuming with her own shovel.

Allie glanced at me, then Juniper. "There's a balance to be had." She hand scooped damp sand into the bucket. "I'm not sure I'd be what I am if my mother hadn't pushed us like she did. But I also think that ballet could have been a major part of our childhood without being *all* of our childhood. Balance would have been good, and I think that's why Dad wanted us out here every summer, to force that balance, but

Mom built the studio and . . ." She sighed. "Well, I love ballet, but I never got to know who I am without it."

Which was probably why she was foundering now.

"Kind of like the café." Caroline nodded. "I get that."

I was still hung up on Allie's confession. True, she lit up like a star on that stage, but she brightened every room she walked into whether or not she was in pointe shoes. I shook my head. "You're smart," I said, knowing damn well I should have kept my mouth shut, that I was blurring the lines between what she considered a fake relationship and my very real feelings.

Allie sat back on her heels. "What?"

"I said you're smart." I doubled down, staring into my own reflection in her sunglasses and wishing I could see her eyes. "And kind, protective, observant, tenacious, compassionate, an oxymoron of hesitance and bravery, and a thousand other things that have nothing to do with ballet. I knew all of that about you in the first five minutes we met, and you were nowhere near a studio."

Allie's lips parted.

Caroline fumbled her bucket.

"Mom won't let me do ballet," Juniper announced as she dug the moat past Allie's knees.

Holy shit, she just went there.

Allie stared down at Juniper as she crawled by, her brow furrowing.

"You make it sound like I don't feed you." Caroline finished her bucket. "I feed her."

"Can I ask why?" Allie acted like this was all new information for her.

Damn, she's a good actress.

Caroline shoveled bigger heaps of sand into the bucket. "First off, it's expensive. Secondly, I don't have time to be one of those moms that gossips with the others about whose kid is better than the rest, and third . . ." She finished the bucket and set it aside. "The only ballet dancers I know aren't people I'd really want to spend time with."

"Caroline—" Fuck this. She'd promised.

"No." Allie held up her hand. "I appreciate her honesty. I could say that about a lot of different sports too. But it would be a shame to judge all dancers based off the few you've met, even if I'm included in your sample group."

Caroline moved forward, then dumped the bucket into place before looking over at Allie. "I promised my brother I'd give you a shot, and that I wouldn't judge you based off the actions of your family. Because the truth is, I don't know you."

"Seems like a good place to start, since I don't know you either." Allie dumped another handful of sand in the bucket.

My chest went all tight. Damn, I was proud of her. It was time to cut this session off while she was coming out ahead. "I think we need some water."

"The sand is already wet here." Juniper dug around the back of the castle.

"Not what I meant." I shook my head at Allie, slowly smiling. She'd had a shit day yesterday, and if there was a chance I could make good on that promise of a distraction, I was taking it.

Her eyebrows rose above her sunglasses, and she immediately crouched, then stood. "I know that look, Hudson, and it's cold." She toed off her sandals and glanced to the right, choosing an escape route.

"I'd argue that it's unseasonably warm." I stood and tugged off my shirt, then dropped it on the sand. My sunglasses followed.

She backed up a few steps, then did a double take and stared straight at me, her mouth falling open slightly.

Was that a hitch in her breathing? *Fuck.* I couldn't see her eyes, couldn't read her expression. "I'd drop the glasses if you don't want to lose them," I warned her, stepping over Caroline's tower and narrowly missing the moat.

"Hudson Ellis," Allie warned, retreating another few steps, but she didn't tell me no. We both knew that single word would stop me in my tracks.

"Really. They look like nice sunglasses." I full-on grinned.

"Seriously with the dimple?" she muttered, ripping her sunglasses off and tossing them near the bucket. "Not fair."

"Never said I played fair." That was all the warning she had before I ran straight at her.

She squealed as I scooped her off the sand and threw her over my shoulder. "You have to be kidding me!"

"I'm not." I walked straight at the surf, cutting between Gavin and Eric. "I never kid when it comes to you."

"I swear, if you drop me in this water—" Her hands fought for purchase along my back, and she pushed herself up so she wasn't dangling.

"You'll what? Live a little? Get a little cold? A little wet?" My feet hit the water, and the chill raced up my shins.

"Ugh. A little wet? That's the best you have?" She worked her sandy hands to my shoulders, and I banded my arms around the backs of her thighs so she didn't go sliding down into the water as she held herself upright. "I'm disappointed. You need to work on your game, Ellis."

"You've never seen my game, Rousseau." The water hit my knees, and I walked on. Fuck, it was cold this time of year. "Trust me, if I was trying, you'd know."

"Guys with game don't look like they're trying," she countered as my ear brushed against the side of her ribs.

"You have to stop dating those dancers. If you can't tell someone's working their ass off for you, then they don't deserve you." A wave hit my thighs, and Allie gasped as it soaked her feet.

"It's freezing!"

"Invigorating, right?" I let her slip a few inches as the next wave hit, and she squeaked. "Makes you feel alive."

"You're going to be dead if you drop me in this water!" She caught me completely off guard, breaking through my hold on her and wrapping her legs around my waist. Her strong thighs locked around me, and her hands spasmed like she didn't know what to do with them.

I would have laughed my ass off if I hadn't been distracted by the thought-stealing feel of her body against mine. Her warm, soft skin sent little jolts of awareness through my nervous system everywhere we connected.

"I won't let you fall," I promised, lifting my hands to support her thighs, steering clear of the perfection of her ass.

She drew back, locking her gaze with mine as her hands hovered inches above my shoulders. There was heat in those whiskey-colored depths, and a flare of interest that had my complete attention as her breathing picked up.

"You could touch me, you know." Another wave came, but it didn't reach Allie. "I did promise you a distraction."

"Using sex as a distraction gets messy." She ran her tongue over her bottom lip, then bit it softly.

"Who said anything about sex?" My grip on her thighs tightened as my eyes tracked the movement. I wanted to lean forward and suck that lip free, wanted to trace it with my tongue, wanted to sink inside her mouth and finally know how she tasted. I was used to craving things I could never have when it came to Allie, but the way she was looking at me now had me wondering, had me *wanting*. "I was just trying to save you from looking like an awkward Frankenstein up there with your hands in the air."

She scoffed. "I was abiding by the terms of our agreement. Our rules were that you could touch me in public," she reminded me. "Not that I could touch you. I wouldn't want to take advantage of you in the heat of the moment."

"So you'll admit it's a moment?" Fuck, her lips were only inches from mine. I thought I'd understood the meaning of yearning, but I hadn't really. Not until right now.

"I'll admit that you were having a moment."

"Such a stickler for the technicalities." I tore my gaze from her mouth and found her watching me. Our gazes held . . . and heated. "Agreement amended. My rule is you can touch me whenever you want,

Alessandra. Public. Private. Doesn't matter to me. Any part of me. With any part of you. Anytime you want." Another burst of cold water hit my thighs, and I wished it had been a few inches higher. "Now might be good, since we're putting on a show and all."

Her hands settled on my shoulders with a light touch. "I mean, if it's for the show," she whispered, and her fingers slid along my skin, then interlaced behind my neck.

Need shot down my spine, and I tugged her closer on pure reflex. Nothing more than a touch, than the sensation of her in my arms, and *fire* raced through my veins. There was a reason I'd never flirted with her in our teens, never crossed the line. I'd instinctively known if I ever got my hands on her, I'd never let go.

Fuck, I'd had no idea what to do with her then, but I did now. I knew hundreds of ways to *distract* her, and I had the suspicion she would make every single one of them feel brand new.

Her hands slid into my hair on a soft sigh, and my breath caught. She glanced at my mouth and parted her lips, then blinked twice. "I'm going back to shore." Her thighs slackened as she unlocked her ankles, and I loosened my grip.

"I'll take you," I protested, biting back a groan as she slid down my body. Freezing her in the water had never been part of the plan.

"I'm not a stranger to cold water." Her hands skimmed my chest as her feet hit the sand, the ocean coming up to her waist. True to her words, she didn't even flinch, even when a wave came and soaked her tank top up to her ribs. "And you should probably give yourself a minute out here before you come back." A smirk tilted her mouth as she backed away toward shore, her eyes lighting up as she stripped off her shirt.

Holy fucking pink bikini.

The swells of her breasts made my mouth water, and the slope of her waist had my hands curling. She was right. I needed a few minutes, because I was hard as hell.

"Feel that?" she asked, tilting her head as she continued her retreat.

"What?" I responded, embarrassingly dumbstruck by the sight of her in a freaking swimsuit.

"Game, Hudson." She held her hands out, still grasping her tank top. "Effortless game." She turned and walked toward shore, and I quit fighting my grin and walked deeper into the water to cool off. I wasn't sure what had been hotter, the delicate glide of her fingertips over my skin, or the spark of life I'd seen in her eyes as she backed away.

For a second there, I'd seen *her*.

You're the reason she— my conscience started, but I shut the asshole up with a quickness, sinking beneath the waves and dunking my head. A distraction, that's all that had been. None of this was real to her, she was just fucking with my head, and I'd enjoyed every minute of it. I even considered sending her an engraved invitation to fuck with it some more.

Only when I had my body—and my thoughts—under control did I walk back to shore. Allie was nowhere to be seen.

"Where did Alessandra go?" I asked Juniper as she continued building her sandcastle with Caroline.

"I forgot my sun hat in Uncle Gavin's car, and she said she'd get it because she left her phone in yours," Juniper answered, scooping the sand from underneath the bridge she was constructing.

"That was nice of her."

"That's because she's nice." Juniper shot a look at her mother and moved on to the main tower.

Caroline rolled her eyes when Juniper wasn't looking but didn't utter a single word against Allie as we added to the castle.

A few minutes and two towers later, Allie came back, her bikini covered by a thigh-skimming pink sundress that nearly had me biting my fucking knuckles. She dropped her phone at her chair, then came our way wearing a look I couldn't decipher.

Two lines were etched between her brows.

"Everything okay?" I asked, rising to my feet as Gavin ran by.

"Yeah," she answered, her voice flat again. "Here you go, kiddo." That fake-ass smile curved her mouth as she handed Juniper her hat, and the hair on the back of my neck rose.

"Thanks!" Juniper tugged it on, slipping the strap beneath her chin.

"No problem." Allie backed up my direction.

"Heads up!" Beachman shouted, and I threw out my hand in front of Allie's head, catching the Frisbee inches from her face.

She blinked rapidly, staring at the fluorescent-yellow disk. "Holy crap."

"Watch where you're throwing this thing!" I stepped away from Allie, flicked my wrist, and sent it sailing back to Eric.

"Thank you." She cleared her throat. "Talk about reflexes."

I bent my head, bringing my mouth inches from her ear. "One might call it game."

She snorted, making me grin. It was the closest to a laugh I'd gotten out of her, and I was taking it as my win for the day.

The afternoon passed quickly. Mom and Dad praised the sandcastle and took Juniper on a walk up the beach while Gavin napped. Allie asked Caroline about the diner in a surprisingly bloodless exchange that left me oddly hopeful.

Then I watched, completely hypnotized, as Allie showed Eric how to pull off an arabesque—standing on her left foot and raising her right leg up behind her at a jaw-dropping angle.

God, she was beautiful.

"She's graceful, I'll give her that," Caroline said.

"More like exquisite. I used to watch her practice for hours when we were younger." I leaned forward, bracing my elbows on my knees.

"She made you watch her practice?" Caroline gathered up Juniper's sand toys.

"Allie didn't make me do shit. Don't twist it like that." I laughed when Eric tried his hand at the move, and face-planted in the sand. "I wanted to be wherever she was, which meant hiding out in their studio whenever her mom wasn't looking. But she did her fair share of hiding

out in the Grizzly Bear or my bedroom to spend time with me too."
I caught Caroline staring, out of the corner of my eye. "That ladder
outside my window wasn't just good as a fire escape."

"Remind me never to let Juniper have that room," she muttered.

Around four, we cleaned up the site, and I helped Dad carry the
umbrellas to the car. Once we had everything packed up in the truck, I
headed over to the comfort station to wash off my feet so I didn't track
sand into the car.

Once I'd gotten the sand off, I walked to the edge of the deck and
looked out over the ocean to wait for Allie. We'd made it through an
entire afternoon with my family where Allie hadn't run and Caroline
had held her tongue.

Plus, when I considered that I'd had Allie pressed against me in
the water, it was a damn good day, even if she'd put some noticeable
distance between us after that.

"Oh good, you're still here." Caroline walked over to the railing to
stand beside me, gathering her long blond hair into a low ponytail. "I
wanted to talk to you."

"What's up? If you need me to cover some hours with Juniper now
that school's getting out, I can probably swing it depending on my
schedule." After all, that's why I lived here.

"It's not that." She clenched the railing. "You're my baby brother,
and I love you. You know that, right?"

"What's wrong?" My brow knit.

"I gave it a shot. A real shot." Her face contorted into a look of
abject misery. "And she's lovely, but you can't date her, Hudson."

CHAPTER FIFTEEN

Allie

Andreamaaay: At this point I'm starting to wonder if your sister is even alive, RousseauSisters4.

User60981: If not, maybe there's a place open at the company!

I held my foot under the knee-height shower and rinsed it off, careful not to splash the knee-length hem of my gauzy pink sundress while wiggling my toes to get the sand out from between them. As much as I'd dreaded today, it had actually been . . . fun.

Spending time with a family that clearly loved each other, building a castle with Juniper, even flirting with Hudson—which I'd never thought I'd be brave enough to do—had been a surprisingly good time, and so very different from being with my own.

And I hadn't thought about ballet, not the heavy parts of it at least, not once. Even showing off for Hudson while I taught Eric had been a blast. I hadn't dwelled on the speed of my recovery, or stressed that someone was vying for my place, or worried that Vasily might not show-case our ballet if I wasn't back to full strength. Sure, I'd missed an after-noon workout, but as much as I hesitated to admit—it had been worth it.

It was the perfect balm to soothe the new wounds Mom had inflicted yesterday.

I showered off my other foot, then glanced back at the parking lot. Jessica had swung by to grab Eric after she was done with work, and Hudson wasn't at the truck yet, which meant he was probably waiting for me. The water stopped on a timer, and I slipped my foot back into my sandal, then headed for the observation deck on the diamond-shaped comfort station, passing four separate entrances to private showers on the left and approaching the point where the building angled.

Only one moment had soured my day, and I still wasn't sure what to do about what I'd found in Gavin's car. Or if I had the right or responsibility to do anything at all.

"You said you wouldn't do this!" Hudson's voice stopped me in my tracks.

"I said I'd give her a shot, which I did," Caroline argued, and my heart plummeted.

Maybe they were talking about someone else. There was a chance, right? I pressed my hands against the new siding and stuck close to the building as I peeked around the corner.

"And it's not that she's not beautiful, or smart, or good with Juniper—" Caroline continued, looking up at Hudson with a tortured expression.

"I'm well aware of how great Allie is," he interrupted, folding his arms across his chest.

So much for hoping it wasn't about me.

"—because she's all those things. And under any other circum-stances, I'd think she's fabulous." At least she looked upset about her disapproval.

"Any circumstances that she wasn't a Rousseau." He shook his head. "You are un-fucking-believable."

The happiness of the day faded like it had never been there in the first place. It would always come back to that with her, wouldn't it? Maybe that was the curse of small towns—you were never allowed to outgrow the part they assigned you.

"The fact that her bloodline is repugnant has nothing to do with what I'm trying to tell you." She reached for his arm and he stepped back before she could touch him.

Repugnant? My hackles rose. I was a Rousseau. My last name opened doors in every ballet company across the world, and would do the same for Juniper if she wanted it.

"One day, you are going to regret you *ever* uttered those words," Hudson vowed, and my stomach churned. Caroline had no idea she was maligning her own daughter.

"Listen to what I'm saying, Hudson. Please." Her pleading tone hit me straight in the chest. I *felt* her desperation to reach her brother as if it were my own. "She's lovely. She's just not for you."

My fingernails scraped the siding.

"Don't start on your she's-leaving-at-the-end-of-summer bullshit." He curved the brim of his hat. "We're fully grown adults capable of making decisions about long-distance relationships, or moving, or a hundred other ways to be with the person you want."

Damn, he sold it well. *And I thought I was a good actor.*

"And you think she wants you?" Caroline challenged.

Every muscle in my body locked, and heat flushed my cheeks as though I'd been called out to my face. Wanting Hudson had never been the problem. Him sticking around was the issue.

"Pretty damn sure, and I know Allie better than almost anyone." A muscle in his jaw ticked, and he shoved his hands into the front pockets of his board shorts. It had been years since I'd seen him lose his temper, but his tells were all the same. He was going to blow.

"You *knew* her," she corrected. "You knew her a decade ago. I did some research—"

My stomach abandoned me. What research?

"You fucking *what*?" He dropped his arms. "If you weren't my sister, I would be so damned done with you."

I knew the feeling well.

"She only dates dancers. Only people in her profession, in her elite little level, and in her tax bracket. And you aren't any of those."

She found that out on the internet? How much of this was I supposed to just sit here and listen to? Anger simmered in my chest.

"I already know that." He shrugged, hands still in his pockets. "So what? Until now, I've only dated women I knew wouldn't ask for a ring. Things change, and I don't give a shit who she's dated before, because she's with *me* now."

Okay, that was kind of hot. Really hot . . . if we weren't faking this whole thing.

"She doesn't want you!" Caroline shouted. "You have to break it off before you get any deeper. I've been watching her all day. I watched her at the party too. You touch her, you reach for her hand, you get her food and take care of her, but she doesn't do the same. Has she invited you to that giant party her ballet company holds every summer?"

I retreated and let my forehead fall against the siding, squeezing my eyes shut as fury burned hotter with every condemnation Caroline spoke, pointing out all the ways I'd already failed Hudson. He'd convinced everyone, and I hadn't pulled my weight.

"Should. Have. Been. You." Mom's words weaseled their way in. Seemed failure was the theme of my week. I'd failed Hudson and Lina, and now I was failing Juniper and Anne.

"We haven't talked about it *yet*," Hudson countered.

"Exactly. Hudson, she doesn't touch you. I'd even say she goes out of her way to avoid touching you, and that's not how a woman acts around the man she wants."

Screw her. That wasn't a failure; that was on purpose. I *did* want him, which was why I was careful not to touch him, not to give in to the electricity between us, not to make a mistake that would leave me broken at the end of the summer again. Shit, had I already ruined our scheme because—as usual—I was too careful?

"So, she's a private person—"

And still, he defended me. *Double shit.*

"She doesn't even smile at you! Not once. Maybe you are great friends, and maybe she's bored or lonely, but I'm telling you that she is not invested in this like you are, and she's going to break your heart if you don't end it."

That's enough. I pushed off the wall and took a fortifying breath.

"This is the last time we're discussing this," Hudson warned. "I'm not breaking up with Allie. Not today. Not tomorrow. Not ever, if I get a say. Letting her go was the worst mistake I've ever made in my life, and I'll be damned if your inability to pull your head out of your ass is going to cost me the only chance I have with her."

My heart pounded as I stepped away from the wall. It was time to hold up my end of the bargain. *Just a role. This is just a role.* But it wasn't.

Forcing my mouth into a soft smile, I rounded the corner. "There you are!"

Hudson blanched. "Alessandra—"

"I was waiting in the truck." Before I lost the nerve, I walked straight to him, rose up on my toes as high as my ankle would allow, cupped his stubbled face in my hands, and kissed him.

I felt his quick indrawn breath, and prayed I hadn't taken it too far. We'd never agreed on kissing. Or not kissing. But here I was, pressing my lips against his . . . finally. I lingered for a heartbeat, just long enough for my pulse to leap, for my mouth to register the softness of his, then prepared to retreat and face the consequences of my sneak attack.

His arm wound around my waist, and he kissed me back once, twice, then gently sucked on my bottom lip and dragged his teeth across it, waking every nerve ending in my body and stuttering my breath.

God help me, it was over before I was ready for it to end.

He lifted his head and looked at me like he'd never seen me before. "We're done talking, Caroline." His gaze never left mine.

I couldn't imagine a lifetime when I would ever tire of looking into his eyes.

"Already gone," she muttered. Her footsteps faded as Hudson and I stood there staring at each other.

"You kissed me." His focus shifted to my mouth.

"I kissed you." My voice dropped to a whisper, and my hands slipped from his face. I'd gone too far. "Are you mad?"

"Mad?" He let go of my waist and retreated a step, putting some space between us. "I'm feeling a lot of things right now, but I'm not sure about anger. Depends on how you answer this: Did you hear that argument?"

"Yes." Anyone else, I would have hesitated, pondered what answer they wanted to hear, but I'd agreed to tell him the truth.

"Fuck." He leaned back against the railing and yanked his hat backward. "You kissed me because you were pissed at Caroline."

"Yes." The breeze picked up, and I pinned the hem of my sundress to my thighs. "Kind of."

A family with two young children climbed the steps from the beach and headed for the overlook, stopping to admire the view about ten feet away.

Hudson muttered a curse, then pushed off the railing, grabbing my hand as he walked by. "We're not having this conversation out here."

My heart galloped as I followed him down the side of the building, and through the first door he opened. *You were playing a role.* But was I? Chaotic, complicated feelings rose, and I scrambled to construct the defenses that kept me alive, but it was impossible when my lips still tingled from that kiss.

He dropped my hand and flicked the light switch, illuminating the private shower room with its teal and bright-white tiles, then closed the door and locked it. The sound of the latch reverberated in my head.

We were alone, which meant I had to choose if I was going to play the role and laugh off what just happened or be truthful and give him a genuine piece of me, knowing I might never get it back.

"You heard what she said and wanted to prove a point." He slipped his hands into his pockets and leaned back against the door.

"Yes." It was the truth. Mostly.

The muscle in his jaw ticked, and he knocked the back of his head against the door as he looked up at the ceiling.

"I'm guessing this means you're angry now." Where had all my earlier bravado fled to? God, it was so much easier when I could tell myself we were pretending, but it felt too real in this little room.

"That was not how our first kiss should have happened."

"Never thought you were the romantic type." The joke fell flat.

"I've waited eleven years to kiss you." Inch by inch, he lowered his head, pinning me in place with those sea green eyes. "Eleven years of thinking what it would be like to cross that line, imagining all the ways—" He shook his head. "Did you even want it? Or was it just to prove her wrong?"

"You thought about kissing me for eleven years?" My chest tightened.

"Yes. Did. You. Want. It?" he repeated.

Now was most definitely the time to protect myself and lie. But I couldn't. Not to Hudson.

"Yes." My confession echoed off the tile. "Why do you think I got away from you so quickly when we were out there in the water? I'm not supposed to want to kiss you. This is fake, remember?"

"Not right now, it isn't." His eyes darkened, and my pulse jumped.

"What is that supposed to mean?" Warmth prickled my cheeks. He'd never looked at me like that before, like I was someone he wanted—no, craved. In fact, I wasn't sure any of the men I'd been with had ever looked at me with such blatant need.

"It means I want five minutes." He pulled his phone from his pocket and worked the screen.

"Where we're pretending what?" I folded my arms and fought to control my racing heart. "That I don't hate you? That this arrangement is real? What roles are we playing?" Any mask was better than none.

"Five minutes where we *don't* pretend. Just you and me." He showed me the timer and clicked Start. Numbers started flying as it counted down, and he slipped it back into his pocket. "Can you do that?"

"Five minutes." I fisted handfuls of my sundress just to make sure I wasn't as naked as I suddenly felt. "Fine. No pretending."

He nodded. "Now would be the time to leave if you don't want this." He pushed off the door and stalked forward slowly, giving me ample time to go. To protest. I did neither.

Lifting my chin, I retreated a step, bumping into the sink as he reached me.

"You're still here." He put his hands on either side of me, trapping me between his arms, then leaning into my space.

"I'm still here." My gaze dropped to his mouth as I struggled to breathe. I should go, yet I couldn't bring myself to walk out that door. "What do you want, Hudson?"

"I want that first kiss." He cradled my cheek and skimmed his thumb over my lower lip. "Do you?"

"It's a bad idea." Oh *God*.

"Do you?" he repeated.

Kissing him—really kissing him—would be totally, utterly reckless, and that word *never* applied to me. But I wanted to kiss him more than I wanted the safety of my solitude. I looked up into his eyes and unfolded my arms, placing my hands on his chest. "Yes."

"Allie." He whispered my name as he lowered his head.

Then his hand slid to the back of my neck, and he kissed me.

Yes. This was exactly what I'd wanted, his mouth moving over mine, *with* mine, the pressure achingly sweet. He stroked the center of my bottom lip with his tongue, and I opened for him.

He groaned, and we descended into pure madness. He consumed me with deft strokes of his tongue along mine, laying claim to every sensitive line of my mouth and wrecking my carefully constructed world.

My hands rushed over his shirt and around his neck, pulling him closer. Electricity raced across my skin, and I kissed him back with a decade's worth of longing as heat exploded between us, untamed and dangerously volatile. His grip shifted to just beneath my ass, and he lifted me onto the edge of the sink, keeping his mouth sealed over mine, robbing me of thought and logic and replacing them with urgency and a need I wasn't sure I'd ever be able to sate.

Holy shit, he was *good* at this.

He parted my thighs and moved between them, bringing our mouths together again and again, weaving his fingers through the hair at the nape of my neck and tilting my head for a deeper angle. A few seconds was all it took for the kiss to spin out of control, and we let it. We pushed it with questing hands and stuttered breaths, too desperate for more to stop for such a trivial thing as air.

I nipped his bottom lip.

He sucked my tongue into his mouth, and I moaned.

I knocked his hat off and ran my fingers through his hair, holding his head against mine.

He skimmed his hand under my dress and along my outer thigh, then grasped my hip, and then he pulled me tighter against him. Oh *God*. He was hard and hot, and so *right there*.

"Hudson," I whimpered, and he responded by kissing me harder, deeper, longer, until I knew his mouth like my own, and the taste of salt and Hudson was branded into my memory.

Yes. So much *yes*. This was what a kiss was supposed to feel like. How had I lived twenty-seven years without experiencing this kind of heart-pounding rush? This overwhelming hunger? I wanted him. I *needed* him. He was heat and warmth, and I'd been so damned cold for too long. He could have asked for anything, and I would have given it as long as he didn't stop kissing me. I wanted to give it, wanted to feel every inch of his skin against mine, wanted him to shove the fabric of my swimsuit to the side and touch me.

I wanted everything.

He ripped his mouth from mine only to kiss a path down my throat, returning to the places that made me gasp, sucking where I moaned. My fingernails bit into the back of his neck as his lips skimmed my collarbone, and I rocked my hips, making us both moan at the friction.

This wasn't chemistry. This was combustion. And I was here for it.

"So fucking mine," he whispered before claiming my mouth again.

I hooked my ankle around the small of his back, and his grip tightened on my hip as I kissed him again and again, like I could fit eleven years of fantasies into this single moment.

Eleven years. We could have had this—had each other—for all that time.

But he'd left. Without a word. Like our years of friendship meant nothing.

I cried out at the sudden pain in my chest, and Hudson broke the kiss, both of us panting hard as his eyes searched mine.

"Allie?"

My vision wavered and my eyes stung. "You broke my heart. Maybe we were just friends, but you *broke* my heart."

His chest heaved as he dropped his forehead against mine, his fingers gently stroking the back of my neck. "I know."

"How could you do that to me?" I should have pushed him away, but I tugged him closer instead, like holding on to him now could somehow have forced him to stay back then.

"I'm so fucking sorry." He pressed a hard kiss to my forehead. "So sorry."

The alarm went off in his pocket.

"Shit." He retrieved the phone and silenced the alarm.

Five minutes. Was that all it had been? How had he unraveled me so completely in only five freaking minutes? What could have happened in another five? Why was I so damned weak when it came to him?

"Allie." He tried to catch my gaze, but I wouldn't give it to him.

My hands fell to his chest, and I pushed. "Time's up."

His frustrated sigh filled the room, but he stepped aside, offering me a hand down from the sink. I ignored it and slid off on my own, then walked straight out of the room on trembling legs.

That can't happen again. I repeated the words over and over in my head as Hudson drove me home in what was arguably the most tense, silent car ride of my life. Why had I done that?

Hudson pulled up in front of my house, and I grabbed my beach bag and reached for the door handle.

"Are we going to be okay?" he asked as I shoved the door open.

"There's no real us, remember?" I climbed down from the truck. "But if you're asking if I'm going to punish Jupiter for my asinine decisions, then of course not." Using my elbow, I shut the truck's door, then started up the porch steps.

You only have to hold it together until you're inside.

The screen door creaked as I opened it, and to my surprise, Sadie didn't come running from whatever she'd inevitably chewed to death. I dropped my beach bag on the entry floor, and deflated, my composure completely deserting me, leaving me as raw as an exposed wire.

Five minutes was all it had taken him to strip away the walls I'd built over the years, the illusion that anger and apathy were the only emotions I could have when it came to Hudson.

I opened my eyes at the clicking sound of Sadie's nails on the hardwood, and turned right toward the living room.

Kenna stood in the doorway, wearing a chocolate-colored sleeveless blouse a shade lighter than her crossed arms and a fuck-with-me-I-dare-you expression, a single black eyebrow arched, while Sadie wagged her tail by her side. "Told you I'd send a search party."

She was here. My closest friend had ignored the declined calls, the unreturned text messages, and she'd brought herself all the way from New York when she had an entire ballet company whose orthopedic care she oversaw. She was here, polished and put together, and I was a fucking *wreck*.

I crumpled, covering my face with my hands.

Kenna sighed. "Well. Shit."

CHAPTER SIXTEEN

Allie

NYMargot505: I'm starting to think Alessandra Rousseau might actually be dead or
something. Anyone know if they're filling her
spot, yet?

"That's . . . a lot," Kenna remarked as we stood with our backs to the cliff an hour later, throwing tennis balls into the yard for Sadie to fetch.

"I'm a horrible person, aren't I?" I tugged the sleeves of my sweat-shirt down over my palms.

"You think there's any chance of me dignifying that question with a response?" She shot me a heap of side-eye as Sadie raced back to us.

"I feel horrible." I took the not-yet-slimy ball from Sadie and chucked it again, careful not to throw toward the pool. Turned out goldens really liked water, and they took forever to blow-dry.

"Because you kissed a man who's had you tied up in knots for almost half your life? Because you're sneaking around that girl's mom without her knowledge in order to manipulate her? Or because you ran off from your support system while rehabilitating a serious injury, refused to pick up the damned phone, and forced me to rent a car and *drive* it—which I have not done since moving back to Manhattan—from the world's smallest airport because there's no Uber out here in the beach town of Nicholas Sparksville?" She brushed her long black twists over her shoulder as the wind picked up.

A sour taste flooded my mouth at the picture she'd painted. *Nothing like getting called out.*

"Yes," I finally said. "All of it." Sadie found the bright-yellow ball and bounded back across the grass and around the pool. "What am I supposed to do? About *any* of it?"

"Why would I have any idea?" She bent down and took the ball from Sadie.

"Because you're the smartest woman I know. You graduated college at twenty and medical school at twenty-three, for crying out loud." I'd never even gone to college. The Company had consumed my life at seventeen, the same year I'd earned my high school diploma online.

"And I'm a sports medicine doctor, not a shrink." She threw, and the ball landed somewhere near the vicinity of the shrubs. "And what the hell were you thinking, getting a dog? You know Vasily isn't going to let her hang out at the studio. That man hates anything related to joy. And you're in the building for almost twelve hours a day. You are a freaking mess, Allie."

"I know." I watched Sadie scramble for the ball and wished it was that easy to be happy. "How is Matthias?"

A smile spread across her face. "Still the perfect boyfriend. Still spends a little too much time at the hospital, but that's to be expected for surgical residency. And don't go changing the subject. My life isn't the train wreck. How's your mother?"

Sadie raced back, jumping over a patio lounge chair. "Mean. Rachel said your mom was up to see her a couple of weeks ago." Eloise was the only other name Mom authorized on campus. They'd danced together for over a decade. "She doing all right?"

"She says she is." Kenna sighed. "Throws herself into all the board nonsense for the Company. I think she's both compensating for your mom's absence and keeping herself busy to avoid the reality of the situation that her best friend isn't coming back to New York."

"And yet you're not a shrink." Sadie dropped the ball at my feet, her tongue lolling to the side as she panted. "I'm really sorry I didn't call you back."

"I know you are. Doesn't excuse it, but it's not like I didn't disappear on you a few times too."

"While you were in residency. Not the same." There were friends who could tell if you were having a bad day. Kenna and I knew if the other was in a bad year. "One last time," I told Sadie, then threw the ball as hard as I could. "You going to ask me about the ankle?"

"Not unless you want to talk about it." Kenna looked my way. "I'm not here as the Company's doctor. I'm here as your friend. Paperwork says I'm on three days of personal leave. No one knows I'm here except Matthias."

Wrapping my arms around my waist, I looked from Sadie to the vast expanse of ocean beyond the cliff. The ocean wouldn't care if I danced or retired, if I kissed Hudson or walked away. The waves would come regardless of my relationship with Juniper, and they would keep coming long after we were only memories. In a way, my insignificance was comforting enough that I could finally speak the truth.

"I keep saying I'll be fine, but I don't know if I'll make it back from this." I whispered the confession, letting it past my lips for the first time. Giving it voice . . . giving it power. "I just know that I can't recover in the building while every soloist watches, and either consciously or subconsciously hopes I won't."

"Understandable." She glanced around the backyard. "Not sure hiding out here is going to help. I don't care what kind of equipment you have in there, it's no substitute for me."

"That, I know." I took the ball from Sadie and rubbed her head.

"Do you want my help?" Kenna offered.

179

A burst of hope flared in my chest, but quickly dimmed. "I can't rehab in New York, and there's no way Vasily would let you come out here to work with me alone. You're too important to the Company."

"That's not an answer. And you'd be amazed at what Vasily would do for you. He still has your *Equinox* ballet on the short list for fall, and you're not even back *yet*." She crouched down to pet Sadie, covering her perfectly tailored slacks in dog hair.

"I'd be grateful if you'd check me out while you're here." There, I'd asked for help.

"Then that's what we'll do." She stood, then rose on her toes and peered out over the backyard to the beach below.

"What are you looking for?" I joined her.

"Just looking to see if there's a middle-aged white man wandering the beach, looking for redemption and a bottle of old love letters."

I snorted.

"Don't you scoff at me, Alessandra. I drove through the town. You and I both know the second Thanksgiving hits around here, there's a surplus of Christmas tree farmers just waiting to snatch some Manhattan girl's soul and teach her the true meaning of the holidays." She shivered in repulsion.

We turned to walk back toward the house and found Anne coming out of the back door, holding yet another sample centerpiece. She startled, then smiled. "Kenna! I didn't know you were coming!"

Kenna brandished a smile I wouldn't wish on my worst enemy. "How's it going, enabler?"

"I'm going to change the setting, and let's see how you do," Kenna said two days later as I lay horizontal on the jumpboard in our gym. Up until now, I'd had it at less than my body weight.

"Sounds like absolute torture. Let's do it." My hands fisted at my sides and I braced my feet against the platform.

"I'd rather you struggle here than fall." Kenna popped back up from beside the machine. "And from what I've seen, you're ready." She moved to the end of the board, then leaned over slightly, her gaze focused on my feet. "Bend the knees into plié."

I bent, the shoulder pads of the machine sliding with me.

"Roll up on demi-pointe," Kenna instructed.

I shifted my weight to the balls of my feet, focusing on the articulation of my foot and stabilizing my ankles. Everything below my waist filed a complaint that I didn't bother listening to. It was my second workout of the day, and after the full sessions I'd put in yesterday, my body was loudly reminding me how out of shape I was.

"Up to relevé," she ordered.

My right ankle threatened to tremble, but I extended, straightening my legs as the jumpboard added resistance to simulate my weight. Sweat beaded on my forehead. "I kind of hate you right now," I squeaked out.

"Blah blah. Lower back down."

I slowly brought my heels to the board. "Feels like it's going to wobble."

Footsteps sounded toward the front of the studio, their rhythm telling me it was Anne.

"You've got to start trusting your body at some point." Kenna stood, folding her arms across her chest. "Do it again."

"Are you sure she should be up on relevé?" Anne's brow furrowed as she reached Kenna's side.

"I'm sure I'm the only doctor in the room," Kenna countered.

"Don't fight." I separated myself from the pain and pushed through another repetition.

"It's not a fight when I automatically win. Go again." Kenna studied my ankle as I repeated the motion. "You look steady."

"She's in pain," Anne protested.

"And? Name one time dancing didn't bring you pain." Kenna shifted to my right side and crouched as I did another rep. "I examined her yesterday morning, and again last night after working her out. She's nowhere near a hundred percent, but she's ready to start climbing. It's been almost five months since surgery, and she's done a great job of building back her calf muscles. She's just short on confidence."

"Stop talking about me like I'm not here." I breathed through the next rep, and my phone buzzed on the gym mat to the right side of my head.

"You keep going and I'll check the phone." Kenna picked up the device as I pushed up to relevé. "Ooh, if it's not the fourth text message from one Hudson Ellis since I got here."

"What does it say?" Anne leaned in.

"Love being a spectator in my own life," I muttered, lowering myself slowly.

"Then stop spectating and do something." Kenna handed me the phone.

HUDSON: Can we talk?

HUDSON: Please?

HUDSON: Did I mention that I'm sorry?

Those had all come in the last thirty-six hours.

HUDSON: To clarify, the things I'm sorry for do not include kissing you.

Ugh. It would have been easier to ignore him if I didn't relive that kiss every time I closed my damn eyes. I sighed and sat up, straddling the machine. "Let's have lunch."

We ate at the kitchen island, and I left the text messages unanswered since I didn't know what to say.

"This is really good, Anne." Kenna forked another piece of salmon on my right. "Thank you for cooking."

"You're welcome. It's nice to be useful," Anne answered from the left, stabbing her entrée. "And you know what? I'm not an enabler."

I groaned and bent down to adjust my leg warmers since I had a feeling Kenna would put me at the barre after lunch.

"Still thinking about that one, are you?" Kenna said.

"She was dying in New York," Anne fired back, leaning forward to look past me.

"Was she?" Kenna asked. "Or were you?"

My fork clanged against my plate.

"She'd do nothing but work out, ice her ankle, and sleep. Eva couldn't get her to socialize, or even *go* to the studio for a little human interaction. So yes, I brought her to our beach house, where there's a full gym with the same rehab equipment the Company has, a full ballet studio, and a fresh change of scenery. If you think that's enabling, then fine." Anne threw out her hands. "I'm an enabler."

"Anne," I lectured.

"And to think, you've always been the stable one," Kenna muttered.

"But you and I both know I would do anything for Allie," Anne continued. "Including leave Manhattan and juggle *everything* for the gala from here. And yes, I want her to recover, I want her back on the stage if that's where she wants to be, but it's far more important to me that she's happy than if she's a principal." She sat back.

"Do I need to be here for this discussion?" I asked.

"All valid points," Kenna agreed. "Still enabling. You're a great sister, Anne. You're just not a ballet instructor."

"That, I can't deny." Anne sighed and went easier on the fish. "But Allie has outgrown Madeline's," she joked.

But Madeline's couldn't be the only studio out here. Not with the afternoon-only schedule she kept.

"Who else teaches around here?" I asked. "Not for me, just wondering which studios get invites for the Classic." It was two months away.

"There's a few." Anne nodded. "Gerard's, Winnie Waters, Quinn Hawkins—"

"Quinn Hawkins opened a studio?" My eyebrows shot up.

"Yeah, about a year ago." She waved her fork. "She's out by Cedarville. Why? When's the last time you saw her?"

"Not since Eva's last year at the Classic." She'd been eighteen, if I remembered correctly. "So, seven years ago? Pretty sure she came in second."

Anne nodded. "I think I heard she tore her ACL or something. Whatever it was ended her career pretty quickly."

"That's sad," I muttered.

"It always is," Kenna agreed. "But it's not you."

We finished up lunch, and then Kenna ordered me to the barre.

Barefoot, I took what had always been my place, the third mirror panel, and prepared for pain.

She worked me with the drive of an instructor, as her mother had been, and the eye of a doctor, as Anne watched nervously, jotting down notes of exercises Kenna wanted me to focus on in the next few weeks.

"I can't." I shook my head after her latest command. Sweat dripped down the back of my neck, and every muscle in my body screamed.

"You can," she corrected me. "You just don't want to, which I think is half the problem here." She drummed her fingers on the barre.

"That's not true," I retorted, snapping slightly.

"Prove it." She gestured to my feet.

Fear held me in its grasp and squeezed.

"Come on. You've been here before. You know what it feels like." She leaned in and lowered her voice. "And no one in this room gives a shit if it's not perfect. Sophie's not here. If you don't want this, no one's going to blame you. You want to retire early? Escape the tyranny of the Company? I will send an email that it's a career-ending injury. I'll have your back. But if there's a chance you still want your position as a principal, then let's go. The time to rest is over, and the time to push is now. What do you want, Allie?"

Why was that everyone's question for me lately?

I glanced over at the picture of the four of us, at Lina's bright, infectious smile, then to Anne, who scribbled something into the notebook. If either of them had been in my position, they would've fought like hell to keep it.

Mom would accept nothing less than me returning as a principal dancer at her company.

I moved my feet into first position and dipped into a demi-plié, ignoring the burn above my right heel. Ribs closed. Shoulders down. Then I rose into relevé, shooting to the balls of my feet.

Pain raced up the back of my calf, dull but insistent. I shut it out with my usual method, pretending it was simply my baseline, and tightened my thighs and core. My quads and glutes reminded me it had been far too long.

But my ankle didn't waver, wobble, or tremble. It was pissed, but it did the job I assigned.

Kenna smiled. "Do it again."

I completed every rep she handed out, and by the time we were finished, my ankle throbbed with an insistence I couldn't block out.

"Ice it. You look way better than you give yourself credit for," Kenna said as I went through my postclass stretches. "And twenty weeks post-op? You can totally rock heels at the gala. That should shut Charlotte and the other wagging tongues right up."

"In two weeks?" Anne asked.

"The gala is in two weeks?" I sat with my legs folded over each other, then leaned forward to ease my back.

"Yes." Anne's eyes narrowed. "And I've been working on it for months, so don't even think about skipping out. You will be at that museum if I have to drag you myself."

"See, now *that* is not enabling," Kenna said with a grin.

"Don't take her side." I shook my head and sat up. "Of course I'm going. Vasily sent an email this morning saying he wanted to talk to Isaac and me, which means it's about *Equinox.*"

"I'd say having a role created for you is worth going for." Kenna sat on the green balance ball.

"I already RSVP'd for you and Hudson." Anne tucked the notebook under her arm.

Hudson? My stomach fluttered, and those weren't butterflies. They were more like wasps. "I'm not taking Hudson. Pretty sure our pretend relationship only exists within county lines." Take Hudson to New York? Even if he wanted to go—which I doubted he did—that would be letting him into my actual life . . . where he could actually hurt me again if he wanted.

"Oh yes, you are." Anne nodded with each word. "You told me Caroline already made an issue out of it."

"You did." Kenna bounced on the ball.

"There will be photographers and journalists—"

"Exactly." Anne waved her pen at me. "Caroline will see the pictures, and we'll be one step closer to her accepting your relationship, and by proxy, our family. Which, if you haven't noticed, isn't going well, and we're kind of on a deadline since you'll be back in New York in August."

"So will you. And everyone will see the photos. You're asking me to go public with a relationship that doesn't exist." I unfolded my legs. "A little help here?" I lifted my eyebrows at Kenna.

"I think the entire situation is a ticking time bomb." She bounced. "But if there's a chance I get to see the man who's pretty much sabotaged every relationship you've ever had—without even knowing it—struggle to fit into your world for a night, then I'm on Anne's side for this one. Should make for an amusing evening."

"Thank you." Anne smiled and straightened her shoulders, then cocked her head to the side. "Wait, did you say you think the situation—"

"A ticking time bomb that's going to blow up in your face." Kenna nodded. "I get that she's Lina's daughter, and you probably have some big, complicated feelings about her being the last living piece of her that you should definitely address with your therapists, but hear me out." She stilled the ball beneath her. "If she was your daughter, how would you feel about the absolute shenanery going on here? And what would you do when it came to light?"

I winced. It wasn't anything I hadn't thought before.

"If she was mine—" Anne's voice faltered, and my chest clenched as she cleared her throat and fought for composure. "I would like to think I'd be happy that there were more people in the world to love her. And I wouldn't be so difficult that these morally gray actions are necessary. We just want to know our niece."

Kenna looked my way.

"I care about what Juniper wants." I snagged my water bottle and rose. "It doesn't seem fair to me that she should have to wait eight more years to find out her medical history, or where she comes from. And yes, I have some very complex feelings about what I owe Lina, and whether or not that includes helping her daughter dance like she did."

"I don't envy the position any of you are in," Kenna acknowledged as she stood. "I think we're done for the day."

"You did great, Allie. I'll go grab some ice for your ankle."

"Thanks."

"It's what older, enabling sisters are for." Anne left the studio, and Kenna walked my way.

"You should start actually jumping on the jumpboard, work the resistance up."

I nodded. "Thank you for coming out here."

"Of course. You would have done the same for me." Her gaze darted to the open door. "Two things. You're medically cleared for pointe. I'm not going to infantilize you by telling you how slow to take it. You know your body. Do whatever you want with that information."

I took a quick drink to help swallow the sudden lump in my throat. "And the second?"

"You don't *owe* Lina anything," she said quietly. "Not when it comes to Juniper, or your mother, your sisters, or your career."

Except I did.

"I'm the one who got out," I whispered.

"You living for her isn't going to bring her back." She gave me a sad, knowing smile, then headed out of the studio, leaving me with the cacophony of my thoughts.

I closed my eyes, then centered myself, willing the chaos to quiet so I could make the necessary decisions, starting with the easiest ones first.

First, if I was cleared for pointe, then I'd start tomorrow, period.

Second, I picked up my phone and texted Hudson.

ALLIE: My company's gala is in two and a half weeks. June twenty-eighth in New York. Black tie. It's probably a good idea for you to come with me.

Third, I opened the internet browser and started a search.

HUDSON: Consider it done.

I pulled up the website, and selected the schedule tab. The second it opened, I scrolled through, then sighed in pure angry frustration.

"Damn it, Juniper."

CHAPTER SEVENTEEN

Hudson

OnPointe34: Whoever said you could pull off that outfit lied.

Bright2Lit: This is a bad take. She's killing that leo.

OnPointe34: That leotard is considering unaliving itself.

"You look like you're going to prom." Eric laughed, slinging his arm across the back of the green velvet sofa in the center of Franklin's Formalwear.

"He was shorter at his prom," Mr. Franklin himself muttered as he judged the lines of the third tux I'd tried on this morning.

"I still don't understand why you don't rock the dress whites." He crossed his ankle over his knee. "Women love that whole *Officer and a Gentleman* vibe. At least Jess does."

"Allie said black tie, and whatever she says is what I'm going with." Especially since that invitation had been the only communication she'd given me since last weekend. It had been the first and only time a woman hadn't returned a text or a call after I'd kissed her. *Talk about bursting an ego.*

The kissing itself hadn't been the issue—that had been in a realm beyond perfect. For a second, she'd been right there with me, fire and all. No mask, no walls, just Allie. Fuck, I could still taste her, still feel the thrum of her pulse beneath my lips, still hear the moan that went straight to my dick. We'd ignited the second our mouths met, and as much as I'd loathed bearing painful witness to the hurt I'd caused her, I was also thankful she'd stopped us when she did. My control had been hovering on the edge, and the first time I sank inside her sure as hell wasn't going to be in a public shower stall. After that kiss, I knew there would be a first time. And a thousandth. I'd never felt chemistry like that in my life. We were a foregone conclusion.

Knowing Allie, that was why she hadn't called, because the kiss had been real. And while it made me realize that I wanted *us* to be real, even if it was just for the summer, it had scared the shit out of her.

"Turn." Mr. Franklin gestured with his pointer finger, and I turned, wincing when I looked in the mirror.

"Can we lose the bow part of the black tie?" I felt like I just needed a rabbit and a top hat to complete the act in this thing.

Mr. Franklin looked around me, meeting my gaze in the mirror. "It's fashionable to wear a normal tie as well."

Thank fuck.

"You spending the weekend in New York?" Eric asked, scrolling through his phone one-handed.

"I have no idea." Were we staying together? Separately?

He laughed. "Watching you have absolutely zero control in this situation is amazing."

"Glad you're enjoying it." I turned again when Mr. Franklin told me to. "I got leave approved, so if she wants to stay the weekend, we'll stay the weekend, and I've studied the Company website, so I'm prepared to meet her friends." The idea of getting to see her life, her apartment, her work was utterly fascinating. Our only time together had been spent on behalf of Juniper. Allie hadn't even been to my house. *If it's even going to stay your house.* "You get it yet?"

Eric shook his head. "They're supposed to be out by now. I swear, they do this just to fuck with us."

Mr. Franklin shot Eric a disapproving look, not that he noticed as he hit Refresh over and over.

"They're not going to send out scores on a Sunday." I was both desperate to know and dreading all at the same time.

"Of course you're not nervous." Eric dropped his phone on the couch. "We all know you passed with flying colors. The only question is how high on the promotion list you'll be."

And what duty stations I'd put on the request list that was due in eight weeks. *You have to stay here.* But did I?

If I chose New York, could Allie and I have a shot? *Not with your past between you.* The best I could hope for was a classic summer fling, and I already knew it wouldn't be enough.

"You passed too," I told Eric. "I'm sure of it."

"I think this one complements your frame better than the others," Mr. Franklin noted, walking around the pedestal I stood on like some damned prize pony. "What do you think?"

"Clean lines. All the chaperones will approve. Just don't forget the corsage." Eric gave me a thumbs-up.

"Remind me why I thought you'd be helpful?" I glanced over the tux, then back at Mr. Franklin. "It's great. Can the alterations be done in the next ten days?"

"No problem." Mr. Franklin gestured toward the dressing room.

"Now that your monkey suit has been chosen, am I free to go grab brunch with my girlfriend? Or do you need a second opinion on the shoes too?" Eric stuck another piece of gum in his mouth and started chewing.

"Say hi to Jessica for me." I stepped off the pedestal.

"No way. She's still pissed about you blowing off Beth." He got up from the couch and threw me a wave on his way out the door, and I headed for the dressing room.

My phone rang as I pulled on my T-shirt, and I swiped to answer as soon as I saw Gavin's name scroll across the bottom of the screen. "What's up?"

The sound of running water filled the line. "What are you doing right now?" Gavin asked.

"Finishing a tux fitting," I answered as I sat on the plastic chair to put my shoes on. "What are you doing? White water rafting?"

"Not exactly." Stress practically oozed out of his voice. "A pipe busted at the bar, and the whole damned kitchen is flooded. I'm here waiting for the plumber because Scott's out of town."

"That sucks." I slipped my shoes on and laced them quickly. "And you're calling me because . . ." I gathered up the tux and walked out of the dressing room.

"Because I fucked up."

"Okay." My eyebrows rose. "In a you-sneaked-Melanie-Dunn-in-to-our-room-and-need-to-get-her-out-before-Mom-sees kind of way?" I set the tux on the counter and reached for my wallet. "Or a need-to-bring-a-shovel kind of way?"

"You'll pay when you pick it up," Mr. Franklin told me. "I'll call when it's ready."

"Thank you." I headed out of the store, a sense of dread growing heavier with every second that Gavin didn't answer. "Gav, if it's a bring-your-own-shovel kind of event, calling me on the cell phone is what will get us featured on a true-crime podcast."

"I didn't kill anyone," he muttered, the sound slightly garbled by the rushing water. "But she's going to kill *me* if she finds out."

"Who?" My feet hit the pavement, and I unlocked my truck with the key fob. Main Street was already flooded with tourists, and there was a line outside the restaurant across the street. The café was no doubt packed too.

"Caroline."

I froze at the edge of the curb. It was Sunday. That dread exploded into a full-on alarm blaring in my head. "Where's Juniper?"

"Look. I know you'll be pissed, but she asked me to help, and I didn't want to tell her no. You're not the only one capable of showing up for her. And I've never forgotten to pick her up. Not once in five months, but this situation's kind of out of my control. I won't make it in time, and I don't want her sitting there waiting, you know?"

"Where is she?" I jogged around my truck and threw open the driver's side door.

"You have to promise you won't tell Caroline." He sighed. "It's not like I was doing anything worse than what you are with Allie."

"Gavin, where the fuck is our niece?" I climbed into the truck and pushed the start button, then dropped the fob into the cup holder.

"She's in Cedarville. If you leave now, you might get there before she's done. I'm texting you the address."

My phone buzzed with a text message and I quickly opened it. I stared at the name of the place for two seconds before putting it into my GPS. Then I lifted the phone back to my ear. "You're not going to have to worry about Caroline—"

"Thank you—"

"Because I'm going to kill you myself." I hung up.

Nineteen minutes and four broken traffic laws later, I pulled into the only empty parking spot in front of the strip mall and killed the engine. There were still nine minutes left of her class when I walked into the ballet studio.

That irresponsible asshat.

How fucking dare he compare what I was doing with Allie to what he'd been hiding for the last five months? I waded into a sea of waiting parents, most of whom were seated in front of the glass that partitioned the waiting area from the studio, and cut through the ones who stood along the back, carrying on conversations.

I glanced over the full front row of seats, then stared as the woman on the left, closest to the wall, tilted her head slightly and revealed the face beneath the black baseball cap. *Allie?*

What in the actual fuck was happening?

I made my way to the wall, then maneuvered myself up the narrow aisle along its edge, dodging purses and cups of coffee until I reached the front, where Allie sat. The brim of her hat had been tugged down low, and she'd covered most of her hands with the oversize sleeves of her dark sweatshirt, which she held clasped in front of her mouth.

She looked *pissed*.

"I'll take it from that look, you don't approve either?" I asked.

Her face whipped my direction, her gaze pinning me to the wall before she turned it back on the class. "Get down, or she'll see you."

"I kind of hope she does," I admitted, folding my arms across my chest. "At least then she'll have an inkling of how much trouble she's in."

"Well, I'm observing the class, and I don't want her to see *me*," she retorted. "So get down."

Okay then. I crouched, jostling Allie's chair with my shoulders as I crammed my body into a space fit for a toddler. The scent of Allie's perfume hit me like a shot of perfect tequila, and I breathed deep, more than ready to be drunk. At least there was one positive to come from this morning. "When did you find out?"

"I saw her bag in Gavin's car at the beach and figured the rest out about five days ago, but wanted to be sure before I told you," she said, bracing her elbows on her knees and leaning forward. "What about you?"

"Gavin called about twenty minutes ago and let me know he wouldn't be able to pick her up." My jaw flexed. "So I'm still processing." I surveyed the class of what looked to be about two dozen girls and spotted Juniper in the front row. "Is she in pointe shoes?"

"Yep." Allie bit out the word, her gaze shifting to the clock above my head. "For all of another seven minutes, she is."

"I can't believe he went behind my back," I muttered.

"I can't believe *she* did." Her huff reeked of sarcasm. "What am I saying, of course I believe she did. Look at what she has *us* doing."

"True." I glanced at my watch. Six minutes left and I needed to make the most of them. "I got my tux today."

"Oh." She looked back at me, then jerked her face forward again. "Thank you."

"Did you want to stay the weekend in New York?"

"You don't have to. I have a couple of appointments on Friday afternoon, so as long as you're there by Saturday evening, we should be good." She tugged her sleeve over the heel of her hand when it slipped.

"I took leave so I can go down with you," I offered awkwardly.

"Okay, that would be nice."

I let a few moments of silence pass, but I had to ask, had to know. "Will your mother be at the gala?"

"No." She shook her head, keeping her focus on Juniper. "I doubt she'll ever step foot in New York again. She chose where she wants to be."

Right, because she was teaching somewhere. Well, that was one less complication.

The teacher yelled, the sound muffled by the glass enclosure, and Allie's eyes narrowed as the girl next to Juniper started to cry.

"I'd love to see her raise her voice to Juniper," I muttered.

"Megan, I think Olivia's crying," one of the moms to the right called out.

"Again? She really needs to learn how to take constructive criticism." Allie's fists clenched.

"Do you want me to get a hotel for New York?" I asked her, and damn if my stomach didn't go all queasy on me.

"No." She shook her head. "The hotel prices there are ridiculous. Just stay at my apartment."

Victory. "Sounds good." I fought a smile.

The teacher's voice escalated as the girls repeated some choreography, and then she threw a water bottle down the line of mirrors.

Oh, I think the fuck not.

"Quinn's in another one of her moods today," a mom noted like it was nothing.

I moved to rise, but Allie threw her arm over my knees. "Don't. You'll just make it worse."

"I'm just supposed to watch a grown-ass adult throw shit four feet away from our niece?" I growled.

"Yes." Allie's arm locked like she was the seat belt and I was the kid in a car seat. "And then you trust me to handle it. This is *my* ocean."

My eyebrows rose. I'd never seen Allie so much as raise her voice to anyone but me. "Fine, but if the next thing she throws hits Juniper—"

"It won't. She doesn't want to hurt the girls physically, just emotionally." She withdrew her arm.

What kind of sadistic shit was that?

Four minutes left. Timing was crap, but we had a modicum of privacy here in the corner, and it had to be said. "Look, about what happened at the beach—"

"Don't mention it." She tensed.

"Allie—"

"I mean it, Hudson. Don't mention it." Her chin titled upward. "As far as I'm concerned those five minutes never happened."

Damn it. My ribs constricted, making it difficult to draw the next breath. "But they did happen. You felt it too. It was real. At least be brave enough to admit it. We aren't kids anymore."

Precious seconds ticked by before she responded. Three minutes.

"Fine. It was real, and utterly foolish." She turned her head, and our eyes locked. "If we want this to continue, it can never happen again."

The feeling of victory fled as quickly as it had appeared.

"Is that a rule?" Because we were going to break the shit out of it. I would happily use every weapon in my arsenal—including our chemistry—to get another real moment out of her.

Her brow knit, and she faced forward again. "If we need to be affectionate like that in public, then fine. We'll keep it short and impersonal."

"Allie, nothing between us is short or impersonal, especially not when we get our hands on each other."

"Precisely the problem." She folded her arms, and I could almost see her throw brick after brick into the very walls I wanted to crush. Two minutes.

"You're really fighting for your life in there, aren't you?" I asked.

She stiffened.

"That kiss scared the shit out of you." I waited until I was sure she wouldn't answer. "Why? Because you enjoyed it? Because we both lost control? Or because for five blissful minutes I got behind that mask you love to wear?"

She slipped her hands into the sleeves of her hoodie and leaned forward, resting her elbows on her knees.

"Here's the thing. I'm not scared to admit that I want you." It was the easiest of the confessions I owed her.

Her lips parted.

"I haven't earned my way out of you hating me yet, and this *arrangement* is a summer thing. You made that clear. But you want me too. I know it. You know it." Her pulse leapt in her throat, and I swallowed. "And when you're ready to admit it, five minutes won't cut it. I'll devote hours, days, nights to being *incredibly* personal with you."

"Hours?" She arched a brow my direction, but even her perfect control couldn't keep the blush from rising in her cheeks. "I'd almost forgotten how arrogant you can be." She shook her head.

"It's not arrogance if you can back it up." I held her gaze. "Say the word."

Pink stained her cheeks and she ripped her gaze from mine. "Oh look, class is over."

And so was the moment.

She stood, gathering her purse and an aluminum water bottle from under her chair as girls in the studio beyond the glass took off their pointe shoes, grabbed their bags, and began exiting the studio through the door on the right.

I rose to my feet, then folded my arms and waited for Juniper to see us.

It took all of three seconds.

She paused on the other side of the glass, her eyes widening as her gaze jumped back and forth between Allie and me. She clutched the thick canvas strap of her bag and retreated a step.

"Yeah, I'd run if I were you too," Allie mumbled.

I crooked my finger at Juniper.

She moved forward slowly at first, then lifted her chin and picked up the pace, coming through the door like it was just an average Sunday. If I wasn't so mad at her, I would have grinned at the pure sass.

"Outside, now," Allie snapped.

Juniper pursed her lips, then did as instructed. We followed the flow of traffic out of the building and into the parking lot. "If you're going to yell, then just get it over with and yell."

"The last thing you want is a piece of my temper," Allie warned.

Juniper's gaze dropped to the asphalt.

I looked over her head and locked eyes with Allie, giving her the choice to make the next move, more than ready to make it if she wanted.

"Bring her to my house. Now." She turned, her ponytail swinging as she walked across the aisle to Anne's Mercedes.

Juniper sighed and lifted her gaze to mine. "Are you going to yell?"

"I think I'll let the professional handle this one." The truck beeped as I unlocked it. "Get in. Because I love you, I'll drive slowly, and if I were you, I'd spend every minute of the trip hoping she cools off before we get there."

CHAPTER EIGHTEEN

Allie

RousseauSisters4: dancers should make their own choices about their bodies, especially their feet.

By the time I walked into the house, the anger that had threatened to burn straight through that glass at Quinn's studio had lowered to a simmer: still hot enough to burn the shit out of someone but controlled.

I walked up the back steps, then quickly dressed in leggings and a sports bra, throwing on a light wrap sweater before going downstairs and waiting, giving me just enough time to type out a quick email to my contact at NASD—the National Association of Schools of Dance.

"Throw a water bottle near my niece," I muttered under my breath.

It wasn't long before Hudson pulled in and walked Juniper up the front steps. She'd put on a zip-up jacket but still appeared to be in her tights and leotard as I opened the door.

"I know you're mad—" Juniper started.

"Go to the studio." I gestured to the doors on the right as Anne came in the back door with Sadie.

"Hey, you're back!" Her tone shifted as her footsteps approached. "What's going on?" She reached the foyer, then stared into the studio, her eyebrows rising as she saw Juniper. "She's here?"

"She was taking class with Quinn Hawkins," I told her, bending to pet Sadie.

"She was taking class?" Anne's mouth dropped, and she shot an accusing look at Hudson.

"Don't look at me. I found out this morning." He hooked his thumbs in his pockets, and I quickly looked away before I got the slightest bit distracted by staring at him. This was not the time or place.

"What are we going to do?" Anne asked, unhooking Sadie from her leash.

"I'm going to handle it," I promised.

Anne's eyes flared for a second, and she opened her mouth, then appeared to think twice about whatever she was going to say. "All right. I'll be in the kitchen."

A tiny gust of a sigh blew through my lips. I hadn't realized how much I needed her to trust my decision, my agency, until she did.

"Feel free to follow," I said to Hudson as I entered the studio, finding Juniper standing dead center, picking at her jacket nervously. "You lied to me."

Juniper startled, her gaze flying to Hudson in an obvious plea.

He walked by me and leaned back against the wall across from the third mirror panel, then folded his arms across his chest, staying silent.

"You. Lied," I repeated.

"I never told you I wasn't taking class, just that Mom wouldn't let me." She wrung her hands.

"A lie by omission is still a lie." I would know.

"I just thought if I could take class and compete in the Classic, then one of her reasons for not letting me dance would be gone." She shifted her weight.

"Because the girls who place usually get scholarships," I guessed.

Juniper nodded. "I wasn't trying for the elite levels. I'm not delusional. But the beginner and intermediates usually score a tuition discount at Madeline's."

Next year, right? She had to mean next year.

She twisted, turning toward Hudson. "I went to Uncle Gavin because I knew you'd say no. Working to change Mom's opinion was already pushing it, but taking class would never fly."

"You were right. I would have said no. But this discussion doesn't involve me." He pointed my direction.

"How long have you been planning this?"

"Four months."

She'd thought she was my daughter at the time, not Lina's, but she'd had more than a DNA test in place for this plan.

"And you went to Quinn because she was out of town?" I guessed.

She nodded. "She had some bad reviews. Fine, a lot of bad reviews, but two of her girls and one boy placed last year in the Classic, and I figured I'd already been learning from YouTube videos—"

"You thought YouTube was a good replacement for a teacher?" I managed to keep my voice calm. There had been more than enough raised voices in this room over the years, and I didn't need to add to them.

"Don't get all elitist." She crossed her arms. "Not everyone has access to professional mothers and private teachers and their own studio. You're lucky."

Lucky wasn't the word that came to mind.

"So instead of heeding your mother's worries, you went to a poorly rated studio with an emotionally abusive teacher who throws things to get your attention—"

"She only does it when they're empty, and it's just—"

"Once or twice a class?" I finished for her. "And always down the line of the mirror during the rehearsal portion, but not when you're at the barre, right?"

Juniper blinked. "How would you know that?"

"Because she learned it from *my mother*." The words escaped, and I immediately wanted to snatch them back and stuff them into the dark places of myself that weren't up for observation. My fingernails bit into my palms, and I saw Hudson tense from the corner of my eye. "Which is ironic considering my mother wouldn't approve of the horrific technique she's teaching."

"My technique isn't horrific!" Juniper threw her arms down at her sides.

"Out of the three of us in this room, I'm the only one with the expertise to judge that." I took carefully measured steps toward her. "And you have *no* business being en pointe."

Juniper gasped, drawing her head back at the verbal blow. "I worked really hard, and Miss Quinn said I could if I felt ready. You can't tell me that I don't feel ready."

"I can sure as heck tell you that you have no business in pointe shoes at ten years old." Heat flushed my cheeks, but I swallowed most of the anger.

She tilted her chin. "There's no definitive answer within the community about when to start en pointe. And dancers should make their own choices about their bodies, especially their feet."

"I don't know who you're listening to—"

"Eva said it in a Seconds." She threw her arm out, pointing at the photograph near Hudson.

Of freaking course she did.

"Sure, because she's the youngest and was always angry Mom made her wait, and she likes to say controversial things for views. Get off Seconds." I breathed, deep and even, and reminded myself that she was ten, and the indignant anger that puckered her brow and clenched her fists was something I knew all too well. Finger by finger, I uncurled my hands.

A figure moved in the mirror, and I glanced over my shoulder to see Anne hovering silently in the doorway, watching Juniper with a mix of surprise and what looked like awe. This was usually the part of an argument where she'd step in and take charge, but she hung back because I'd told her to. It made all the difference.

"You think you're ready for pointe? Put your shoes on," I ordered Juniper, then walked back to Anne. "Am I wrong?" I asked quietly.

"No." She shook her head, then brushed her curls out of her face. "You're absolutely right, and I'm loving the assertiveness. She's a smart one, and I don't doubt she's already back there thinking about how to run verbal circles around you."

"She's Lina."

A smile slowly curved Anne's mouth. "So handle her like you would Lina."

"Like *anyone* ever handled Lina." I scoffed.

She squeezed my arm gently. "Best of luck."

Lina had constantly argued with my mother. She hadn't been the stereotypical eldest, somehow that personality type skipped straight to Anne, but she'd definitely been the most outspoken. And she never changed an opinion—even when she was wrong—without cold, hard proof.

Juniper needed data.

She tied the ribbons of her pointe shoes, and I bit my tongue about her particular selection as I made my way back to her. No wonder her feet had looked a little raw at the beach. "You don't have to stay," I told Hudson.

"I'm enjoying the show from my favorite seat in the house." A corner of his mouth lifted.

Naturally, he was standing in the same place where he'd watched me for hours whenever Mom wasn't around. But the last time he'd stood there I hadn't known how he tasted, and now I most certainly did. I shut those memories down and focused on Juniper as she rose to stand on flat feet.

"Go ahead. Show me what you've got."

Juniper swallowed, then moved her feet into first position and rolled up onto her toes. "See?" Her ankles wobbled, and she stepped forward to catch her balance. "I'm fine."

Anne groaned behind me, voicing my exact feelings.

"No teacher worth her salt would ever have allowed you en pointe." I rubbed the bridge of my nose. "It's Quinn's fault. Not yours."

"That's mean!" Her legs started to tremble.

"That's the truth, and that's what ballet is, Juniper. A few gorgeous moments built on a foundation of a lot of stinging truths, not just between you and your teachers, but you and your own body. I'm not going to baby you, nor am I going to fill your head with false praises that will ultimately get you hurt."

She plopped back down to her flat feet with a thud. "Just because you got hurt doesn't mean I will."

Ouch. "And here I thought you respected my opinion because I'm one of the best dancers in the world. Or have you found someone with a higher level of expertise from which to get your advice?"

Her mouth snapped shut.

"Arguing with me will not change the fact that you don't have the strength, the control, or the alignment to be en point. Not to mention you're wearing the wrong shoes."

"They're Blochs, like you wear." Juniper folded her arms and pursed her mouth.

Okay, that was kind of sweet, but I refused to give into the warmth spreading in my chest. "And here's your first lesson: just because another dancer likes something doesn't mean it's right for you. You're wearing a narrow box when you have nontapered toes, and that shoe isn't the right height for the thickness of your foot, which I've seen. It could be the right brand, but it's definitely the wrong model for you. You need to be fitted, Juniper."

Her eyes lit up. "Will you take me to be fitted?"

"Sure, when I think you're ready. Take them off." I moved to the barre and did a few quick stretches since it had been a few hours since my morning workout.

Juniper walked over, and I outright sighed at the condition of her feet.

"Take the position by the first mirror panel," I instructed when she stood in front of the second.

"Why?" She backed up a few steps to comply. "I thought beginners were supposed to take the middle and leave the ends to the better dancers."

"True." I nodded. "But you were standing in Anne's place. Now you have your mother's."

Her eyes brightened, and her chest swelled as she glanced around the space, her gaze skimming over the mirror and the hardwood floor, finally landing on the barre. She took the lower of the two options.

"Still warm from class?" I asked.

She nodded.

"Good. Let's start. Pliés." I worked through the basics with her, mirroring my moves to demonstrate while I silently evaluated her strengths and weaknesses.

By the time we were done, she'd stopped arguing and now stood silently, waiting with expectation in her eyes and a slightly raised chin. "You're phenomenal, but I already knew that."

"Yes." I nodded. "You can be, too, if you're ready to listen."

She glanced over at Hudson, who still stood against the wall as if he'd been built into the support structure of the house, then nodded at me.

"You're a beautiful dancer. I watched the entire class, not just barre. And for only having five months of instruction, you're remarkable, Juniper."

She smiled wide. "I'm a Rousseau."

I nodded. "But talent has to be paired with fundamentals, and you haven't yet developed the ones that make pointe possible. I'm not just talking about the fact that the bones in your feet haven't developed enough. Please trust me when I say if you continue to do so, you will sprain or break your ankle."

She sighed, but didn't argue, which I was going to take as progress.

"You need to work on your foot articulation, need to be able to work each part of your foot, move each toe." I pointed my right foot, then glided it over the floor in an arc as I swept it in front of me. "There's a difference between that"—I moved back to first position, then pointed again and jutted my foot forward—"and that. We do the basics over and over for this reason."

"What else?" Her chin rose another half inch.

"Strength and control. You roll up into relevé, which means you need to strengthen your muscles so you rise in one burst of motion, and then you need to slowly roll your foot down with control, all of which takes time and practice to develop. Your alignment needs work too. Any flaws you have while flat will only be exaggerated en pointe, which leads to imbalance."

"So everything." Her hand fell away from the barre. "I suck at everything."

"No." I moved closer to her. "I've already told you that you're remarkable. You've only been doing this for five months. Give yourself grace, but check your ego. I just told you why you aren't ready for pointe, not that you suck. You don't. Ballet is a lifetime of development, of never settling for the skills you have now, knowing that you might be phenomenal, but still striving for that unattainable feeling of perfection."

"And fun," she added. "It should be fun."

"Yes." *In theory.* "And I'm sure next year you'll be ready for the Classic, and *you'll* be phenomenal because you will have honed your fundamentals. In slippers. Beginners compete all the time in slippers. Both Eva and I did until we were thirteen."

"But Miss Quinn signed me up for the Classic this year."

I somehow kept my face blank. "Did she?" After only five months? What the hell had she been thinking? Juniper would be going up against dancers with *years* of experience and training. "As one of the exhibition dancers?"

"No, in the beginner category." Juniper rubbed her finger along the barre.

I glanced up at Anne in a plea for guidance, but she put her hands up, looking as stunned as I felt. "Okay, and how do you feel about that?" I asked Juniper.

"I don't want to embarrass myself." Her voice dropped to a whisper. "I thought that if I was already en pointe, I'd have a better shot at reaching top twenty."

At getting hurt, maybe.

"I don't want to pull out of the competition. What do I do?"

I reached for the lone strand of hair that had escaped her bun and tucked it back behind her ear. "I really think you should consider talking to your mom."

Juniper stiffened. "She won't understand. You know she hates ballet."

"I know she loves *you*. And I bet she gives really good advice."

She seemed to think it over, then shook her head. "I can't. If I make the top twenty, it will show her that I'm good, that I could be as great as you are if she just lets me dance. And by then it will be the middle of August, and she'll love you too. So, by the time you're ready to go back to New York, maybe she'll let me visit you and Aunt Anne."

Anne took a deep breath and pressed her lips between her teeth.

"Eva, too, of course. It will all work out."

"Juniper . . ." The further we got into this charade, the worse I felt about it.

"I won't dance en pointe," she rushed. "I'll do whatever you say if we can just follow the plan."

My heart clenched as I floundered and looked to Anne for the right answer, the right words.

"How about we give Aunt Allie a minute to think, and you help me put together some energy bars in the kitchen?" Anne offered. "They're chocolate."

Juniper glanced between us for a second, then at Hudson. "Okay."

"Excellent." Anne led her out of the studio, then closed the door behind them.

"I think we should tell Caroline," I said to Hudson.

"I agree." He walked across the studio in his socks.

My ribs threatened to squeeze the air out of my lungs. "It could mean Juniper wouldn't see us again for eight more years."

"This far into lying to her? Probably." He lifted a hand, then dropped it, as if thinking twice about reaching for me, which was probably for the best considering the fact that I'd nearly screwed him in a shower the last time he'd touched me. *And he wants hours. Days. Nights.*

"And she'd pull her out of ballet." The barre dug into my back as I leaned against it.

"Not sure that's a bad thing after what I saw at that class." He folded his arms.

"Not everyone teaches that way." Shit, that was defensive. I looked over at the picture of Lina, and my chest tightened another degree.

"What are you thinking?"

"Lina loved to dance." I studied her smile, the little lines that crinkled her eyes. "I mean, she really loved it. She'd been born a dancer, not told she was one. She woke up in the morning excited for class every day, and she spent more time in this studio than any of us. It was her oxygen, her food. She *loved* it in a way I never . . ." I shut my mouth so quickly my teeth clicked.

"You loved it too," he whispered.

I dragged my gaze from the picture to meet his.

"I was there, Allie. You loved it too." He cradled the side of my face, and I struggled not to lean into the warmth, not to lean on him. I scrambled for my defenses and came up empty. "You came alive on that stage in a way I've never seen. Maybe not the days your mom harped on you, but the day you danced that routine from *Giselle* instead of whatever she'd picked out for you . . . that was love up there, and passion, and excitement. I saw it in your eyes."

"Variation," I muttered, dismissing most of his words. "It's called a variation."

"Fine. Variation. Whatever it was, you loved it the same way she did. If you don't anymore—"

"It's not about me." I stepped out of his hand. "Juniper's just like Lina in so many ways that it's uncanny, and if you'd cut Lina away from ballet, she wouldn't have survived it. If Juniper feels that way—and considering all she's done to get around Caroline, she probably does—then . . ." I sighed. "Lina should be here, but she's not, and I owe it to her to help Juniper, but there's no good solution in any of this."

"I know." He slipped his hands into his pockets. "And I've done my best to honor the promise I made to Sean that Caroline's fears wouldn't hold Juniper back, but I'm telling you right now that she can't go back to that studio. I'd rather break her trust than watch someone break her down."

There were two months left before the Classic, and Juniper was determined to compete. "So it's either she quits dancing, or goes back to Quinn's and gets herself hurt, or you tell Caroline, which leads to her quitting by force . . ." I blew out a long sigh. She'd never be able to hide attending at Madeline's, and I didn't know any of the other local studios well enough to send Lina's daughter there, which left the only viable alternative. "She's done with school for the summer? How does she spend her time?"

"Last week." He studied my face. "She's in the local activity program on the days Caroline works, and Gavin and I usually try to grab her when we're off so she's not stuck there until seven."

I nodded. "What's your schedule like?"

"Suddenly interested in my actual life?" He dared a smile.

Too close. "You wish. What's your schedule?"

"I do wish. And it's usually as close to nine-to-five as it gets. I pull four to six twenty-four-hour shifts a month, and I get a couple days off a week—not always Saturday and Sunday. Why?" He tilted his head, and I absolutely did *not* look at his mouth.

Liar.

"Bring her here." I pushed out the words before I lost the nerve. "I'll teach her. We'll just hope she knows her mom better than we do. Hopefully by August I've won Caroline over, and at this point . . . in for a penny and all that." If we were going down, then we may as well do it with giant flames.

His brow knit. "You mean that? You have time for that?"

"I'll make time." I nodded.

"She needs a consequence for going around our backs. I'm not sure rewarding her with the best private tutor in the world is the right move here." Two lines formed between his brows.

"What do you have in mind that doesn't involve asking her actual parent?" I challenged.

"Not sure yet, but I'll have to come up with *something*. She's broken the rules, lied, schemed, and manipulated every single person around her to get what she wants." His jaw ticked.

"Yeah, and she's only ten." I started toward the studio door. "Not excusing her actions, but you know there's a label for that kind of behavior in adults."

"Criminal?" he guessed. "Don't even *think* reckless. This isn't me."

"Maybe." I opened the studio doors. "I was thinking CEO."

CHAPTER NINETEEN

Hudson

WestCoastPointe: Not going to lie, I would die for an invite to the MBC gala.

This place was a black-tie zoo disguised as an art museum. I wove my way through the checkerboard-dressed crowd, and along what I hoped would be the narrowest exhibition hall, careful not to bump into anyone or spill any of the thirty-dollar martinis they were carrying.

I cataloged every face I saw.

"Hudson!" Anne waved from the end of the hall, and I slowly made my way to her. "I'm glad you made it." Her smile held an edge of nerves. "Allie's in a meeting with Vasily, otherwise she would have met you herself."

"Sorry I'm late." I fought the urge to adjust my tie. "I meant to come down with Allie yesterday, but one of the other swimmers fell off a ladder and broke his leg, and another's wife went into labor, so I got called in from leave."

"Don't care." She patted my arm as we walked into the center of the museum, an open space easily five stories high, lined with balconies in galleries on the other floors. Round tables for ten filled the floor, with the exception of what was clearly a stage on the far end of the hall. "You're here now, and that's all that matters. Do you like it?" She gestured to the room. "I spent the last eight months designing the color scheme. I figured the dark-pink lighting would look great since everyone is dressed for the white-and-black theme. And I think I went through a dozen sample centerpieces before I decided on the orchids and dahlias."

"It looks spectacular." I offered what I hoped was a reassuring smile. "And you look great too."

"Thank you." She glanced down at her long white dress, then smiled. "Do you need a crash course on who everyone is? Kenna's around here somewhere. She's Allie's closest friend, so I'm sure she'd help you out. Actually, I'm not sure. She might watch you fumble just for the fun of it."

"I think I'm good." I shook my head, and she led me past most of the tables. "I checked the website, and Allie's been quizzing me with photos off her phone every time I pick up Juniper. Though I'm pretty sure I saw a couple of movie stars back by the exhibit who weren't on her camera roll."

"Don't worry, they're not in the Company," she teased. "Word of advice, if you think you're supposed to know someone and you don't, just tell them you're a huge fan of their work, but don't get specific." She walked us around the edge of the three-foot-high stage, and to the bottom of a wide staircase flanked on both sides with art. "She should be out right about—there she is! Mission accomplished; I will see you later." Anne walked away.

I looked up the staircase and tried not to swallow my damned tongue as Allie descended ahead of two men, looking back over her shoulder in conversation.

She was sheer perfection.

Her long black dress looked like it had been poured onto her curves, then gathered at the left side of her waist, and then—fuck *me*—sliced clean open from the curve of her hip to the floor, exposing the impossibly long line of her leg with every step. She'd pinned one side of her hair back behind her ear, and left the rest down, the waves brushing over the tiny straps of her dress and the heart-shaped neckline that lifted her breasts up like appetizers.

I was suddenly starving.

She faced forward, and her eyes flared as she saw me. Head to toe, her gaze raked over me in clear appreciation, her lips parting as she slowed her steps, pausing so we were the same height. "Hudson."

"You look like a fucking dream, Allie." A dream that, for the next few hours, I was not only allowed but encouraged to touch. I palmed her waist and tugged her against my chest, hovering my mouth inches from hers. "Truly breathtaking." I brushed my lips over hers, careful not to smudge her makeup.

"Thank you." A corner of her mouth tilted as I set her safely back on her step. "You look entirely too good in a tux to ever wear one in public again."

Even knowing she was just playing the role, I couldn't help but grin.

"Ugh. Especially when you do that." She stroked my dimple with the tip of her finger.

"I don't believe we've been introduced." The taller of the two men reached the bottom of the steps. The lights turned his silver hair and pale skin a pinkish hue. "Vasily Koslov, artistic director of the Metropolitan Ballet Company."

"Hudson Ellis," I replied, shaking his soft hand.

"Ah! Alessandra's new boyfriend!" He gave a polished grin that made me think everyone in Allie's ballet company went to the same smile class. "You're the subject of quite a bit of gossip in the building. Hope you won't mind when we steal her back come the fall."

"Whatever makes her happy makes me happy." Gossip?

"Now that's the right answer when you're dating someone as extraordinary as Alessandra." He sent an adoring look her way. "Have to admit, I had my doubts when you said you were bringing someone. I know how you are in love affairs"—he lowered his voice playfully—"which is why I told Anna to make sure his card still said *guest*, just in case you changed your mind."

My eyebrows rose. What a weird-ass detail to pay attention to.

"Anne," Allie corrected him with a flash of teeth. "And Hudson and I go back over a decade. You could have put his name on the card."

"No matter." His gaze shifted to the left, and his smile deepened as he raised his arm. "Ah, my dear." A woman with black-and-silver hair went to his side, her arm wrapping around his waist as his did hers. "Allow me to introduce my wife, Danica, the Company's executive director. Dani, this is our Alessandra's current beau. He's a lifeguard or something."

Oh, for fuck's sake. Good thing my ego wasn't fragile.

"Coast Guard rescue swimmer," Allie clarified, her smile still sharp. "He jumps out of helicopters and rescues people when their boats sink." She moved down a step and shifted her clutch to the other hand to lace her fingers with mine, and it was all I could do not to lean in and kiss the shit out of her. "It's actually one of the hardest jobs in the world. Most people never qualify, let alone make it through training."

"How remarkable!" Danica tipped her head my direction. "Do you save many people?"

"From time to time." I nodded.

"He saved me," Allie said, her thumb stroking along mine. "That's how we met when we were kids."

"Charming." Danica patted Vasily's arm. "Darling, we really should say hello to the Jemonds before the performance starts. They're already chatting with Maxim, and they're such big donors that it would be a mistake not to."

"Duty calls." Vasily smiled at Allie. "I cannot wait to have you back in the building and gracing the stage. This fall will be your triumph." He glanced at the guy standing close to Allie, who appeared entirely comfortable occupying her personal space. "Both of your triumphs. I can't express how much I'm looking forward to showing the world what you two have created."

"Thank you," Allie replied, color flushing her cheeks.

"Now that you've met the old man and the walking prenup he calls a wife"—the guy bounded down the last two steps and thrust out his hand—"I'm Isaac Burdan."

I shook his hand, glancing over his short black curls, golden brown complexion, and blinding smile, placing him instantly from Allie's pictures. "The choreographer. Nice to meet you."

He laughed as his hand fell away, his gaze darting to Allie. "Is that all you've told him? How fascinating. Well, I'm off to find a celebratory drink," he told me, then turned back to Allie. The softening of his expression told me the details Allie had left out. "You headed back to the beach tomorrow?"

She nodded. "I'll be back before September for rehearsals."

"I will count the days with bated breath." He picked up her free hand and brushed a kiss across her knuckles. Acid rose in my throat. "New York's shine is but a glimmer until you return to make it sparkle again, Alessandra." One last smile, and he disappeared into the crowd.

What the actual fuck?

"Sorry." Allie stepped off the last stair, her heels bringing her nearly to my chin. "He can be a little much, but he's truly brilliant."

"Did he talk to you like that in bed?" My brow furrowed.

"What?" Her mouth dropped open for the slightest second. "And take that look off your face."

"What look?"

"You look like you just caught a whiff of a trash pile in the middle of July."

It was a pretty accurate description of how I felt. "Seriously, though. That's what does it for you? Bated breath and glimmers? Let me guess—he doesn't tell you he's about to come, he declares that he's arriving."

Allie snorted but stopped tantalizingly short of a laugh, then batted her eyelashes at me. "And I suppose you're more of the first variety?

Have to warn a girl that she'd better rev her own engine because your race ends before the first turn? Or are you the silent, grunty kind?"

Oh, she had jokes, did she?

I yanked our laced hands against my chest, whipped my arm around her waist, and turned, pressing her against the wall on the far side of the staircase, just short of a plaque marking a piece of artwork. "Want to skip the rest of the gala and find out? I promised you hours, if I remember correctly."

Her breath stuttered and her gaze dropped to my mouth. "We can't."

Not "I don't want to." Interesting.

"No need to rev your own engine unless you want to." I lowered my head to hers. "You'll come at least twice *before* I fuck you, Allie," I promised. "I'm far from silent, and I know how to use my mouth to ensure you aren't either."

Her pupils dilated and the color in her cheeks shone red even under the pink lighting as she opened her mouth, then shut it.

"Now, should we go do whatever it is you do at these things?" I had to put at least a couple of inches between us, or these pants were going to start cutting off circulation to my dick.

She nodded slowly, and I backed up, keeping her fingers entwined with mine as we faced the growing crowd of people finding their seats.

"Our table is this way," she said as we walked into the crush. "I should have warned you about Isaac. I'm sorry."

"You have nothing to apologize for. I didn't exactly hand over a list of the women I've slept with either."

"At least none of them are in the same room with us." She gave a fake smile and wave to someone who called her name.

"That you know of." I dodged some drunk asshat who stumbled backward, then angled my body so he didn't bump into Allie.

She looked up at me with raised brows.

"Relax. I'm kidding." I shrugged. "Maybe, since I haven't seen the guest list or anything. Why? Does the thought of me having slept with someone here bother you?" The aisle cleared, and we started walking again.

"Does the fact that I've slept with at least two of the men in this room bother you?" she countered.

A slight twinge of jealousy tightened my collar. "Are you planning on sleeping with them while we're together?"

"This isn't real," she whispered as we passed another table at the edge of the stage.

"Semantics. Answer the question." I tucked her close to my side when the crowd thickened again.

"No." She shook her head. "Once I'm done with someone, I'm done. I don't like things . . . messy. It's one of the reasons I only date dancers. Same lifestyle, same schedule, same priorities. No mess."

"We're messy, and you like me just fine when you forget you still hate me." Keeping my hands off her tonight was going to be fucking impossible.

"We're messy because I lo—" She shook her head, and I stared at her long enough that I nearly collided with two women who weren't watching where they were going either. "I cared about you. That was a mistake I never made again. Sex is fun—necessary, even—and keeping the same partner allows for a certain level of comfort I prefer. But I don't get jealous because I don't get attached."

She probably meant it as a statement, but I heard it as a warning.

"Which works out because Vasily doesn't want you to," I noted.

"He likes me focused—likes all of us focused." She pointed ahead. "That's our table, just beyond the one in the center. And now you're ducking the question."

"I realized something during that kiss." We passed the center table. "Not the first, when you caught me off guard, but the second—"

"I know what kiss you're talking about," she interrupted.

"Good." A grin crept across my face, and I spotted our place cards. "It hit me that it didn't matter if the first one was fake, because that one was real. It doesn't matter who had your first, or my first . . . anything."

We stopped behind our chairs, and I picked up my card. *Alessandra Rousseau Guest.* My chest tightened. The *guest* somehow bothered me more than the choreographer had. Vasily had given the direction, but Anne had still printed it as if she hadn't believed Allie would actually bring me.

"Firsts are overrated," Allie said, setting her clutch on her chair.

Guest. My chest burned like a struck match at the sudden awareness that I wanted my name on that card. I didn't want to be some anonymous, fleeting, erasable guest in her life like the others who had come before me. I wanted to be engraved, etched, and carved so deeply into her soul that she'd never get me out.

She'd given me her fake summer, but I wanted it *all,* and my heart didn't seem to care how unattainable that was. I was just going to have to find a way to make it possible.

"Glad we agree." I nodded to myself, then set the card down and turned to Allie. "So while sure, it makes me jealous that there are a couple of guys here who have seen you naked, I actually feel sorry for them because they'll never have you again." I tugged her close and let the words fly like the revelation they were. "But I will. First means nothing. Last means *everything.*"

And that right there is why you get called reckless.

"You can't say things like that to me." Her fingers curled around the lapels of my jacket. "Even for show," she whispered. "Keep to your part, Hudson."

It wasn't for show. That was the very complicated, very *messy* problem for which I had no solution. Yet.

"I thought we agreed not to lie." I trailed my fingertips down her bare spine and her breath hitched as she shivered. My dick stirred in response, just like it always did when she showed the first sign of interest. "And as you reminded our niece, omission would be just that. I told you I want you. I'm done hiding from it. Public. Private. Don't care. This is real for me. It's about to get messy." I held her gaze, watching her expression shift from surprise to confusion, then fiery annoyance as she stepped away.

There's my girl.

It was the first slip in her mask I'd seen all night.

"Alessandra!" Her name was the only warning before we were *engulfed.*

There were at least half a dozen people reaching for Allie and pulling her into hugs and taking selfies. Not once did her mouth curve genuinely.

These were her people. Shouldn't she be happy?

"We've missed you!" A woman with black hair and a kind smile clasped Allie's shoulders, and my mind flickered through the pictures from the website. Reagan Huang, principal dancer, which equated to the same rank Allie was. "It's not the same without you."

"Yeah, there's no one around to make us look bad." That joke was offered up by a blonde with catlike eyes and a hard-to-read smile. Harlow Oren. Soloist. One rank below Allie.

"Please, like you need Alessandra showing you up to look bad." A lanky guy with blond hair and a monochromatic tux pulled Allie into a hug. "Ugh. I've missed you. You don't call. You don't text. You don't respond when I call *and* text." He leaned down, setting his chin on her shoulder. "It's bullshit, really." Everett Carr. Principal. "I'll only forgive you if you come back."

"Stop hogging her, Ev." A brunette in a black ballgown tugged Allie away from Everett and hugged her quickly before cupping her face. Candace Baron. Principal. "Tell me you're taking care of yourself."

"I am," Allie promised with a nod, and I couldn't tell if she was lying.

The last guy looked like he'd just stepped off a billboard. Black hair, blue eyes. Jacob Harvey. Soloist. He smirked and opened his arms. Allie walked right into them.

My gaze focused on his hands, which were well above her lower back. Probably not mystery ex number two, then.

"It's a little overwhelming, isn't it?" a woman said to my right, pulling her long black hair over her shoulder. "Not knowing who's genuine and who's not. I'm Kenna, by the way."

Allie's closest friend.

"It is." I offered my hand. "Honored to meet you. I'm Hudson—"

"I'm one of the only people in this room who *actually* knows who you are." She shook my hand, then tilted her head and studied me. "You make your move yet? Your real move, that is. Not this fake bullshit or a shower stall."

I instantly liked her. "She told you about the kiss?" A flame of hope caught behind my ribs.

She lifted her brows. "Whole-ass beach out there just waiting for some cinematic romantic moment, and you choose a *shower stall*?"

"No regrets. Had to know she wanted it, that she wasn't performing." I slipped my hands in my pockets, keeping watch on the people gathered around Allie from the corner of my eye. "And she's skittish when it comes to real moves."

"Wonder why." She shot me a look that would level cities.

"Guilty." I nodded, then peeked Allie's direction and found the same beautiful but bogus smile on her face as she talked to the other dancers. "Any advice?"

"Hell no. I'm her friend, not yours." Kenna's brown eyes narrowed. "But you *are* going to make a move, aren't you? Because she needs to get with you or get *over* you. Hear me?"

"Heard." Allie wasn't getting over me, the same way I was never getting over her.

"Good." She nodded, then glanced at Allie. "And you'd better be ready to fold yourself into her life, because the only time ballerinas bend is onstage."

"I'll fold," I promised, my voice lowering. "I'll turn myself inside out if it means I get to be hers." Saying it out loud took *pounds* off my shoulders and untwisted the first of about three million knots standing between Allie and me.

"Okay, then." Kenna's shoulders relaxed, and she turned to stand beside me. "Everyone, this is Hudson Ellis," she announced to the dancers. "Allie's boyfriend."

Every set of eyes turned toward me, more than one appraising me in a way that would have made my mother blush. "Nice to meet . . . everyone."

"Would you look at those eyes," Everett muttered. "Allie, where did you find this delicious specimen?"

Allie huffed, then tucked herself into my left side. "At the beach when I was sixteen."

"Technically you were off the coast about a mile," I corrected her with a wink, wrapping my arm around her and sliding my hand over her hip.

Reagan lifted her hand to her chest and sighed. "Oh, Alessandra, please tell me you're bringing him back to New York."

"Hold that thought." Kenna stepped in front of us and lifted her phone. "Smile."

We posed and she clicked. Tonight's goal had been accomplished.

"You two have fun. I've got Matthias for a whole night and I'm not wasting him." She waved, then disappeared among the tables.

Jacob's gaze tracked a blonde with a pixie-shaped face. "I'll see you guys afterwards." He made a beeline for the woman.

"Really?" Allie lifted her brows.

"Oh, they started fucking as soon as summer rehearsals started," Everett remarked.

"Don't be jealous." Harlow kissed his cheek.

"Please, I've got all I can manage with Michael right now." He shook his head. "Speaking of which, we should find our seats. Candace and Reagan are here with you, but I'm over there at the other principals' table."

"You could be back with the soloists," Harlow teased in a way I wasn't sure was teasing. "Good to see you, Allie." She headed back a row.

Everett leaned in and kissed Allie's cheek. "Get your ass back to New York."

"Working on it," Allie assured him as the others filed off. She leaned into my side. "I guess I forced you to learn their names for no reason."

"I like knowing who your friends are." I bent and brushed a kiss over her forehead just because I could.

She sighed and leaned into me. "Besides Kenna, I'd only consider a couple of them friends," she said softly. "Reagan"—she nodded across the wide table—"and Everett."

"I told you that dress would look *killer* on you." Eva walked between the tables, a brunette with a predatory look in her eyes following about ten feet behind. "Holy shit, Hudson Ellis."

"Hey, Eva." I nodded.

"I told you he was coming." Allie swirled her finger. "Turn around, your straps are twisted."

"I wasn't sure he'd actually show." Eva did as she ordered, and Allie unhooked two of the dozen straps crisscrossing Eva's back, then hooked the correct ones together.

"I go wherever your sister beckons." I looked over Allie's head and noted the other brunette hovering in the background. Pointed nose. Shrewd blue eyes. Charlotte Larsen. Soloist.

"You're all set," Allie told Eva.

"Thanks." Eva turned my direction and looked me over. "Were you always this gorgeous? I mean, I remember you being pretty hot, but *wow* did you grow into all that." She waved her hand my direction. "Five stars. No notes."

My eyebrows shot upward.

"Eva," Allie snapped, but her sister only smirked. "No."

Eva tsked. "A good sister would share, you know."

"A possessive sister *will* cut you," Allie warned in a sing-song voice, and I barely stopped myself from pulling her into a kiss.

"Relax." Eva rolled her eyes. "I was just kidding. Like I'd ever dream about coming between the two of you when you took so damned long to get together."

I blinked. Allie hadn't told Eva the truth.

"Did you find your seat?" Allie changed the subject.

"Back with the steerage? I mean corps? Of course." She reached for Allie's hand, all pretense falling from her face. "Charlotte took your locker."

Allie tensed. "I'm sorry?"

"This morning after rehearsal, she moved all of your stuff from your locker, and put hers in." Worry lined the space between Eva's eyebrows.

"What exactly did she do with my things?" Allie clipped her words.

I shot a look at the brunette, who was creeping closer.

"She just dumped them on the bench. I stuffed everything into my locker. Don't worry, it's all there." Her shoulders dipped. "Allie, she already took your barre spot. She's coming for that principal role. Tell me you're healing. You'll make it back, right?"

Allie nodded and squeezed her sister's hand. "It's all right. Vasily already told me that *Equinox* is on the fall program. I'll be ready." She forced a smile for her sister. "Don't worry about Charlotte. Not on my behalf. Principals rise and principals retire. If someone is better than I am, then they'll take my place. It's as simple as that."

"I can put laxatives in her yogurt if you want." Pretty sure that was a genuine threat.

Allie scoffed. "Knock it off and go find your seat."

Eva sighed, then walked away, heading toward a table another row back and to the left.

"So, nothing much has changed there," I remarked.

"She's pretty much a sour patch kid." Allie took the step that separated us. "How do you like my world, Ellis?"

"Feels . . . slippery." I grabbed the back of her chair and pulled it out. "You're kind of a chameleon here, aren't you? Putting on whatever disguise the person in front of you compels so you don't get eaten?" She blended in a little too well. "How many people in the world actually know who you are, Allie?"

"Very few," she admitted softly. "And unfortunately for me, I think you're one of them."

"Look out," I warned her as Charlotte approached.

Allie pivoted, then weaponized the fakest smile I'd ever seen. "Hi, Charlotte."

"Good to see you feel well enough to come tonight," Charlotte replied, her smile razor sharp. "Since you haven't been able to sit in on any rehearsals or even take class with us."

"You did a marvelous job with Giselle." The muscles in Allie's back tensed, and her chin rose. Juniper didn't just take after Lina in that regard.

"I know." She glanced past Allie and all but eye fucked me.

I narrowed my eyes to let her know it wasn't welcome.

"You should know"—her attention focused back on Allie—"that we all want you to take as much time to heal as you need. One ruptured Achilles is a disaster, but two?" She grimaced. "Imagine if you rushed it and suffered a third? That would be career ending, and none of us want that for you. You're practically Company royalty."

Allie's shoulders straightened. "Thank you for the concern, but I'll be back before fall for rehearsals, as I'm sure you've asked and I'm certain you've been told."

A corner of my mouth tugged upward.

"Well, just in case, I don't want you to worry." A saccharine-sweet smile spread across Charlotte's face, and she lowered her voice. "I've been learning the choreography to *Equinox* after hours with Isaac. That variation in the first act is just scrumptious. Probably a little hard on someone with an ankle injury, though."

Equinox . . . Wasn't that Allie's ballet? The one Isaac had choreographed and created for her?

To Allie's credit, she didn't flinch.

The same couldn't be said for me. What the fuck kind of viper's nest was this, and why was Allie so hell bent on returning to it?

"You should take your seat, Charlotte. I think the performance is about to start." Allie's tone could have frozen a volcano.

"Enjoy your night." She wiggled her fingers at Allie, then headed toward one of the soloists' tables.

If this room was a shipwreck, Charlotte was the person I was putting on the helo last.

"Allie?" I whispered.

"Everything okay?" Reagan asked, leaning to the side to see past the centerpiece. "Was Charlotte being an ass?"

Allie startled, then blasted that fake smile. "She was just wishing me a speedy recovery." She grabbed her clutch and sank gracefully into her seat before I did the same to her right.

"Think I just figured out why you build walls. They're more like barricades. Ironic that I'm in the military," I told her quietly, leaning in as she stared toward the stage, her face a rigid mask of control. "But I suspect you're the one fighting wars."

She looked back at me as Vasily took the stage, and for a second, the mask slipped, and anger shone through. "I would care."

"About?" I reached into her lap and took her hand, spearing my fingers through her clenched fist, then holding tight.

"If you'd slept with someone in this room. If someone like her had you—" Rage burned in her eyes. "I would care, Hudson." She jerked her head toward the stage, and Vasily began his speech before I could reply.

Allie seethed, her posture rigid, gripping my hand like a vise all through Vasily's remarks, and didn't let up as the kids from the Company's ballet school took the stage and began their performance.

"I can't be here." She gripped her clutch and looked back at me. "I'm done. Take me home. Now."

I didn't need to be told twice.

CHAPTER TWENTY

Allie

SanFranFouette: OMG. I'm living for these updates RousseauSisters4

Hunter4lights: If she can't sit through dinner, there's no way she can handle rehearsal. How embarrassing.

I threw my keys onto the entry-hall table of my apartment and kicked off my heels once I hit the living room. The sun was setting, giving a dusky glow through the two-story windows that looked out over the city as I ditched my clutch on the surprisingly clean coffee table. Either Eva was making an attempt at picking up after herself, or our housekeeper deserved a raise.

Anger crawled beneath my skin, the heat of it cracking the carefully constructed mask I worked so hard to maintain when in the city. I hadn't even made it through dinner.

"You want to talk about it?" Hudson asked, the sound of his footsteps behind me softening as he reached the area rug. What did he think about this place? My mother had hand selected the apartment for its proximity to the studio and had decorated for Lina, only to hand the keys over to me a month after her death.

Did he like the subtle acts of rebellion Eva and I had committed in the street-vendor art on the walls and messy photos of messier nights in their mismatched frames along the bookshelves? Or did he only see the polished surfaces presented for first glance?

"Allie?" He walked past the wicker baskets of pointe shoes we kept near the sofa just in case we felt like breaking them in while streaming a Netflix marathon.

"I'm still processing." Moving to the windows, I looked down twenty-two stories and watched people go about their lives, walking their dogs, taking their children to the store, maybe arriving at the restaurant on the corner for a date night.

"You can process out loud." He appeared at my side.

"We're off the clock." Funny, but I'd thought that if he were here in my apartment, with its high lofted ceilings, he wouldn't feel so much bigger than life. I was wrong. He was everywhere, his ocean-salt scent in my lungs, his voice in my ear, his touch imprinted on my skin. I was constantly torn between putting as much space between us as possible, and yanking him closer. Damn it, I was a mess. "You found the guest room when you got here, right?"

He nodded. "Thanks for asking the doorman to let me in."

A wry half smile twisted my lips. "I know you're close to superhero status and all, but I figured it was too much to ask you to Clark Kent it in a phone booth."

He unbuttoned his tux jacket. "Your friends seemed nice for the whole three minutes I spent with them. I like that Kenna's protective." The jacket slipped from his shoulders, and he folded it in half before laying it over the back of the leather armchair.

"I can handle myself." I folded my arms like it would keep another piece of facade from cracking. "Just because I'm quiet or controlled doesn't mean I don't know how to fight back or defend my place in the Company."

"I'd never accuse you of being quiet. At least not around me. Observant and thoughtful, but not quiet."

"I always have to be careful what I say and who I say it to here. There's always an ear lurking nearby. Always a phone with a record button." Looking over at him was a mistake. On a normal day, Hudson was beyond beautiful. Without his shirt on? Mouthwateringly sexy. The sight of him in a tux had rendered me speechless. But the sight of him standing there so casually in the black vest, rolling up the sleeves of his dress shirt, stole every coherent thought and took my sex drive from *sure, that would be fun* to *how fast can I get under this man*. Instant heat.

And I could have him if I just *asked*. He'd made that achingly clear.

"Being on all the time has to be exhausting." He looked out at the view, taking in the New York skyline.

"It's been harder since I fell," I admitted. "The culture of the Company changes from year to year as dancers come and go, but for the most part, we're all very supportive of each other while still keeping our competitive edge." My hands balled, and my nails bit into my palms. "But the second I fell, it was like seeing blood in the water, especially with Charlotte." Anger flared again, rising from a simmer to a boil. "She's been working with Isaac." I knew Hudson had heard before the performance, but I needed to say it, let the reality, the very real danger of it, sink in. "He's been teaching her the choreography he'd created for *me*. I've never had a role created for me. Sure, some choreography changed here and there in certain pieces, but never a full ballet. It's one of those career moments that might never happen again, and he's teaching *her*."

"She's a piece of work." He turned that gaze on me, and the heat racing through my blood shifted into a very different kind of burn.

Shit. He was too close, too accessible, and way too dangerous to my peace of mind.

"I shouldn't have told you any of that." I walked away before I could do something entirely foolish, like jump him. Didn't stop me from thinking about all those mouthy little promises he'd made back at the gala, though. Gathering handfuls of my dress so I didn't trip, I headed into the kitchen.

"You can tell me anything. I'm not going to use it against you, Allie." He followed me in, but stayed on the opposite side of the island as I opened the refrigerator.

"You hungry?" I moved around a couple containers of takeout. "I promised you dinner, then dragged you out before the first course."

"I'm more worried about you than I am food."

"What do you want me to say, Hudson?" I pushed aside some very questionable milk, only finding containers of yogurt and prepped snacks to take to the studio. Shit. Slamming the refrigerator door should have been my first clue that I was losing my hard-fought self-control. Letting Hudson in was a hard second.

"Whatever you're feeling is a good start." He crossed one ankle over the other and leaned back against the counter near the sink.

"Feeling? I'm angry. How is that for feeling?" I turned toward the freezer, whipping the door open.

"Excellent start."

"Everything I've worked for is inches from being taken away. I risk losing my contract, my ballet, my mother's . . . God, it's not like I had her approval or pride to begin with. I'm just a stand-in for Lina because Anne couldn't dance, and if I falter, she'll move on to Eva. At the end of the day, I'm just another Rousseau girl, completely and utterly replaceable." I located two pints of ice cream, a few bags of frozen vegetables, and a half dozen containers of prepped broth. "And why is there no fucking food in this house?" I slammed that door, too, then pivoted to face Hudson. He stood there all calm and controlled, watching me like I was the tornado and he was the storm chaser waiting to see which way I'd turn.

We'd flipped roles, and yet we were both . . . ourselves. There was no point bothering with my carefully constructed defenses. I didn't have to be poised around him or present the illusion of perfection because he already knew I was neither of those things at my core.

Inside, I was imperfect, and unkempt, and chaotic, just like him.

And he alone had the power to quiet the chaos. That kiss at the beach had consumed me in a way no other kiss had, taken up too much space to feel anything but him. Even the hurt of our past was all about him. There was no ballet when I was in his arms, no company politics, no disappointed mother, no pressure to recover. I couldn't worry about my future when he demanded every ounce of my present.

And if it was only the present, then there was no risk of getting hurt, right?

"What are you thinking over there, Allie?" He braced his hands on the edge of the counter.

"What if I want five minutes?" I walked around the side of the island.

"What are we pretending this time?" His knuckles turned white as I approached.

"That you want me." I put myself directly in front of him.

His gaze heated. "That's a very real fact of life. I live in a constant state of wanting you. I have since I was seventeen years old. Wanting you is all I know."

I ignored the burst of . . . something . . . that confession made me feel. "I remember you saying something about coming twice. Was that a brag? Or bluster?" My eyes searched his, and my skin prickled with anticipation.

"It was a promise." He lifted a hand and skimmed the backs of his fingers down my cheek slowly. I leaned into the touch. "For a time when you aren't looking to hide from your feelings with sex."

My heart flipped. He was getting all noble on me, and that wasn't something I could handle at the moment. "I'm taking a page out of your book and breaking the rules. You had the last five minutes. These are mine." I retreated two steps.

"Allie . . ." His jaw ticked.

"So if you want me, I'd take the offer. Because this is the only time I'm making it." I reached under my arm, undid the hook and eye closure with a snap of my fingers, then dragged the zipper down my side. "You're the decisive one, so choose. Now, or never."

"I'd like to do the right thing here." He watched the progress of my fingers like he hadn't eaten in months and I was about to take the silver top off a buffet.

The look alone was enough to jump-start my pulse.

"The right thing is overrated." I reached my waist and the dress parted along my ribs.

"I want you," he growled.

"I think we've established that." I slipped one spaghetti strap off my shoulder.

He shook his head. "I want all of you. No masks. No walls. No more pretending what's between us is fake when we both know it's excruciating, and terrifying, and amazingly real. I want more than five minutes."

Panic shot into my blood like ice, but it quickly melted in the overwhelming heat coursing through me. "That's not going to happen." I'd never be foolish enough to let him in all the way again, not when he had a track record of leaving.

"It is." The certainty in his gaze didn't stop me from lifting my hand to my other shoulder. "And I wish I was above using sex as a way to get you, to keep you. But I'm not."

"Don't worry, you can't." I tugged the other strap over the curve of my shoulder and let it fall to rest against my arm, relishing how he tracked the movement. "I won't let you. I told you I don't do messy." Sex wasn't emotional for me, and he wasn't going to change that.

Hudson shook his head slowly. "It's not a debate. It's a disclaimer. Only truth between us, remember?" Every line of his body tensed. "You're using this as a way to run, and I'm saying I'll use it to keep you."

I arched a brow. "What are you going to do, Hudson? Fuck me so well that I never want to leave your bed? That I'll be willing to forget everything in our past because you're that damn good at dishing out orgasms?" Never going to happen. My vibrator dished out orgasms and I had no problem replacing it every year.

"Yes." His gaze dropped to my neckline and I let the dress slip an inch. He bit back a groan, and my mouth curved slightly. I had him. We both knew it.

"Then by all means, give it your best shot." I lifted my chin.

He surged toward me and I braced for impact.

It didn't disappoint.

His mouth collided with mine in the same instant his hand reached for my face and the other splayed across my back, pulling me against him.

Yes. Every cell in my body screamed the word as my focus, my very existence, narrowed to the feel of his lips on mine.

He pressed down on my chin with his thumb, and my mouth opened, immediately invaded by the skillful slide of his tongue. It was just as hot and consuming as the first time had been, and for a split second, I worried he might just be able to do what he threatened, and addict me.

That thought scattered when his hand slid down my throat, across the swell of my breast and along the skin my zipper had bared. His touch woke every nerve, raising goose bumps in its wake. He deepened the kiss as he grabbed my ass with both hands, then adjusted his hold to my hips and lifted.

I wound my arms around his neck, and the straps of my dress pulled tight across my arms as I kissed him back with everything I had, licking into his mouth to stake my own claim. My ass landed on the cold granite of the island, and I didn't so much as flinch at the temperature as he kissed me again and again. He drowned out the noise of the outside world by becoming the center of mine. There was only his mouth, his tongue, his hands, and the all-consuming need burning between us.

Heat pooled between my thighs as he moved his hands across them, one of them grazing my skin through the slit in my dress. Then he pushed them apart to make room for his hips, filling the space and then some, spreading my legs wider to accommodate him.

He tugged on my bottom lip with his teeth, then moved to my ear, brushing his lips over the sensitive shell. "You want this to stop? Tell me. Don't like what I'm doing? Tell me. I get close to a boundary, tell me." His eyes met mine as he lifted his head. "Understand?"

"Yes." That was the only word he was going to hear from me.

His hand caressed the nape of my neck before sliding into my hair. "You're so damned beautiful. There's *no one* like you, Allie."

I took hold of his vest and pulled him back to my mouth. He groaned into the kiss, the sound flooding me with a feeling of power as I worked the buttons free, then tugged the garment off with a little help from him. I started on the buttons of his shirt as his mouth fell to my neck, and I fumbled once or twice as he worshipped every sensitive place he'd discovered at the beach, drawing a gasp, then a whimper from my lips.

He'd remembered exactly what I'd liked and used the knowledge to flip every switch I had until I was practically humming. My thighs clenched in anticipation. This was going to be so damned good. It already was and we were both still clothed.

I yanked his shirt free from his pants as he moved into new territory, his lips brushing over every inch of skin beneath my collarbone, slowing to explore the swells of my breasts as his hand slid along the slit in my dress and up my thigh.

"Off," I demanded, tugging on his shirt.

He grinned against my skin, then let me go only long enough for the shirt to hit the floor. I splayed my hands across his chest when he leaned in to kiss me and pushed gently. He took the hint and stood straight.

Holy fucking *yes*.

I sighed in pure feminine appreciation as I looked, and looked, and looked, taking all the time I'd deprived myself of at the beach.

Dancers were long and lean—even the guys. Hudson was massive, packed with perfectly chiseled muscle, from the curved lines of his pecs to the sculpted ridges of his abdomen. I'd seen him shirtless, but now I *stared*, fighting off the one word that wouldn't leave my brain: *mine.*

I'd never felt possessive over anyone except him, and now I had him.

"How are you real?" My eyes locked with his as I traced the dips along his abs. They tensed under my touch.

"You're surrounded by professional dancers," he reminded me, a smirk playing across his lips. "You see athletic bodies all the time."

"Not like this." I followed the deep fuck-me lines to his waistband. "Not like you." My body burned a degree hotter just looking at him.

He pounced, capturing my mouth in a dizzying kiss. "I'm trying to be good, but saying things like that will get you fucked, Allie."

"Yes, please," I replied against his mouth.

We lost control of the kiss as it turned blatantly carnal, and I worked my arms out of the straps of my dress, trusting the boning in the bodice to keep it upright as his hand stroked up my thigh. I ripped my mouth away, gasping for air when his fingers skimmed the sensitive line along the silk fabric of my thong.

He sank his other hand into my hair and tugged. My back arched as I threw my hands out behind me, and my dress slid to my waist, leaving my breasts bare.

"Damn," he muttered, his gaze moving over me with a look of pure hunger that made my heart pound even faster. "Could you be any more perfect?" His mouth closed over a nipple, flicking it with his tongue, and I moaned at the jolt of white-hot need that streaked through me.

God, that felt good. It was somehow even better when he moved to my other breast and started all over again. My hips jerked and he traced the elastic of my underwear from my hip all the way down my inner thigh to my center. An inch to the left and he'd be right where I needed him.

He was turning me into a puddle, melting me with his mouth and with the light, stroking teases of his fingers. I needed more. I'd never felt this urgent before, like the world might actually end if he didn't touch me, didn't appease the steadily growing ache between my thighs.

"Now would be a good time to tell me to stop." His fingers stroked over my core, a tiny scrap of fabric separating us, and he scraped his teeth over my nipple before lifting his head to look me in the eye.

"More." Like hell were we stopping.

"Allie?" He leaned in and brushed his lips over mine as his fingers dipped beneath the edge of my underwear. "I think those first five minutes are up. Want to extend?"

"Oh my God, Hudson, just touch me." I balanced on one hand and held on to the back of his neck with the other.

He studied every detail of my expression as his fingers found me, and then his eyes slid shut as he groaned. "Fuck, *Allie*. You're soaking wet."

I gasped as he brushed my clit.

His eyes flew open, and I wasn't sure what turned me on more, the circles he started tracing with his fingers around but not over my clit, or the way he looked at me like I was the answer to every question he'd ever asked. "Soft." Circle. "Hot." Circle. "Slick." Circle. "Flawless."

He moved his hand from the nape of my neck and down my back, fully supporting my weight when my back arched and my hips rocked, looking for friction, for pressure, for something to release the spiraling tension he constructed with each swirl of his fingers. I hooked my left leg around his hip and used the leverage to change the angle so his next stroke hit me right where I needed.

Holy *shit*. Pleasure shot through my veins, sharp and sweet.

My moan echoed off the walls. Again and again, I rocked against his hand, setting the pressure, the rhythm the way I liked it, chasing the high, the climax that hovered so close I could almost taste it.

"Tell me, love." He ghosted his mouth over mine as he withdrew slightly, denying me what I wanted. "Are you used to taking what you want?"

I threw my arms around his neck, kissed him in answer, and rocked my hips again, whimpering in frustration when he kept the touches light and teasing despite my best efforts.

"You are, aren't you?" His eyes searched mine, and I hated that he could speak coherently, that he was in full control while I squirmed. "You know exactly what your body needs to get there, and you take it. Quick. Easy. You have partners, not lovers."

"Yes." I bucked my hips again, and he backed off. I cried out in sheer frustration as the climax I'd been chasing slipped away. "What are you doing?"

"Denying you the little orgasm you almost took so I can ruin you with the one I'm going to give you." His fingers circled my clit, rebuilding what he'd flat-out stolen from me, and he lowered his mouth to my breast, swirling his tongue in the same pattern until that coiled need flared brighter and hotter than before.

Then he did it again, backing off right when I reached the edge and beginning over, building a hotter fire, winding a tighter spring until I was a writhing mess. My fingernails raked into his hair and down the back of his neck.

"Hudson." It was a plea.

His eyes flared, edged with hunger. "Say it again." His fingers slipped lower, and it dawned on me that I'd given up control . . . and gained power.

"Hudson." One long finger slid inside me. I gasped, and my walls clenched around the welcome intrusion. "Hudson." A second finger joined, and I whimpered at how fucking good the stretch felt. It had been so damned long. "Hudson," I whispered and arched my hips.

"So fucking hot." A groan rumbled through his chest, and I made it my life's mission to hear that sound again. "God, you're on fire for me, aren't you?"

I pulled his head down to mine and kissed him, then whispered, "Hudson."

"Yes." He claimed my mouth in a deep kiss as his fingers started moving, stroking deep and hard, keeping a steady, delicious, addictive rhythm that let me know exactly how he'd use his cock. It was too much and not nearly enough.

"I want you," I cried out against his mouth.

"I'm right here." His thumb stroked my clit as his fingers pumped, and that bright, spiraling tension drew all my focus inward.

My eyes fell shut as my thighs locked around his hand.

"Eyes on me, Allie," he demanded, and I complied, keeping my gaze locked on his as he curled his fingers to hit my G-spot.

Oh God. If he stopped, I'd die. I'd simply combust right here and cease to exist. My breaths came in ragged pants and my hips bucked for more.

He gave it, and the tension that enveloped me built to a breaking point. "You're right there, aren't you, love?"

"Hudson." It was barely a whisper as every muscle in my body tensed.

"Yes. So fucking mine," he whispered, and the next stroke was all it took.

I shattered. Wave after wave of pleasure broke over me, each just as intense as the last, cresting again and again as I cried out, holding on to Hudson like he was the only thing keeping me tethered to the world.

He brushed a kiss over my lips as I came down, then withdrew his hand. "You're stunning. A complete damn revelation. I could watch you come apart all day, every day, and never get bored." His gaze raked over me in awe and I smiled.

"You can't possibly say that after just one time." I reached for his belt.

He froze, staring at me with the strangest expression. Wonder? Shock?

"What?" My hands fell, inadvertently brushing his very hard cock.

"Do it again."

I found the buckle of his belt.

"Not that. Smile," he begged.

"What?" My mouth curved at the incredulous widening of his eyes.

"There she is. God, I've missed you." He kissed me long and hard, his fingers hooking into the straps of my thong and pulling the silk down my thighs, his mouth only leaving mine when he tugged the fabric completely off.

The absolutely ravenous look he gave me sent heat flooding through my body again, taking me by surprise. Usually, I was a one-and-done kind of girl, but need sparked deep within me as he moved between my thighs. Holy shit—I didn't just want to get him off, I really *wanted* him.

I sat up and fused my mouth to his, stroking my tongue behind his teeth. His fingers dug into my hips as I reached between us and gripped him through his pants. Hot. Hard. Thick. Exactly what I needed.

His groan was the kind of sound I wanted to record and play back over and over, but he caught me off guard when he captured my hands and pulled them off his body.

"Hudson?" I asked between kisses as he laid me back against the granite.

"I keep my promises." He slid off me and sank between my thighs, then shoved the wreckage of my dress up to my waist.

Oh *shit*. "Hudson, I'm not usually able to come twice."

"Challenge accepted." He settled his mouth over me, and I cried out at the first drag of his tongue over my hypersensitive clit. Our eyes locked as he did it again, and my back arched.

"You taste better than I ever dreamed. And I dreamed for years, Allie." He pulled my thighs over his shoulders and dragged my ass to the edge of the island. "Eleven long years."

My head fell back as he licked and sucked, teased and tortured. Every stab of his tongue had me keening, every flick against my clit had me gasping for more. I writhed under the intense pleasure as it built and spiraled, bordering the point of pain, and I speared my fingers through his hair to pull him away, but held him closer instead. "Oh my God, don't stop."

He didn't.

"Hudson," I whimpered, my head thrashing as he drove me relentlessly toward a peak I didn't know existed. He stopped teasing and flat-out devoured me.

And when my legs tensed, he only went harder, using the flat of his tongue and thrusting his fingers inside me until I trembled, my body so impossibly tight that my choice was either come, or die right there on my kitchen island with Hudson between my thighs.

He drove the point of his tongue against my clit and I shouted something that sounded like his name as my body flew apart, the tension within me snapping violently. My hips bucked against his face and he threw an arm over my lower stomach, pinning me in place as he stroked me through the most intense orgasm of my life.

By the time I came down, I was completely limp, a puddle of satiated bliss.

"It wasn't bluster," I managed between the gulping breaths I took to steady my heart.

He fucking grinned, that dimple in his cheek appearing for a heartbeat as he gently took my legs from his shoulders and let them dangle off the edge of the island as he stood. The heat in his eyes as he looked me over had me pushing against the granite to sit up.

"Now." I undid his buckle before he got some wild idea to see if he could ruin me for a third time.

"Allie," he whispered with an edge of desperation, his cock straining against his pants as I—

The sound of a key turning in the lock registered a second before the front door opened, slamming into the doorstop.

I *froze*, my fingers poised on Hudson's waistband.

"Fuck," he growled, then moved faster than I'd ever seen. He jerked my bodice upright and yanked me off the island, setting me on my feet so my dress fell into place, then pinning my hips to the counter with his to steady my wobbly knees. His cock was harder than granite and pressed against my stomach in a screaming denial I agreed with.

This was *not* happening.

"You guys here?" Eva called out, her heels clicking on the floor as Hudson pulled my zipper up. She rounded the corner into the kitchen. "There you—" Her eyes flew wide and she spun, turning her back to us. "Oh my God. Are you two seriously . . ." She whipped back around. "We *eat* in here." She gestured to the barstools at the end of the island, then did a double take, staring at Hudson's torso, and I shifted my body to block any potential view of his cock. Clothed or naked, it was mine, not for Eva's to see. "Wow. I mean. *Wow.*" She gave me a thumbs-up. "Good for you, Allie."

I wanted the floor to swallow me whole. Right now.

Her gaze dropped to the floor, but it wasn't Hudson's shirt that had her attention. I followed her line of sight and promptly wished for death. She pointedly lifted her brows at my hot-pink thong. "And good for you, Hudson."

"Eva!" My voice cracked.

"Right." She turned her back on us. "Sorry to interrupt what was clearly a good time. I saw you race out of the gala and left right after dinner in case you needed an ear, but clearly you have something *much* better to comfort you."

I buried my head in Hudson's chest, and he pressed his mouth to my hair.

"Anyway, I guess I'll head up to bed." She walked down the hall toward the steps that led upstairs. "I think Anne is staying at her place tonight, so feel free to continue the kitchen escapades. Just keep it down. The walls are thin, and I do *not* need that in my life. Oh, and for fuck's sake, bleach those counters before you cook anything on them."

The sound of her bedroom door closing let me finally take a full breath.

"That didn't just happen." I lifted my head.

"Oh, it did." Hudson grabbed his clothes off the floor, then handed me my underwear. "Which is precisely why I live alone."

Because he didn't want to be interrupted with the multitude of women he brought home?

The thought gave me the instant ick.

But he was entitled to do whatever he wanted, as soon as our charade was up. In seven weeks he'd be free and clear . . . because I wasn't going to keep him. I couldn't. There was no way to trust someone who'd already abandoned me at my most vulnerable.

And yet, I'd just blatantly used him. Twice. And he'd *let* me.

What the hell was wrong with me?

"Whatever you're thinking, stop." He took my chin between his thumb and forefinger and tilted my face toward his. He really did have the most remarkable eyes.

"I used you to quell my anger." Guilt twisted around my rib cage. "I'm sorry."

"I'm not." He backed up a step, letting his hand fall from my face. "But I am glad we stopped. I'd like you to fuck me because you want me."

Mortification curved my shoulders. "I did want—"

"Only want," he clarified, tilting his head to the side. "No, need. Need is better. None of the other bullshit, just need." He glanced down the hall. "I'm going to sleep in the guest bedroom. Don't worry, I'll be up before Eva notices."

"Are you . . ." God, I'd felt how hard he was. "Okay?"

He nodded once. "Nothing deflates me faster than the sight of your little sister."

"Right." I wrapped my arms around my waist. "I'm really sorry. It won't happen again."

"Don't threaten that." He shoved his arms through his shirt and crossed the distance between us. "I meant what I said. Every word of it. And if you want to use someone for an escape, then it's me you'll be using. Sure, I'd like you to fuck me because you need me, but I'll take you however I can get you, Allie."

"I feel like an ass."

"Really?" He glanced down my body like he'd seen me naked. Which he kind of had. "I would think you'd be feeling nice and relaxed after I got you there twice."

My lips parted.

A cocky smirk played across his face as he backed away. "What was it you said I should do? Fuck you so well that you'd never want to leave my bed, and dish out orgasms? Two down, and infinity to go. Sounds to me like it's going according to plan." He turned away and walked down the hall to the guest bedroom.

Ugh. He'd definitely delivered on the orgasms.

Present me officially hated past me. We couldn't do that again.

This time I meant it.

CHAPTER
TWENTY-ONE

Allie

TigerPrideTendu: INCREDIBLE technique.
They should have put YOU in as understudy,
or just given you the role to start with.

June rolled into July, and I settled into what I'd called my Haven Cove routine, rehearsing all day, teaching Juniper in the evenings, and keeping at least ten feet away from Hudson at all times.

Especially right now, since he was working out shirtless in our pool as Juniper moved through a new routine in the studio. Thank God the only windows that looked into the backyard were at the end of the room—the gym, and not up here, where I needed to concentrate.

He hadn't brought up our night in New York, probably because we hadn't had a reason to be alone, nor had we faked it, since there were no family events for Caroline to pick at me. Then again, no family events meant I hadn't had a chance to win Caroline over yet either. We were getting further and further into this charade, and all I'd done was get way too attached to a little girl I had no right to. At least three times a week, Hudson brought Juniper by the house after work, then swam until it was time for her to head home.

I glanced at the clock. In a few minutes, he'd get out of the pool, walk up the porch, and head into the downstairs bathroom, where he'd get changed into dry clothes. Which meant I could stop fighting the impulse to run a sporadic mile on the treadmill just for an excuse to stare. Not like I needed a reminder of what he looked like; I saw him hovering over me, gloriously shirtless, every time I closed my eyes.

I couldn't go there again, not with him wanting this to be real, but in a way, it already . . . was. Without a reason to put on a show, we were simply ourselves, and while I wasn't exactly letting him, I wasn't cold-shouldering him.

Juniper finished the routine with a flourish, and I hit pause on the remote in my hand, killing the classical music.

Her smile fell and her shoulders dipped. "I did it better earlier."

"Earlier you weren't as tired, and I think you did great."

"You always say that," she muttered, picking at her skirt.

"No, this afternoon I said your turnout was lazy." I walked to the closet beside the studio doors and tucked the remote away next to the stereo. "When I give you a compliment, I mean it."

We moved through a stretching session for cooldown.

"Are you excited to come camping this week?" she asked as we moved into our legs.

"I don't know enough about the trip to call it excited." I couldn't afford to take the days off training for the trip, not with Charlotte breathing down my back and scheming to take my role, but I couldn't lose an opportunity to spend time with Caroline either. Three days of being examined by Hudson's sister only to be found wanting wasn't exactly my idea of fun, but it was our last scheduled chunk of time together, so I needed to make what progress I could before this whole thing blew up in our faces.

"It's the best." Juniper grinned, leaning into another stretch. "We rent these little cabins right by the lake. They're not fancy, no electricity or anything, just a couple twin-sized beds with kinda lumpy mattresses." Her nose crinkled. "The center one is the best because it's closest to the outhouse, for—you know—"

"Gotcha." I moved into position to work my hip flexors. "Lumpy mattresses, twin beds, outhouse."

"Grandma and Grandpa push their beds together. Mom and Dad used to do that too." Her voice trailed off. "I used to sleep with my cousins in cabin four, with the bunk beds, but after Dad died, Mom got nervous about me being so far away—the lake and all—so now I sleep in hers. But maybe this summer she'll let me go back with Mason and Melody."

"Maybe." A pang of sympathy smarted in my chest. It was understandable that Caroline had anxiety when it came to Juniper. "When my dad died, the three of us took turns staying at Mom's house until she felt ready to be alone. It's really nice of you to be a comfort to her."

Her brow furrowed as she twisted, stretching her back. "How did Grandpa die?" She flinched. "You don't have to answer. I don't want you to have a panic attack."

Like I had when talking about Lina.

"No, it's okay. Talking about his death is easier since I wasn't a part of it, I guess." That pang bloomed into an ache. "He slipped coming out of their brownstone in the snow. Hit a patch of ice and broke his neck. He died instantly, which I'm thankful for, but it felt like a really stupid way to die when it happened." Pointless, even.

"I'm sorry," she said softly, then twisted to the other side. "Nothing genetic, though."

"Just an accident." I shook my head, and my stomach hollowed. She needed to be tested. Genetics and medical history were the least of what Juniper was owed, and we could only give her half of that without knowing who her father was.

"Back to camping," Juniper said as we both settled in to stretch our calves.

"Bug spray and sunscreen?" My muscles screamed, but I kept my face flat. Too much time on pointe meant I was going to have to use the ball tonight to release the muscle.

"Absolutely, and you should bring a good sleeping bag, because it can get cold," she added. "Oh, and lanterns are really good too. Cabin two is probably second best because it's closest to the pavilion, so you can smell breakfast cooking in the morning." Her eyes lit up, and I couldn't help but smile. Her excitement was contagious. "Mom always makes me eggs in a basket, which are my favorite, and then usually packs a picnic lunch, too, since we don't usually stay at the campsite all day."

"What do you do?" I muscled back a grimace and started working the left.

"Hike. Zip-line. Rope swing into the deeper part of the lake— you're going to love that." She grinned.

"Ummm . . ." I pressed my lips between my teeth.

"Allie here isn't what you'd call a risk-taker," Hudson answered from the doorway.

My gaze flew to his. Man, he looked good. *Really* good. His hair was still wet, and his blue T-shirt stretched across muscles I hadn't had nearly enough time to explore. Knowing I could if I wanted to yet choosing to abstain was a particular brand of torture.

"I'll take you however I can get you."

Yeah, those words had starred in some pretty detailed dreams this week.

"That's not true," I argued. "I take risks."

"Says the woman who didn't learn to ride a bike until sixteen." When he'd taught me. He lifted a brow at me.

"Mom wasn't keen on anything that could possibly lead to injury." I stood and tried like hell to ignore the appreciation in Hudson's gaze as it skimmed over my leggings and sports bra combo.

"Or fun," he added. "Let's see if I can remember correctly. No bikes, no scooters, definitely no motorcycles. No trampolines—"

"You remedied most of that, and if you had any idea how many kids are injured on trampolines, you wouldn't fault her for that one." I hadn't caved on the motorcycle until I was seventeen.

Juniper traded her slippers for flip-flops and put the rest of her things in her bag.

"—no sports—" Hudson continued.

"I'd argue that ballet is a sport," Juniper interjected, and I held up my hand. She high-fived it as she walked by, heading for Hudson.

"Oh, and definitely no boys." He shook his head. "How does she feel about men when it comes to her daughters nowadays?"

"She trusts us to make our own choices." I shrugged. "And I don't tell her a lot. She knows about us, though."

He tensed, and it must have been a lighting thing, because it looked like he paled a little too. "And how did she take that?"

"Like Mom." There was no chance I was repeating her heinous remarks.

"Yeah, that's what I'm worried about," he said slowly, patting Juniper's head as she walked out the studio doors.

"Relax." A smile tugged at the edges of my mouth. "She's not going to burst in here and throw you out or threaten to ground me for a million years. She made some snide comment like always and then dismissed it." I walked his way. "I didn't exactly tell her the truth, and I guess she figures we won't last long enough to throw a fit over. Besides, she's mostly still angry at me for blowing the *Giselle* performance and embarrassing her." The admission slipped out. Shit, it was getting too easy to do that around him.

His brow knit. "Your Achilles snapped. How is that embarrassing to her?"

I tugged my bottom lip between my teeth and debated a flippant reply that would keep some emotional distance between us. But in this house, in this room, it was almost easy to forget the last decade had happened. He was just Hudson, the boy who'd pulled me out of the water and forced me out of my comfort zone, who'd given endless support without a single hint that he'd ever wanted more than my friendship.

"I've waited eleven years to kiss you." I'd never had a clue.

Unless that's what he'd wanted to talk about that night.

"Can you meet me at the cove tonight?" A younger version of Hudson's voice slipped through my head, and I blinked at the patchy memory. Trying to remember that day felt like hiking in thick fog. Wisps of clarity came and went without ever getting a full picture. But I remembered he'd asked me to skip the end of the Company social—where contracts were ceremoniously awarded like trophies—to talk that night.

And I couldn't remember why, but I knew I hadn't showed. Lina and I had been on our way back from the social when she—

"Allie?" Hudson prompted, leaning into my space. "You okay?"

I blinked. My ankle, we'd been talking about my ankle. "I should have prevented it." So much for a flippant reply. "I knew I needed to rest it, that the responsible move was to call in Charlotte and take the night—maybe the rest of that month—off. I ignored the signs and went on, anyway. I took a risk, lost my footing, and now I have to deal with the consequences." I heard the front door open, then close. "Did Juniper just leave?" I started toward the doors.

"I have the keys, so at least she can't drive off." His hand brushed my lower back as we passed through the studio doors.

We walked into the foyer and my stomach hit the floor.

Juniper hadn't left, and she wasn't alone.

Eva stood just inside the door, her sunglasses perched on her head, a canvas bag over her shoulder as she stared down at Juniper in clear confusion.

"Aunt Allie, look!" Juniper beamed. "Aunt Eva's here!"

Oh *shit*. Hudson's hand flexed on my back.

"*Aunt* Eva?" Eva repeated, her gaze jumping to me, then toward the living room as Anne scurried in, tugging off her reading glasses. "I know you two have been here all summer, but one of you seriously had time to produce an entire kid?"

This was bad. So, so, *so* bad.

CHAPTER TWENTY-TWO

Allie

Ballet4Life97: Are you trying to mix Vaganova with Balanchine? Because it's not working for you.

"You should have told me you were coming," Anne said, clasping Eva in an awkward hug. "I would have made up your room for you."

"Or at least put away the kid," Eva muttered as Anne stepped back, sending a worried look my direction. "Seriously, though. What's going on?" She let her bag fall from her shoulder to the ground.

"I'm Juniper Mecarro," Juniper answered. "Sean and Caroline Mecarro's daughter, but Lina was my biological mother. Or first mom. Or birth mom. Depends on what terminology you like. I prefer biological mother, but I reserve the right to change my mind as I grow."

"Lina?" Eva's startled gaze flew to mine and I nodded. She got the same response from Anne. "Lina had a kid no one knew about, then—"

Her plucked brows furrowed. "Caroline Mecarro, as in your sister?" she asked Hudson.

"That would be her," Hudson answered, his hand warm and steady on my back.

"Let me guess, Gavin's her father." She studied Juniper as a science experiment.

My heart stuttered at the possibility, but Hudson shook his head. "No. I took a DNA test after Allie did just to rule him out."

"You never told me that," I whispered, which seemed foolish, since everyone could hear.

"Figured it wasn't a big deal since there's no blood relation." His thumb stroked down my bare spine in a soothing rhythm.

"Great, so who's her father?" Eva asked, tugging her long brown hair over her shoulder.

"We don't know," Juniper answered, and her brow furrowed. "Your Seconds this morning was kind of mean."

Eva's head snapped toward our niece. "I was showing proper technique in piqué turns, and aren't you a little young for social media?"

"Looked to me like you were showing that you could have danced *Giselle* better, since you used performance footage to compare. Didn't even monitor the comments trashing Allie." She shrugged. "But what would I know. I'm ten."

Eva had *what*? My back stiffened.

"Huh." Eva flashed a performance smile at Hudson. "Cute kid."

"Thanks." Juniper grinned, flashing a set of little dimples at the lower edges of her mouth, and Eva's eyes narrowed.

"Let's go before this gets any more awkward." Hudson's hand slipped from my back, and I pretended I didn't immediately miss it. "Allie, I'll pick you up Monday?"

"Eight a.m.," I agreed. "See you in a couple days, Juniper."

"Bye!" She waved at us. "You're going to have so much fun camping with us!" she promised as Hudson ushered her out the door, then closed it behind them.

"Eva," Anne started.

"Don't you think it's time to take off the rings?" Eva interrupted, leaving her bag in the foyer and heading for the living room. "I know a few guys, if you're ready to get back out there. A few girls too."

"Oh." Anne ghosted her thumb across her wedding and engagement rings. "No. Not yet."

I stared at Eva like the wild card she was. What would she do with the information about Juniper's existence? She could be petty when pissed, but I didn't see her running to Caroline out of spite.

"So, I don't know what's weirder." Eva picked up Anne's book from the armchair and shut it, then set it on the end table as she sat. "That Lina apparently had a kid when no one was looking, or that you're going camping."

"I'm happy to see you, but what are you doing here?" I perched on the edge of the couch, far enough from my phone to not give in to temptation and see what people were saying under whatever scathing video Eva had posted. Anne took the seat beside me.

"As if my showing up at the family beach house is more peculiar than what just happened there?" She gestured to the foyer. "We finished the summer performances last night—thanks for coming, by the way, Allie."

I dropped my gaze, regret gnawing on my insides. The only thing going back to New York had shown me was that I wasn't quite sure I liked who I was when I was there. If I even *knew* who I was. I'd only felt like myself around Hudson.

"I already told you, it's hard on her," Anne chastised.

"Don't cover for me." I looked Eva in the eye. "I'm sorry. I'll do better next time."

"You'll be back for next time." She shrugged, kicking off her shoes before tucking her legs under her. "I brought you a few bagels from that shop you like down the block, since I thought you might be missing the city."

"Thanks." As an apology for whatever she'd posted? "That was sweet of you."

"Oh, and Vasily announced the fall program." She looked at me knowingly.

"On the website?" *Breathe.* Vasily frequently changed his mind. Just because he told me *Equinox* would be one of our three selections for fall didn't mean it actually would be. Not until he made it public.

"On the website." She grinned and her eyes lit up. "He listed *Equinox*, Allie. You'll finally have a role created just for you! Congratulations!"

The air rushed out of my lungs.

"That's amazing!" Anne leaned over and squeezed my shoulders. "I can't wait to see it."

Joy, disbelief, pride, every emotion flooded me simultaneously, but anxiety fisted my heart hardest. "He listed it. We'll really get to do it." I smiled, choosing to let the joy win.

"Casting is TBD, of course, not that everyone doesn't know it will be you and Everett, but . . ." Hope flared in Eva's eyes. "I figured if you helped me for a day or two, I'd have a leg up when rehearsals start and I'd have a shot at getting soloist. Please say yes."

"Did Isaac put out the choreography?" That should still be six weeks away.

"No, but everyone knows he's fucking Charlotte, and she's been . . ." She shifted in her seat uncomfortably. "She's been practicing, Allie. I've seen her in the studio hours after everyone else, with Isaac. If you're not ready, she's gunning for your part."

Nausea turned my stomach. "She's a soloist. If I'm not ready, the part will go to Reagan or Candace. They're principals."

"You'll be ready," Anne declared.

No, I was about to take *days* off to frolic in the woods. Shit.

"So Lina really had a kid?" Eva changed subjects so fast it gave me whiplash. "Why would she give her to Caroline? She hates us." Her nose scrunched. "Caroline's cool with her being here? I'm pretty sure she'd rather set fire to our house then let her daughter hang out."

"She doesn't know," Anne told her. "Not yet. We'll tell you every-thing we know—"

"No need." Eva shrugged. "She's cute. Totally looks like Lina's pic-tures, but I doubt I'll see her much."

"We're hoping to change that." Anne flashed an optimistic smile.

"Why?" She took Anne's water bottle from the end table, twisted the lid, and took a drink. "If she's happy, then leave her be. Obviously Lina didn't want us interfering or she would have told us." She set the water down. "But you really don't know who her father is?"

"No." Anne stiffened. "We figure it has to be someone from San Francisco."

"Huh." She stood, then threw her arms above her head, stretching. "I'd ask Jacob. I think he was out there around that time. Spent a couple years in their corps. He might know who she was screwing. Are you seriously going camping?" She addressed that question to me.

"Yes." I nodded. "Trying to get in Caroline's good graces so she won't file a restraining order when we tell her we're Juniper's biological family." She was right: Jacob would be a good place to start. Everyone else I knew and trusted had started and stayed in New York.

"For how long?"

"Three days," I answered.

"You're going to take *three days* off training to go hang out in the woods?" Her voice rose. "You can't afford the time off."

"She can," Anne argued, tucking her curls behind her ears. "She needs a life outside the Company. We're encouraging this, Eva." Her tone shifted into something close to Mom's.

"We're encouraging her fucking off and not taking her position or upcoming role seriously in order to spend time with a kid Lina didn't *want* us to know she had?" She scoffed. "Super responsible, Allie. Mom would be so proud."

"Low blow." I stood. "I'll make up the days, and my therapist thinks it's a good idea. Getting out of the studio and camping," I clari-fied. "Not the lying to Caroline. I'm going to go pack."

"I don't get how you can have *everything*, and not fight to keep it," Eva said, following me out into the foyer. "I would kill to have half your talent, and you just piss it away. It's so unfair."

"Stop fighting," Anne ordered.

"Is that what the video was about?" I reached the first step, then turned around. "Retribution for not going last night? Or showing the world that you're more talented? Are you so desperate to prove your worth that you need a million people to tell you that you're better than I am? Is the validation you get worth throwing me under the bus of the internet?"

Her face fell. "Our follower count was stagnant, and you hadn't filmed any rehab content, and you agreed to let me use footage of you—"

"I agreed to help my sister!" The shout filled the empty halls of the house.

"We both know they just want to see *you*!" Her hands curled. "You're *Alessandra Rousseau*—everyone in the world loves you, worships you, validates you! I'm just the little sister the Company let in to keep you happy."

"That's bullshit, and you know it." I shook my head. No one knew me well enough to love me—except my sisters. "Vasily doesn't do nepotism. He didn't hire Lina that first season, remember? He'd made her work for it, develop another year before trying out again, just like you. Stop playing the pity card, Eva."

"Right." Eva drew the word out sarcastically. "Because Maxim's last name has nothing to do with his role as a choreographer." She rolled her eyes. "Drop the humble facade and admit it for once. You're the queen—"

"Stop it!" Anne put herself between us, throwing out her arms and flaring her hands. "You will stop it right now! We're *never* out here together, and you two will not do this." Her gaze jumped between us. "This isn't what Mom had in mind when she wanted us to spend more time together—"

"Let's call up Mom and ask her." Eva reached for her pocket, then looked at me. "Or are you only getting one-word answers? She's still ashamed of you, isn't she?"

My fingernails dug into the banister.

"Enough!" Anne snapped. "You know damn well Dad wouldn't stand for you talking about her like that, and Lina would have—" She snapped her mouth shut and took a deep breath.

Guilt slammed into me with the force of a semitruck, and Eva looked away, wrapping her arms around her waist.

"We're all that's left, guys," Anne said softly. "It's just the three of us. No one has had an easy year, but we have to do better, be better for each other. We just do."

I deflated. We were the only three pylons left on the pier. We wouldn't make it through another storm if we didn't lean on each other. If it made Eva feel better to post an already public video of my injury, then fine. It was a small price to pay for my sister to get whatever she needed from that stupid app.

"I'm sorry," Eva whispered, slowly raising her eyes toward mine. "I'll take it down."

"Thank you. And I'm truly sorry. I should have gone last night." I glanced at Anne and sighed at the desperation in her pleading eyes. Out of the three of us, she was the one whose world was in upheaval, and she deserved better than this. The least I could do was help smooth things over. "I'll help you," I told Eva. "I have two days before I leave with Hudson, and I'll teach you what I know about the soloist parts for *Equinox*."

"Thank you!" Eva lit up, but it was the relief in Anne's eyes that made it worth it.

Metal clinked above me, and I looked up the stairs to see Sadie trotting down, freshly awake from her nap. "Hey, girl."

"Holy shit, you have a *dog*?" Eva exclaimed. "What the hell is going on around here?"

"Just go with it," Anne lectured. "That's our new motto."

We worked all weekend, taking breaks only to ice our feet, and by the time Eva left Monday morning she had a good grip on most of the choreography. She'd left her room a mess, and ransacked Lina's closet when she needed an extra sweater, but at least she'd felt more confident when she left for the airport.

My motivation for working myself to the bone had been Charlotte. Like hell was she taking the role that had been created for me. But while the days in the studio had invigorated Eva, they'd shown me how far I still had to go in my recovery. I'd fallen more times than I cared to admit, mostly due to being out of shape for pointe, lack of confidence, and fear of reinjuring my ankle. Out of the three, the fear was a real career killer. If I couldn't get past it, I may as well retire.

"You've been quiet the whole drive," Hudson said as we pulled into the gravel parking lot near the lake. "Should I worry?"

"No. Just preoccupied." We got out of the truck, and I stared up at the thick canopy of beautiful foliage from the trees. It was peaceful out here. "I forgot to tell you. I called Jacob a few days ago—you met him at the gala—"

"Harvey. Principal dancer. I remember." Hudson reached into the jam-packed truck bed and tossed me my backpack, a framed little number Anne had insisted I buy for the trip.

"Thanks." I slung it over my shoulders as I took stock of whose cars were already in the parking lot. *Everyone's.* "He said he remembers Lina getting injured in January and taking a leave of absence to heal. Apparently, it was why he hadn't questioned why I don't rehab at the Company. He figured it was just the way our family recovered."

"He didn't know she was pregnant," Hudson guessed, grabbing his bag.

"Nope." I clipped the strap across my chest. "Back to the drawing board."

"Shit. Well, let's get you a tour and settled in at the cabin, and I'll come back for the rest of the gear," Hudson said, slipping on his own pack.

"I'll follow your lead." I offered a small smile.

He grinned, then laced his fingers with mine as we started down the wide graveled trail. "Just in case anyone's watching," he whispered, then lifted the back of my hand and pressed a kiss to it.

My chest went all warm and gooey. There was no one out here and we both knew it, but I didn't snatch my hand back.

"You ready to spend three whole days with the Ellis crew?" he asked.

"I'll be Caroline's favorite by the time we leave," I promised, mostly to hype myself up.

"You're already mine."

I rolled my eyes, but the warmth in my chest burned brighter. "This isn't real, you know."

"You keep telling yourself that, Allie." He squeezed my hand. "Besides, for the next three days it is. By the time we leave, I will have convinced you to give it a go for the summer."

"So arrogant." I fought a smile as we started down a steeper portion of the trail and the edge of the lake came into view. "We're not pushing our beds together."

"How would you know about pushing beds together?" He glanced sideways at me with a definite smirk.

"Juniper told me all about it." My thighs protested the angle of decline, and I fought to push the pain away. Every freaking muscle in my body ached from too many hours in the studio with Eva. "And that the best cabin is four because it's near the outhouse."

He laughed, and the sound did absolutely nothing to dispel the sweet, inconvenient pressure behind my ribs. In fact, it freaking *fed* it. "I like seven, personally. It's closer to the water, but we're late, so I'm sure one of my uncles already took it. And don't worry. We won't push the beds together until you ask."

I waved away a flying bug. "Not happening." I'd liquefy into a puddle the second he put his mouth on me, and my survival required I remain in solid forms at all times. Rigid, even.

"We'll see." This time his dimple popped and I quickly looked away. The man was too gorgeous for his own good, and way too gorgeous for mine.

"Hudson! Allie!" Mrs. Ellis called out, grinning wide as we reached the pavilion. The covered patio held four picnic tables and a grill, and had a stellar view of the tree-lined lake. She hugged us both, and I accepted the warm embrace a little more naturally than I had at the beach. "It's good to see you two." She handed Hudson a key with a mini canoe paddle attached. "You're in nine."

"That's yours," he argued. "I'm not taking your favorite cabin."

"Well, the rest are all full"—she peeked over her purple-striped glasses—"so he who arrives late will take what is offered to him with grace and gratitude. Everyone else is unpacking, so get to it."

"But it's *yours*." He glanced at me like there was any chance in hell I was getting in the middle of this, and I put my hands up. No way was I causing a fight before we even unpacked.

"Your dad wanted four. Nine is the farthest away, and apparently, he ate something last night that just—"

"Say no more." Hudson's hand closed around the key. "Looks like we're in nine."

"Lead the way." I adjusted my backpack on my shoulders.

"Oh, and they remodeled nine, eight, *and* seven this year," Mrs. Ellis noted with an excited smile. "Tell us what you think. I bet six, five, and four will be done by next summer."

"Will do," he promised.

"Lunch is at twelve," she reminded him before turning to me. "Allie, we're so pleased you could join us. If at any time Caroline acts like a sour fish, treat her like one and toss her ass in the lake."

My mouth dropped open, but she turned and headed down one of the paths to what I assumed was cabin four.

A five-minute hike later, we stood just inside the open doorway of cabin nine, staring at the cozy primitive-style interior with more than a little shock.

"This isn't happening," I whispered.

Hudson rubbed the back of his neck. "Let's ask someone to trade."

"Absolutely not. They'll think I'm an asshole," I hissed, looking around the twelve-by-twelve space like there was any other solution. Somehow we'd stumbled into every cliché in one of Anne's romance novels.

"I mean . . . on the bright side, we won't have to push the beds together," Hudson noted.

"Kind of impossible when there's only one of them."

CHAPTER
TWENTY-THREE

Hudson

NYFouette92: OMG. No way. The way I RAN
to the comments!!!

Waking up next to Allie ranked as one of my favorite lifetime moments. It was right above graduating from rescue swimmer school, and just below the first time I'd seen her clinging to that sinking boat, all flustered cheeks and big brown eyes.

I propped my head on my hand and shamelessly watched her sleep, her body curled toward mine even though we were in separate sleeping bags, and noted the dark circles her long lashes rested against. We'd come to bed early when I'd realized she'd fallen asleep against my shoulder next to the campfire, but even a good ten hours of sleep wasn't going to help the exhaustion she'd driven herself into. It had nothing to do with yesterday's hike, or the late-afternoon swim either.

"I don't want to wake you," I whispered. "But I know you love bacon, and if we wait any longer, there won't be any left." Not with my nieces and nephews running amok.

She rustled with a deep breath, then sank farther into the pillow.

"Allie," I said softly.

Her eyes fluttered open, and my heart lurched as she smiled at me. "Hudson," she murmured, then fell right back asleep.

Yeah, I could get used to waking up like this every single day for the rest of my life.

You can't even get her to agree to a summer. But I would.

If it wasn't for our mission to humanize Caroline, I would have let Allie sleep and brought back breakfast, but unfortunately, my sister would see that as Allie being spoiled instead of me being thoughtful.

"Hey, love," I tried again. "You'd better wake up or you'll have to catch the only protein you'll get for breakfast with a pole and a lure."

"I don't know how to fish," she muttered as her eyes opened again.

I grinned. "Well aware. We need to get moving."

She nodded with a groan of protest, and we both unzipped our bags. "Look at us, making it through the night without falling prey to the one-bed trope." Her feet hit the floor.

"The what?" We both rummaged through our packs on separate sides of the queen-size bed, pulling out clothes.

"You know, like in a book or a movie where the couple can't stand each other, but there's only one bed left at the inn, and they end up sleeping together." She turned her back, and I did the same, repeating the same awkward dance we'd done last night to get ready for bed. One-room cabins didn't exactly leave room for privacy, and neither of us was willing to risk being caught out on the porch while the other changed if any of my family happened to walk by.

"Don't worry." I yanked my shirt over my head. "We still have tonight."

"Shit," she muttered as I pulled on my shorts.

"Problem?" I focused on my socks and shoes to keep from turning around.

"I got marshmallow all over the front of my sweatshirt trying to help Juniper with s'mores last night, and now everything in the forest is stuck to it."

I reached into my bag and pulled out my black hoodie, then threw it backward over my head to her. "Take mine."

"I'm dressed. You can turn around," she said, a hint of—dare I think—happiness in her voice. "And thank you."

I tucked my phone into my pocket, just so I could snag some pictures, then turned and stared as Allie walked around the end of the bed.

Holy fucking hell was she perfect.

"Should we get going?" She pulled the wavy mass of her hair into some kind of topknot.

My hoodie swallowed her, shorts and all, leaving the impression that she was naked underneath, and drawing all my focus to those long flawless legs. Perfect, toned, silk-smooth legs I'd had over my shoulders, her thighs locking so beautifully tight around my head as I licked—

"Hudson?"

I swallowed. "Yeah, we should go."

"You all right?" She pushed the sleeves up her arms.

"Yep." I followed her out the door and into the crisp morning air. "Just remembering the way you taste." Honesty was the best policy . . . when possible.

She startled. "Well, good morning."

"Would have been a way better morning if I'd woken you up with an orgasm." We started down the worn path toward the other cabins. "I do enjoy breakfast in bed."

"You can't say things like that." Her cheeks flushed, and birds chirped in the trees.

"You like it when I say things like that." We passed cabin eight. "You also like it when I call you love, when I kiss the side of your neck, and you definitely like it when I use both my fingers and my tongue—"

She covered my mouth with her hand, bringing us to a standstill. I leaned into it and kissed the center of her palm.

Her eyes flared and her hand fell away. "Someone could hear."

"Is that your only protest?" I grinned.

She glanced at my mouth once. Twice. Then she sighed and whipped her head forward, pulling the sleeves of my hoodie down over her hands. "That's not happening again."

I caught up as she walked down the trail, picking up the pace as we passed seven. "So you said the first time."

"What is this, anyway?" She pointed to the logo above her chest.

"Nice change of subject. It's the rescue swimmer emblem." I looked her over, then put my eyes solidly on the trail. "You look good in my clothes." Shit, I was *not* prepared for the immediate swell of possessiveness in my chest.

"So others may live." She read it upside down.

"It's our motto." We passed six.

"As in you're willing to *die*?" She glared up at me.

"Kind of comes with the territory." I couldn't help but smile right into her narrowed eyes. "Come on, you knew what I wanted to do. You knew it was dangerous."

"Contemplating dream careers at sixteen is a little different than you actually flying off into potential death every day." Two lines appeared between her brows as she looked forward and we passed five.

"How's the reality of your dream career measure up to what you thought it would be?" We broke off the main path and took the smaller one toward what she'd called the outhouse but which was a full bathing station, indoor plumbing and everything.

"I don't know." She shook her head. "It's everything I wanted, and sometimes even better than I could have dreamt, especially when performing. But it's also so much worse."

"Hold on." I reached for her arm, stopping us just in front of the building. "Are you not happy?" Was I wrong in thinking the injury had sucked the joy out of her?

"Define happy." She lifted her brows. "I'm at the top of my game—or will be once I'm fully healed—and have a contract as a principal dancer at one of the most prestigious ballet companies in the world. I get to do what I love every single day and they pay me for it."

"Not that you need the money," I reminded her.

"I'm happy. Or at least content." She headed into the restroom.

"Right," I muttered as she closed the door.

A few minutes later—with brushed teeth—we headed into the chaos of the pavilion, which was in full breakfast mode.

Dad and Caroline stood at the flattop, laughing as they cooked, while Mom stacked the camping dishes to prepare to serve.

"Allie!" Juniper raced over and slammed into Allie, throwing her arms around her middle.

"Hey kiddo." Allie hugged her back, then smoothed the hair out of her eyes. "How did you sleep?"

I caught Caroline watching from the corner of my eye.

"Not bad!" She bounced back on her heels. "We're rope swinging today!"

"Oh." Allie tensed. "That sounds . . . exciting."

"You're going to have so much fun!" She ran off to play with the twins.

"And suddenly, I'm chopped liver." I brought my hand to my heart.

"Awh." Allie clasped my hand, leaned into me and smiled, crinkling her freckle-spattered nose. "Is Hudson not the favorite for the first time in his life?" Her eyes lit with mischief, and if I hadn't fallen for her eleven years ago, that look would have done it. Hook. Line. Sinker.

"Fine. You can be Juniper's favorite." I locked my arm around her waist and bent my head to hers. "As long as I'm yours." I kissed her, slow and sweet, savoring the hint of mint that clung to her lips. She rose up and kissed me back, and I seriously debated telling my family to fuck off so I could carry her back to our cabin, but I kept my tongue behind my teeth.

I was never going to get enough of this.

"Why did you two even bother getting out of bed?" Gavin asked as he walked by.

"Good question," I said against her mouth as I broke the kiss.

"Behave," Allie ordered, her smile turning my heart end over end.

"Not in my vocabulary." I let her go reluctantly so we could grab food, then mentally groaned when Allie sat at Caroline and Gavin's table. *Time to work.*

"Nice hoodie," Gavin said with a grin.

"Like it?" Allie glanced down. "I'm thinking of adding it to my Hudson's Hoodies collection." She bit into a piece of bacon.

If she used her teeth on me, I'd give her every hoodie I owned.

"So when's the big day for your promotion?" Caroline asked me.

"You're getting promoted?" Allie raised her eyebrows at me.

"You didn't know?" Caroline countered, then sipped her coffee.

"I hadn't told her." I narrowed my eyes on Caroline before turning toward Allie. "Because I don't know when it will happen. I made the list, but *when* you actually make rank depends on how many people they promote a month and how fast the list moves, so probably not until September. Maybe October."

"Congratulations." She smiled. Yeah, I was never going to get enough of *that* either.

"And where are you thinking of heading next, since your duty-station preferences are due like what . . . in a few weeks?" Gavin asked, side-eyeing Caroline.

"Your what?" Caroline fumbled her coffee but kept it from spilling. "You're not leaving, are you?"

"You get to choose where they assign you?" Allie asked.

I shot Gavin a look, and he had the nerve to shrug. "Kind of. My three years are almost done here. We give them a list of our top duty stations and they try to pair us according to the needs of the Coast Guard."

"Cape Cod is your top, right?" Panic crept into Caroline's eyes. "And what do you mean *try*?"

Allie slid her hand to my knee.

"Of course, I'll put Cape Cod as my top choice—"

Allie tensed and her hand spasmed.

"—but just like the rest of the military, I serve at the needs of the military. My promotion means I'll be looking to manage my own shop."

"Okay?" Caroline's brow furrowed.

"It's a job title. I don't just swim. We already have someone who manages the shop here, and if he stays, there won't be a slot for me. And if they let me stay anyway, it would . . ." Fuck, how did I say this to her?

"It would hold back his career," Gavin finished, setting his metal mug on the table. "Baby brother's gotta fly the coop if he wants to keep climbing the ladder."

Caroline stared, panic leaching into her blue eyes.

Fuck. I had one favor I could call in at the assignments desk, and that look meant I'd probably have to use it to stay.

"Is there a slot for you in Sitka?" Allie asked.

"There might be," I answered softly.

"It's what you've always wanted." She stroked her thumb along the outside of my knee and nodded, the corners of her mouth curving. I slid my fingers over Allie's and we both ate one-handed.

"You can't go to *Alaska*." Caroline shook her head. "What would . . ."

"You do?" Gavin interrupted. "That's what you're worried about, right? What *you* would do if he went and lived his life. You could, I don't know, take Mom and Dad up on their offer to help, or hire a babysitter like every other working parent in America."

Oh, shit. "Don't," I warned Gavin. "I can fight my own battles."

Caroline flinched. "Staying near your family is a *battle*?"

"That's not what I meant," I said quietly.

"You know the café makes almost *nothing* with the overhead," she hissed at Gavin.

"Sell the fucking thing. We all know you hate it." He gestured at Allie. "Even Allie probably knows you hate it and she only ate there when she was a kid."

Allie quickly took a drink of her coffee to avoid answering.

"Keep your voice down. Mom and Dad will hear you." Caroline dug in to her scrambled eggs. "They built it from the ground up and, contrary to popular belief, I love that place. It's just been harder to run on my own than I thought it would be. I never imagined I'd be doing it without Sean. I know how much you guys do for Juniper and I hate that I have to lean on you."

"We know," I said gently, and Gavin backed off.

"Is there anyone else you trust to keep an eye on her?" Allie asked carefully.

"Absolutely not." Caroline shook her head. "I've seen too many crime documentaries."

Allie cleared her throat. "She's welcome at our house if you need extra hands."

"Thank you." Caroline stiffened. "But we're not a charity case to take on so you Rousseau girls can feel good about yourselves. And I don't want a houseful of professional ballerinas distorting her body image or putting ideas into her head that I can't afford and don't support." She cringed, which was the only thing that saved her from me losing my shit. "Respectfully. Sorry, I've seen too many of those documentaries too."

"I understand." Allie popped a piece of bacon into her mouth, and I squeezed her hand supportively, then glared at Caroline.

She shot me an apologetic look and sagged in her seat.

The rest of breakfast passed in awkward silence, and I kept Allie's hand in mine the entire time.

"How about you and I do the dishes?" Allie asked me once we were done.

Caroline's jaw dropped.

"Excellent idea. I'm down for anything that gets you wet," I teased.

"Excuse us," Allie said to my siblings as she got up from the table. "I have to go wash his mouth out."

I happily followed.

"Don't tire him out," Gavin called after us. "We're rope swinging this afternoon!"

"Oh goody," she muttered.

"I don't think so," Allie said as we sat on a blanket near the lakeshore that afternoon, watching Gavin pull the rope swing up the steep embankment at the base of the giant tree. Years had washed away some of the dirt on the lake side of her roots, but she was still standing.

"You'll love it," Juniper promised, sitting between Allie's outstretched legs. Their toenails were the same color of pink. When had that happened?

"How deep is that water?" Allie asked, her fingers deftly braiding Juniper's hair. "What happens if he smacks into a tree? Or lands on someone? And it's humid today. What if your hands slip on the rope?"

"You're about as fun as Mom," Juniper accused.

"Meaning she's utterly delightful?" Caroline dropped down on Allie's other side and I shot her a warning look. "Thank you for braiding her hair. You didn't have to."

"No problem." Allie tied it off with an elastic. "Three sisters. I can braid in my sleep."

Three. She still counted Lina.

Gavin swung out on the rope, sitting on the barrel-top-size wooden disk that served as a seat, then let go at the highest point of the arc. He flew for no more than a second, then splashed into the water cannonball-style.

"Solid eight," I called out and clapped, and Juniper hollered.

"Mom, can I?" she asked.

"Go ahead. Just make sure there's someone in the water!" Caroline finished in a yell, because Juniper was already running for the tree where the twins waited.

"Takes after you." Allie nudged me, then drew her long legs up and wrapped her arms around her knees. She'd ditched the hoodie, and the hot-pink straps of her bikini peeked out of the collar of her MBC T-shirt.

"She does," Caroline agreed. "Maybe she'll be a rescue swimmer too."

"Or you could let her dance," I countered, my ire from this morning getting the best of me.

"Don't start." Caroline pulled her hair up.

"She could be one of the greats," I prodded, wrapping my arm around Allie's hip. "She'll never know if you don't let her try."

"Your perception is skewed by your proximity to the Rousseaus," Caroline replied, watching Juniper. "Talent like Allie's is rare."

Allie blinked. "While I think that might be the nicest thing you've ever said to me, I'd argue that Hudson's talent is far rarer."

Holy shit, was that a compliment? My head swung toward hers, finding her attention fixated on Mason as he swung out over the lake and splashed into the water.

"Than a professional ballerina?" Caroline reached for her backpack, taking out her sunscreen.

"Sure. There's about four thousand of us throughout the country, but only three hundred and fifty Coast Guard rescue swimmers." She leaned into me. "Makes him far more precious."

"Hmm." Caroline studied Allie for a second. "You're a principal, right? The top of your field?"

"Yes." Allie nodded, tensing slightly. "As long as I can fully recover."

Caroline's gaze skimmed to Allie's feet. "And what's left to accomplish? What motivates you when there's no competition, no promotion to attain, no"—her focus shifted to me—"fantasy duty station?"

"I'm not a prima, let alone an assoluta." A wry smile twisted Allie's mouth. "Which my mother loves to remind me. So there's that to work toward. And if by some miracle that title is bestowed upon me, then I'd still compete with my biggest rival, as always." She glanced at my sister.

"Myself. There's always something I can do better, some technique I'll always strive for but never perfect."

"Because perfection is the goal?" Caroline asked, but there was no bite in her tone.

"Always." Allie's smile slipped, but she quickly bolstered it. "And it's unobtainable, so there's never a shortage in motivation."

"You're pretty perfect to me." I brushed my lips over her temple.

She scoffed, but her eyes sparkled. "Says the man who had to teach me to ride a bike."

"Allie!" Juniper called, cupping her hands around her mouth. "Will you braid Melody's hair before she swings?"

Allie nodded. "Have an extra hair tie in that bag?" she asked Caroline. "Mine are all back at the cabin."

Caroline dug into the bag and handed the elastic to Allie.

"Thanks." She brushed a quick kiss over my lips and pulled away before I could grab hold of her to deepen it. "Be right back."

"How many principals?" I asked as she climbed to her feet on the blanket. "There's three hundred and fifty of me, but out of the four thousand professional dancers, how many of them are principals, like you?"

"Oh, honey." She backed away with a smirk. "Don't make me hurt your feelings."

I scoffed, and she headed down the slope.

"Something's different between you two," Caroline noted, spraying her legs with the sunscreen. "She's . . . lighter. I don't mean skinnier, or anything about her weight—"

"I know what you're saying." I watched as Allie reached Melody, then started braiding her curly blond hair. "Her injury was devastating both physically and mentally, but she's coming back to herself. Little by little, she'll get there."

"She's smiling too." Caroline sprayed her arms. "I would guess that's all you."

"I wouldn't mind being the reason." I smiled when Juniper laughed at something Allie said. "But I'm not taking credit for the work she's put into herself."

"Were you always in love with her? Or just this time around?"

My gaze flew to Caroline's.

"Oh, come on, you're about as subtle as a hippo in a pet store." She offered the sunscreen, and I shook my head since I'd already applied some. "No judgment. I'm just being nosy."

"Always," I answered as Allie finished up Melody's hair. "It took me until that second summer to realize what the feeling was, but I fell for her the first day I met her. She was clinging to the side of the world's oldest rowboat, and she lifted her chin and demanded I get Eva to safety first, even though she was bleeding. She asked if I had siblings and said there was nothing more important to her than her sisters. I was a goner and didn't even know it."

Caroline's head tilted as her gaze bounced like a ball between Allie and me. "That's . . . annoyingly relatable. And admirable."

"Because you're determined not to like her?" I took my hat off and set it next to Allie's, then started on my shoes.

"I know she's not her sister." Caroline's mouth pursed. "But there's just something about her—about that whole family—that sends warning signals screaming through my brain. They've always used their money, their influence, to further themselves. Screw whoever got stepped on."

"Because her mother cut your best friend from your ballet class?" I set my shoes and socks on the blanket. "And yes, I know about that. It's kind of fucked up that you got to take ballet and you won't let Juniper."

"Taking those classes is one of the reasons I won't let her," Caroline argued. "It was two years, and the girls were mean. The teachers were mean. You heard Allie. There's an impossible standard of perfection that always leaves you feeling like you'll never measure up. You think I don't see the circles beneath Allie's eyes?"

I couldn't fight her on that last observation. "But you think she's admirable, so we're getting somewhere."

Caroline rolled her eyes. "I think what she *did* was admirable, but the Rousseau girls always stick together, so I'm not surprised." Concern puckered her forehead. "I'm still worried she'll break your heart when she leaves, just like the first time."

"That's not what happened." I stripped off my shirt and stood, watching Allie shake her head at Gavin as he gestured to the rope swing.

"I was there," Caroline countered, stretching her legs over the blanket. "I didn't know why you were crushed and silent before you left for basic, but now it makes sense. I remember the devastation on your face, and the emptiness in your eyes. You wouldn't talk to me—to anyone—and Gavin told me not to poke." Her tone sharpened. "So don't tell me she didn't break your heart. I saw the truth with my own eyes."

"You saw your truth." I pivoted to look down at my big sister. "But mine? I left *her*. I broke *her*. She was in the hospital, for fuck's sake, looking at months of rehabilitation. Her sister *died*, and I didn't show up for her. She woke up and I was gone. I was the prick and broke my own heart. Not Allie."

"You wouldn't do that." Caroline's jaw dropped, and she looked at me like I'd suddenly become a stranger. "You save people, Hudson. You don't leave them."

"But I did." If she knew that I was constantly lying to her, she wouldn't be so certain about my character. I was currently the hero in Juniper's story, but I'd be the villain in Caroline's once she learned that particular truth. I crouched to look her in the eye. "Truth always differs depending on who's telling the story, and in complicated situations, there are countless variations. But when it comes to that summer, in every single variant, I'm the asshole who wasn't strong enough to hold on to her."

A splash sounded in the lake behind me, and the kids cheered Gavin's name.

"Why would you . . ." She shook her head.

"I was a selfish fuck who cared more about what I wanted than what she needed." My chest constricted like a vise. "I'm the one who has to earn her back, not the other way around, and it would really help if you could just lay off and be one less obstacle to overcome, because she's it for me, Caroline. This summer might be all I have with her, but she's it."

Caroline blinked in surprise, then glanced at Allie. "Okay," she said slowly, then nodded at me. "Okay."

"Thank you." Relief lifted at least a hundred pounds off my back.

I walked down to the shore as Juniper went flying off the swing, then came up with a shout of victory as Gavin treaded water nearby.

"We're up after Melody," I told Allie when I reached her side.

"Very funny." She watched, completely rapt as Mel caught the rope and started dragging it up the slope.

I knew that look. She'd worn it the night I met her at the bar with Gavin's motorcycle. My girl wanted to swing and thought she shouldn't.

"I'm dead serious."

Allie snorted. "No way. I think Gavin flew fifteen feet through the air on his last jump. If I come down wrong . . ."

"It's water, not concrete. Your mom isn't here, Allie. You can have a little fun. It'll be good for you." I watched the expressions change on her face, her brow furrowing at first, then rising slightly as she pressed her lips between her teeth and tilted her head to the side. "The lake's a good twenty feet deep around there. It's safe."

She side-eyed me. "It's a God-only-knows-how-old rope tied to a God-only-knows-how-healthy tree that can bear God-only-knows how much weight, into—" She sucked in a breath as Mel hopped onto the seat and swung down and out, letting go at the perfect time to fall into the lake, squealing until she hit the water.

"You want to," I prodded. "I can see it."

"Like you know when I want things," she muttered, folding her arms. "I have a great poker face." Which she immediately ruined by raking her gaze over my torso and biting her lip.

"Maybe to everyone else." I palmed her waist and turned, tugging her against me. "The water's just how you like it, love. Wet. Deep. Safe. Come play."

"You did *not* just make a sex joke." Her gaze darted to the water.

"You can trust me. I won't let anything bad happen to you." All traces of teasing left my voice.

That got her full attention. She winced, then quickly smoothed her expression. "You can't promise that."

I brought my left hand up to her cheek and cupped her face, getting the feeling that she wasn't just talking about the swing. "That's exactly what I'm promising. We'll do it together."

"And what if I'm too scared to let go? Are you just going to fly off and leave me hanging?" She swallowed.

"I won't let go until you do," I promised, stroking her cheek. "We'll swing back together, relaunch, and try it again. As many times as you need." My stomach clenched. "You just have to have a little faith in me."

She searched my eyes. "Do you think I'm absurd for being nervous? I mean, the kids aren't scared."

"You're not absurd." A smile tugged at my mouth. "They were scared the first time too. You're just getting a later start."

"Were you scared? Wait. Don't answer that." She threw up a hand and stepped out of my arms. "You're never scared, which makes you a shitty barometer." She blew out a slow breath. "All right. Let's do it."

"Really?" My grin was instant.

"Stop asking and let's do it before I lose my nerve." She yanked her shirt over her head, and I did my absolute best to keep my eyes off the swells of her breasts.

Damn my memory, I could still feel the hard buds of her nipples in my mouth, hear her little gasps of pleasure. *Not right now.* For fuck's sake, we were surrounded by my family, and I was twenty-eight years old, not some hormonal teenager. This was most definitely not the time.

She shimmied out of her shorts.

Never mind. I was a kid in a candy store and Allie was pure sugar. Every inch of her was delectably perfect. Somehow, I managed to shut my mouth without drooling, and walk her down to the rope.

The kids climbed out, and Gavin trailed after them. "I don't know how the hell you tread water constantly," he griped. "I've got to go to the gym."

I laughed, then took hold of the rope as Allie leaned out over the ten-foot embankment. "You ready?"

"We both can't sit on that thing." She motioned to the wooden disk.

"We're going to stand." I held the rope steady. "You hop on first, and I'll pull us up the hill, and then jump on with you."

She stared at the disk. "You could just let me go."

"I could, but that would make me an asshole." I crooked my hand at her. "Come on, Allie."

"This is the stupidest thing I've ever done." She gripped the rope with both hands, then stepped onto her side of the disk.

God help us if I ever took her bungee jumping.

"Good girl." I locked eyes with her, then dug my heels into the ground and backed up, dragging her up the hillside. "I'm not going to jump on until you want me to."

"Your exact word was *need*, if I recall," she muttered.

"Now who's making sex jokes?" I bit back a smile and we reached the sweet spot for taking off. "You tell me when."

She took a deep breath, then another, and another, adjusting her grip on the rope. "How will I know when to let go so I don't hit the shore down there instead of the water?"

"I'll tell you."

"Okay. Let's go." She nodded.

"You're sure?" I prepared to launch.

"Right now!" she ordered.

I jumped with both feet and landed on the disk, then momentum swung us down the hill.

Allie shrieked, and I let go with one hand, wrapping my arm around her waist as we cleared the shore and shot out over the lake. I waited for the water to turn that deep blue that equaled depth, and shouted, "Now!"

The second I saw her let go, I did the same, and we flew.

The lake rushed up to meet us, and I held my breath before we hit. Water engulfed us, rushing over our heads. I slid my hand from her waist and grabbed her hand before I kicked for the surface.

I popped up a second before she did.

She gasped when she hit air, and I let her hand go so she could tread water, remembering that what was second nature to me wasn't to her. "That was . . ." Her eyes locked on mine and she smiled wide. "That was incredible!"

And then she laughed.

I fell in love with her all over again. Not the quiet, observant girl she'd been, or the friend I'd let down, but the woman she'd grown into, beautiful and strong, scarred and still laughing.

She launched forward, threw her arms around my neck, and pressed her mouth to mine.

I kept us afloat, and then kissed the shit out of her, tilting my head and stroking my tongue into her mouth. I groaned at the taste of her, the delectable scrape of her fingernails along the back of my neck, and the heat of her body pressed against mine.

She whimpered, and the sound had me hard in seconds.

Need barreled down my spine, and I grasped the nape of her neck as she wound her legs around my waist, trusting me fully to keep us above the surface. I'd never wanted anyone—anything—the way I needed Allie. I kissed her like she was air and I'd spent the last decade swimming for the surface.

"Hey! There are kids out here, you know!" Gavin called out.

Allie pulled away, breathing hard and fast.

Fuck the rest of this day, I was taking her straight back to the cabin.

She must have seen my intention in my eyes, because hers flared, and she untangled herself, then swam slowly for shore.

I took off after her and prayed the water would cool my dick down enough to not scar my family for life. It was close, but I was in presentable shape by the time we got there.

Allie and I walked out of the lake and onto the little beach beneath the drop-off, where we were momentarily hidden from view. I pulled her into my arms, and she brought her hands to my chest, but didn't push me away. "I want you." I lowered my forehead to hers. "I will do anything to be with you, to keep you, to make this work. I have never felt anything more real in my life."

She sucked in a breath. "It would never work. I'm going back to New York."

"I don't care. You're here *now*. Give me your now." My hands flexed on her waist. "Tell me you feel it."

She squeezed her eyes shut, then nodded. "I feel it. It's real."

Thank you, *God*.

A shape flew over our heads, and our heads turned as Juniper swung out over the lake, then shouted happily as she let go. She hit with minimal splash as Mason and Melody cheered from above.

"She's not supposed to do that unless there's someone in the water," I muttered, staring at the surface of the lake. My brow furrowed when she didn't immediately pop up, and I started counting as the hair on the back of my neck rose.

"Hudson," Allie whispered, her hands falling from my chest when I reached nine.

I turned fully toward the lake, then strode in, making it to twelve by the time the water reached my waist.

"*Hudson!*" Caroline screamed from above us.

"Stay here," I called back to Allie, then dove.

CHAPTER TWENTY-FOUR

Allie

Dancegrl6701: Oh how the crown has fallen.
Sorry, RousseauSisters4, but you're a wreck.
Time to step aside.

My heart thundered as Hudson cut through the water like a knife, swimming faster than I'd ever seen.

"If you're up there, she could use some help," I whispered to Lina.

Hudson's head rose, and then he disappeared beneath the surface around the same place that Juniper had.

I wrapped my arms around my waist, like that could stop my stomach from sinking lower with every second he was underwater. He did this every day. He did this in twenty- and thirty-foot seas. If he found that captain who'd jumped off the boat in the middle of the ocean, he could find Juniper in a lake. He had to.

Dirt skidded down the steep path to my left, and Gavin flew past me, racing into the water. Caroline stumbled down the trail and stopped at my side.

"She's wearing bright orange," she whispered, lifting her hands to her chin. "Hudson always said she needed to swim in bright colors in case . . ."

I sidestepped and wrapped my arm around her trembling shoulders. "Three hundred and fifty," I reminded her. "There are only three hundred and fifty people in the country as good as he is. He'll find her." I treated the panic like I did pain, shoving it into a mental box.

There wasn't a world where Hudson would let his niece—our niece—drown. He simply wouldn't allow it.

"How long has it been?"

"She can hold her breath for a really long time." I rubbed her shoulder, my eyes locked on the surface. "I've seen her do it for over a minute at my house when she's swimming with Hudson."

This wasn't happening. Not again.

"A minute." She started full-on shaking. "Has it been a minute?"

"I don't think so." It was a tiny lie, only because I wasn't certain. "Hudson hasn't come up for a breath, so that's a good sign," I babbled. How long *could* he hold his breath?

I didn't know. I'd been too focused on keeping him at arm's length to ask those kinds of questions, or even see his house. He'd put maximum effort into whatever this was, and I'd pushed him away at every turn unless it involved Juniper.

And now Juniper was—

Don't think like that. My heart pounded in my ears and my stomach twisted as my mind ran amok. Juniper would never be able to meet Lina because I hadn't been able to save her, and now Hudson was her best chance to keep her here where she belonged, and not with Lina.

Gavin was almost there.

"Please, please, please," Caroline whispered over and over, my thoughts echoing her plea.

Hudson broke the surface, facing the opposite direction, and my heart lurched into my throat. "Got her!" he shouted, then started swimming in a sidestroke toward us, Gavin at his side.

"Oh, God!" Caroline ran into the water.

"She's breathing!" Gavin called out.

I heard Juniper cough, and my knees gave out, hitting the sand instantly. "Thank you," I whispered up at Lina. "Thank you. Thank you."

Hudson lifted her into his arms once he was able to touch the bottom, then carried her out of the lake as she coughed again.

"Juniper!" Caroline got out of Hudson's way, then quickly followed him back to shore, her clothes soaked to midchest.

"She's all right," Hudson assured his sister, looking down at Juniper before glancing over at me. "She's all right."

Juniper coughed again as Hudson sat her down on the sand a couple feet to my left, then crouched in front of her. "How you feeling, June-Bug?" He picked up her foot.

Caroline knelt next to Juniper and stroked her head as Gavin walked out of the water, dropping down on Hudson's other side.

"I'm okay." Juniper took deep, ragged breaths, and glanced at her mom. "I went so deep that my foot got tangled in a branch or something. I couldn't see. I tried, but I couldn't pull it free." Her breaths started to slow. "Uncle Hudson got it, though."

My chest clenched.

"Okay." Caroline pressed a kiss to Juniper's forehead. "Thank you, Hudson."

He nodded. "It's a decent scrape." He peered down at the raw patch on the top of her right foot. "But I think you'll live. You suck in any water down there?"

Juniper shook her head. "I held my breath the whole time."

"I'm proud of you." He smiled at her, the curve falling as he looked over at his trembling sister. "Hey. She's okay. The orange made it way easier for her to spot. You did everything you were supposed to. We were all here. She's okay," he repeated.

She swallowed and nodded.

"You were not supposed to swing without an adult still in the water," Hudson lectured, then rose to his feet and helped Juniper to hers, Caroline and Gavin quickly following.

"I figured you were close enough," she muttered as Caroline pulled her into a bear hug, locking her arms around Juniper. "And in my defense, you were. But I'm sorry. I'll be more careful next time."

Caroline tensed, and I saw the words in her eyes that there wouldn't be a next time, but to her credit, she just nodded. "I love you."

I wasn't sure I could have done the same.

"I love you too." Juniper sagged against Caroline.

"We need to watch her for coughing, fever, lethargy, any of the signs that she's got water in her lungs, but barring that, I think she's fine," Hudson told Caroline. "Why don't you take her up and get the scrape cleaned out?" He nodded up the trail.

"Can you walk it?" Caroline asked Juniper.

"I think so." The two started up the steep trail, Gavin walking close enough behind to catch Juniper if she fell.

I watched them until Hudson stepped into my line of sight.

"Allie?" He offered a hand and I took it on reflex, rocking back onto my feet and standing with his help. "Hey. You okay? You're shaking."

Was I? "I love her," I whispered, my eyes stinging.

"I know." He wrapped his arms around me, pulling me against his chest.

"I didn't want to. I just thought I'd help her, and that would some-how make up for me living and not Lina, but I love her, Hudson." My voice broke.

"She's okay." His hand swept up and down my back.

"Are you okay?" I asked through rattling teeth.

"Scared the shit out of me for a second before I saw her, but I'm more concerned about you at the moment." He rested his chin on the top of my head. "Just give it a second, the adrenaline will work its way out of your system."

God, I was leaning on him.

"I'm all right." I moved to push out of his arms.

"Will you just let me hold you for once?" His arms tightened. "You don't have to handle everything on your own, Allie. You can be scared, and you can love Juniper even if it's messy. Messy is good, love. Messy is where the best parts of life happen. You don't have to be in control at all times. It's okay if you fall apart. I promise I will be right here to put you back together if you just let me."

Maybe it wouldn't hurt if I gave in, even if only for a moment.

I relaxed against his chest, my ear to his slow, steady heart. Juniper's incident might have scared him, but it didn't shake him. I was starting to think nothing did. "Thank you for saving her."

"It's what I do," he said into my hair. "Plus, I'll admit I have a vested interest."

A half smile curved my mouth and the tremors lessened, but he didn't let go. This is what he did, but I barely knew more than that about his real life. "Where do you live?"

"On Warren Street, about four blocks from your house. It's the dark-blue one with the white door. Why?"

"I've never asked." But I knew which house it was. I'd walked by it every summer when we headed to his parents'—Caroline's—café.

"Hmm." His strokes down my spine slowed. "Want to see it when we get back?"

It was a step in a direction that didn't involve Juniper . . . or the deal we'd made. I closed my eyes and let the rhythm of his heart slow mine, and God love him, he didn't push or press me to answer quickly. It made it easier when I finally nodded. "Yes. I'd like that."

The rest of the day passed without anyone else nearly dying. We hiked, played cards in the pavilion until the wind picked up, and cooked dinner amid a chorus of laughter and chaos that I was beginning to adore—especially since Caroline wasn't just being civil, she was . . . nice.

And really funny when she wasn't hell bent on picking at me.

As the campfire died, Hudson's aunts and uncles filed off to bed around the same time his parents headed to their cabin, leaving Caroline and me sitting on a log around the embers. I watched Hudson spin Juniper on a tire swing about twenty feet away, near the edge of the lake.

"He's really good with kids," she mentioned not so casually. "He'll be a great dad. You know, if you want kids."

Kids?

"I . . ." My mouth opened and shut a few times as I imagined Hudson holding a baby—our baby—and I clutched my Hydro Flask. What was that feeling hovering just below the immediate nausea that accompanied her comment? Was that interest?

"You look like you might vomit." She chuckled. "It's okay to not want kids. I was just saying Hudson is really good with them."

"You don't have to sell me on his qualities, I promise." I sighed. "Having kids isn't something I've really thought about. Most everyone I know waits until we retire. That's actually what stopped Mom. She got pregnant with Lina and married our father."

"Ahh." She leaned forward and poked the embers. "Makes a little more sense as to why she seemed to drive you four relentlessly."

I nodded. "Juniper is phenomenal," I said to change the subject. "She's headstrong, and witty, and smart. You've done a good job with her."

Caroline sat back and stared down at Juniper swinging. "She's reckless like Hudson," she muttered. "Sean was like that, too, always jumping before he looked, but yeah, she's more stubborn than I could ever dream of being and gives me a run for my money every day. Tenacity must run in her genes. Guess we'll find out when she's eighteen. She'll probably march her butt down to the lawyers and ask for her file on her birthday."

My throat tightened, and I took a quick drink. "Do you want her to wait that long? Aren't you ever worried about stuff like medical history?"

"A little." She nodded. "It will be good for her to have access to that information, or at least where to go to start asking the questions, but the adoption was closed for a reason. I don't know her birth parents, or what they'd do if she . . ." She tensed. "Waiting until she's eighteen protects Juniper, and it protects their privacy too."

Lina was dead, but what about Juniper's father?

Caroline sighed. "I know everyone thinks I'm horrid when I won't let her run out searching for her birth family—"

"No one thinks you're horrid," I promised.

She scoffed. "They do. But no adult throwing their two cents in has lost their husband, watched the father of their child die in their arms because his body just couldn't fight anymore. That pain belongs to me, and to Juniper." A sad smile curved her mouth as Hudson spun Juniper on the swing. "I don't think I could breathe through another loss like that, and the idea of anything happening to her makes me want to surround her in bubble pack. I can't risk losing her, not when I've already lost Sean, and watching her grieve—" She took a shuddering breath. "Sean and I made promises, and I'm the only one left to keep them, to make sure she grows up safe and loved. Call me overprotective, but she's only ten, and for right now, I'm okay with being horrid if it keeps her from feeling that kind of pain, that heartbreak again, and that includes ballet. Can you really tell me that dancing has never broken your heart?" She looked over at me. "Or your body?"

I pulled the sleeves of Hudson's sweatshirt down over my hands. "It's not without its challenges," I admitted, finally starting to see Caroline clearly. She wasn't horrid—she was still grieving, still scared.

"Right." She nodded. "I know you lost a sister. People who have suffered like us know that there's no such thing as having everything, and when it comes to the unknown, there are prices I'm unwilling to let Juniper pay. So for now, I'll make the tough choices. I'll be the bad guy."

"I get it." I cleared my throat and decided not to push my luck by asking anything else. "I'm going to walk down to them."

She nodded. "Tell Juniper I'm waiting for her, would you? I want to be sure the fire's out."

"Sure thing." I stood, and Hudson's hoodie fell to my thighs as I walked around the campfire, then down to the shore. Thankfully the moon was out and full, lighting the way and allowing me to dodge the roots and rocks that could have twisted my ankle.

Juniper laughed as Hudson spun her again, and my heart clenched. She might not be here if Hudson wasn't so good at what he did. I'd figured we'd have time for me to tell her more about Lina, time for her to know us, but if today had shown me anything, it was that time wasn't a given.

"Hey," Hudson said, smiling at me as Juniper wound down from her last whirl, giggling.

"Hey." I glanced back at the campfire quickly. "Please do me a favor and go keep Caroline busy for a second?"

His smile faded, but he nodded, then headed up to the campfire.

Juniper recovered from her laughing fit with a sigh, hugging the top of the tire swing, and I crouched down in front of her.

"You feeling okay after today?" I asked softly.

Her expression sobered. "For a second, before Uncle Hudson found me, I thought I might die . . . like my mother."

My heart seized. "But you didn't."

"No." Her forehead puckered. "But all day I was thinking that my last words would have been *watch this*, to Melody. And then I thought that at least I'd have last words, but no one remembers my mother's," she finished in a whisper. "It's weird, I know. But I wish somebody remembered them."

"Me too." I nodded. "Would it help if I told you what I do remember?"

"Not if it hurts you."

"Let's see how far I can get." I forced a smile. "A lot of why it hurts so much is because what I remember doesn't match all the evidence, so I wasn't allowed to talk about it." Not until I'd hired my own therapist a few years ago.

"Okay," Juniper said slowly. "I'd like to know."

I breathed in and fought to steady my heartbeat. "I don't remember anything solid after the Classic. I remember winning, and the contract offers, and seeing your uncle. We made plans to meet up that night, but—" I swallowed. Obviously I hadn't shown, which had probably contributed to him walking away. "Anyway, I was told we were on the road home from the Company reception. I remember listening to Coldplay, and Lina laughing as we took the curve—she was always laughing, always the first with a joke. I think out of the four of us, she was always the most . . . alive, the most certain of herself. Like you."

"Like me," Juniper whispered.

"Yeah. There's a lot of her in you. Your smile, and your laugh, and your grace in the studio . . . that's Lina." I glanced over her shoulder and noted that Hudson was pouring water onto the fire. "Basically, I remember the feelings from that night, even if the events are kind of spliced together out of order in my mind like a bunch of messed-up film."

She leaned forward, resting her chin on the tire.

I chose my next words very carefully.

"My memory says that she told me that she loved me, and to follow my heart." My throat didn't tighten like it usually did when I denied the memory. "And she tucked her ring into my front pocket and asked me to take care of what she'd left behind." I squeezed her hand. "I used to think she meant Anne and Eva, but now I wonder if she meant you."

She squeezed back, her wide eyes locked on mine. "She left you a ring?"

"Yep." I looked over her shoulder and saw Hudson and Caroline walking this way, a definite apology lining Hudson's face. Time was up. "It's an heirloom from our great-grandmother. Your great-great-grandmother. My father gave it to my mom as a promise ring, and she gave it to Lina when she won the Classic her year. Guess it was more like a promise to marry our dreams instead of a guy. Lina wore it every day. Only took it off for rehearsal." I sighed.

"And then you won the Classic and she gave it to you," Juniper guessed.

"I think so. When I woke up a few days later in the hospital, the nurse gave me a bag of the belongings I'd had when the ambulance brought me in, and the ring was there. So, I know that part is true, but head wounds are weird." She didn't need to know the rest, the bits and pieces that came screaming back in my dreams, or whenever a song played on the radio.

"Did you show them as proof?" She wiggled on the swing.

I shook my head. "No one but you knows I have it." I'd been too afraid that Mom would take it back and I'd have nothing left of Lina. "Point is, I choose to believe that her last words were asking me to look after the people she loved, and I think it's okay if you choose to believe that too."

She nodded.

"Getting late, don't you think?" Caroline called out as they came closer. "What are you two talking about?"

Juniper blinked twice. "I was asking Allie about how she tore her Achilles when she was performing."

She even lied like a Rousseau. Impressive.

I stood as Caroline reached us, her mouth hanging slightly agape.

"Juniper, that's not something you just ask someone," she chastised.

Juniper shrugged and climbed out of the swing. "It's not like it's not on the internet. Do you think it was overuse?"

"Umm. Yes." I nodded, and the four of us started up to the trail. "I knew I should have rested it, and made the bad choice to dance instead."

"And it just . . . went?" Juniper asked.

"Allie, I'm so sorry," Caroline apologized, shooting a look at her daughter. "You've been more than kind with what you've already shared."

"It's okay. I got a little distracted, lost my spot during the piqué turns, and that probably didn't help." I shrugged, and Hudson stiffened at my side. "But I don't remember falling out or anything that would have caused it. It just tore. And had it not torn at the end of the variation, it would have in act two." We reached the trail. "When you don't give your body time to heal, it will take the time from you."

Juniper nodded.

"And on that note, we're headed to bed." Caroline put her hand on Juniper's back. "See you two tomorrow."

We said our good nights and started back toward our cabin, stopping at the outhouse before going the rest of the way.

"I don't think we should tell Caroline," I blurted in a whisper as we walked back to the main trail.

"What?" Hudson paused, and I turned to face him.

"She's scared for Juniper on so many levels after losing Sean. I think we can't just tell her that we're not a threat, or tell her that Juniper has a gift. Caroline is a lot like Lina, in a way. She needs the evidence, she needs to be shown. So we prove it to her. We let her see just how talented Juniper is for herself, at the Classic. With how stubborn Caroline is, it might be the only way Juniper ever gets to show her."

Hudson lowered his head, his eyes shifting in thought. "It could work, and I can handle the fallout, but there's every chance Caroline will go right back to hating you for the deception, even if she realizes you aren't coming to steal Juniper away."

I nod, my stomach hollowing. "It's a risk I'm willing to take. This should be about Juniper, not me. Not Anne. Being cut out for eight years is worth it if it means Juniper's happy." And I'd be able to sleep knowing I did what I could, which was the least of what I owed Lina.

"Okay." Hudson nodded, and we started back up the trail to our cabin. "You got distracted?" he asked as we picked our way through the moonlight. "During the *Giselle* performance?"

Heat stung my cheeks. "Yeah."

"But you don't think that had anything to do with the tear?" His brow furrowed.

"No." I shook my head. "I did at first, but I was just looking for something to blame. I faltered a little bit, but nothing that would have caused the tear." A wry chuckle worked its way up my throat. "Funny thing, and I've never told anyone this, and I don't even want you to respond because it's so embarrassing, but . . ."

He glanced my way.

"I thought I saw you." I shoved my hands into the front pocket of his hoodie and definitely did *not* look over to see the way he gawked at me. "I thought I saw you in the back row, and when I looked again, you weren't there, of course. It was just my brain playing tricks on me, probably because you'd been there the only other time I'd performed the variation for an audience."

He kept staring, and I wished I could go back about thirty seconds and undo that confession. What was *wrong* with me? Just because he said I didn't have to be in control all the time didn't mean I needed to jump from zero to Mach one on the oversharing train.

"Did you know that I didn't think about training today? Not once." I blurted out the first thing that came to mind to change the subject.

"Allie—" He reached for my arm, but I sped up.

Foolish didn't begin to cover how I was feeling. "Not once. I didn't feel guilty about not working out, or not spending all day in the studio. It's the most fun I've had in . . ." I laughed. "Probably since you used to drag me out and make me do fun things. I stopped doing fun things after you . . . it was just dancing after that, but hey, I'm a principal, so it worked out."

"You can balance it, you know," Hudson said, catching up as we reached the steps of our cabin. "You can be at the top of your game and still have a life. Still have days like this. It doesn't have to be all or nothing."

"I don't know how to do it any other way. But it's a beautiful thought, balance." It really was. I walked in ahead of him and immediately fumbled in the dark.

"Don't move. I don't want you to trip," Hudson said, his hand skimming my lower back as he walked around me to his side of the bed. A couple clicks later, the lantern turned on. "There we go." He turned and came straight back to me, his jaw ticking as he curved the brim of his hat.

What the heck did he have to be nervous about?

"I know you said you didn't want me to respond—"

Kill me now. "Please don't."

"But I have to." He cupped my face.

"You really don't." I glanced at the door, the wall, the ceiling, anywhere but at him.

"Look at me." His thumbs stroked my cheeks. "Please, love."

I somehow climbed out of a pit of mortification to meet his gaze.

"It was me." He took a breath, and I held mine. "It was me, Allie. I was there."

CHAPTER TWENTY-FIVE

Allie

OuchPouchhtr5: What a fucking liar. She's not recovering. She's done.

"You what?" I stepped back, and his hands hung midair for a few heartbeats before he lowered them.

"I was there," he repeated slowly.

"No, you weren't." I grabbed onto the thick wooden rail of the footboard to steady myself.

He sat on the edge of the footboard and gripped the unfinished wood. "I was two rows from the back. Dead center. You saw *me*."

My lips parted and my stomach fluttered straight out of my body. "I don't understand."

"I tried to buy the back row center seat, but I couldn't get it. It must have gone within seconds when they put the tickets on sale." He stared straight ahead at the closed cabin door. "I was so pissed when whoever bought it didn't bother to show up. I saw your mom in the box with

Anne, saw Eva in the corps, saw you—" His eyes drifted shut, and my nails bit into the footboard. "You were so beautiful."

Breathe. I had to remember to breathe.

"I saw you fall to a knee at the end, a little more uncontrolled than I remembered it being when we were younger, but I didn't question it until you screamed." His head hung. "You screamed. The orchestra stopped. The whole place went silent when they carried you offstage. I climbed over every person in that row to get to the aisle, but they don't exactly let ticket holders backstage to see one of the most famous dancers in the world, you know."

"You were there?" A sweet, stinging ache threatened to crack my chest open, threatened to dig its way out of the decade I'd spent ignoring it, and expose an inconvenient and dangerous truth I wanted no part of. But I was so over being numb, over not allowing myself to feel anything but anger and sadness.

"I was there." He looked up at me, tracking my movements with those gorgeous eyes as I slowly made my way to stand in front of him. "Of course I was there. You told me once that you needed me in the audience for that piece, remember?"

"Before the Classic," I whispered. Mom had told me to pick something else because Lina had just been offered the role in the fall program for MBC and she didn't want any comparisons made since members of the Company were there judging. I'd done it anyway, my first and only true act of defiance.

Hudson had snuck into the back row to watch so my mother wouldn't see him. That part of the day was still crystal clear in my memory.

"I'd already let you down in the worst way." His voice lowered. "I knew it wouldn't make up for it, that you'd never see me, but I was there."

"How did you even know I had that role?" My brain tried to make sense of it, but my heart was quickly shoving logic out the door.

"I have . . ." A flush crept up his throat. "I have an alert set to email me if your name is in the same headline as *Giselle*, but I didn't know that you were still out, how bad the injury had been, until Juniper told me you were at the beach house." He searched my eyes. "I didn't know you'd see me, and I sure as hell never thought I'd distract you. I'm so sorry."

"It wasn't your fault. The turns didn't cause the tear. It would have happened whether or not you'd been there." I stepped forward, between his knees. "You've really had an alert for all these years?"

He nodded.

The silence grew thick as my heart continued the battle with my head, then finally won. He'd been there. He'd come. Juniper hadn't forced his hand, he'd come to New York for *me*. "The middle seat of the last row is always empty. It's in my contract."

Two lines creased the area between his brows.

"And if you'd gone to will call and given them your name, they would have handed you that ticket. That's in my contract too. It's always your seat. Every venue. Every performance. I don't even know why I did it, except I guess I never gave up hope that you'd walk in one day." There, I'd said it.

"All these years?" His voice came out like it had been scraped over the campfire embers.

"All these years." My gaze dropped to his mouth and my pulse quickened. I wound my arms around his neck and accepted the simple fact that I would always want him, and for this moment, I could *have* him. "Hudson?"

"Allie?" His hands moved to my hips.

"I need you."

He didn't hesitate, not even for a heartbeat. Our mouths collided, and I melted at the first thrust of his tongue, surrendering completely as he kissed me breathless. Heat and need exploded between us like a match tossed into a vat of gasoline.

His hands slipped to the backs of my thighs as he stood, lifting me against him. I wound my legs around his waist, locking my ankles at the small of his back, then knocked his hat to the ground so I could sink my fingers into his hair.

My back hit the wall, and I used it as leverage, breaking the kiss so I could get his shirt off. Watching him walk around shirtless the last two days had been *torture*. I lowered my mouth to his throat, his two-day stubble rough against my lips, and I savored every one of his indrawn breaths as I reached the curve of firm, warm skin where his neck met his shoulder.

Before I could demand another kiss, he took hold of my hoodie and started to tug it upward. "As delicious as you look in my clothes, I need it off."

Me too. I lifted my arms, and he made quick work of removing it. It hit the floor and I grabbed the bottom of my tank top and hauled it over my head, then threw it so I could feel his skin against mine.

Our mouths fused, and I kissed him long and hard, running my hands down his arms, his back, across his chest—anywhere I could reach—as he kneaded my hips and thighs, growling when my shorts blocked the access he sought.

He speared his hand into my hair, banded his arm under my ass, and then we were moving again. The room spun momentarily, and I felt the bed at my back, then the perfect weight of him above me.

I let my ankles fall from his back, leaving my knees bent so my thighs bracketed his hips. His hands skimmed over the fabric of my bra, and I whimpered in frustration. That needed to come off too. Right now. I tugged at his bottom lip with my teeth, pushed at his chest, and rolled.

He got the message, flipping us so I sat astride his hips.

"You want me." I grinned against his mouth, then ground my core against the hard ridge of his cock, gasping at the jolt of pleasure. His answering groan was absolutely everything.

"Every day since I met you." He sat up and kissed me until I wasn't sure what day it was. Time began and ended with him. "You are the subject of every fantasy I've ever had." His mouth moved down my neck, and I rocked my hips when he found that sensitive spot. "Fuck, you're killing me."

"Good." I reached behind my back and unfastened my bra, then slipped it off my arms and tossed it.

"If you knew half the things I want to do to you . . ." His hands slid from my waist to cup my breasts, and I sighed as he stroked the hard peaks with his thumbs.

"That sounds good." I kissed him once, then slid off his lap to stand in front of him, quickly kicking off my sandals. My fingers moved to the button of my shorts, and he captured my hand with his.

"You're sure you want this now?" The heat in his eyes scalded me.

"Yes." I slipped my hand free, then flicked open the button.

"You don't want to wait until I can get you into a real bed?"

"Looks real enough to me." I tugged the zipper down slowly and watched his jaw flex as he followed the movement with his eyes. "Do you want to wait?"

"I'm not thinking about me." His hands fisted in the fabric of his sleeping bag. "I wasn't kidding when I said I would take you however I can get you. My bed. Your bed. This bed. That wall. The back seat of my truck. I don't care, if it means I get to hear your breath hitch right before you come."

My core clenched, and heat gathered in my stomach, low and insistent. "Those all sound good too." I hooked my thumbs in the waistband of my shorts at my hips, catching the strings of my underwear, then dragged them both down at the same time. I kicked them aside and stood up straight. "But no, I don't want to wait."

"Oh *fuck*." His gaze ran over me like a caress, heat licking my skin everywhere he lingered. "You're absolutely perfect, Allie. So damned stunning." Our eyes met. "Come here, love."

My heart galloped as he gripped my hips, his fingers digging in slightly as he lifted me onto his lap. He claimed my mouth with a deep kiss that had me whimpering for more, chasing his tongue with mine as he lay back, my hair falling around us as I followed him down.

His hand slid between my thighs, and I felt his moan vibrate through his chest as my own answered at the touch of his talented fingers. "Hot and slick." He nipped my lower lip, then licked over the soft flesh before sliding his open mouth down my neck. "How many times do you want to come, Allie? How many ways? Tell me, and I'll give it to you."

I fought for breath as he stroked and teased, then gasped as he flicked my clit with his thumb. "I don't care as long as you don't make me wait for the first one."

"First one." His hands shifted to my hips and he dragged me up his torso. "You're learning."

"You're going to ruin me for anyone else, aren't you?" I fell forward, bracing my palms on the bed above his head as his mouth caressed my breasts, the curve of my ribs, sending little shocks of bliss throughout my body.

"There's no one else." His lips ghosted across my stomach and his hands slipped under my shins. "Never was. Not for either of us." He kissed the crease of my hip, then dragged my knee over his shoulder. "They were all just placeholders."

I shivered as he turned his face into my upper thigh and sucked, leaving a mark before hauling that knee over his shoulder too.

"The only thing that's ever mattered is you and me." He hooked his arms over my thighs, then arched his neck and ran his tongue from my entrance to my clit.

I gasped, my hips rocking on pure instinct.

"Sit up so I can watch you come." It wasn't a request.

I fought against every impulse to melt into a puddle right there, and sat up on my knees, hovering inches above his mouth. My pulse skyrocketed and my breath caught as our eyes locked.

"Sit," he ordered.

Every muscle in my body clenched.

"Sit, Alessandra." He tugged on my thighs, and I buckled.

He rewarded me with a groan, then pulled me against his mouth and stole my entire soul with his lips and tongue. Heat and need spiraled through me. I muffled my first cry with my fist, but my second slipped as my hand fell away.

There was no thought, only feeling. I existed only for him, my hips rocking, my breaths ragged, my vision consumed with the mind-blowingly erotic sight of him beneath me, watching my every reaction. He adjusted immediately to what drove me higher, wound my body tighter, and then drove me relentlessly out of my mind.

He was absolutely ruining me, and I was letting him.

"Hudson," I whimpered, then slammed my hand over my mouth, remembering we weren't alone out here. "It's too good." And that was *too* loud.

He reached up, covering my mouth with one hand and pulling me harder into his mouth with the other, holding me prisoner for every lash of his tongue.

I held on to his arm for balance as my muscles locked, and that spiral of tension stuttered my breath into shallow pants. He worked me relentlessly to the edge of the cliff, then sent me flying. The release took me in colossal waves that arched my back again and again, drowning me in pleasure so sharp I almost forgot to breathe. His hand muffled my shout and every moan that followed as he stroked me down, dragging out every last aftershock until I fell to the side, gasping for air.

He followed, rolling me to my back, then lightly traced my clit with the tip of his tongue, setting off another shudder of pure bliss. "I can't get enough of you." He repeated the caress, and my stomach tightened.

"I want *you*, Hudson." I ran my fingers through his hair and tugged. "Inside me. Now."

"And I want you desperate." He gave me another series of gentle licks, and my back bowed as that sweet tension built within me again. God, it felt so *good*. "Writhing and needy and begging for me."

I propped myself up on my elbows and watched his next strike. "I don't." I gasped as he dragged his tongue over my swollen clit. "Beg."

His slow smile was the sexiest thing I'd ever seen. "You will," he promised, sliding off the edge of the bed and stripping out of his remaining clothes.

I watched like the show it was, my tongue wetting my lower lip as he pulled off his shorts, then the black boxer briefs underneath. Every inch of him was cut, defined by hours in the water and gym. He was beyond words, beyond my ability to grasp what I'd thought perfect was. My core clenched just looking at him, my gaze lingering on the hard length of his cock as he stepped free of his clothes. "You are . . ." I swallowed. "You're beautiful. Please tell me you had more foresight than I did and brought condoms."

For the first time in my life, I wasn't sure I cared. I was on birth control, trusted Hudson more than any partner I'd ever had, and needed him inside me. It was that simple.

"I'd call it more like wishful thinking than foresight." He reached into his pack and brought out a foil packet.

I sat up and took it from him.

His eyes flared as I ripped it open and threw the wrapper on the nightstand next to the lantern. Then I rolled the thin layer of latex over him slowly, my mouth curving as his breath caught, his abs tensed, and his hand fisted in my hair. Finally, I reached his base, then wrapped my hand around him.

His low groan gave me life.

"Sure you want to wait until I'm begging?"

"Holy shit, Allie." He grabbed my waist and all but threw me back onto the bed, then prowled over me, positioning himself between my thighs. "Writhing. Needy. Begging. We've waited too long for it to be anything less."

He kissed me with an urgency that demanded my response, and I gave it, arching up for his mouth again and again while his hands roamed over me, setting me on fire with every touch. I arched as he worshipped my breasts with his mouth, then cried in frustration when he flipped me to my stomach and trailed kisses up my spine.

I reared back when his mouth reached my neck, pushing my ass against him in clear invitation. The ache winding within me *throbbed*.

"Fuck, you're almost there. Almost but not quite." He flipped me again like I weighed next to nothing and ran his hand up my inner thigh.

"Hudson . . ." My hips squirmed, trying to put his hand where I needed it.

"Do you need me?" His fingers dipped between my thighs and I cried out when he stroked the hypersensitive nerves. "Your body sure as hell does. God, you're drenching my hand."

"I need you!" The man had the self-control of a saint, and I was going to burn alive if he didn't give in.

"Right now?" He swirled around my clit, then sank a finger inside me. My core locked around him, and I moaned. So, so, so good, but not enough.

"Right. Now." My hips rocked, my nails dug into his shoulders, and when he slid in a second finger and curled them upward, stars winked in my vision. "More. I need more." If it wasn't for the way he looked at me, the way his arms trembled, I would have thought he was completely unaffected. "Hudson." My hands slipped up to his stubbled cheeks as I writhed. "Don't make me wait. *Please.*"

His fingers withdrew, only to be replaced by the blunt head of his cock at my entrance.

Finally.

He braced his weight on his forearms, leaned down, and brushed his lips over mine. "Are you desperate?"

"Yes." I drew my knees up, so consumed with wanting him that I didn't care what he needed me to confess. I'd give him any truth he wanted.

"Wild?" He pushed in, consuming that first tight inch.

"Yes!" Holy shit, he felt *incredible.*

"Like you won't survive the next heartbeat without me?" Another brush of his lips.

"Yes." My hands slid to the back of his head and I swiveled my hips.

He groaned low in his throat, dropping his forehead to mine. "Good. Because that's *exactly* how I feel every minute of every day. I'm losing my fucking mind over you."

"I'm right with you." Even if it killed me.

"Yeah, you are." He cradled the back of my head and drove into me in one powerful thrust, taking every inch I had and stretching me for more. He was too much, and it was *divine.*

We muffled each other's moans in a kiss, and he shuddered, the muscles of his back rippling under my fingers as I splayed my hands wide.

"My Allie." He lifted his head, locked his awe-filled gaze with mine, and withdrew, hitting every nerve ending within me. "You're so hot. Tight. Perfect. Fucking *made* for me, and I want to be gentle—"

"Don't." My hands slid to his ass. "Don't be gentle or careful. Fuck me like you mean it, Hudson."

His eyes flared again, and he slammed home. The pleasure of it rattled my wits and a cry slipped free. "Like that?"

"Just like that." God yes.

He kissed me deep as he withdrew, then snapped his hips, setting a hard, deep rhythm that had me straining for the next thrust, meeting him every time, curling my leg over his hip to take him deeper.

"Don't stop," I begged. I wouldn't survive it if he did.

"I'm never going to get enough of you," he said against my mouth as his hips drove into me again. My cries softened to keening pants as sweat slickened our skin. "You feel. So. Damned. Good. Allie." He punctuated every word with a thrust, and I lost the ability to form sentences.

"More." It was my only demand. My only thought.

He drove us across the bed, then wrapped his arm around my back and lifted, straightening us. "Headboard."

I threw up my hands, then grabbed the wood and braced, using it for leverage to rock back into his thrusts so he'd hit harder. Deeper. And he *so* fucking did. Wood creaked as he surged over me again and again, and the sight of his wild eyes, his body moving with mine, sent my temperature skyrocketing. Each thrust coiled that sweet tension tighter within me, stringing me like a bow until my body vibrated and pulsed. I felt Hudson everywhere. He was in the very marrow of my bones, the breath in my lungs, the demanding beat of my heart—they were all his.

"I want you from behind, so I can watch this perfect ass bounce as you take my cock," he growled as his hips continued to swing, wringing soft, keening cries from my lips. "And against the wall. And on top of me, riding me hard. Once isn't going to be enough. I want everything."

"Yes. All of it." I rocked faster, demanding he pick up the pace. This slow, thorough fucking was exquisite, but I wasn't going to survive if he made me wait much longer for my release.

"Next time." He kissed me hard and gave me what I wanted, swinging his hips faster but just as deep. "This time I want your eyes." He kept his gaze locked on mine, then reached between our bodies. "You're right there, I can feel it. Every muscle is tight, every breath shallow. I need to feel you come around me, Allie." He strummed my clit, and I stopped meeting his thrusts, only capable of receiving as my body locked at the new onslaught of sensation, my thighs clenching around his hips. "That's it, love."

He pressed lightly, and I saw stars. The edges of my vision darkened as the orgasm tore through me, breaking me apart while Hudson somehow kept me together, never ceasing the relentless drive of his hips as he covered my mouth with his to capture my cries. My body arched again and again.

Only when I fell back against the pillow, gasping for breath and completely wrecked, did his control break.

He curled his arm under my shoulder to keep me from sliding into the headboard, and then unleashed, losing all rhythm in a handful of hard, voracious thrusts.

I brought my hand to his face and took his line as he came undone. "So fucking mine."

His eyes flared, and he kissed me hard, smothering a moan. The sound rumbled through his chest, low and guttural, as he found his release with a final, deep thrust that struck my very soul. He collapsed onto me for a heartbeat before rolling us to the side, holding me close.

We never took our eyes off each other as we came down, our breaths gradually slowing as the sweat cooled.

"We're really good at that," I said once my heart finally stopped slamming.

"Yeah. We are." He ran the backs of his fingers down my cheek. "I've never felt anything like that in my life."

"Me either." We let the words hang between us for a perfect quiet moment I knew couldn't last.

"Let's stay tomorrow," he suggested, catching me off guard. "My family is taking off, but I have one more day of leave, and I rented the cabins for an extra day just in case plans needed to shift. Let's shift them."

I swallowed. "And do what?"

"Not leave this room for anything but the necessities." He stroked his thumb over my swollen lower lip.

That sounded absolutely scrumptious, but I had to get back. I needed to be in the studio. But I also wanted to be here. Maybe he was right, and I could balance. I could be the best, and have a life—have him, even if only for now.

"Okay." I nodded.

He grinned, and I didn't feel the slightest ounce of guilt over playing hooky when that dimple popped in his cheek.

We stayed in bed that night, muffling each other's moans over and over, then spent the next day in the shower, on the shore of the lake, and on one of the picnic tables after his family left.

By the time we pulled in my driveway the day after, I was sore in places I'd forgotten existed and thoroughly . . . happy.

"Who's here?" Hudson asked as he parked next to a car I didn't recognize.

"Not sure." We walked hand in hand up the steps, Hudson carrying my pack for me.

The door swung open before we reached it, and Anne stepped into the doorway. "Where have you been? We've been trying to call you since yesterday."

"Not a lot of service in the woods, so I turned it off." The panicked look on her face sent my stomach into a deep dive. "What's wrong?"

Kenna appeared over Anne's shoulder, then squeezed by her to step onto the porch.

"What's wrong?" I repeated. "Why are you here?"

"I have a month of use-or-lose vacation and a best friend in dire need of help." Her expression softened with . . . Wait, was that *pity*? "I'm guessing you haven't been on the internet?"

"No." I shook my head. I'd been too wrapped up in Hudson to check in on the real world.

Kenna swore, then took her phone from her pocket and swiped open the screen. "I don't know what bug crawled up Vasily's ass, but he announced partial casting for *Equinox*."

"He never announces this early. It's only the middle of July." Dread perched on my shoulders. "Please don't tell me Charlotte . . ."

"No. She didn't." Kenna's shoulders drooped as she turned the screen to face me.

I read the casting announcement, and my stomach twisted. Saliva filled my mouth, and bile rushed up my throat. Ripping my hand from Hudson's, I leaned over the porch railing and vomited up my breakfast into the bushes.

"What the hell happened?" Hudson grabbed my hair as my stomach heaved.

"Eva took her part."

CHAPTER TWENTY-SIX

Hudson

It was a special kind of hell to spend days tangled up in Allie, to finally see what we could be if we gave it a real shot, only to be shut out emotionally in every way possible once we got back to Haven Cove. She hadn't returned a single call or text in two days.

I brought Juniper to the house in the pouring rain after I got off work as planned, only to find Allie sweat drenched in the studio with Kenna.

"Good luck with that one," Anne muttered, patting me on the shoulder, then returned to an enormous pile of paperwork spread out on the living room coffee table.

"Is this a bad time?" I asked from the studio doorway as Allie walked in a small circle, her hand on her lower back, wincing with every step.

"I'd say it's the perfect time," Kenna replied, pushing off the wall. "She needs to take a break."

"Taking a break is what got me here," Allie snapped.

Shit. My eyebrows rose.

"Your sister being a back-stabbing—" Kenna's words died off as Juniper came in behind me. She glanced from my niece to me. "Try to talk her into resting."

Somehow I doubted Allie was going to listen to me.

"Hey, Aunt Allie." Juniper walked over to the window and dropped her bag in the same place she always did.

"Juniper . . ." Allie's mouth opened and shut before she sighed, her shoulders dropping. "I need about five minutes and then we'll get started."

"You sure?" Juniper's face scrunched for a second. "You seem . . . angry."

"Oh, I'm furious," Allie assured her, ripping a towel off the barre and putting it around the back of her neck. "Just not with you. I'll be back in a couple of minutes and we'll work."

Juniper nodded, and Allie strode past me without looking my direction, heading into the foyer.

"Aunt Eva stole Aunt Allie's part in the ballet that was created for her," Juniper whispered as she sat next to her bag.

"I know that, but how do *you* know that?" I'd been careful not to say anything to her.

"Because Eva posted a Seconds yesterday with Aunt Allie saying she couldn't do a bunch of choreography yet that looked . . ." She wrinkled her nose.

"Yes?" Shit, was I actually going to have to download that app to know what was going on around here?

"It looked like Eva hid the camera," Juniper whispered. "And then she posted this morning that Allie wasn't getting better, and she'd been hired as a principal for next season, so I looked at the website." She kicked off her sandals and reached into her bag. "No one jumps from corps to principal. He had to have given it to her just because she's Allie's sister and he felt bad since the ballet was created for her."

So that's how Eva got the part. What a wretch.

"Right. Wait here, kiddo." I left Juniper in the studio and headed into the living room. "You okay?" I asked Anne, who sat on the floor in front of the paper-strewn table, Sadie asleep beside her.

"Yep, just going through three decades of paperwork, hoping my mother kept anything pertaining to Juniper's adoption." She moved a manila envelope to a stack on the floor. "And don't ask me why I'm not in the office. As I've told Allie a dozen times, it still feels like our father's. Not like Mom used it, either, since half this crap was stuffed into boxes in her closet."

"And you're looking for the paperwork because . . ." I lifted my eyebrows at her.

"Because Juniper wants to know who her father is." She dropped another folder on the stack with a thud. "And I have the Classic completely planned, so no current job to do, not that I got to *do* the job I went to school for, because after all, I was supposed to be using all my energy to get pregnant."

And we have another Rousseau sister down. Shit.

"And I have one sister out there stealing the other one's parts, changing the password to their joint Seconds account so Allie can't take the video down, and won't pick up the damned phone for me," Anne continued. "And another who couldn't get out of bed for two days, and now is back to putting herself into an early grave chasing something she never really wanted in the first place just because our mother told her to." She held up a finger. "And don't get me started on my mother guarding Lina's secrets like she's the only person who mattered."

Allie couldn't get out of—

"Wait." My hands curled at my sides. "Your mother knew about Juniper?"

"We're pretty sure, though it's not like she'll talk to us about it. I went to see her again yesterday and got nowhere." *Thunk.* Another envelope hit the stack. "She's busy"—she winced—"*teaching*. Can't be bothered with me."

"That's . . . unfortunate." A pit in my stomach opened, and I breathed through the immediate sensation of panic that belonged to a younger version of myself. I was going to have to set some shit straight with Mrs. Rousseau if I wanted a real chance with Allie.

"So instead of sitting around completely useless while Kenna rehabs Allie's ankle, and Eva burns our family to the ground over her ego, I'm going to make *someone* happy, which means finding a copy of the adoption paperwork so I can tell Juniper who her biological father is." *Thunk.* The files slid, cascading in a paperwork avalanche. "Shit!" Anne snapped, throwing a finger at me when I reached for the papers. "Don't try to help me."

Sadie perked up her ears, then decided sleep was more important.

"Heard." I reached over to pet the pup, then continued through the living room into the kitchen, looking for Allie. Kenna sat on the counter, scrolling through her phone, taking bites off a carrot stick.

"Yeah, it's a real shit show around here," she noted without looking up.

"Seems like it." I peered into the dining room, but there was no trace of Allie. "Allie couldn't get out of bed?" Why the hell was I hearing that from other people?

"If a video trashing your reputation went viral with over a million hits, spawning countless stitches and commentary from every wannabe ballerina to contract lawyers, critics, and armchair experts who've never met you or even watched ballet before, would *you* feel like facing the world?"

Fuck. "No one told me." Dinner curdled in my stomach. "She shut the door in my face after we got back from camping. Why didn't she return any of my calls? Better yet, why didn't either of you reach out? I would have been here."

"Anne and I were with her." Kenna peered up at me over her phone. "She declined further support, and we honored her wishes."

"She didn't want me here," I said quietly. Not like I didn't already know that from the declined calls and unread texts, but hearing it out loud felt like having my heart dragged out and scraped across broken glass.

"She's a little prickly today, just to warn you." Kenna sat her phone down on the counter. "Vasily tried to call her twice the day you two didn't come home, and now he won't take her calls."

Shit. This was because of me. I leaned against the counter on the opposite side of the sink as the guilt sank in, knotting in my throat. No wonder she didn't want to speak to me. If I'd just brought her home as planned, this might not have happened. So much for *balance.*

"It's not his fault." Allie walked in from the foyer in a clean set of workout gear, her face a perfect mask of control. Fuck me, she'd thrown her walls right back up. "It's not your fault," she repeated in my direction, but didn't make eye contact as she opened the refrigerator and pulled out the lemonade.

Yeah, lemonade meant she was stressed as hell.

She slammed the pitcher on the island. "It's not your fault that I didn't stay in service. Not your fault that I decided to spend an extra day with you. Not your fault that I taught Eva the very choreography she no doubt went back and used against me."

Those first two stung like a slap, but I held my ground when Allie walked my way. "I'm still sorry that I played any role in it."

"It wasn't you. It was all me. I'm a big girl who made choices and now has to deal with the repercussions of those choices." She tilted her head to the side. "I need a glass."

I moved four inches to the left so the door would clear my shoulder, and Allie arched an eyebrow, then yanked open the cabinet, her arm brushing against mine to reach the glass.

To my surprise, she brought back two glasses, then went back to the island to pour the lemonade.

Maybe she really *wasn't* pissed at me. My throat loosened.

That relief lasted all of thirty seconds, after which she gave the second glass to Kenna, who took it with a mouthed thank-you as she swiped to answer her phone. "Why, Isaac Burdan, were your ears burning?" She tapped a button on the screen and set the phone on the counter.

The choreographer.

"Good to hear your voice as well, Dr. Lowell," Isaac said through the speaker, and Allie tensed. "I'm sorry to bother you, but it seems Alessandra won't take my calls."

At least I wasn't the only one.

"Hmm." Kenna took a sip of the lemonade. "I wonder if that has anything to do with the fact that you handed over the ballet you choreographed for her to Eva? Just a hunch."

Allie folded her arms.

"I had *nothing* to do with it, I swear. You have to tell her." His voice pitched high. "Vasily showed me some footage of Alessandra teaching Eva, noted that she wasn't going to be back in time to perform, and told me he'd made the decision to cast Eva in the role. I think his exact words were *'raise up the newest MBC star.'*"

"This is bullshit," Allie snapped.

"Alessandra? Oh, darling. I'm so very sorry this has happened. You know I created that role for you and you alone. It's the product of our work, our passion—"

Passion? Jealousy burned in my gut, but I managed not to tell the fucker to keep his pet names to himself because she wasn't his anymore. Not that she was exactly mine, either, since we hadn't really hashed out what was happening between us.

"Cut the crap, Isaac. You were already teaching the choreography to Charlotte, no doubt hoping to rework a little with *her* passion." Allie shook her head and pivoted on the other side of Kenna, facing my direction. Icy rage shone in her eyes as she glared at the phone.

"Anger sounds . . . rather delicious on you, darling. You really should let that temper flare a little more often." He sighed loud enough to be heard through the phone when Allie didn't respond. "I was fucking Charlotte, no big deal. Working with her was only a by-product of that."

"And are you still?" Allie questioned.

"Fucking Charlotte? Yes, but I'll stop if you're saying you'd like to resume our—"

I saw red.

"Working with her, Isaac. Are you working with her?" She rubbed the bridge of her nose. "I don't care who you sleep with anymore, nor will I ever care again."

He scoffed. "It's that guy you brought to the gala, isn't it?"

I stiffened, and Allie's gaze shot to mine.

"Have to say I'm slightly surprised," Isaac continued. "He's not really your type. So handsy in public when you prefer discretion. Plus you like your men lean, built for endurance instead of heavy lifting, if you will. I'll be here when you get bored."

Allie's face flushed and Kenna's eyebrows rose.

Had he been here, he would have learned the definition of *fuck around and find out*.

"Isaac, I wish you the best of luck with Eva. We both know she'll slaughter that variation; you'll have to take *everything* down a notch in difficulty for her to have a prayer of making it halfway through." Allie's hand hovered over the screen. "Oh, and as for Hudson, he's built like a Greek god and fucks like one, too, so I'm all taken care of." She tapped the phone and the call ended.

I gripped the edge of the counter to keep from reaching for her, even damn well knowing she'd said it just to piss off Isaac.

Kenna's gaze swung between Allie and me. "And on *that* note, I'll be in the studio." She hopped off the counter and threw me a wave. "I'll be rooting for you."

I nodded in thanks, and Allie made her way back to my end of the island, then put the lemonade back in the refrigerator. "I shouldn't have said that to him."

"Didn't bother me." A corner of my mouth lifted, but I wiped the smirk off my face before she turned to face me. "Bothers me that you aren't returning my calls either."

She flinched. "Did you need to talk about Juniper?"

"No." I folded my arms. "And you know it."

"Then there's really no reason to call." She shrugged. "What happened out there was just two consensual adults working off some pent-up tension. That's it."

"And I thought we weren't going to lie to each other." Her words bounced right off me because I knew exactly what she was doing. I just wasn't going to let her.

"It meant nothing." Her apathetic mask was so well constructed I'd almost believe her if it wasn't for the turmoil in her eyes.

"Lie." I took two steps, putting us toe to toe. Her pupils dilated and her breath quickened. "Back row, center seat for eleven years isn't nothing."

She tilted her chin. "It has to be. You and me . . . we don't fit in each other's worlds, Hudson. Not outside this tiny little town neither you nor I actually belong in. Do you see what happened when I took a few days off? I lost the role of my *life*. I should have been here working. That's what happens when I try to balance my career with anything else, anyone else who isn't in the industry. We"—she gestured between us—"can't be a thing, and I don't have time to argue about it with you."

My stomach clenched. And back to square one. My phone vibrated in my pocket and I pulled it out to check the screen. It was the station. "Hold that very wrong thought," I said to Allie, then answered the call. "Ellis."

"Hey, Chief—"

"Not yet." I cut off that shit quick. I wasn't going to pin for at least a few months. "What's up?"

"I'm sorry to call you, Petty Officer First Class Ellis, I know you just clocked out, but we've got two birds out already and a distress call coming in."

Fuck. This day just kept getting better.

"I'll be there in fifteen minutes." I hung up and shoved the phone back into the pocket of my uniform. "Looks like I don't have time to argue with you about it either. Can you take Juniper home when you're done for the day?"

"Why?" Her brow knit with concern, which only served to frustrate the shit out of me after she'd spewed all that shit about us meaning nothing.

"Because a distress call just came in and I have to go. Can you take her home, or not?"

She blinked, then leaned sideways to glance past me at the window. "You can't go out in this. We're in the middle of a storm."

"Yes, love, and this is what happens during *every* storm." And time was ticking.

Her eyes widened. "You're going . . ."

"Yes." I nodded. "Can you get Juniper home? If not, I'll call Gavin on my way in and ask him to swing by. Allie, I have to go, *now*."

"I'll take her home," she said softly, chunks of her armor falling away. "Hudson—"

"Thank you. Please tell her I had to run, but don't be specific. She worries." I ignored the urge to kiss her and walked away. "I'll call you tomorrow. Naturally it's up to you if you want to answer."

A little before midnight, I pulled my truck into my garage, then cursed my past self for renting a place where I had to walk through the rain to get in my front door.

It wouldn't be the first time I'd been soaked to the bone tonight.

Exhausted, aching, and still more than a little frustrated with the sharp-tongued ballerina I was irrevocably in love with, I walked across the little patch of grass that separated my house from the garage and headed up the steps to the front porch, only raising my head once I was clear of the rain. The sight of Allie stopped me dead in my tracks. She sat barefoot on my porch swing, her arms wrapped around her legging-covered knees, her ballet flats lying discarded next to a giant familiar bowl of water beneath her.

"You're all right?" She lifted her chin from her knees and studied me from head to toe, worry creasing her forehead.

Fuck, if that look didn't drain some of the frustration right out of me. "How long have you been out here?"

"A little over an hour, maybe. I worried for a while I had the wrong house."

"Right house." I crossed the porch and picked up the bowl of water, wincing slightly at the pain in my ribs, then emptied the contents over the railing. Anne's Mercedes was parked on the opposite side of the street.

"I was icing my feet," Allie muttered.

"I've been around you long enough to recognize the foot-icing bowl. And it takes a hell of a lot longer than an hour to melt that much ice." I put the bowl on the swing next to her, and she unfolded her legs. I was too tired to fight with her, but I didn't want her to go either.

She tugged the edges of her cardigan closer. "Fine, it was a couple of hours."

My shoulders dropped. She had to be frozen. "Come inside and get warm." I unlocked the front door, then held it open as she picked up her shoes and walked in.

She looked left, into the living room, and right, toward my office, then glanced up the steep stairs to the second floor. "I like the original woodwork."

"I'd say thanks, but I'm just renting it." I shut the door, and to my surprise, she set her shoes down on the hardwood and walked straight into my office.

"Because you don't plan to stay," she said over her shoulder, flipping on the light switch.

My stomach clenched as I took off my hat and hung it on the coatrack, my jacket quickly following, and I battled the illogical feeling that I was about to be tested. Good thing I kept the place picked up.

"I was only supposed to be here long enough to help Caroline get on her feet. It's taking a little longer than I planned." I followed her in, watching her expression shift to curiosity as she tucked her hair behind her ears and looked over the bookcases, stopping to examine the titles, pausing when she came across a framed photo.

"Savannah," I explained when she looked closer at one of Juniper and me on the beach when she was five. "It was my second duty station. I was there when Sean died, then begged everyone I knew for a compassionate reassignment."

"Did you like it there?" She moved along, her gaze skimming across a handful of awards I'd wedged between books in their padded folders.

"Yeah. I liked living somewhere else, seeing new places, meeting new people—that kind of thing." I would have killed to know what she was thinking. Her being here was an admission that she had real feelings for me, but that didn't mean she'd let herself give in to them, not when she felt I'd jeopardized her career.

Which, in her defense . . . I unknowingly had.

"And these?" She tugged a few of the awards free.

"They're handed out when you save people, but they're just pieces of paper." I shrugged.

"Bravery and valor," she read off one, then closed the folder and put it back with the others. "Sounds like you." Her gaze shifted to the framed map of Alaska above my desk. "You never asked for Sitka?"

"Twice," I answered, fatigue settling into my bones. "But I wasn't highly ranked, and my wants didn't match the needs of the Coast Guard."

"And now that you have the opportunity to ask again, you're going to request to stay here." She picked up a framed piece of Juniper's artwork off my desk. "For her."

"For the same reason you wouldn't get in the boat before Eva." We may have been polar opposites, but we were eerily similar in one respect: our family came first, which was exactly why this thing between us had about a zero percent chance of lasting past August.

"I'm second-guessing that choice lately." She pivoted and walked between my desk and the worn leather armchair, passing right by me and walking into the living room. "Do you ever second-guess coming back?"

"No." I followed, my right side throbbing as her gaze swept over the space, no doubt cataloging everything, from the art I'd picked up during a drunken trip to Miami with Beachman to the potted plant I'd somehow managed to keep alive in the corner.

"Do you ever think about leaving?" She ran her fingers over the soft throw blanket draped over the armchair and cracked a yawn.

"Every day." But I wanted her with me, spending weekends curled beside me on the sofa, her laughter filling these rooms. I wanted to bicker about everything and nothing, and then make up and decide what we'd make for dinner. I wanted the mundane interactions of a relationship. An ache of longing sliced between my ribs and cut straight into my heart. Even if I convinced her that we could make this work long term, eventually our past would have to be dealt with. She'd never forgive me for what I'd done. It was only a matter of time before it tore us apart.

"Maybe you should go." She turned her attention to the photographs on the gallery wall, and yawned again.

I raked my hands through my hair. "Allie, I love that you're finally here, but I'm exhausted from fighting thirty-foot seas and a really panicked family who thought I was a ladder they needed to climb, and my ribs are killing me—"

"What happened to your ribs?" Her face whipped toward mine and her eyes flared.

"Nothing a couple nights of good sleep isn't going to take care of."

"Let me see." She strode over and tugged my top up, then yanked my T-shirt free, and I lifted my arm because I didn't have the energy to argue with her . . . and I loved her hands.

She inhaled sharply. "Hudson."

"It's fine. Just a bad bruise." I'd had way worse. "People do irrational things when they're scared."

Her hand hovered over the foot-size contusion, but she didn't touch it. "I'm sorry."

"You didn't do it."

"That's not what I meant." She dropped my clothes back into place. "I owe you an apology. There are very few people in my life I trust with . . . me, but I've never guarded myself against my sisters. And when Eva crawled over my corpse to get ahead, I took my anger out on you, and I shouldn't have. I'm sorry." She dragged her gaze back to mine.

"Apology accepted."

Her eyebrows rose. "That easy?"

"That easy." I nodded. "And I'm sorry I kept you out of the studio."

"That wasn't your fault. I wanted to stay with you." She huffed a frustrated sigh. "I always want to stay with you. That's the problem."

"Then let's go to bed." I held my hand out.

She drew back slightly. "I didn't come over for sex, Hudson."

"I figured." A smile tugged at my lips. "I'm tired. You're tired. And unless you feel like going out in that storm again, you may as well come to bed so we can both get some sleep." I lifted my brows when she furrowed hers. "You want to stay with me? Then stay."

"Just for the night?" she clarified.

"For as long as you want. I told you I'd take you any way I could get you, even one night at a time." I crooked my fingers, well aware that I was treading on exceptionally thin ice with an exceptionally skittish woman.

"That sounds good." She nodded slowly.

Thank fuck. I turned the lights out, checked the doors and windows, then took her up the creaking stairs, past the guest room where Juniper slept occasionally, and into my bedroom.

She took in the space, with its dark furniture and hunter green accents. "Sometimes I forget how neat you are. Nothing's out of place."

"More efficient that way. Come on." I took her into the bathroom, then pulled out a new toothbrush from the cabinet.

"You keep toothbrushes for your overnight guests?" She glared at the bristles.

"I keep toothbrushes stocked the same way I keep everything else." I opened the cabinet and showed her the organized rows of supplies before shutting it. "There's no one else. You know that. Stop looking for a reason to bolt."

She sighed, and we did the domestic things that couples take for granted, like sharing a sink and scooting past each other in the doorway.

Then I completely forgot how tired I was when she walked out of the bathroom in my T-shirt. My body temp rose by at least a full degree. Yeah, I definitely had a thing for seeing her in my clothes.

She slid under the covers, then lay on her back, staring up at the ceiling. "I don't suppose you have a phone charger?"

I carefully shifted to appease my pissed-off ribs, opened my night-stand drawer, and pulled out my spare, then handed it over.

"Thank you." She plugged it in and set her phone on the night-stand, then went back to staring at the ceiling. "You really missed your calling as a Boy Scout."

"Always prepared."

She drummed her fingers on top of the comforter.

"For fuck's sake, Allie, come here." I rolled toward her on my unbruised side, wrapped my arm over her ribs, then tugged her across the bed.

She promptly snuggled back against me, stole half my pillow, and pushed her incredible ass right against my dick as she got comfortable.

"What do you want to do about Eva?" I asked, resting my hand on her bare hip.

"Besides throttle her?" She sighed. "Once it's announced, it takes an act of God to change Vasily's mind. I'm not sure there's anything to do besides never speak to her again, which also is just . . . unconscionable."

"Yeah, I don't know if I could cut Gavin or Caroline off either." I stroked her skin absentmindedly. "You could leave the Company."

"You could leave the Coast Guard," she retorted.

"Point taken." I fought a smile. "But I move duty stations and still do the same thing. You can dance anywhere in the world. Are you still under contract?"

"For another month," she answered. "August fifteenth."

"Day of the Classic." It was coming up quickly.

She nodded. "I sat in the dark for two days, trying to decide if I should change my name and move to another country, or metaphorically beat the shit out of my sister."

"And what did you decide?"

"I want my role back." She shifted.

"Then be an act of God." I groaned. "And stop wiggling your ass or all my honorable intentions will disappear."

"As I recall, you did some *very* dishonorable things to me a few days ago."

"That's not helping." I kissed the top of her head, burying my nose in her hair and breathing in the unique floral scent that had haunted me for over a decade. "Go to sleep."

"You should put Sitka at the top of your list."

"One, Caroline isn't ready for me to go. Two, it puts me on the other side of the whole fucking country from the only person I'd like to be close to, who—in case you missed it—is you. And three, go to sleep." I draped my arm over her waist.

She tensed for a second, then burrowed closer, which I didn't mind in the least. "I didn't mean it. When I said we meant nothing, I didn't mean it. All I could think for those hours was that you were out in that storm and I'd . . ."

"I know. I knew it when you said it." I kissed the spot behind her ear. "And I have a hundred-percent return rate when it comes to storms."

She turned in my arms and looked at me. "I don't like it when people get too close," she whispered.

"Also something I know." I stroked her hip. "In fact, I've known that for about eleven years. And while it's probably one of your most frustrating qualities, I have to admit you keep it interesting. And in your defense, you warned me from the get-go." Guess we weren't sleeping, but I couldn't bring myself to care, not when I finally had her in my bed. "But you could do us both a favor and stop fighting it."

Her mouth opened like she wanted to say something, and she struggled for a few seconds. "Would you really take me any way you can get me?"

I was instantly, fully awake. "Yes."

"What if there's a way for this to be real but . . . safe." She tucked her hands against my chest.

Holy shit. Was this actually happening?

"It's already real. What do you need to feel safe?" I grazed my hand up her back.

She swallowed hard. "It has to be easy. Simple. No one gets hurt."

"Okay." I was already going to hurt, but as long as she escaped unscathed, I'd give her whatever she wanted. "No mess," I guessed.

She nodded. "Everything in my life is in upheaval, and I need you not to be." She brought her hands up beneath her chin. "And I know that's not fair—"

"Any way I can get you," I reminded her, and guilt started gnawing on the edges of my stomach. There was so much history between us.

"Even if it's only until I go back to New York?" She tensed.

Fuck. "You only want this to last for five weeks?" But hadn't that always been my plan? To use the summer to bring some life back into her eyes? Then why did it feel like having a section of my heart carved out?

"I can only have this for five weeks," she clarified. "I have to be fully focused once I go back. I'll be fighting for my place in the Company, and—"

Make it easy for her.

"I get it." I brushed her hair back from her face, and the guilt bit harder. This was a taste of everything I'd ever wanted, and talking about the past would risk *everything*, but I had to. I couldn't tell her this was real and not *be* real. "We should talk about the way I left you, and if you don't forgive me—"

"Don't." She shook her head quickly and cupped the side of my face. "I forgave you the second you told me you were at the performance. We were kids and we've both made mistakes, Hudson."

"Not like me." I gripped her hip, and she pressed her fingers to my mouth. I ceased breathing. She couldn't forgive me, not that painlessly.

"Simple and easy, remember?" she whispered. "It's all I can handle right now. Let's just agree that now is all that matters. The past is over, and we can't have a future. I won't give up New York, and you won't leave your family if you can help it, and if you can't, God knows where you'll be assigned." She tried to smile and failed. "So, unless you can think of something that prevents you from being mine for the next five weeks, please don't make me ask again. This is the only chance we'll get, and I want it." Her fingers slipped to my chin. "As long as you do."

The panic filling her eyes stole my words and my best intentions. She'd never been more vulnerable with me, even when we were teenagers. If I misstepped now, she'd turn those walls into a fortress.

"Hudson?" She drew back.

"Five weeks isn't long enough." My voice roughened. If this was longer than five weeks, if we were going the distance, I would have begged her to listen to me grovel. But digging up our past would bring a storm she couldn't weather, not now, not when she was about to wage war to get her role back. But after, when this was all over, she needed to hear me out. "But I'll take it."

She beamed, then leaned in and brushed a kiss over my lips. "Good. Now we can sleep." She turned in my arms and snuggled back against me.

I had five weeks to make her the happiest I could, and I wasn't going to fuck it up. Whatever she needed, I'd give her.

Our breathing evened out, and I was almost asleep when I heard her say, "Your dreams matter, too, Hudson."

The only dream I cared about was the one I was currently living, where I got to fall asleep next to her. It was the dream I blinked out of at five a.m. as Allie's phone rang.

She rolled out of my arms, slapped the top of the nightstand a few times, then finally answered the damn thing. "You'd better be dead, Anne. Yes, I'm at Hudson's. Because I'm a grown woman who can sleep wherever and with whomever she chooses."

"As long as it's me." I pulled her back against me. I wasn't due in until 0900 after last night's mission, which meant I had enough time to watch Allie come a couple of times and catch a couple more hours of shut-eye. Perfect morning.

"What do you mean, you haven't slept?" Allie tensed. "You what? You're kidding. No, that doesn't make sense. No way it's him." She sat up and my arm fell away. "No, I'll call him in a few hours. Because not everyone is up at five!" Her spine stiffened. "No, you did *not*. You didn't tell him why? Fine. I'll be home by nine." She hung up the phone and slid it back onto the nightstand.

"Feel like sharing?" I cracked an eye open.

She looked at me with wide eyes. "Anne found Juniper's original birth certificate."

CHAPTER TWENTY-SEVEN

Allie

Bright2lit: She deserves whatever she gets.

The clock ticked as I sat in the armchair of our living room, scrolling through Instagram, liking a few of Reagan's and Harlow's posts as they geared up for summer intensives.

Good for them. I'd spent my morning having two spectacular orgasms while riding Hudson, pushed over the edge on the second by watching him lose complete control under me—after I made him beg, of course. Surely, that counted for cardio.

Anne sat on the couch across from me next to Kenna, her back twisted so she could look out the window, her fingers drumming a quick rhythm on the upholstered back.

Kenna and I shared a look, and then she swiped on her iPad. "Anne, you are going to have to find some other outlet for the nervous energy, because you're giving *me* anxiety."

Anne's fingers paused, but she didn't look away. "Just nervous."

"We can tell," I noted, tucking my feet under me and reaching for my water bottle so Kenna wouldn't get on me about hydrating.

"One of you could read to me," she suggested.

"Would you like to hear about a new minimally invasive procedure for rotator cuff repair that's showing good results in clinicals?" Kenna asked. "Because that's what I'm reading about."

"I thought you weren't a surgeon?" Anne finally gave up on her pretzel maneuver and twisted onto her knees toward the window.

"I'm not. I'd rather treat the whole patient and find ways to prevent getting cut open in the first place. Doesn't mean I don't read about what's out there." She swiped again, then glanced pointedly to the end table next to me. "That banana isn't doing you any good just sitting there."

I rolled my eyes and quickly peeled the fruit.

"What are you reading, Allie?" Anne asked. "Anything good?"

"Looks like Candace is engaged." I smiled and turned my phone around so they could see the picture of the brunette showing off her ring. Anne looked over her shoulder, then spun back around like the car wouldn't pull into the driveway if she wasn't personally watching.

"Look at you on social media again, and good for Candace!" Kenna nodded. "Jillian's great, and she's wonderfully talented too. I stopped by her new gallery last month and the place was packed."

"An artist? Huh. I always figured Candace would marry another dancer," Anne said.

"That's your mother talking," Kenna chided before looking my way. "Some people like having lives outside the studio, having a partner who can help them anchor their life outside ballet so they survive life *after* ballet."

"Don't start." I scrolled with my right hand and snacked on the banana.

"She has a point. You know what they say," Anne muttered. "A dancer dies twice." Once when they retire, the second when they expire. "I like that you're breaking your no-dancer rule, Allie, and I love getting to see your smile again."

"But?" I took another bite and opened the Seconds app.

She folded her arms across the back of the couch, and rested her chin on her hands. "I can't help that I'm protective of you, and I know you said Hudson was there the night at *Giselle*, and that goes a long way to climbing out of the hole he dug when we were kids, but—"

"But you've never entirely trusted him." It was nothing I hadn't heard before. I logged in to a new, anonymous Seconds profile, then checked out the RousseauSisters4 page and stared. The account had gained another two hundred thousand more followers since I'd come to Haven Cove in May, and forty thousand in the last two days. Hopefully the video was slowing down.

"People make shitty decisions before their frontal lobe develops," Kenna interrupted, saving me the trouble. "He couldn't handle seeing Allie hurt and dipped out for basic. That makes him an immature dick at eighteen, not irredeemable. It's not like he caused the accident or something." She looked up from her tablet. "He didn't, did he? There wasn't some second set of tires or something?"

"No, that was all Lina. Never could obey a damned speed limit." Anne sighed. "Or any rule, for that matter."

"It was just us out there," I confirmed. "That much I remember." I searched RousseauSisters4 and clicked on the first video, turning the volume down so the others wouldn't hear. It started as the video Eva had secretly taken of me explaining why I wasn't comfortable with grand jetés—or any leaps yet—through the edits she'd made of my embarrassing errors during our weekend, and then WestCoastPointe stitched it, adding their commentary as they walked through the halls of a ballet company in California. Thanks to the subtitles, I kept my humiliation to myself.

"So let's break down the latest MBC drama. Do I think Alessandra knew she was being recorded? I doubt it. But that doesn't change the fact that she's clearly still in the early stages of rehab, and from what I'm hearing at MBC, she flat-out lied to *everyone* at their gala about being ready to return for the fall, which brings up some major ethics issues, in my opinion."

The banana lost its flavor. That wasn't true. I never lied.

The creator's face twisted in disgust. "Look, it's not like MBC wasn't going to hold a spot for her if she told them she's taking longer to heal—she's *Alessandra Rousseau*—but lying to her company about her injuries when they developed their entire fall program around her is just . . . It lacks integrity, you know? No respectable company is going to touch her after this. Look, I've said it before, she's as pretentious and haughty as they come, but she used to be one of the greats, and I'm disappointed. She's supposed to be an idol. Let me know what you think in the comments."

I never asked to be. Despite the immediate nausea, I chewed the banana because I needed the fuel, then attempted to reach expert-level masochist and tapped the comments.

PenchePrincess: Damn. Bet she never thought she'd get caught.

AdrienneAdage14: This is why you should have to rehab at your company if on contract.

WestCoastPointe: AdrienneAdage14 Totally agree.

AraThomas9164: They should be able to sue her for fraud

Dulcinea4ever: She's disgusting and I hope they don't renew her contract

OnPointe34: Why isn't anyone talking about the fact that they replaced her with her sister? Can't MBC stand on its own without a Roussseau?

> **Pardonmypasse:** OnPointe34 Doubt it. The whole place would crumble without that $$$

Tutucutex20: I stopped supporting her forever ago.

ReeseOnToe: I think her sister did a really shitty thing by posting that video.

> **WestCoastPointe:** ReeseOnToe Disagree. Eva did the community a service.

> **ReeseOnToe:** WestCoastPointe she's her SISTER.

> **WestCoastPointe:** ReeseOnToe Right, so imagine how hard it must have been for Eva to hold Alessandra accountable. I have so much respect for her.

> **TanyaThomas97:** ReeseOnToe, absolutely agree with you. Obs she didn't know about the recording.

BrandoQueso: Not sure how I ended up on ballet Seconds, but I'm here for the drama.

ReaganHuang: If Alessandra says she'll be ready by fall, then she will. She's not a liar, and you're not helping your professional image by calling her one, Lila.

"Allie?" Kenna called my name like it wasn't the first time she'd tried to get my attention.

"Huh?" I jerked the phone to my chest, hiding the screen, and found her standing over me.

"I was asking why Hudson wasn't here, considering this involves him too." She held out her hand. "Give that to me."

"Why?" I clutched it tighter.

"Because you went pale as hell, stopped listening to us, and now you're the shade of a cherry, so unless Hudson is in there sending you dirty text messages that startle the shit out of you, hand it over." She flexed her hand.

I swallowed my pride and embarrassment, and showed her.

She read through the comments, alternating between scoffs and sighs. "You do not need to be reading this shit." She shook her head. "I'd love to see someone say any of this in person."

"I told her to stop looking," Anne said, still staring out the window. "Stick to the baby-goat videos if you need dopamine. Or that one guy who cooks."

"Love that Reagan has your back," Kenna said, handing the phone back. "Want me to hop in and defend your honor?"

"No. They'll just call you complicit. I'm already on fire, no need to strap yourself to the pyre." My fingers hovered over the screen, and for the slightest heartbeat, indignation won and I debated replying to set the record straight. I tapped the Comment button.

"Don't do it," Kenna warned. "I have no doubt this feels shitty, but you enter that fray personally and the sharks will feast. They'll twist whatever you say to fit their narrative and set off a new wave of monetized content. Don't pay their rent. We both know next week there will be something else new and shiny for everyone to comment on. Now, where is Aquaman?"

I scrolled up and closed the app. "Hudson couldn't get out of work."

"He's here." Anne pushed back so hard that she slid clean off the couch, and I winced as her knees hit the floor. "He's here!" She scrambled to her feet, and I rose to mine.

"Stop it." I ditched the phone on the end table and put myself in front of Anne. "We have a plan. You *will* stick to the plan. You have no idea how he'll respond to this."

Anne pursed her lips, then snatched the manila envelope off the coffee table and sat down on the couch.

"Thank you," I told her, then headed to the front door and opened it as Everett hauled his Louis Vuitton suitcase up the steps in a fitted teal polo and plaid shorts. A knot of anxiety formed in my throat.

"Oh my God, there she is!" He abandoned his luggage at the doorway, shoved his sunglasses onto his blond hair, and rushed me with his last few steps, carrying me into the house in a hug. I held on, knowing it might be the last one he willingly gave me. "Ugh, Alessandra." His arms squeezed tight. "I was waiting for you to reach out, but when Anne called, I hopped on the first flight." He set me down and lifted his hands to my upper arms.

"Hi, Everett." I smiled and found myself searching his face for signs that Anne's discovery had any basis in truth.

"What Vasily did is just . . . it's a steaming pile of shit. The whole Company's pissed. Since when do we announce casting in the middle of July? And you should have *seen* the fit Charlotte threw that Eva had been yanked through the ranks up to principal above any of the soloists. Reagan said she shattered one of the mirrors in the women's locker room. Pretty sure Vasily is hoping it will all blow over by the time everyone's back in the building after summer intensives, but I've heard a couple soloists might not renew their contracts. It's all very dramatic." His eyebrows raised scandalously. "Did Vasily at least explain himself to you, or did he send Maxim to do his dirty work?"

"I missed his call and now he won't take mine." That knot in my throat doubled in size.

"Of course he won't." He rolled his eyes and dropped his hands. "He knows the board isn't going to fire him while his wife's the executive director, so it's not like he has to own up to whatever fuckery this is. What the hell happened? Did your mother make a call or something? Not that I think Sophie would screw you over in order to . . ." He cocked his head to the side. "Well, I wouldn't put anything past your mother."

"She didn't call." I stifled the absurd bubble of laughter that tried to rise at the accusation. "For the first time in my life, I can honestly say my mother had nothing to do with this. It's all Eva."

"Fucking Eva." He pulled his suitcase in and shut the door. "So what's the plan to get your role back?"

"I . . . don't have one." Short of becoming the act of God Hudson had suggested.

"Please. You have Dr. Lowell here with you. Everyone knows it. If you don't have a plan, she does. Don't you, Kenna?" He raised his voice with the last question.

"I do," Kenna answered, appearing in the doorway. "But my plan depends on three things going right."

"Well, I'm here, so obviously you have one." He gestured to his suitcase. "I assumed Anne called because you needed a partner to practice with, because hell is freezing over before I partner with your sister come October. And before you ask, of course I'll stay for the month. Michael will have to come visit, of course, but who doesn't love summers in Cape Cod? God, I haven't been here since that last intensive your mother taught. How old were we?" He surveyed the foyer like he was looking for changes and peeked into the studio.

I cleared my throat. "I was seventeen that summer. Lina was nineteen."

"That's right." He didn't so much as flinch. "So what's the second variant to your brilliance?" he asked Kenna.

"That's a bit more—" she started.

"How do you explain this!" Anne charged out of the living room, waving Juniper's original birth certificate.

"Way to stick to the plan," Kenna muttered.

Everett's manicured brows lifted as she thrust the paper inches from his face, and I held my breath as he scanned the document that listed Juniper simply as Baby Rousseau. "Well, shit. I'd pretty much forgotten about that."

My jaw dropped along with my stomach, "That's all you have to say?"

He glanced at me, then Anne, his features slackening. "Oh, shit, you didn't know. In that case, anyone feel like a drink? I might need one for this."

Five minutes later, I handed Everett the fourth glass of lemonade I'd poured as he'd settled into the matching armchair, then took mine to my own seat and found a text message on my phone.

HUDSON: Just thinking about you.

I smiled despite the circumstances and typed out Take it easy on your ribs today, then gave all my attention to Everett on my left, who was avoiding Anne's glare like a professional.

"Start talking," she demanded.

"I was sitting right where Kenna is when Lina asked me to play daddy." He ran his finger over the rim of the glass. "She said it would only be on paper, and I'd only be responsible for a few hours. Just long enough to sign the termination of parental rights."

My heart clenched. She'd told him, but not us.

"So you aren't Juniper's father?"

"Is that what they ended up naming the kid? Her parents, I mean." He took a drink, then realized we were staring. "Of course I'm not her father. That would require me having sex with a woman. No, thank you." He shook his head.

Anne sagged like a balloon that had lost all its helium.

"Like you didn't know it was a long shot," Kenna muttered at her.

"Do you know who it is?" I asked Everett.

"No." Everett leaned forward and took a coaster from the stack on the coffee table. "She said it was a one-night stand when she got to San Francisco and couldn't remember his name." He set the coaster on the end table, then put his glass on it. "I can't believe you guys don't know this. I thought you shared everything."

"Apparently not, so please keep going." Anne stared at her glass. "When was this?"

"I think it was the first week in May," he answered.

"And she was here?" I looked around the living room like Lina would magically appear.

"Yeah." He nodded. "Said she'd been here for a month or so."

"She must have come once we went back to New York after spring break," Anne muttered. "Records said Juniper was born a few towns away. She stayed in Barnstable County."

"Sounds right. I agreed to come up once she'd had the baby, and when that happened, I signed whatever the lawyers put in front of me."

"Why would you do that for her?" I asked.

"She was pregnant and needed help. The lawyers said the adoption would go through easier, faster, if the legal father signed off on it, and Lina made it sound like she had the perfect family picked out for the kid. And when I hesitated . . ." He struggled for words, then took his sunglasses from the top of his head and set those down too. "You're going to think I'm a piece of shit."

"I could never." I reached across the end table and squeezed his hand.

"I could," Anne mumbled.

"Knock it off." Kenna threw a pillow at her, and Anne deflected, then hugged it to her chest.

"I didn't make the cut for the MBC summer intensive that year," Everett admitted, running his fingers through his hair so it stuck straight up. "I auditioned in January, and didn't make it."

"Impossible." I shook my head. "You were here that summer, and Mom only allowed kids who were accepted into that program to come . . ." My ribs tightened around my lungs.

"Yeah. That." He nodded. "That was the price. I could train with the Rousseau girls, and she'd cover my room and board in town, as well as secure me a place in the Classic so I could compete for an MBC contract."

I forced myself to breathe, then drank down half my glass of lemonade, focusing on the tart, sour flavor.

"Machiavelli had *nothing* on your mom," Kenna said.

"I really thought you knew," Everett said to me. "I thought that's why you were always so nice to me."

"I've always liked you because you're . . . you." I could hardly fault him for keeping secrets when I kept so many of my own.

His gaze whipped to Anne. "They said it would be confidential. Your mother promised me no one would ever know."

"She only kept this copy of the birth certificate, from what I've found," she told him. "But you were always going to be found, Everett. They changed the law a few years ago. Once she turns eighteen, Juniper will have access to her records."

"Well, that's . . ." He swallowed. "Good to know."

"I thought I knew her," Anne whispered. "And every day I'm realizing I knew *nothing*."

"No one knows everything about everyone," Everett said. "We all keep things to ourselves."

Gravel crunched in the driveway, and we all looked out of the window as a black Range Rover pulled in.

"Are we having a house party I don't know about?" Anne asked.

"That's the third element of getting your role back," Kenna said, unfolding from the couch and walking across the living room. "I can rehab your ankle, but what you need is an instructor."

"Did she call your mom?" Everett whispered.

She wouldn't. My stomach lurched.

"Doubtful," Anne replied. "Mom is a little . . . self-absorbed at the moment."

"What did you do?" I asked Kenna as I stood. Every instructor I knew was teaching intensives this time of year.

"I'd never call your mother," Kenna called back from the foyer, then opened the door.

"Baby!" Eloise stepped into the house in a red sheath dress and hugged Kenna, then looked over her sunglasses at Kenna's athletic wear. "What *are* you wearing? No matter. My bags are in the car. I'll take Sophie's room, of course."

Oh, holy *shit*.

She hadn't called my mother. She'd called *hers*.

CHAPTER
TWENTY-EIGHT

Allie

When the time came for summer intensives as a kid, and Mom spared no expense for bringing her hand-selected instructors to the cape, she'd always save the hardest, the most demanding teacher for last.

It was no coincidence that teacher was her best friend.

Eloise unpacked, told Anne to prepare lunch, and ordered Everett and me into the studio.

"We have our work cut out for us, don't we?" That was all she said as she changed the music in the stereo.

The next two days passed in a blur. Once Kenna confirmed my ankle was cleared without restriction, Eloise was *merciless*. She demanded perfection, and when we didn't give it, she put us through combination after combination until we got it right or she decided we were too exhausted to continue.

When Hudson brought Juniper over the evening of Eloise's third day, the teacher hung back as I worked with her. She watched, she assessed, and to my surprise, she smiled once we were done.

"Do you know who I am?" Eloise asked as Juniper put her slippers into her bag. "I only ask because you were staring in that mirror like you did."

"You're Eloise Lowell," Juniper whispered reverently. "You were a soloist at MBC before you became an instructor."

"That's right." She nodded. "Would you like me to help teach you while I'm here?"

"Think carefully before you answer, Juniper." I took off my own slippers, wincing at the sight of my feet. That blister on my right foot had popped in the last hour despite the cushion I'd wrapped onto it, and Eloise wasn't a fan of Ouch Pouches. "Eloise is the best, but she's not afraid to hurt your feelings."

Eloise arched a brow.

"Yes, please," Juniper responded, lifting her chin. "I can take it."

Eloise chuckled. "I think you can. Now run off to your . . ." She threw a glance toward the doorway, and I looked up to see Hudson waiting, his hair still wet from showering after the pool.

My pulse jumped, and that sweet, biting pressure I refused to name filled my chest. It was beyond liking him. Beyond caring for him. But I wasn't giving it the power of a label.

"Uncle," Juniper supplied, then shoved her feet into a pair of neon-green Crocs and grabbed her bag. "Thank you!"

"Don't thank me yet," Eloise warned, her gaze sliding to mine.

I stood, disassociating from the pain as I walked toward Hudson. As much as I hated to admit it, I'd missed him the last few days.

He grinned, that dimple appearing in his cheek as I approached, but his expression quickly fell when he looked down. "What the hell happened to your feet?"

"It's nothing. Paying the price of a few lost calluses, but they'll rebuild." I rose up and kissed him, quick and fast. "This is Eloise, Kenna's mother."

He offered his hand, and Eloise took it, shaking it slowly. "I've heard a lot about you, Mrs. Lowell."

"If you're who I think you are, then I'm afraid I can say the same." She folded her arms over her pink sweater. "You were a thorn in Sophie's side."

"Proud of it." He nodded.

"Hmm." She walked back into the studio as Juniper rushed by, her bun already falling out in places.

I walked them out, rolling my stiff shoulders and neck, then said goodbye to Juniper as she hopped into Hudson's truck.

He wound his arms around my waist on the front porch. "Looks like you've decided to go with the act of God strategy?"

"Something like that." I placed my hands on his chest. "You know how you're always talking about balance?"

He nodded, two lines creasing his brow.

"There's not going to be any balance. Not for the next month." I swallowed as the pressure tightened in my chest, mixing with the bitter taste of fear. "Eloise, Kenna, and Everett are all out here for me, and I have to show up every day for them. My focus has to be on what happens in that studio if I want any shot at getting my role back."

He pulled me closer. "You cutting our time short?"

"I don't want to." My hands slipped up his T-shirt and around his neck, and my chest constricted. "But it would mean you draw the short stick. The only time I'll have is at night. I'll be pulling eleven-hour days and sleeping at least eight hours at night to recover. Give or take the hour or two it will take me to wake up and eat meals, and there's not much else."

"Am I an asshole if I ask for the leftovers?"

"No." I shook my head and barely kept from sighing with relief. The skeptical part of me had screamed that he'd walk away.

"Then short stick it is." He bent down and kissed me. "If this was a movie, you'd be heading into your training montage. I get it. I have no problem counting sleep as quality time. Your place. My place. I'll make it work."

"Thank you." I smiled, and that ache started freaking throbbing in the area of my heart.

"Any way I can have you." He kissed me again, taking the time to deepen it just enough that my breath quickened and I leaned into him. "Try to make it nine."

"Nine what?" I asked as he let me go and started down the steps.

"Nine hours in bed," he replied over his shoulder. "You give me that extra hour and I promise you'll sleep better the other eight."

I snorted. "See you tonight?"

"You want me to knock? Or do I have to climb up the trellis?" He grinned as he reached his door.

"I'll let you in," I promised.

"Don't make promises you can't keep. See you in a few." He climbed into the truck, and I walked back into the house after his taillights disappeared down the drive.

Eloise was waiting in the foyer. "That little girl looks awfully familiar."

"Does she?" I closed the door and fought to calm my racing heartbeat.

"She looks like Lina. Same eyes. Same smile. Even steps out of her pirouette at the same place when she loses her balance." She stared at me. "Anything you feel like telling me?"

Mom hadn't told *her*. "Nothing comes to mind."

"Hmm." She nodded. "And her uncle. Is he a distraction?"

My spine straightened. "No, ma'am."

"Good. Hate to waste all this work on a summer fling." She headed up the stairs.

No wonder Eloise was such good friends with my mother. Their words were eerily similar. It was on the tip of my tongue to argue that it wasn't a fling . . . but that's exactly what we were doing. That's all I'd asked for, all I could handle, and everyone—even Hudson—knew it.

But just because I knew it wouldn't work out once I went to New York didn't mean I didn't want it to. I simply knew better than to open my door to the inevitable destruction our failure would cause. So I concentrated on what we had, and I threw everything into *now*.

Days spun into weeks, whirring by in an unending cycle of work, pain, and recovery. Slowly, my body adjusted. My calluses thickened. My ankle strengthened.

Every morning I was home, I'd pull open my nightstand drawer while Hudson showered, peek in at Lina's ring to remind myself why this was all worth it, and get to work. I spent my days in the studio and my nights with Hudson, burrowing deeper into the tangled mess of my feelings for him instead of running, like every instinct demanded. He fit himself into my life like sand poured into a jar full of pebbles, settling seamlessly into the spaces between the rocks. He was everywhere without making himself the priority.

Whether at his house or mine, we spent every night he wasn't on duty in the same bed. He held me to a strict eight-hour policy, never once letting me lose sleep in favor of indulging in him, which only made me head to bed earlier, determined to savor every second we had together. He kept a phone charger on his nightstand at my house. I kept clothes in a drawer at his.

July became August. Michael came out to spend weekends with Everett, and Matthias flew in whenever his schedule allowed. Storms rolled in, and Hudson flew out every time, and I slowly learned how to breathe around the fear and trust that he'd come home, slowly started to trust *him*.

Juniper flourished under Eloise, learning faster than I ever had at that age, and though Eloise never mentioned Lina again, I'd catch her watching Juniper with a sad smile from time to time and knew . . . she knew.

"She's talented," Eloise remarked one Friday in August as Juniper packed up after rehearsal. "She won't win, but she won't embarrass herself either. I think at least the top twenty in her division."

"I hope so," I agreed, trying to ignore the guilt that sat in my stomach like lead. Day by day, we crept closer to the Classic, and dug a deeper hole when it came to Caroline. We'd all become horrifyingly comfortable in the lie, selfishly unwilling to risk the delicate happiness that came with being in each other's lives. I just hoped we'd made the right decision, that showing Caroline how easily our lives could blend for Juniper's sake, we'd assuage her fears.

"I had something made for her," Eloise said with the flash of a smile. "For the Classic. It will be here tomorrow so she can practice in it. Took her measurements while you were busy staring at her uncle in the pool last week."

My gaze whipped to hers. "You didn't have to."

"Of course I did. I saw what you two were looking at online. Can't have a Rousseau girl dancing in just any costume, can we?" She leveled the same look on me that Kenna used.

"Who said she was a Rousseau girl?" I tugged off my demi-pointe shoes and wiggled my toes. The muscles were still warm, but they'd lock up soon enough.

"Who indeed?"

The next week arrived without permission, sneaking up on us like the end of summer always did—before any of us felt ready.

Juniper danced in the pink confection with the widest smile I'd ever seen, and any guilt I felt about hiding her secret from Caroline evaporated. The second she saw her daughter this happy tomorrow, she'd let her continue. There was no doubt in my mind.

"She looks like Lina," Anne whispered as we watched Juniper twirl.

"Yes and no." A slow smile spread across my face. Juniper took more risks than Lina did at that age, put more of her own personality into every move. Lina and I stepped into roles and became them, but Juniper somehow made the roles bend to her. "She looks like herself."

"You ready for tomorrow?" Anne glanced my way.

"Physically or emotionally?" I asked.

"Emotionally." Anne bumped her shoulder against mine. "I know you're physically solid."

"No." I shook my head. "Too many things can go wrong." It wasn't just the Classic or Caroline; it was the official end of the deadline I'd set for Hudson and me. But I couldn't think about that, not if I wanted to survive the next twenty-four hours.

"They won't." She hooked her arm through mine.

"And if Caroline bars us from seeing Juniper for going against every single rule she's put in place for her daughter?" My stomach roiled.

"She won't." Anne shook her head with a smile. "We'll beg her forgiveness, and everything will be okay. It's one of those ends-justifies-the-means situations."

I wished I felt that certain.

"If only you looked that ecstatic during rehearsal," Eloise said as she walked our way, motioning toward Juniper. "Should I order one in your size?"

"If you think it will help," I replied.

"As long as you let yourself shine on that stage tomorrow, you'll do just fine, Alessandra." She glanced at Juniper. "You both will. Now I'm off to call your mother so I can relay all the gossip coming out of the Company. It's my favorite time of the week." Eloise left the studio.

"At least she's nice to her," Anne muttered.

I grabbed my phone, which practically lived on the windowsill since Eloise would have tossed it into the pool if I'd wasted rehearsal time looking at it, and found two missed texts.

REAGAN: Just checked into the hotel. This sucks without you. You're coming to the reception tomorrow night, right? He has to renew your contract.

My thumbs hovered over the keyboard. Every MBC principal dancer had reached out, but not once in the five weeks since Vasily announced the casting had he called. Neither had Eva.

ALESSANDRA: I'll see you there. Promise.

With a swipe, I switched to Hudson's thread.

HUDSON: Gavin's on his way to pick up Juniper.

ALLIE: I'll make sure not to get confused and let him into my bed.

"Seven o'clock. Time to hang it up for the evening," I told Juniper. "Awh." She danced by to a melody only she could hear. "Already?" "Yep." My phone buzzed. "Time flies when you're having fun."

HUDSON: Don't even joke about that. It would be a shame to break my mother's heart by committing fratricide.

I scoffed.

ALLIE: I hate that I can't see you tonight.

Hudson was on twenty-four-hour duty and wouldn't get off until just before the Classic in the morning. I breathed through an irrational swell of panic. We hadn't had enough time, and yet we'd had exactly what we'd agreed upon.

"At least I get to wear it tomorrow for real." Juniper sighed, then took her bag out of the studio, hopefully headed to the bathroom to change.

Dinner smelled scrumptious as I headed into the house, dodging one of the suitcases Anne had already packed in preparation for our departure. She'd been a godsend, cooking to Kenna's exact specifications all day, playing with Sadie when I spent too long in the studio, and even prepping the endless pointe shoes I went through.

Sadie trotted over to me from the living room with a stuffed bear in her mouth.

"Hey, girl." I bent down to scratch behind her ears.

"I hope Vasily is ready to have a dog in the building," Everett said, walking down the stairs, his hair still wet from a shower.

"You think he'll let me bring her?"

Everett grinned. "I think he's going to give you anything and everything you want after tomorrow." He pulled me into a hug. "We're ready, Allie. You're ready."

I squeezed him back. "In case I forget to say it tomorrow, thank you." My phone buzzed and I pulled away to read the text.

HUDSON: Me, too. But I'll be dead center, back row tomorrow.

I was counting on it.

CHAPTER
TWENTY-NINE

Hudson

BriellePiers73: Best GRWM I've seen lately.
Good luck today!

"I cannot believe you're making me do this," Caroline muttered as we waded through the crowd at the Haven Cove theater and I protected the bouquet of pink peonies that cost a hefty chunk of my pay. "Remind me why?"

The last time I'd simultaneously anticipated and dreaded a day had been when I'd left for basic. Seemed fitting this time revolved around the Rousseau girls too.

Today was the last official day of my relationship with Allie. Every cell in my body rebelled at the thought of walking away. I'd somehow managed to battle last night's impulses to go AWOL, bloody my hands climbing the trellis to her room like I was eighteen, and lay out a full, exhaustive, thought-out argument as to why she should give us a real chance. I'd saved that for tonight.

"First, because we're here to support our brother, and secondly, culture is good for you." Gavin nodded to a year-rounder and his costumed son as they hurried past us with excited smiles.

"Says the man who preaches that *Die Hard* is a classic." Caroline shifted sideways, making room for a train of four girls in various colors of tutus. "Not a single one of those girls is a local. Didn't any local girls enter the contest?"

"I'm sure they did," I answered.

"I don't recognize any of them." Caroline scoured the halls, and I prayed Juniper was already out of sight.

"Trust me, there are more ballet studios around here than you realize," I muttered.

"Besides, you can't hate the hand that feeds you," Gavin argued. "Whether or not you like Sophie Rousseau, you have to hand it to her for bringing in a *shit* ton of business to a small town. This is the kind of thing that happens in New York or Boston. Not here."

"Fine," she grumbled as we turned left into the theater. "I can admit that we made some record-breaking money this week at the café, which is where I should be."

"Thought you were training a new manager," I said, skipping over the programs on the table and leading my siblings to the back row. "Part of your whole work-life balance thing."

"He's not . . . ready," she muttered.

"Or you're just a control freak," Gavin noted.

"Possibly," she admitted. "I'm working on it. Just not there yet."

I scoured the theater, both dreading and hoping for sight of Allie's mother, but didn't see her. "Fuck," I muttered as we slipped past the others in the back row, making our excuses until we reached the dead center, and then I sat, settling the tissue-paper-wrapped bouquet in my lap.

"Who are you looking for?" Caroline asked. "Maybe I can help."

"Sophie Rousseau." The judges' tables were still empty, so maybe Allie was wrong and she'd show.

"You really going there?" Gavin leaned forward in his seat and lifted his brows.

"Don't really have a choice." Fear and determination were dangerous when combined, and I'd walked hand in hand with them for the last few weeks, ever since I changed my preference list for duty stations. "If I want a shot at making it work with Allie, I'm going to have to have it out with her mother. The school she teaches at said she's not interested in speaking with me, and I'd like to get it over with." Before Sophie realized I was in Allie's life to stay and destroyed whatever chance Allie and I had. "And I know Allie said she wasn't coming, but how do you not show up to watch your daughter's comeback?"

"She's always been a viper. Sophie, not Allie." Caroline glanced at the pink roses in Gavin's lap. "Do you really think it's appropriate to bring your brother's girlfriend flowers?"

Shit, those were for Juniper.

"Allie deserves two bouquets." Gavin shrugged.

"Weird, but whatever. Okay, explain . . ." Caroline set her purse down and gestured ahead of us. "How this works. I never got to this stage."

"Dancers compete in their division." I readied my CliffsNotes explanation and searched the theater for any sign of Allie. "Youth all the way to senior. In this case, ten to nineteen. Official judges sit there." I pointed to the line of judges' tables four rows down, the empty chairs lit by small table lamps, each marked for the companies who'd been invited to send judges. The others were scattered around the theater, clipboards in their laps, and from experience, I knew it was only a portion of the ones who would show up for the finals tomorrow. "Winners get prizes."

"Like scholarships to Madeline's," Caroline said with a nod. "I know that part."

"No." A corner of my mouth quirked. "Madeline will award some scholarships to the local dancers who come in around the top twenty." Which would hopefully be Juniper. Nausea made me shift in my seat. "Pretty sure Sophie Rousseau only ever invited them to give the appearance of being inclusive. The top winners get to move on to the Grand Prix, where the actual prizes are."

"And some of them get contracted right out of this theater," Gavin added.

"So it's like an opportunity for a team to sign someone before they actually enter the draft." She nodded. "Got it."

"Eh . . ." Gavin's head tilted and his face puckered.

"Close enough." I smiled for the first time in six days, but it quickly fell as judges and professionals filed in. London, Paris, New York, San Francisco, and Houston all took their places, leaving the center table empty.

"Excuse me." Eva and a few of the soloists from MBC worked their way down the row below us. She startled, then froze when she saw me and sat immediately, taking the seat in front of Gavin.

"Et tu, Brute?" Gavin flashed a smile when she looked over her shoulder.

"And Allie is competing in this?" Caroline's brow knit. "Isn't it . . . you know . . . a little beneath her?" She finished in a whisper.

"Allie's doing an exhibition," Gavin said loudly.

Eva whipped around, her mouth falling open as her frightened gaze met mine. "Allie's what?" Her outburst drew the attention of the other Company members.

"Doing. An. Exhibition," Gavin said slowly, dragging out the last word.

"That's not in the program," Harlow Oren noted, flipping through the pages. "And why are there only three local studios? I thought we usually accepted four."

"Quinn Hawkins shut down," Jacob Harvey answered from Harlow's right, bent over his phone. "Whole big drama about a month ago, remember? Ate up the Haven Cove Classic hashtag for like three days."

"Oh, right." Harlow nodded, still searching the program. "Something about NASD getting a complaint about abuse, and you know if NASD is getting involved, someone big in the community filed it."

Allie. I bit back a smile. She'd handled the teacher who'd thrown the water bottle.

"Seriously, Allie's exhibition isn't anywhere in this." Harlow waved the program and turned to Eva. "Is she even healed?"

"Of course not," Eva snapped. "So why is she performing?" She aimed the question at me, but I didn't trust myself to speak to her.

"Because you've entered the find-out portion of your relationship," Gavin answered. "You know, because you fucked around, and now—"

"I know what that means," she snapped. "Hudson?"

I let my anger slip its leash just enough for her to see, and she paled in the house lights, but I kept my mouth shut. Allie would handle her, just like she'd handled Quinn.

Caroline's gaze jumped between Eva and me, and then she bristled. "Look, I don't know what the hell you did to earn what my brother is dishing out—"

"She threw Allie's reputation in the mud, then stepped on it to steal the role that had been created for her," Gavin supplied.

Caroline's mouth unhinged. "But . . . you're her *sister*." Her tone implied that a worse crime didn't exist. "She defended you. She made sure Hudson pulled you out of the boat first. She—" Caroline's mouth snapped shut. "You know what? You don't exist to me. From now on, Allie is the only Rousseau girl as far as I'm concerned."

"You sure about that?" Eva arched a brow at me.

"Nawh." Gavin shook his head. "Anne's pretty fucking great, too, and Lina . . . well, I can say on pretty good authority that Lina would be ashamed of you."

Eva drew back like she'd been hit, and Caroline looked at Gavin like she'd never seen him before. "Look," Eva hissed, "if Allie can't hack it, then she needs to graciously depart so her inability to perform doesn't hold back Isaac. It's his ballet too."

For a second, I wondered if he also called her *darling*.

"You're a sh—" Gavin started, then fell quiet as the house lights dimmed and Anne walked out onto the stage with a handheld microphone.

She smiled brightly as the audience clapped. "Thank you. I'm Anne Rousseau, chairwoman of the Haven Cove Classic and daughter of our event's founder, Sophie Rousseau. It's my honor to personally welcome you on behalf of our family to the Haven Cove Classic!"

"I thought she was married?" Caroline whispered as we applauded.

"Divorcing," I answered, noting Anne's bare left hand. That was a new development.

"But neither of you dated her, right?" Caroline darted a glance at Gavin. "Because I think I'm picking up on a trend."

I shook my head as the applause died down.

"Mother is currently occupied dedicating herself to the next generation, so you'll have to deal with me instead." The audience chuckled. "She founded the Classic to foster the spirit of community, spread the beauty of ballet, and give dancers at every socioeconomic level access to professional critique, advancement, and scholarships from local instructors all the way to international companies."

She paused for another round of applause, and a flare of pink caught my eye to the left. Juniper peeked over the edge of one of the boxes.

My stomach jolted. Holy shit, she was going to get us caught before she even *started*.

"As usual, our thanks goes out to our sponsor, the incredible Metropolitan Ballet Company!" She gestured to the auditorium, and a spotlight swung to the door. Reagan Huang and Candace Baron walked in with wide smiles, followed by Vasily, who simply nodded as they took their seats in the center of the judges' row. "Naturally, this morning's festivities will focus on our juniors, starting at the beginner division, before our seniors compete this afternoon. My sister and I thought our up-and-coming generation might like to see what's possible when you follow your passion." Her smile sharpened as she looked to the judges, like it was directed at Vasily. "From the Metropolitan Ballet Company, please welcome to the stage principal dancers Everett Carr and, for the first time since her injury, my sister Alessandra Rousseau!" Anne gestured to the side of the stage, then quickly retreated into the wings as Everett and Allie walked out hand in hand.

The theater erupted with overwhelming applause, and Caroline put two fingers in her mouth and whistled. I brought my hands together again and again as I drank her in.

She was as radiant as the sunlight she represented in her sunset-colored costume, the jewels and metallic embroidery reflecting the stage lights as she dipped into a low, elegant curtsy, and Everett bowed in black and silver, the personification of night.

Allie stood, her smile lighting up her eyes as her gaze swept the auditorium, pausing on Vasily, then jumping up to me.

I clapped harder, and my chest drew tight. Ten years ago, I'd sat in this very seat and watched the very same woman take the same stage, and held the very same feelings, but now they'd grown tenfold. I could barely breathe around the enormity of what she meant to me. This couldn't be the last day of our only chance. Not when it felt like this.

Wait and see how she feels after you confess what you've done. I shut my conscience down. I'd handle that later, and who knew if I'd get my first selection anyway. But I still had to tell her. I owed her every ounce of the truth.

Everett said something to her, and she broke eye contact, the applause quieting as they took their positions center stage.

"Wow. She looks great," Caroline whispered. "You're sure you don't want to move up to the front?"

"This is the best seat in the house."

The music started, and within the first few notes, Vasily tensed up like a steel rod had been shoved up his ass, and Eva fell back against her seat. "She wouldn't," Eva whispered.

"Find-out portion," Gavin reminded her in a hush.

All my focus shifted to Allie as they began, moving effortlessly through the pas de deux from the first act of what would be *Equinox*.

They were beautifully matched, clearly comfortable with each other, and set the stage on fucking fire as they acted out the love story between day and night, the reluctant sun and the darkness desperate to feel her warmth.

Allie landed every leap, nailed a series of Italian fouettés, and moved seamlessly with Everett, completely in time and absolutely flawless. Her joy was palpable as he followed her through the piqué turns, and my stomach clenched when he finally captured her as the music built to a peak. I knew the feeling of chasing daylight all too well.

My breath froze as she rose onto her right toe and lifted her left leg to over a hundred and eighty degrees to point at the ceiling, her arms arched gracefully as she held a perfect penché. Every ounce of her weight was exquisitely balanced and supported by the ankle that had betrayed her seven months ago.

And it didn't so much as wobble.

Pride swelled in my chest, numbing the heartache as Everett turned her in place as though the night wanted to see his prize from every angle, then swept her into his arms and carried her offstage as the music ended.

The room rose to its feet and the applause rattled armrests, the lights on the judges' tables, the very world.

"Oh my God." Caroline clapped as we stood. "She's . . . she's . . ."

"Perfect," I finished for her, cradling the bouquet awkwardly in one arm so I could clap.

The noise escalated as Allie and Everett took the stage for a bow, and I felt her smile in every cell of my body as she looked over the audience, her eyes crinkling when she caught sight of Juniper.

Our eyes locked and she nodded, her smile never waning as Everett led her back offstage, and slowly we all took our seats.

"And that," Anne said from the edge of the curtain, "is how it's done. Please stick around, we'll be starting our beginners in five minutes. Naturally, we'll adjust our expectations accordingly."

Everyone chuckled except Vasily. He turned in his seat and leveled a look of utter, complete disdain at Eva, who shrank back in her seat and stared blankly ahead.

"Now that was a performance," Caroline noted, slipping her purse onto her shoulder. "I'm really glad we got to see her." She rose and glanced down at Gavin. "Are we going?"

Oh *shit*. Anne had arranged for Juniper to be in the first few, but we hadn't thought through how to keep her seated until the performance.

"Uhh . . ." He lifted his eyebrows at me. "Sure. But I need to stop at the bathroom first."

"Seriously? You can't hold it? Are you five?" she asked, and I forgot my siblings even existed when Allie walked by the main doors.

I jumped over the back of my seat like a teenager and ran into the hallway to catch her, dodging a couple of latecomers. "Allie!" I shouted as a photographer urged her outside.

She said something to Everett, then turned and came straight for me. My grin echoed hers as she crashed into me, throwing her arms around my neck. I held her tight, one hand across the bare skin between her shoulder blades and the other careful not to squash the fortune I'd spent in flowers.

"You were perfect." I whispered in her ear as she buried her face in my neck, and just like ten years before, I gave two fucks about the stage makeup on my dress shirt. "Stunning. Exquisite. Flawless."

Her chest shuddered against mine. "Thank you for being here. Seeing you in the back row meant everything."

"I'm just so fucking proud of you." I pulled back and cupped her face, letting myself drown in her eyes. "I'm so glad the rest of the world gets to see you shine the way I do."

She rose up and brushed a kiss over my lips. It took every ounce of my control not to deepen it, but I'd smear the shit out of her lipstick, and she had photos to take. Besides, this wasn't about what I wanted.

"They're not from a grocery store this time," I said as she pulled back, and I handed her the flowers.

"They're beautiful." Her smile beamed brighter than the stage lights as she took them, lifting the peonies to her nose and breathing in deeply. "And I love them just as much as the last ones you brought me. Thank you."

"How fucking *could* you?" Eva snapped, storming into the hallway with wild eyes, my siblings walking out behind her, trailed by a few of the MBC soloists wearing big grins.

My hands fell from Allie as she turned toward her sister. "How could I what, Eva? Dance the role that was created for *me*?"

"You did it just to upstage me!" Eva's face flushed the same scarlet as her blouse. "You did the same thing to Lina, showcasing the Giselle variation before she was supposed to perform it."

Allie's eyes widened. "Lina *told* me to dance the variation from *Giselle*. We never competed with each other, and we sure as hell never stole each other's roles."

"So this is your retribution? Making a fool out of me in front of Vasily? God, Allie, for once, can't you just get the fuck out of the way so I can maybe see the sun?" Eva shook her fists.

Everett leaned against the wall to my left, tapping on his phone— no, wait, that was Allie's phone—as if none of this was happening.

"Is that what you were doing when you secretly filmed me, then posted some of my most vulnerable moments for the world to see? That you were getting me out of the way because you can't find a patch of sunlight anywhere but New York?" She took a step toward Eva, who retreated. "You fed me to the internet and let them brand me a liar. Mom would be so very proud."

Eva's mouth snapped shut, and music started in the theater. The first beginner was performing.

"The worst part is, I would have given it to you." Allie's voice broke, and she clutched the bouquet tight. "If you'd told me how you felt, I would have had Isaac work with you, craft the perfect part to highlight your talent so you would have shined on your own and risen through the ranks, instead of fueling the incessant gossips wondering exactly what you did to leap over every other dancer at MBC. I would have taken care of you the same way I've done since the day you were born. Upstage you with that pas de deux? You're so damned lucky I didn't perform the variation."

"That would have been something to see," Vasily said, walking past Gavin and Caroline in his open-collared gray suit, and lifting his brow at the other company members before turning to Allie. He took her hand and kissed the back of it. "I am, as always, completely stunned by you, Alessandra." He grinned, flashing a set of dimples at the corner of his mouth. "I daresay that you surpassed your mother today on that stage. Naturally, your part is yours."

Allie's shoulders straightened and she dipped into a curtsy. "Thank you, Vasily."

I held back a fist pump. She'd done it—climbed back from an injury that would have retired most dancers and reclaimed her place as the best.

"But it's announced!" Eva argued.

Vasily's eyes hardened, and he looked past her to the other company members. "Find your seats, *now*." They scattered, throwing looks of pity Eva's way, and I saw more than one fumbled phone. "Eva, I gave you that part as a kindness to your mother, and you lied to me about Alessandra in return. Tell me, what else have you been lying about?"

The blood rushed from Eva's face. "Nothing. I'm good enough for the part. I can hit every element of the choreography—"

"Good enough pales in comparison to perfection. We'll speak about this after the competition. I need some air." He straightened his tie and walked out the glass double doors.

"Please, Allie." Eva turned and clasped Allie's shoulders. "Please don't do this to me. Tell him I should have the part. He'll listen to you. It's not like you just performed at the Met—we're in Haven Cove, for crying out loud. This can all be undone. Just tell him you don't want it." Her face fell when Allie remained silent. "Oh my God. You *don't* want it, do you?"

My eyes narrowed slightly, catching the faint purse of Allie's lips as the music faded from the auditorium.

"She may not have performed at the Met, but one point four million followers are watching her kick your ass on that stage right now," Everett said, flipping Allie's phone around to display the screen, where a video played on Seconds.

CHAPTER THIRTY

Hudson

"No," Eva whispered, her hands flying to her mouth, her eyes bulging as she stared at the screen, where Allie and Everett danced.

"What?" Everett shrugged. "Could have sworn you were the one bitching that Allie never helped you with content creation. Even Anne did her part by texting that video over as soon as the performance ended, and it wasn't hard to guess your new password, especially when you used *Equinox* and your birthday."

My eyebrows shot up. I hadn't seen that coming.

Eva's gaze dropped to the floor for a couple of awkward seconds, and then she fled back into the theater as another performance began, bumping into Caroline on the way—who was reading the program, completely unbothered.

Oh shit. My hand flew to the small of Allie's back as Caroline's eyes bulged, and I braced for impact.

"What the hell?" Caroline shouted, her gaze jumping between the three of us. "Tell me this is a joke!"

Gavin thew out some jazz hands. "Surprise?"

"No." She shook her head and crumpled the program in her fists. "No. She can't." Her gaze whipped to mine. "Go get her. She can't."

"She is," I said softly. Her panic cut me to the quick.

"We figured if you saw how good she is, you'd relent on your stupid rule," Gavin said. "And it wasn't like you were going to give her the option to show you, so here we are."

"Allie, photographer?" Everett asked, nodding toward the door.

"I need a minute," she answered, her voice shaky.

He nodded and tossed her phone. She caught it with one hand and juggled the bouquet with the other as Caroline turned on her.

"This is all you, isn't it?" She shook her program at Allie.

"Hey." My tone sharpened and I moved slightly, putting Allie just behind my right shoulder. "It wasn't her. It was me."

"Actually, it was me first." Gavin preened. "She trusted me to take her to class. What do you think we were doing on Sunday mornings? Just wait until you see how good she is—Caroline, you're going to cry. Seriously, I know you hate it and whatever, but it doesn't matter what *you* hate if she loves it, does it?"

"You don't get it." Caroline shook her head and backed up a couple of steps, fear sliding through her eyes. "None of you get it! Do you think I like making her miserable? Do you think I want to have the same fight over and over?" She pinned a look on Allie. "Do you think I'm such a shitty mother that I would deny her joy because I can't get past some spoiled rich girls from my childhood?"

"I did," Gavin stated. "Except the shitty-mom part."

"Not helping." I shook my head at him.

"No," Allie said quietly, worry creasing her forehead as she looked at Caroline. "You're an excellent mother, Caroline. I just thought you were scared that she wouldn't be good enough and it would break her heart, and showing you was better than telling you that she is more than good enough."

"I know we went behind your back," I added. "I'm sorry. *We're* sorry. We just wanted to give her a chance. And Caroline, she's astounding."

"You fucking idiots." Tears welled in her eyes, and she crushed the program in her grip. "I didn't want her to fall in love with dancing because it would break her heart to stop. Sean and I had to make two promises *in writing* in order to have her placed with us. The agency called us out of nowhere and said they had a beautiful baby girl and we'd been chosen by the birth parents to adopt her, but we had to sign the biological parents' conditions if we wanted to move forward."

"You've never told us this." My stomach careened like it knew we were all about to crash and burn.

"Of course we didn't," she snapped. "The document was signed under terms of nondisclosure."

"What were they?" Allie tensed and stepped forward. "The conditions?"

"Besides secrecy? The first was that she could never do ballet," Caroline told her, blinking back tears.

"Not possible." Allie shook her head. "That's simply not possible." She looked up at me, and the denial in her eyes hit me straight behind my ribs. "Hudson, she'd never do that."

"People do irrational things when they're scared." I reached for her hand and squeezed. "You don't know what went through her mind."

"She wouldn't." Allie turned back to Caroline, and my heart stuttered at the horror dawning on my sister's face. "Lina wouldn't do that! She loved dancing. She lived and breathed to be on the stage. She'd never limit her own—" Allie pressed her lips between her teeth and her eyes flew wide. Paper crunched in her arms.

"Her own what?" Caroline asked, her voice deceptively soft. "Her own *what*, Allie?"

Fuck, this had gone so wrong, so very quickly.

"Daughter," Allie finally said. "Lina wouldn't do that to her own daughter."

"Oh my God." Caroline staggered backward, pinning Gavin, then me, with an accusatory glare before shifting to Allie. "You're her aunt. How did I miss it? She looks just like the four of you. You're her aunt . . . and you *all* knew." She folded her arms like she needed protection. "From the time she was a baby?"

"No. None of us knew about Juniper or that Lina had placed her with you." Allie shook her head. "Not until May. Juniper figured it out long before any of us. She thought I was her mother to start with, but it's Lina."

"That . . ." Caroline started breathing faster. "That was the second condition. That she not search for her biological family. That the birth parents retain complete anonymity. What did you *do*?" She charged at Allie.

I stepped in, catching Caroline's shoulders and dipping my head to look her in the eye. "None of this was Allie's fault. Juniper sought her out. Juniper took the DNA test. You want to be mad at anyone, then bring it to me or Gavin, but Allie's been on your side since day one. Remember what I told you at the lake? Truth is different depending on who's telling it. Give her a chance and see it from her side, because she's done nothing but look at it from yours."

Caroline sagged.

"Letting her perform in the Classic for you is on me," Allie clarified. "I know you wanted a closed adoption, and this is probably your worst nightmare. And I'm sorry we didn't tell you. You'd always hated our family, and we thought you'd ban us from seeing her. We were always going to tell you. We just hoped you'd like me first, that you'd see that we weren't a threat so we could stay in Juniper's life. It got so out of control, and I'm truly sorry."

"I never wanted a closed adoption," Caroline corrected her, and the music stopped. "It was always a comfort to me knowing that she could legally seek out her records at eighteen, and I would have been happy with an open one in the first place, but I signed—"

"Lina's dead," Allie interrupted, "and Everett's listed as Juniper's legal father. You're safe. No one is going to hold you to whatever you signed before the adoption. No one is going to fight you for custody, or visitation, or do anything that risks your family. And none of us care if she dances. We just want to see her happy."

"Legal father?" Caroline's jaw slackened and fear flooded her eyes. "Not her biological father?"

"We don't know who that is," Allie admitted.

"Oh my God." Caroline retreated, shaking her head. "If her biological father was never informed of her birth, of the adoption, he can contest it. And if he knows she exists, that I haven't abided by the promises Sean and I made . . . we're not *safe*. He could walk through the doors of the county courthouse and petition to take her from the only home she's ever known. What have you done?" She leveled a murderous look on each of us.

The three of us fell into a stunned silence, and I tried to swim through the heaviness of my own ignorance. None of us had thought that part through.

"Caroline, I'm so very sorry," Allie whispered. "Lina told Everett it was a one-night stand, so the chances of him knowing are incredibly small."

"But not nothing," Caroline countered. "Otherwise, why would they have demanded we agree to those terms?"

"They had to have been to protect Lina," Allie said. "No one is looking for Juniper. We'd know, because *we've* been looking for him."

Another song started, and I immediately recognized it. "Juniper's onstage."

Caroline glared us all into the ground as the first tear slipped down her cheek. "If anything happens to her, I'll never forgive you. Not any of you." She swatted at her cheek, then walked into the auditorium.

The three of us followed silently, then lined up against the back wall next to Caroline, who stood with her arms wrapped around her waist, her program clenched in her hand.

"We fucked up," Allie whispered to me as Juniper danced.

"On every level possible." I watched my niece with a sad smile, realizing what this performance had potentially cost her—cost all of us. But damn, did she look happy up there. Happy and graceful and utterly charming.

Caroline watched in awe, and Allie's head bobbed with the rhythm, her face strained with worry like she was the one up there. She flashed a smile when Juniper nailed a move, then smiled wider in encouragement when she didn't.

"You can definitely tell she's a Rousseau," Gavin whispered from Allie's other side.

"Yeah, she is," I whispered in reply.

"She's a Rousseau." Allie's face fell, and her focus shifted to the audience. Her gaze jumped from person to person with a speed that bordered on panic by the time the music ended.

"What's wrong?" I asked Allie as we all clapped for Juniper.

"Professional ballet is a very small world," she whispered. "And there are at least twenty scouts in the audience. Boston." Her eyes shifted right, then left. "Houston. Atlanta. San Francisco." Color drained from her face.

"She's beautiful," Caroline said with a watery smile, alternating between clapping and batting at tears. "So very lovely. And good." She looked around me to Allie. "She's good, isn't she? Or am I just her mom? Am I biased?"

"She's extraordinary." Allie's smile shook. "And if you let her dance, you'll never have to worry about paying for any of it. We'll help take care of her if you let us." Caroline's smile slipped, and Allie walked in front of me to take her hand. "Juniper isn't going anywhere, I promise. I'll fix this." She let her go and retreated.

"Allie?" I reached for her hand but she drew it back. "Don't you want to see Juniper?"

"I do, but it's more important that she sees Caroline. I have to go. I think I know how to fix this." She clutched her phone and flowers, and backed away. "Trust me to fix this, Hudson."

I had no idea what the fuck I was agreeing to, but the plea in her eyes had me nodding.

"Thank you." She turned and ran.

CHAPTER
THIRTY-ONE

Allie

ReaganHuang: Told you Alessandra wasn't a liar. Pretty sure a new cast sheet will be posted soon.

I had to fix this. If Hudson and I had put Juniper into any uncertainty or danger, then I had to fix it. I needed the only person who'd known Lina better than I had—Anne.

After changing into my street clothes, I bagged my costume and set the peonies in a sinkful of water in my dressing room. Then I went looking for Anne and found her offstage at the edge of the curtain.

She took one look at me, handed the mic off to an assistant, and came my way, offering a polite smile to everyone she passed along the way. "What's wrong?"

I pulled her down the hall and into a storage closet, then flicked the light switch and shut the door.

"Well, this is rather cloak-and-dagger, don't you think?" She eyed the myriad of cleaning supplies and tucked one loose curl of her updo behind her ear.

The door flew open. "I thought I saw you. What are you two doing in a cleaning closet?" Kenna asked, lifting her brows. "Mom, they're over here."

Shit.

"Just . . ." There was no time to think this through. I shook my head and went with Hudson's tried-and-true method of impetuousness. "Get in here." Anne and I moved to the back while Eloise and Kenna squished themselves in and shut the door.

"And to think"—Eloise scanned our surroundings and folded her arms over her custom Prada dress—"out of everywhere in this tiny town, *this* is where you want to celebrate a most decisive victory?"

"We'll get to that," I promised. "Look, Lina made Caroline secretly promise two things in order to adopt Juniper," I blurted, immediately getting everyone's full attention. "That she'd never do ballet and wouldn't search for her biological family—"

"No way." Anne shook her head.

Eloise blinked and tilted her head, and Kenna followed suit. *Like mother, like daughter.*

"She did," I assured Anne. "Naturally that last part legally expires once Juniper is eighteen, but she got it in writing—"

Anne balked. "Not do ballet? Lina would never. Everything we did this summer was because Lina would *never* keep her daughter from dancing."

"I think she would." My voice dropped to a whisper as apprehension skittered straight down my spine. If I was right, things had the potential to go incredibly bad. "Think about it. Juniper looks just like us—"

"She would have no way of knowing that," Anne argued.

"Stop running me over and *listen*," I snapped.

"Valid point," Kenna noted.

Anne blinked. "Okay, then. Please continue."

"Mom's genes are strong. All four of us look similar enough to garner notice. If Lina had even suspected Juniper would be the same, and didn't want anyone to know she existed, she'd have to make sure no one in the community ran across a little girl who looked and danced just like a Rousseau, hence the rule." I folded my arms and hoped I didn't sound like I'd completely lost my mind.

"Oh, that cat left the bag the second she stepped onstage. You can definitely tell she's a Rousseau," Eloise said. "Especially in a room full of people who have known two generations of you over the last five decades and happen to be at the Classic started by your family. Tongues will be wagging tonight at every company reception."

"That's what I'm afraid of." My throat threatened to close.

"For hypothetical reasons, I'll go along with this." Anne nodded. "Closed adoptions are disappointingly common, but fine, let's say Lina was adamant she never be found. Why?"

"Do you think Lina was embarrassed?" Kenna asked.

"Lina was impossible to embarrass." I shook my head, and my stomach hollowed. "I thought of three potential reasons she'd impose that rule about Juniper dancing. First, she knew we'd get involved if we knew about Juniper . . . which we did."

"Guilty." Anne winced.

"Second, to protect the adoption. We knew Everett wasn't her father the second we saw the certificate, but . . . Can Juniper's biological father really contest the adoption? That's Caroline's fear right now."

Every head swung toward Anne.

"Um . . ." A set of lines appeared between her brows. "In Massachusetts? I'm a little out of practice, but as far as I know, there's no paternity registry here. If the father didn't know about Juniper's birth, and then established paternity, he could file a suit. What Lina did is technically fraudulent. Everett had no right to sign as Juniper's father."

My throat spasmed. Then Caroline had every right to be afraid. "Okay, but if Lina could keep Juniper from searching for her family, no one would ever know about Everett. No one would file a suit. And after she's eighteen, no one's coming for custody either."

"Both of those make sense," Kenna agreed. "What could possibly be her third reason for not wanting Juniper to find you?"

My heart sank, and I opened my mouth once, then twice, but I couldn't bring myself to say it, to voice the lowest possible opinion I'd ever had about my sister's actions.

"Allie?" Anne prodded, taking my hand.

I dragged my gaze up to the only person in this room who might not dismiss my thought process just because she loved Lina, the only person who might actually agree because she thoroughly understood the variable in this equation—Mom.

Eloise arched a single brow as I looked over at her, then narrowed her eyes like she was thinking, and wasn't sure she liked the direction of her thoughts. "Say it," she commanded. "I'm not standing around in a broom closet for you to *not* say what you're thinking, Alessandra."

If I did, I could never take it back, but if I didn't, there was a very real chance I was leaving Juniper vulnerable. *I'm sorry, Lina.*

"I think she used Juniper as leverage." The words tripped over themselves on their way out of my mouth.

Kenna's eyebrows shot up.

Anne gasped and pulled her hand from mine. "She wouldn't."

Eloise turned a knowing look on Anne. "For all of Lina's wonderful qualities, are you forgetting whose daughter she is?"

Anne paled, and she lifted her hand to her stomach. "I think I might be sick."

"Mom knew," I reminded her gently. "Mom orchestrated Everett. It wasn't just Lina making that list. It was our mother. I think Lina did her best to protect Juniper. She put her with a family in which two men we loved were raised. She knew she'd be safe. She might not have gotten along with Caroline, but she had to have known what a protective mom she'd be. She definitely knew that Gavin and Hudson would watch out for her, but, Anne . . . I'm pretty damned sure she also used Juniper's existence to her advantage." My heart sank as I put the most plausible pieces together. "And I don't think she's the only one."

Anne paled. "You know who her father is, don't you?" She searched my eyes. "It's Jacob, isn't it? He was with Lina in San Francisco, and his mother sits on the board out there. She wouldn't want anything to jeopardize his career."

"Are you still certified to practice in Massachusetts?" I asked, ignoring her question.

"Yes." Her forehead crinkled. "Why?"

My phone vibrated in my back pocket. "Because we have to do what Lina wouldn't and protect Juniper legally." I pulled out my phone and opened the text.

REAGAN: You were AMAZING. You're coming to the yacht for the reception, right?

"We need Jacob to sign a termination of parental rights," Anne said. "A handful of NDAs wouldn't hurt to help convince him."

"And a medical history form," Kenna added.

"Good idea." Anne nodded.

"Leave the father's name blank," I said to Anne. "Just in case."

She nodded. "All right. I'll get them done this afternoon as long as Eloise doesn't mind taking over as emcee."

"Of course. I never turn down a microphone." Eloise smiled. "And I'd do just about anything to get out of this closet."

We filed out as nonchalantly as four grown women could when exiting a broom closet.

Anne and Kenna split off toward the parking lot and Eloise headed toward the stage as I typed out a reply to Reagan.

ALESSANDRA: Thank you! I'll see you on board.

Then I swiped to Hudson's thread and sent a text.

ALLIE: Mind being my date tonight?

Blackmail required backup.
He was quick to reply.

HUDSON: Every night is my preference.

"Allie," Eloise called out, and my head shot up to find her watching me. "I don't think *you're* wrong, which could be dangerous. I also think you need to put your eyes on your sister."

I nodded without needing to ask which one.

I found her within thirty minutes, but let her sulk another few hours before heading upstairs.

"Stop crying and get up," I ordered Eva, peering down at where she'd curled herself into a ball in the bottom of Lina's closet.

"How did you know I was here?" Eva dragged the forearm of her crimson blouse over her splotchy face.

"Because this is where you always go when shit hits the fan." I stepped out of the doorway and into Lina's room. "It's like you forget that Lina isn't around anymore to cover for you. Now get up. You have to get ready so we can go to the Company reception."

"Since when do you care about Company events?" She stood, jostling what remained of Lina's clothes on the rack.

"Since always. I've been there far longer than you, remember?" I glanced around Lina's room and remembered why I avoided coming in here at all costs. Grief lived in this room. It had dug its claws in deep, settled in, and built itself a home, lingering in her pictures and dust-covered trophies.

A sour taste filled my mouth when I thought about what she'd done, or at least had been a party to, and tried to believe what Hudson repeatedly told me. That people do irrational things when they're scared.

Or maybe the truth was that the Lina I thought I knew wasn't the same Lina Mom loved, wasn't the same Lina Anne cried over, wasn't the same Lina Eva had hidden behind. Maybe she was a dozen different things to a dozen different people, switching out her mask as necessary.

Maybe only Lina had truly known Lina.

And until I'd come back here, until Juniper had shoved Hudson back into my life with two enthusiastic hands, I'd been dangerously close to saying the same thing about me.

"You hate the Company." Eva sniffled and walked out of the closet.

"I don't . . . hate it," I said quietly, looking over Lina's pictures. "I'm just not always sure I like who I am within it." I glanced her way and found her clutching her phone. "And I know I don't like who you are within it. What are you doing with that phone?"

"I'm getting canceled," Eva admitted, sitting on the edge of Lina's bed and holding her phone in her lap. "There's at least fifty videos already, and I'm sure you'll say I deserve it."

I sat down next to her, depressing the old mattress. "Yeah, that sucks. My best advice is to avoid the comments at all costs."

"I kind of hate you," she whispered, swiping the app closed.

"I figured that out right around the time that you orchestrated *my* cancellation. Fortunately for us, I think it's a case of jealousy eating your common sense and not actual hatred." My gaze caught on a framed picture of the four of us from the one and only time Dad had snuck us out to a theme park.

"What's it like to be the chosen one?" She raked her sleeve across her cheek again.

"What's it like to be the whiny one?" I countered. "Seriously, Eva. You're twenty-five, not fifteen. No one's left you behind. No one's dancing en pointe while you look on longingly. I understand wanting to step out of the shadows, but maybe the answer is to look for another source of light."

"It's the Company," she whispered. "Mom's company."

I sighed. "I speak from experience when I say the validation you're starving for isn't going to come from her—"

She shriveled.

"—or anybody in there." I pointed to her phone. "You and I both know she isn't capable of telling us she's proud, and that's complete and utter unfair shit that's going to take a few years and a lot of hours in therapy to unpack."

"How long did it take you?" she asked.

"Considering I just nearly broke myself to prove to Vasily that I'm still one of his principals? I'll let you know when I get there." I glanced at her phone. "I'll also give you the new password, so you can at least take the video down."

"You're not mad at me?" Her brow scrunched.

"Yes, I'm incredibly mad at you." I shrugged. "But unfortunately, I still love you. You're my sister. You bring me bagels from New York and save my stuff when Charlotte throws it out of my locker, so I will give you the password and *one* chance to make this right between us."

"There's no point to taking it down. It has all those stitches already." Her shoulders sagged. "And it's just you dancing. You didn't do anything wrong. I did." She slowly looked my way with swollen red eyes. "This is horrible."

"Yeah. It hurts." I reached over and clasped Eva's hand. "Real life is what happens out here, you know. With me, with Anne, with your friends, at the barre, on the stage. That . . ." I glanced pointedly at her phone. "That is just a sparkly hall of mirrors, and staring too long through the lens of how other people perceive you is bound to start distorting how you see yourself. Delete the account, or at least deactivate it for a while, if only so you don't live on Lina's closet floor."

"It's a lot of followers," she whispered, covering her phone defensively.

"It's just an idea." The hardwood squeaked beneath my feet as I stood, letting go of her hand. "But I can't give you the luxury I had of retreating to bed. I need you to get ready for the reception while I shower and do the same, because we need to help our niece. Apologies are more than words, Eva, and I'm giving you *one* chance to fix what you broke, or I swear I'll go no-contact on your ass. Do you understand?"

She nodded. "What do I have to do?"

I picked up the picture of us and sighed. "Unfortunately, I'm pretty sure it's nothing you haven't done before."

CHAPTER THIRTY-TWO

Allie

CassidyFairchilde1: They're both incredible dancers. I hope they figure out their family issues.

"Have I told you how incredible you look tonight?" Hudson's hand warmed my lower back through the thin green silk of my asymmetrical dress as we made our way through the packed marina. We needed to be on board in the next ten minutes, or we'd miss departure.

"Have I told you the same?" I glanced over at his suit, more than admiring how it hung on the broad lines of his shoulders.

"You guys are nauseating," Eva remarked from behind us as we stepped onto the wooden pier.

"You nauseate me," Gavin countered from her side. I'd figured two pieces of backup were better than one, and he'd agreed to tag along as Eva's date.

Hudson shot his brother a warning look, and I concentrated on not catching my heels in the gaps between the boards of the pier. I spotted members of at least four different companies from around the US as we walked toward the slip with the yacht MBC had rented for the reception tonight.

"Alessandra!" someone called out, rushing at us off a boat to the right.

I clutched the manila envelope Anne had given me like my life depended on its contents, and shifted so Eva wouldn't be hit head on by the energetic blonde. An eerie sense of recognition tickled the back of my brain.

"Hi!" She grinned and waved. "I'm Lila Morris from the Los Angeles Metropolitan Ballet. I was sent out to help judge the Classic, and just had to tell you that your performance was exceptional."

"Thank you, that's very kind of you to say." I blinked at the name, and my throat tightened as it hit me. "You're WestCoastPointe."

"You've seen my content?" Her smile dazzled, only slipping when her gaze momentarily darted to Eva. "I just wanted to say that I think you're one of the best of our generation, and I hope we get the chance to work together."

"Funny, I could have sworn you said she was pretentious and haughty," Eva said, straight faced, staring Lila down.

Gavin stifled a snort, and Lila flushed crimson as we walked away.

"That wasn't nice," I chided my sister.

"I know." Eva shrugged as we reached the slip with the MBC logo and found the yacht's engines already purring. "This must be us."

"Holy fuck," Gavin muttered. "Seventy footer?"

"I bet it's over ninety," Hudson responded. "You sure about this?" His hand moved to my waist.

"I'm never sure about anything." My heart started pounding as we approached the ramp. "I usually leave that part to you." The staff was too busy readying the boat for launch, so no one checked names, and we walked right onto the enormous party yacht and into the bustling gathering that started on the back deck by the small dinghy, and continued both inside and upstairs.

"Where do you think he is?" Hudson asked.

"Usually in a private room toward the bow." I nodded toward the front of the boat and started moving.

Hudson wrapped his arm around my waist and tugged me out of the path of a group of kids racing through the crowd in ties and summer dresses, scurrying for the steps that led to the upper deck.

"Thanks." I lifted my hand to my chest to calm my racing heart.

"You guys have kids on this thing?" Hudson asked as we moved forward into the cabin.

"Some attend the school," I answered, nodding and smiling to colleagues as we passed by. "Most are the ones who placed in the top five or so in their category today."

"Juniper came in seventeenth," Gavin announced proudly.

"She did," I agreed with a smile. Best text I'd gotten all day, considering I'd had to chase down Eva.

"Allie!" Everett stepped away from Michael and the group of soloists they'd been standing with at the bar. "Are you ready to celebrate? They're pouring excellent martinis." His face puckered when he saw Eva. "Guess they let anyone on."

"Go easy on her," I said. "She's having a rough day."

"As she deserves." He offered Eva a sharp smile as the boat's horn blew. "Ooh, we're sailing." He leaned in and kissed my cheek. "You know he's waiting for you. Get that contract and come party."

"I have something to take care of first, but I will." I nodded. "Do me a favor and let Hudson and Gavin hang with you for a minute?"

Hudson stiffened. "That was not the deal."

"Relax," Everett said. "Boyfriends don't go to contract meetings. Let her handle business, and then you two can sneak off *after* we toast." He lifted his eyebrows at me.

"We'll toast as soon as I actually have an offer," I promised.

"Of course you will." Everett rolled his eyes. "And if it's anything like mine, well, we're sitting pretty. I think Jacob is in there right now, but I'm sure he'll be out in a second. They've been locked away for a hot minute. You should head back."

Perfect timing. I turned to Hudson.

"I don't like this," he grumbled as I straightened his tie.

"I think you look quite sexy in it." I tugged on the fabric, and he leaned down, his face inches from mine. "If we're not back in twenty, come looking."

"You want me to wait twenty minutes?" His brows lowered, and he bracketed my waist with his hands as the boat began to move, pulling out of the slip. "Anything can happen in twenty minutes."

"Count it out in five-minute intervals, if that helps." I clutched the manila folder between us and pressed a quick kiss to his mouth. This wasn't how I wanted to spend our last night together, but I was glad he was here with me. "I'll be right back."

He looked torn, and his hands flexed once before he let go and nodded, reaching into his pocket and retrieving his phone.

"Eva?" I looked over at my sister.

"Let's go." She put on a polished smile.

"Hey, Caroline," Hudson answered. "We just got to the party."

I gave Hudson another once-over just because he looked too damn good not to, then left him with Gavin and Everett. Company members waved to me as we moved through the cabin, but their hands faltered when they caught sight of Eva.

I looked through the windows that lined the cabin as the sun set and we headed out into open ocean. If this didn't go well, the next few hours of this cruise were going to be horrifically awkward.

The anxiety I'd been fighting off all afternoon flared to life in the form of a stab of pain behind my sternum as we approached the door to the private cabin. "Tell me one thing," I said to Eva as I spotted Maxim hovering near the door with a few members of the Company.

Here went nothing. "How did you figure it out so quickly? You only saw her for a few minutes."

"The dimple," Eva answered, and my brows lifted in surprise. "What? I took biology. I understand enough about genetics to figure that one out. Plus, it made sense when I started lining up dates."

"Now that, I get." My heart fluttered at the speed of a hummingbird's wings as we reached Maxim.

His smile didn't reach his eyes, but it never quite did. "Well, if it isn't the topic of the hottest conversations today." His gaze jumped between Eva and me. "Didn't expect to see you guys here together."

"I'm heading in," I informed him, reaching for the door handle.

"Best of luck." He raised his glass in salute.

"I'll let you know when it's clear," I whispered to Eva, then opened the door to the private room, and stepped inside.

"There she is!" Vasily smiled and clapped Isaac on the back from where they sat behind the long ebony table, six or seven manila envelopes stacked in front of them. The door on the starboard side was closed, but port was locked in the open position, letting in the ocean breeze from the deck that wrapped toward the bow.

Jacob closed his own folder and stood in front of that open door, then pushed his chair in and ran his fingers through his dark hair. "Alessandra. I was just leaving. Remarkable performance today."

We hit a rather large wave, and I grabbed the chair in front of me to steady my balance.

Fucking boats.

"Thanks. It's good to see you, Jacob," I said.

He nodded, then slipped past me and out the door.

"Alessandra, you're going to be so pleased with who we're offering a contract to," Vasily said with a grin. "He's the best I've seen in years." He leaned over and grabbed an envelope off the booth to the left. "And of course I had your new contract drawn up."

My gaze darted to Isaac, and he inclined his head. "Darling."

"Not your darling," I reminded him.

"At present," he acquiesced.

"Would you mind stepping outside? I have some family business to take care of." My smile could have cut the table in half.

Vasily pushed my envelope across the table, then sat back in the booth. "Go ahead, Isaac. The terms of Alessandra's contract are always private. A courtesy to her mother, of course."

"Naturally." Isaac got out of his chair and walked my way. "Not going to lie and say I wasn't annoyed to see you decided to debut one of my numbers without telling me, but the execution was superb, and it's piqued some great interest online."

"Flawless," I corrected him, catching his eye as he walked by. "I was flawless. Eva's waiting out there—would you send her in, please?"

"Flawless." He nodded with a cocky smirk. "And of course. Though I do hate to miss what's sure to be a delicious little catfight."

I opened the envelope I'd brought with me and pulled out the two Anne had put inside as the noise of the party flooded the room. Eva walked in and shut the door, cutting out all the noise except the waves that crashed against the hull.

"Are we negotiating a family rate?" Vasily shifted in his seat, his eyes narrowing as he glanced between us. "Does Eva require an empty seat in her theater as well?"

Eva moved to my side and remained quiet.

"You have a choice to make." I held up the first envelope in my right hand. "You can accept these signed nondisclosure agreements in return for filling out a nonidentifying medical history form and a release of parental rights—"

He rocked forward and slammed his hands on the table, and my pulse leapt. "Not you. I expected this from your mother and Eva, but not you."

"Oh. Did Lina catch you off guard?" I asked, tilting my head. "Or did she have Mom do the dirty work for her? Please, do tell me which one of them had the temerity to look you in the eye and blackmail you so you'd offer Lina a contract that year?"

He drummed his fingertips on the table, then sat back.

"He's not going to answer," Eva said softly.

"Of course not, he wouldn't want to admit it. Would you?" I lowered the envelope to the table. "That's okay. I put it together. Lina came begging for another shot when you didn't sign her at eighteen. We all know that."

He didn't flinch.

"And you don't give her one, of course. You only accept the best, and you'd already found her lacking. But you did abuse the power dynamic and take her up on what she was offering, didn't you? Fast-forward a few months and she fakes an injury to get a leave of absence from San Francisco because she's pregnant, and instead of calling you, she called our mother. Am I close?" *Click. Click. Click.* I tapped the corner of the envelope on the table. "I'm fairly certain you don't know any of the details for very good reason, so let's skip ahead to you getting blackmailed. I'm guessing it was Lina."

He held my stare unnervingly, but his right eyebrow twitched.

"And I'm guessing she said something along the same lines as my sweet baby sister here did about a month ago, which was probably *I know you have a child that violates your very public, very ironclad prenup. A child that would cost you the company you've dedicated your life to building. I know where this child is, and if you give me what I want, the secret will stay between us.* Does that sound right?"

"It's annoyingly accurate," Eva noted. Her calm tone was at odds with the white-knuckled grip she had on the back of the chair as the boat dipped.

Movement caught my eye to the left, and I grabbed hold of the chair again. Water splashed up over the deck as we rose up into the next wave. It was always choppy as hell for the first half hour, and tonight was no exception.

"Is that what *you're* saying to me, Alessandra?" Vasily laced his fingers in front of his chest.

"Not at all." I shook my head. "Though I am mildly curious to hear if it's how my mother secured *my* contract as well."

"Mildly?" A corner of his mouth quirked. "Knowing you, that question must be eating you alive. Are you worthy of your position? Are you good enough?"

My stomach *nearly* flipped.

"A few months ago, that would have ruined me," I admitted. "But not anymore. And I'm not here about a contract or a role. Not mine. Not Eva's." I let go of the chair and pushed both envelopes across the table. "Choose. Envelope one: everyone who suspects you're the father of this child has signed an NDA, and you can have them for the price of signing the release of parental rights and a medical form. Or envelope two: our signed statements and a copy of said child's original birth certificate get dropped into the hands of whoever grabs it first when I walk out this door. I mean, assuming you have no desire to parent said child, but I'm guessing that point would have been made about ten years ago." I lifted my chin and mustered all the bravado in my body to hold this particular mask in place.

He studied me in awkward silence for a good minute, then leaned forward and took the paperwork on the right and reached into his suit coat for a pen. Silence filled the cabin as he opened the folder. "Baby Rousseau," he repeated, reading over the release.

"You don't get to know their name." I shook my head. Anne crafted the release to match the details of the original birth certificate, minus the gender. It wasn't foolproof, but it would be enough to give a judge if Vasily ever changed his mind.

"I don't know who you're talking about. I'm simply signing a document releasing paternal rights over a child that was never mine to begin with. Though had it been, that lapse in judgment would have cost me dearly when it came to my reputation, had it not been for the casual disrespect of simple traffic laws."

My entire body locked, and I forced myself to swallow the bile that swiftly rose in my throat at his casual mention of the accident.

"I only take the best, as you're aware. Good thing I never had such a lapse in judgment." His pen moved quickly over the release, and then the medical form, and I took short, shallow breaths until he stuffed both back into the folder and slid it across the table.

I caught it at the edge, then tossed the other one his direction. "For your records to do as you see fit. Thank you." Anger was quickly replaced as full-hearted relief shot through me so quickly my head lightened. Juniper would be safe. Caroline would never lose her.

"Do take your contract, of course." He motioned to the paperwork in front of me. "We wouldn't be the Metropolitan Ballet Company without you as one of our principals. I mean that wholeheartedly, Alessandra. I only take the best, and you are unequivocally the best, as you proved today. You have my word that what happened here will never be mentioned. Rehearsals begin in two weeks. Come back where you belong and dance the role that was created for you. Who knows, it may make you the next prima of our time."

I stared at the envelope like it might grow teeth and bite me.

"Three years. Incredible pay raise. Center seat, back row as always," Vasily said, tucking his newly purchased envelope into his pocket. "I'm not oblivious, Alessandra. I know you've already had calls from San Francisco, Houston, and London."

"And Paris," I added. "Or I could go freelance and choose them all."

"And Paris. But none of them are us. None of them are your family, and I know how much you enjoy dancing with your sister. Her contract isn't up for another year. Perhaps . . ." He tapped his finger together and glanced Eva's direction. "Perhaps she'll find herself in a soloist position this season. Just look it over, approve it, and sign, or write an email to my assistant and she'll send you an electronic version."

"Allie," Eva hissed, and she was right to. It was everything I'd worked for, everything our mother had dreamed of, and it would secure Eva too.

"I want to bring my dog to the studio."

Vasily's nose wrinkled. "I can have that included."

The contract felt heavy as I picked it up. "Thank you for your offer."

"I'll see you in New York." New York. My home. My apartment and my life. My sisters and Kenna. My company and my role. But no Hudson. "I mean it, Alessandra. This never happened. That child does not exist."

A whimper sounded to the left as the boat dipped again, and my head whipped toward the door.

No, God, no. My soul left my body as Juniper's head disappeared from the doorway, and through the window, I watched her back away, her hands covering her mouth as she retreated toward the railing, like she couldn't get away from us fast enough.

"Stop!" I shoved all the paperwork at Eva as I ran for the door.

Juniper stumbled backward, her eyes frozen in shock, staring past me into the cabin. The boat rose into the next swell and water crested the deck, pouring over the railing and Juniper's lilac dress. My heels slipped as I reached the deck, and I lunged for her—

But she wasn't there.

"No!" The boat pitched as I hurtled to the side. A flash of purple in the water below had me scrambling over the water-slick railing.

"Allie!" Eva shrieked behind me.

I jumped.

CHAPTER THIRTY-THREE

Allie

ReeseOnToe: They're sisters. Hopefully they'll figure it out. Watching their videos has been so helpful in my own journey.

WendyCook52: Agreed. They're so inspirational, but they're human, too.

The Atlantic was fucking *freezing*.

The cold knocked the breath from my lungs as I fought to the surface, kicking with all my strength, clawing my way through the water.

I gasped when I broke the surface, then swiveled my head, looking for Juniper. It took less than a second to spot her a few yards to my left, sputtering as she treaded water, disappearing for a second as a swell separated us. My heart pounded as I swam, trying to remember two summers' worth of boating and swimming lessons from over a decade ago.

No time for fear, no bodily resources to waste over it either. I had to be as calm, collected, and decisive as Hudson.

"Allie!" Juniper shouted as I reached her.

"Swim!" I ordered, grabbing a fistful of the back of her dress in one hand and propelling us away from the boat as it passed.

We battled through the water until I counted to ten, and then turned back toward the yacht as the tail end of it went by.

"What are we going to do?" Juniper cried as I held on to her, kicking to stay at the surface while I searched the passing boat.

There. The setting sun cut through the windows of the cabin, silhouetting its occupants, and I barely made out a racing figure darting through the party—Eva. Two seconds later, Hudson and Gavin burst onto the back deck and ran toward the railing.

"Hudson!" I screamed, waving my left arm.

"Help!" Juniper shouted simultaneously.

Hudson lurched over the railing, and Gavin dragged him back, shouting something we couldn't hear over the noise of the party and the engines as they pulled ahead of us.

"They're leaving!" Juniper shrieked, her voice so high it threatened to pierce my eardrums.

"It's okay," I assured her as everyone on the back deck mobilized.

Hudson reappeared at the railing and threw up his hand, splaying his fingers and mouthing something that looked like *five minutes.*

"It's okay," I said to myself as the boat left us behind. "We're about to hit the wake, so stay above the surface. Don't fight the waves, just ride with them." I turned all my attention to Juniper. "Understand?"

She nodded, and I tightened my grip on the back of her dress, treading water with my other three extremities. The water swelled from the opposite direction of what we'd been fighting, and I kept my eyes locked on hers as we rose and fell with the first wave, and then a second.

The horn blew on the boat, but it continued onward, sailing straight.

"They're not coming back!" Juniper sputtered, water dripping off her forehead.

"They will," I promised her as we rode far more gentle swells. "Your uncles aren't going to leave us out here. We just have to make it five minutes treading water. Can you do that?"

Juniper nodded, treading water like she'd been taught by the best. "I lost my shoes."

"Me too." I forced a smile. "Gives us a reason to go shopping when we make it out of the water."

"I wasn't supposed to be on the boat," she admitted.

"I know." Cold seeped in my muscles, but I held tight to her dress. "And we're going to have a very long talk about that."

"That man . . ." Her lower lip trembled, and I hoped it was from emotion and not cold. "He's my father, isn't he?"

I nodded my head. It wouldn't help to lie to her. "How much of that did you hear?"

"I was with some of the other kids on the bow. We'd just come down the stairs when I heard your voice, and when I listened at the door, you were asking him if Lina caught him off guard." Water tracked down the little lines between her eyebrows.

My heart sank. "You heard it all."

"Is that what I am?" Her teeth chattered. "A ticket into your company?"

"Not to me." I shook my head vehemently. "There is no excuse for what other people have done, but I love you, Juniper."

"Was that what you were doing? Using me to get your part back?" She recoiled, and I held fast, refusing to let her go and risk our separation out here.

"No." Treading water with only three of my limbs was exhausting. "I went to get him to sign some paperwork that would protect you, that would make it so he couldn't take you from your mom. My contract had already been printed when I went to confront him." I left Eva out of the discussion and prayed Juniper hadn't heard every detail.

Tears welled in her eyes. "They didn't want me. They didn't love me."

My throat clogged. I was so ill-equipped to handle this discussion, but it wasn't like I had the option of staying quiet out here. "I can't speak for him, but Lina loved you," I said, and prayed it wasn't the wrong thing. "I know she loved you because she chose your mom and dad. She knew Uncle Gavin and Uncle Hudson. She chose your entire family, people she knew would love and protect you, and she placed you where she'd be able to check up on you. She put you in one of her favorite places in the world so you could grow up surrounded by the things and the people she loved too."

Her tears mixed with the ocean. "You don't know that."

"I can't imagine anyone knowing you and not loving you, Juniper. Your mom and dad, your grandparents, your uncles and your cousins, they all love you. Anne and I love you." A high-pitched whine sounded from behind us. "And I know that might not be enough to soothe the hurt you're feeling, and I'm so sorry."

Her forehead scrunched as the noise grew louder. A boat motor. "Those papers you gave him? Do they mean I have to be a secret?"

My jaw started to shiver uncontrollably. "No," I forced out. "They mean there's a few of us who can't say he's your father. But you?" I tugged her closer. "You get to say whatever you want, whenever you want to. You have choices. We took the power from him, never from you."

She nodded. Her lips had taken on a bluish tinge.

I looked over my shoulder as the rescue dinghy approached and nearly sank with relief. "They're coming."

The driver killed the motor, and Hudson appeared at the edge of the stern as the small vessel drifted toward us. Fear was etched into every line of his face as the boat slowed, the tip of its bow pointed about ten feet away from us. "Allie! Juniper!"

"We'll swim!" I shouted before he got any ideas about jumping into this freezer called an ocean. "Can you do it?" I asked Juniper.

"Yeah." She nodded, and then we swam.

I kept one hand on her dress and moved through the water in a sidestroke, ignoring the cramps that were slowly seizing my muscles as we rounded the stern of the bobbing boat.

Both Hudson and Gavin waited on the small swim deck, Gavin crouched and Hudson on one knee.

"Take her!" I shouted at Gavin when we reached him first, then put both my hands on Juniper's waist and shoved her up toward the deck, kicking as hard as I could.

"Got her!" Gavin shouted, and I let go, sinking back into the water.

"Allie!" Hudson shouted, and I wrenched my gaze from Juniper's rising body to Hudson's outstretched hand, then looked back as Juniper's bare feet emerged from the ocean. "He has her. Now get in the damned boat, or I'm coming in!"

I kicked, forcing my body left, and reached for Hudson.

He clasped my right hand, then my left, and hauled me out of the water with unthinkable strength, plastering me against his chest before throwing his arms around my back one at a time, leaving my hands to fall to his shoulders as he twisted and set me down on the swim deck. "Are you all right?" His gaze raked over me.

"F-f-fine," I chattered out.

"Okay." He nodded, then hauled me into his arms and stood. The boat swayed as he carried me into it, then sat me on the U-shaped bench that took up the stern.

I shook uncontrollably as I searched for Juniper and found her wrapped in a silver blanket on Gavin's lap a few feet away. Two of the yacht's crew were on board with us, one at the helm and the other shaking out another silver blanket.

Hudson wrapped it around my shoulders and then crouched in front of me. "Anything broken in the fall?"

"Check her first," I demanded, my frozen fingers clutching the edge of the blanket.

"She's with Gavin. I'm checking *you*." He studied my eyes, then put his fingers to my wrist, quieting for a moment before he nodded. "Did you breathe in any water?"

"I don't think so? Maybe? It happened *really* fast."

A muscle in his jaw ticked. "Don't move." He crossed the small boat to Juniper, then sat beside her and checked her over as the engines gurgled to life.

"Two survivors on board. We're headed back to the marina," one of the crew said into the radio. The reply was muffled by the engines, and we started moving, cutting across the ocean in the opposite direction of the yacht.

Hudson returned a few minutes later, and tucked me into his side, wrapping his arm around my shoulders. His warmth trickled into me, and he pressed a kiss to my temple. "God, Allie, you jumped in after her."

"If you even *think* about lecturing me," I shouted over the roar of the engines.

"Thank you." He tucked my ice-cold forehead against his neck. "Just . . . thank you. But please. Just don't. But thank you. Fuck, I'm a wreck."

"Does Caroline know she's here?" The marina came into sight.

Hudson shook his head. "She thinks she's at a sleepover, but trust me, she's about to find out. Pretty sure our niece is going to have an ankle monitor by the end of the night."

"She knows," I said, loud enough for him to hear. "She knows about Vasily. She heard the whole thing." I looked her way, but Gavin had her tucked against his chest, both arms enveloping her small frame as she faced away from me.

"Fuck." Hudson held me tighter.

That word covered it, so I let the rest go and simply soaked up the heat radiating from his body as we bounced our way back to the marina.

When we arrived, there was an ambulance waiting.

Two hours and a hot shower later, I felt mostly human as I walked out of the kitchen, brownie in one hand and a bottle of water in the other.

"You have to stop hovering," I lectured Sadie as she kept pace at my side into the living room. Gavin had dropped me off an hour ago after I refused to go anywhere near the Haven Cove ER, and Sadie hadn't been more than two feet away since I came through the door. She'd even sat on the bathroom rug as I showered.

The intuition of dogs was indisputable.

I already had three text messages from Hudson, checking on me, and the tone of the messages was anything but pleased since I'd demanded he accompany Juniper to the ER to meet Caroline. I typed out a response to his latest message and dodged two of the packed boxes Anne had left beside the far armchair.

ALLIE: Eating. Drinking. Everything is fine.

It was quietly odd yet freeing to be in the house alone. It would be hours until everyone else returned from the reception. "Go lay down, honey," I said to Sadie, motioning to her fluffy bed at the edge of the living room as I walked through the baggage-strewn foyer that only served to remind me that the summer was over. So was my time with Hudson.

My heart rebelled against the thought as Sadie gave a sigh of resignation, and I looked over my shoulder to see her turn a circle and collapse with a huff onto the bed as I headed into the studio.

I flipped the second light switch, and the wall sconces turned on, illuminating the studio with a soft glow instead of the bright overhead lights that spotlit imperfections when we trained at night.

We. I polished off the brownie as I pondered that particular term. *We* had trained here. *We* had been broken and remade. I just wasn't sure what each of us had been shaped into. Even me.

I hadn't even called my mother to tell her I'd won my part back.

Putting the bottle on the floor, I moved to Lina's barre position, searching for any trace of her in my own reflection as I stood barefoot in cotton pajama pants and a tank top. But I didn't see Lina, or even my mother. I only saw myself, principal dancer at whatever company I chose from the stack of contracts I'd been offered. I could go to Paris, or San Francisco, or I could go back to New York, sleep in the apartment my mother had chosen, work for the company she'd worshipped, and dance the role that had been created for me. I could secure Eva's position too. I'd have to see Vasily every day, but I could go *home*.

My chest buckled, and I rubbed my hand over my sternum like I could somehow ease the ache accompanying the simple truth that every choice took me far from Hudson. He was expecting orders any day. At best case, he'd be in Sitka, six hundred miles away from the nearest professional ballet company, and *God* I wanted that for him, even if it cut me to the quick when we said goodbye.

At worst case, he would remain here, stifled but surrounded by the love of his family, and even if I wanted to be with him, to throw caution to the proverbial wind and let him all the way in, it would kill the career I'd just victoriously reclaimed. The nearest company was in Boston.

The best company was in New York.

There was no solution that even let me ponder keeping him.

Unless he gets stationed somewhere with a company, like San Francisco. But would either of us be happy, knowing our relationship had come at the cost of the very things we'd dreamed about?

A pair of headlights shone through the studio windows, and I turned to watch Gavin's car roll up the long drive from the main road in the dying evening light. But it wasn't Gavin who parked in front of the house and charged up the steps like a man possessed.

It was Hudson.

The front door blew open and was shut with the same energy a second before he walked into the studio, collar of his dress shirt undone, tie missing, and hair mussed like he'd ripped his hands through it a dozen times. His eyes held a wild desperation that made my heartbeat trip over itself as we locked eyes.

How was it possible that this was my last night with him?

"I wanted to bring you home." He strode toward me, his gaze roving over my body. "And you let *Gavin*?"

"Shoes," I reminded him, heat flooding my body as I retreated a step for every one he took. "And you're the one with medical training. It only made sense to send you with Juniper, seeing as Caroline was meeting you at the ER."

"Fuck the shoes." He kicked them off. "And you refused to be seen—"

"The EMT cleared me at the scene," I reminded him, passing Anne's barre spot and entering the familiar territory of mine, where I stopped retreating and stood my ground. "And I have enough memories of that hospital without making any new ones, thank you very much."

He flinched, and I immediately regretted reminding him. "Seeing you in that water?" He shook his head, crossing the distance between us. "You scared the shit out of me."

"It scared the shit out of me too," I admitted as he reached for me. "Juniper—"

"Not just Juniper." He cupped the back of my neck and leaned into my space. "You, Allie. You scared the *shit* out of me. Do you have any idea what you mean to me? You're my air. And I know you don't even want to think about going there when it comes to us, that you need things all neat and tidy, but I'm already there. Messy. Tangled. So wrapped up in you that I couldn't *breathe* in that ER because I needed to be here with you."

My heart swelled, beating so loud it almost drown the insidious doubts that shook the bars of their cage, demanding I keep that very heart right where it was, safe within my own chest. I couldn't surrender it to Hudson, not when ruin was our only possible outcome. But damn it . . . I wanted to.

"Hudson," I whispered, my hands rising to his chest, but I couldn't bring myself to push him away.

"I'm the one who needs you." He lowered his head toward mine. "I need you, Allie. I always have."

CHAPTER THIRTY-FOUR

Allie

USER HAS DISABLED COMMENTS

The words broke me, snapped the tethers of self-preservation, and left me anchorless. I fisted my hands in his shirt and surged upward, pressing my lips to his.

He groaned low in his throat and took my mouth with an urgency that flooded my veins and set my nerves on fire. The kiss was blatantly carnal, all twisting tongues and clashing teeth as we strained to get closer.

I tore at the buttons on his shirt, and reluctantly surrendered the kiss for the whole three seconds it took Hudson to strip off my tank top, leaving me bare from the waist up. Then his mouth was fused with mine again, and I sucked on his tongue as I worked his shirt off his shoulders. I was rewarded with another groan as fabric hit the floor.

His hand cupped my breast, and the skim of his thumb over my nipple hardened the peak instantly. A shiver rolled up my spine and I arched into his hand as he kissed me deeper, longer, centering my world with him as my only compass point.

I knew the carved lines of his torso by heart and traced them with my fingertips as my hands slid down his body, quickly finding his zipper and tugging. There were too many clothes, too many layers between us. I needed him as naked as I felt, and only all of him would do. A quick flick of my fingers on the hook closure of his dress pants, and they were unfastened. I slipped my hand between the rigid muscles of his abs and the elastic of his boxer briefs and found him hot and hard.

"Fuck, Allie." His moan echoed off the mirrored walls as I wrapped my hand around his cock and stroked from the tip all the way to his base.

My thighs clenched, heat centering between them as I swirled my thumb over his tip, and then stroked my tongue into his mouth, flicking the sensitive line behind his teeth in time with the motion of my hands. I lived for his swift intakes of breath, the clench of his hand in my hair.

I abandoned his mouth to kiss down his chest and worship at the altar of his perfect abs. My tongue dipped into the line that ran from the edge of his stomach down past his waistband, and I hooked my hands at his hips and dragged the clothing from his body in one long pull, hitting my knees in front of him.

"Love . . ." There was awe in that tone, but also a touch of warning that let me know I was playing with absolute fire.

"Off," I demanded, and he stepped free of his pants and boxer briefs. Once I stripped his socks off, I sat back on my heels and looked up and up, marveling at the perfection of his body. "I don't think I've ever seen a more perfect form."

"Al—" he started, but ended on a rumbling groan as I rose onto my knees and sucked him into my mouth.

His cock slid over my tongue, and a heady sense of power flushed my skin as his hips rocked once. Twice.

"Holy shit." His hands fisted in my hair. "Allie. Love. You have to."

"Hmmm?" I took him deeper and reveled at the flare of his eyes, the flex of his jaw, the knowledge that I had the complete and total ability to unravel him.

"Stop," he managed to say.

I flicked his tip with my tongue and released him. "Are you sure that's what you want?"

"I know exactly what I want." The heat in his gaze would have set a glacier on fire, and I was already kindling, ready to burn at the first touch. He slipped his hands beneath my arms and hauled me to my feet, then stripped my pajama pants and underwear right off, adding the garments to the sea of discarded clothing around us.

"Do you?" I asked, more than a little breathless.

He nodded, his gaze devouring me as he reached into a pile of his clothes. "I've been fantasizing about what I would do to you in this room for far longer than I care to admit."

"Is that so?" I swallowed hard and stepped backward over my forgotten tank top, kicking it aside to clear his path. "What are you looking for?" Whatever it was, he was taking too long.

"Wallet." He grabbed his pants. "Condom."

"Forget it." I retreated until my back hit the barre. "Don't need it. I'm on birth control." And I wanted him *now*. "It's like ninety-nine percent effective."

He retrieved a foil packet from his wallet and shook his head at me as he ripped it open. "Not risking that one percent." He rolled it over his length.

I blinked. Right. Of course he wouldn't. We weren't even in a long-term relationship—

"You want kids?" he continued. "I'll give you kids. Say the word." The thought should have frozen me, but the conviction shining in his eyes, shouting that our futures were already intertwined, had my heart beating double time as he stalked forward, gloriously, beautifully nude. "Until then, I'm not risking everything you've worked for because I'm impatient."

The ache in my chest flared bright and so sweet that I bit my lower lip to keep the words from spilling out.

"God, the things I have pictured doing to you," he murmured, his gaze raking over me with palpable hunger. He consumed my mouth with a soul-rending kiss, then dropped to his knees at my feet, hooked an arm around my left leg, and lifted it to settle on his shoulder.

My breath hitched as he leaned in and kissed the sensitive skin of my inner thigh. "I'd watch you for hours, perfectly composed, completely disciplined, and wondered what you would do if I—" He dragged his tongue from my entrance to my clit.

I cried out, and my back bowed as I caught fire. My hands reached for his head, but he shook it.

"Hands on the barre, Allie," he ordered.

I immediately did as ordered.

"Perfect," he praised, then worked me over with his mouth, pleasure coiling within me with every scrape and swirl of his tongue. I gripped the barre as my hips rolled on their own accord, chasing the high I knew only he could give me.

He kept one arm locked around my thigh, holding me in place, and guided my hips with the other, using it to haul me into the rapturous assault, then hold me at bay when I came close to the edge, until my muscles shook and my desperation spiraled into needy pants and whispered pleas.

"This is exactly what I pictured," he said, then swirled his tongue around me. "You trembling, gasping, flushed with need."

"Hudson, please," I begged.

He slid two fingers inside me and stroked. "But the sound of you moaning my name? That's beyond anything I ever could have imagined, Allie. And now it lives in my dreams." He used his hand and tongue to drive me straight over the cliff.

I broke apart, shattered by waves of mind-numbing bliss, and would have fallen if Hudson hadn't held me upright, wringing every last shudder from me and somehow igniting a whole new fire as he finally, slowly stood.

My chest heaved and my leg rose with him. He dipped his shoulder, and my thigh slid off only to be caught at his elbow, then lowered to the floor.

"Turn around."

I flipped to face the barre, then took two steps back, meeting his gaze in the mirror.

"Fucking flawless," he said, running his fingers down my spine before taking my ass in his hands.

I leaned forward in blatant invitation and spread my feet, keeping my eyes locked with his. "Hudson," I whispered. "I need *you*."

"Feeling is more than mutual." He slipped his fingers between my thighs, and I shuddered at the fresh wave of urgency that washed through me and held fast, demanding appeasement. Thankfully, he didn't make me wait this time. He bent his knees, and I felt the head of his cock nudge my entrance, then pause.

"Yes." I nodded my head and pushed back, using the barre for leverage and earning the first inch of his intrusion.

"You are so fucking *mine*." He clasped my hips and drove into me.

I called out his name, and my eyes slid shut at the sublime pleasure. He hit so deep, so perfectly.

"Eyes," he demanded. "Watch us."

The words alone had me melting, but the way he withdrew only to slam home again turned me *molten*. He set a rhythm that had me gasping, keening for the next thrust, the next dose of the bliss I was shamelessly addicted to.

"Every time. You're. In a. Studio." He punctuated the words with the snap of his hips. "I want. You to. Remember. Exactly. How this feels." His face flushed, and sweat beaded on our skin, and the only time he looked away was to stare down at where we were joined. "What. We do. To each other."

Fuck, I was *doomed* to never look at a mirror the same way again.

When his gaze found mine again, he looked *starved*.

"I need your mouth." He withdrew completely, and I whimpered in protest at the loss, but he gripped my waist, and the barre flew from my hands as the world spun and Hudson filled my vision.

His mouth consumed mine as he lifted me into his arms, and I wound my arms around his neck, my legs around his waist. My ass hit the barre, and then he was inside me again, stroking deep, feeding the wild desperation that had me moaning into his mouth.

Every stroke was better than the last. Every thrust sent me higher, wound me tighter.

"Fucking barre," he groaned against my mouth, and then we were moving. My back hit the section of mirror where the barre ended, and then he drove so deep I saw stars, and our kiss muffled our shouts.

"More," I demanded, using the mirror to arch into every thrust, and he braced one hand beside my head and gripped my hip with the other, delivering everything I needed.

God, this was *life*. This was the meaning of breath, and the purpose of existence. Just Hudson.

Tension built, coiling so tightly that I lost the ability to rock back into him as my muscles locked, then started trembling. And still he took me, kissed me, sent me up in flames, and became the very air I drew on.

"Hudson," I cried, riding a painful edge.

"I've got you, love." His hand slipped between us, and the next touch sent me careening into pure light.

I fractured into a thousand tiny pieces, but somehow Hudson held me together. My hips arched again and again as the orgasm pulsed through me, crashing like endless waves on a beach. I felt him tense, and hung on as he found his own release, spearing my fingers into his hair and cradling his head.

We came down together, gasping for breath, staring into each other's eyes like the beginning and end of everything in the universe was held between us. My heart rate descended slowly, and I fought the very real logic that tugged at the corners of my mind, knowing there were things that needed to be said, decisions that had to be made. Knowing I didn't want to give him up.

"Allie." Hudson pushed my hair back from my face. "We should—"

I cut him off. "Take me to bed. Before anyone gets home. Just take me to bed."

Anything and everything could wait until tomorrow.

I wanted tonight with him.

He carried me upstairs, and gave me exactly what I asked for, looking at me like we had forever and making love to me like we lived on borrowed time.

I was barely conscious when he slipped out of bed, and when I cracked an eye open, I saw pink through the window. "What time is it?" I burrowed deeper into my pillow and smiled at Hudson's scent.

"Six," he answered, already dressed in one of the uniforms from my closet. He sat on the edge of my bed and stroked his hand across my hair. "I'll take Sadie out so you can sleep. Beachman is picking me up for a meeting, and Gavin will be by in about an hour to get his car. I'll only be gone a few hours."

"You should stay." I caught his hand and pressed a kiss to his palm.

"Trust me, I would if I could, and when I get back, we have to talk." His brow knit. "About the bags you have packed, and us, and . . . things I need to tell you. We just have to talk."

"Okay," I agreed begrudgingly. "But it's hard to have a serious conversation when we don't even know where you'll be living."

"Yeah." A corner of his mouth rose, and he stole a quick, soft kiss. "Hopefully I'll hear today."

"I know you put Cape Cod first," I said, rolling to my back. "But I really hope you get Sitka. You deserve to catch that dream, Hudson."

"Dreams can change." He smiled as he stood, then backed away toward the door. "I meant to tell you sooner, but I changed my first choice right before I sent the list in."

"To Alaska?" I propped myself up on my elbows as he opened the bedroom door.

"No." The dimple in his cheek popped. "New York."

He was gone before I could even process the words, what the location meant. My stomach fell. No, he didn't. *He couldn't.* He wouldn't do something that impulsive, that . . . reckless.

Why didn't he choose Sitka? Cape Cod I understood, but New York? We'd never even discussed the possibility.

We can be together. I immediately stuck a pin in that particular childish bubble of joyous thought and popped it. New York would take everything I loved about us and muddle it, wreck it. My life there would ruin Hudson. Stealing scant hours with me for a month was one thing, but we couldn't build a life on it. Oh *God.* He'd just given up a chance at his dream duty station to live out what would end in a nightmare with me, and now he'd have to wait another three years before he could make another request.

I got up, showered, and dressed as my mind spun. When the town's lone taxi service pulled into the driveway an hour later, I was already sitting on the front porch steps with Sadie curled at my side.

Gavin would set this right. He wouldn't let Hudson throw himself away on . . . me.

"What's wrong?" Gavin asked as soon as he stepped out of the taxi. "You look like something's wrong. Is Hudson okay? Did something happen? He just texted me an hour ago—"

"Hudson's fine," I assured him as the taxi pulled away. "At least until I get my hands on him. Did you know he changed his duty-station preference to New York?"

Gavin's posture sagged in relief. "No, but that doesn't surprise me." He rubbed the back of his neck. "Shit, you scared me. I thought something was *wrong,* from the look on your face."

"Something is wrong!" I stood.

"Because he wants to be near you?" His arms dropped to his sides. "Are you seriously pissed that he's willing to uproot his whole life, and piss off our sister—which I fully support—in order to be with you?"

I shook my head. "No, I'm pissed because he didn't choose Sitka! That's been his dream since I met him, to get as far away from this town as possible." My shoulders drooped and I fought the growing, bittersweet ache in my chest I couldn't name for the sake of my sanity. "He should get to have his dream, too, Gavin. And I get putting it on hold to come back and help Caroline. He's an incredible brother. But putting it on hold for *me*? You have to talk him out of it."

"I don't think that's how that works." Gavin rocked back on his heels and stared at me like I'd grown a set of horns. "Damn, Allie, you really don't get it, do you?"

"That he's selfless? Yeah, choosing a career where he literally risks his life for other people clued me in." I folded my arms.

"No, that *you're* his dream. He's in love with you," Gavin countered.

My breath abandoned me in a rush. "He's not." I smothered the sudden rush of warmth behind my ribs.

"He is." Gavin nodded, throwing out his hands. "Of course he wants to be stationed where you are. Would it really be that bad, being in a real relationship with my brother? Or were you just playing around with him for the summer?"

"I would never do that." I drew back at the insult. Hudson and I had an agreement. We both knew what this was.

"Are you sure you're not looking to ditch him now that the Classic is over? Rousseau girls specialize in yanking out an Ellis boy's heart and throwing it back when September rolls around." His gaze narrowed.

I jabbed my finger his direction. "That was uncalled for."

He sighed. "You're right. I'm sorry. Would it really be so bad if he got New York? Forget your fear and your need to keep everyone but Sadie at arm's length. Would it be the end of the world if you went home to Hudson every day?"

I breathed through that thought, trying to push past the logic of what my life would do to him, and focusing on that growing pressure in my chest. "No." I shook my head. "It would be pretty great." That was a *selfish* answer. "But it would be too hard on him."

"Let him decide what's hard." Gavin's fists opened and closed, jingling the keys. "Look, I was there. I saw what losing you did to him the first time, so I can't blame him for grabbing hold with both hands and holding on. For fuck's sake, just let him hold on, Allie. He's strong enough for the both of you."

My brow scrunched. "What do you mean, you were there? I don't remember you being at the Classic that year."

"No." He shook his head and looked at me like I'd grown two. "Who the hell do you think picked him up at the hospital that day? Me." He tapped his chest with his hand. "I'm the one he called. I'm the one who had to coax the words out of him when he walked out of the emergency department covered in *your* blood. I'm the one who had to make up some bullshit story to our parents about why he wouldn't speak for the next four days before he left for basic. So excuse me if I just want him to finally be happy!"

I stared at Gavin and tried to breathe, tried to make any sense of his words. "*My* blood?"

Color drained from his face, and he retreated a step. "Shit," he muttered, his eyes sliding shut.

"What the hell do you mean, *my blood*?" My voice rose and I fought the nauseating sensation of gravity shifting.

"Just . . ." He retreated down the steps, keeping his eyes on me like I was a mountain cat he knew better than to turn his back on. "He thinks you won't forgive him, and you have to, Allie. Just let him hold on this time, and not just for him. You need each other. You two are the shit poets write about."

What was *that* supposed to mean?

"Gavin!" I shouted as he reached the car.

He pulled out of the driveway and left me standing on the porch, second-guessing everything I thought I knew about the last ten years.

CHAPTER THIRTY-FIVE

Hudson

Devon2Sharpe: RousseauSisters4, just wanted to know the meaning of your handle. I thought there were only two of you?

ReeseOnToe: Devon2Sharpe, there are three alive. One plays an admin role in the company, and they lost their oldest sister in a car accident that Alessandra survived.

Devon2Sharpe: ReeseOnToe oh shit, I didn't know. Thx

ReeseOnToe: NP. Alina was a spectacular dancer, too. You can find some of her stuff on YouTube.

She's on the beach. That was all Anne was willing to tell me when I got to Allie's, but the look she dealt out said it was my fault. Yeah, dropping that New York information on her and splitting probably wasn't my best course of action, but I'd been feeling all hopeful and shit.

Not so much anymore.

I blew out a slow breath, accepting my fate, and made my way through the backyard and down the steps. Good thing I'd stopped at my house to change out of uniform. Sand was a bitch when it got in my boots.

Allie sat on the end of the pier, staring out over the ocean. My chest clenched as I crossed the wooden expanse. This morning's hope had transformed into tonight's problem when my email pinged during the morning meeting, and what seemed like an easy hurdle to jump now felt a canyon. Orders had come in, and I wouldn't be going anywhere soon.

I'd be in Cape Cod, while Allie most likely took the New York contract. This was going to suck, but we could handle a fight. The fight would be good for us, force us to define what we were really doing, which had left the fling department weeks ago, somewhere between me giving her a key with her drawer and her freeing up closet space for a few of my uniforms. Flings didn't make room for each other in their lives the way we had.

"Hey," I said so I didn't startle her, then lowered myself to sit at her side, letting my legs dangle above the water.

She fidgeted with her hands but didn't look over.

"I'm guessing you're pissed that I asked for New York," I started, "but it turned out to be nothing. I got my orders, and I'm staying here." Caroline would eventually be thrilled once she was done being pissed at me. "I hope you know I'd never expect you to take the Boston contract or anything. I fully support you going back to MBC if that's what you want."

No response.

"Allie?" I studied her profile and flinched when she didn't so much as look my way. Shit. She'd thrown her walls right back up in the three hours I'd been gone. "I know I should have talked to you about changing it, but . . ." I took the deepest breath of my life and dove straight into what was going to be the most important fight of our lives. One I wasn't willing to lose. Not again. "But I don't want this to end. I know you're leaving in the next few days, but we can make this work. I have a favor I can call in at the assignment desk, and if that doesn't work, I'll come down on weekends so you don't lose studio time. I'll fold myself into your life—"

"My father always told us that waves come in sets," she interrupted, staring out at the ocean as those very waves broke against the pylons beneath us.

My stomach tensed. Holy shit, I was in bigger trouble than I thought if we were talking about science. "They can," I agreed, "depending on if they're caused by wind or storms, and the shape of the ocean floor—"

"He told us that individual waves move faster, but when they group in deep water, they move slower because they're connected by the same energy." Her left hand moved over her right, spinning something around her finger. "They're bound as a set, traveling through the water until the landscape changes with the shoreline." She paused. "And then they break one by one."

"Right." Where was she going with this? I braced my hands on the pier and held on to the edge as I listened, looking for any clue in her expression, but she was fully masked. Untouchable.

"And I understood the metaphor he was making, but I always thought that we were more like the pylons," she continued, her fingers moving faster. "We were stronger together, more capable of taking the hits, holding the pier through storms, as long as we supported each other. But the longer I sit here, the more I realize that losing one pylon might damage the pier, but it doesn't lessen the integrity of the others. They're connected by purpose, not energy."

She looked down as a wave crashed into the wood, the spray rising to just beneath our feet. "And now I think Dad was right. The four of us were a set, moving through life bound by an unbreakable force, at times unintentionally holding each other back so we could push forward together, not realizing the picture-perfect beach we were racing toward would break us one by one, and the others would be doomed to watch, powerless to help or prevent our own ruin." The evening light brought out the gold in her eyes as she looked past me toward the beach and the breaking waves. "We aren't the pylons. We're the waves. Lina broke first, and in our own ways, the three of us are now careening toward the shore."

"Allie, what happened?" A deep sense of foreboding sent chills up my spine, the feeling identical to the moments my tires had lost their grip on an icy road, and all there was to do was wait for them to find purchase—or wreck.

"That's the problem. I don't know." Her eyes locked with mine, and the hair rose on the back of my neck. "But you do, don't you, Hudson? Because you were there."

"What do you mean?" My grip spasmed so hard I half expected to leave handprints in the wood.

"Gavin let it slip that he picked you up at the hospital"—she tilted her head—"covered in my blood."

Oh *fuck*. My stomach crashed into the waves below, and for the first time in my life, I didn't know what to do. I froze.

"You. Were. There." She spit it like the accusation it was. "At the accident. That's the only way you could have had my blood on you."

I wanted to run, to rewind time two days, two weeks, *two months*, and do it all differently. My ribs clamped down on my heart so hard it pounded in protest, but I'd never told Allie a lie, and I couldn't start today. *Except by omission.*

"Yes," I admitted. "I was there."

Her eyes widened, and my heart screamed that I'd just cost us any chance at a future. "Were you in the car?"

"No." I shook my head and fought the boulder of a lump forming in my throat. "I was behind you. We left the beach at the same time—"

"The beach?" Her brow knit.

"The cove where we kissed." I grimaced at the way she instantly tensed. "Kissed now, not then. Then, I wanted to wait until we faced your parents, to do everything the right way, and then it all went so. Fucking. Wrong."

"The cove." Realization flared in her eyes. "I showed up that night?"

"You were late, but you showed up." I nodded. God, I'd wanted to tell her so many times, and I should have. Damn the consequences. She never should have heard it from Gavin. "It's the same road, so everyone just assumed you'd been coming back from the reception."

"Did you see the accident happen?" Her hands clenched.

"No. You disappeared around the corner probably thirty seconds ahead of me. By the time I rounded the curve . . ." I looked away, my brain recognizing I was here on this pier, but my memory fighting to convince me otherwise, filling my vision with mangled metal and my lungs with smoke. "You'd hit the tree."

"Was . . ." Her voice broke, and I snapped my gaze back to hers. "Was Lina alive when you got there?" Her lower lip trembled.

"Yes." My chest tightened painfully. Her head had been turned toward Allie, her bloodied face flush with the steering wheel, but I left that detail out. Allie didn't need my nightmares.

"What did she say?" Her eyes filled with tears, and my ribs threatened to break.

"She told me to save you."

"But I was already safe." Allie blinked, then shook her head. "Why did she go back to the car? What was she looking for?"

"Back?" My eyebrows jumped. "What are you talking about?"

"She went *back*!" She pushed up on the pier and stood.

I quickly did the same, a chill rolling up my spine. "You remember something, don't you?"

"Yes!" she shouted. "It was my fault." The wind gusted and she shoved the loose tendrils of her hair out of her face. "She pulled me out of the car, and then she carried me up the embankment to the shoulder of the road and sat with me."

Every muscle in my body tensed, but I kept quiet.

"She held something to my head to help stop the bleeding, then told me to hold on because help was coming." She spoke with complete and utter certainty. "She told me that she loved me, and to follow my heart, and to take care of what she'd left behind, and then she put her ring in the pocket of my skirt."

Fuck. My soul left my body. Lina had said at least two of those things at the cove when I'd walked Allie back to her car.

"But then she told me I'd be okay, and she went back to the car for something, and I couldn't stop her. I tried, but I couldn't move. God, my mom just kept crying that I'd saved myself and left her there to die . . ." She shook her head violently. "I couldn't tell her the truth was so much worse, that I couldn't get her to stay."

"Allie, it wasn't your fault. That's not what happened." I shook my head.

"It is!" She lifted her right hand and the ring flashed in the sun. "See?"

"Holy shit, you have it." Breathing took more than a little thought.

"Why did she go back?" She stepped backward. "You were there, Hudson. Why?"

"She never went back. She never left the car." I took the steps that separated us and clasped her shoulders so she didn't stumble off the pier. "And you didn't leave her to die, Allie. I did." And there it was.

She startled.

"I left her." I'd only ever said those words to one other person.

"I don't understand." Her forehead crinkled. "She pulled me out—"

"No, love. *I* pulled you out," I said slowly, so there was no chance of misunderstanding.

Her face slackened.

"When I got there, the car was already on fire. It took all my strength to rip open your door. The frame had been bent in the crash. Lina was conscious, and you were dazed. She told me to get you out, to save you, and I didn't argue. I didn't even hesitate." I cradled the side of her face for what I feared might be the last time. "You were . . . God, Allie, you were essential to existence. Of course I was going to save you."

"You?" she whispered, studying my eyes.

"Me." I nodded. "I cut through your seat belt with my pocket-knife, somehow got you out of the wreckage, and carried you up the embankment." Even now, I could feel the heat of the fire on my back, the slight weight of her in my arms. I saw her eyes, watching me with absolute trust even as they unfocused and she started to slip into unconsciousness. My heart pounded like we were still there, on the side of the road I avoided to this day. "I was going to run straight back, but your head was bleeding so fucking fast. The wound was pulsing, and all I could think was it had to be arterial, and I was terrified you'd bleed out before anyone could find us. You were my world. Nothing mattered beyond you." Even Lina. "I sat you down, took off my sweatshirt, and put pressure on the wound."

"You." This time it wasn't a question.

"I told you to hold it there, and then turned around to go back for Lina . . ." My throat closed, and I had to take a deep breath and swallow so I could finish confessing. "But the fire had reached the gas tank and the car exploded."

"Oh my God." Her face crumpled, and her eyes watered.

"Listen to me, Allie." I leaned in. "You didn't leave her or let her do anything. None of it was your fault. Whatever you remember is just your mind trying to protect you, piecing together bits and pieces of what she said to you at the cove to give you one last memory of her. I'm the one who made the choice, and I chose you."

"But I have the ring," she whispered.

"I gave you the ring at the beach." God, if I'd only known that's how she remembered everything, I would have said something *years* ago.

"No." She wrenched out of my hands and sidestepped before turning her back on me and walking toward shore.

"Lina gave me the ring before the Classic!" I followed her, pausing when she did to give her space. "You can ask Anne. She saw us in a hallway and thought we were sneaking around behind your back or something. But Lina told me to give you the ring."

Allie pivoted to face me. "Why would she do that? It was her heirloom."

"Because . . ." Now I was the one who needed a second, and Allie watched as I struggled for the words. "Because I was in love with you." How, out of everything, was *that* the hardest truth to tell? "And Lina, she saw what I thought I kept pretty well hidden."

"We were just friends." Allie hugged her arms around her waist.

"Until we weren't." I reached up to shape the brim of my hat, then ripped it off my head and whipped it into the ocean out of pure frustration. "The fact that you don't remember what might have been the most pivotal moment of our lives has haunted me for ten fucking years."

"Haunted *you?*" she snapped. "Tell me what happened, Hudson."

I turned to face her. "I was leaving in four days, and Lina told me to take the ring and give it to you as a promise that whatever we started, we'd finish once I was out of basic training. She said it would be a message to your entire family that she had your back, and she was so certain you'd choose me because you loved me, too, even if you didn't realize it." My ribs did their best impression of a vise. "She was right. You did. And you don't remember."

"I chose you over ballet." She searched my eyes like she was looking for a lie.

"You chose me over your mother's company." I nodded. "You chose *us*. You didn't sign the MBC offer at the reception, and said you'd wait to accept whichever company's contract was closest to wherever I'd be assigned, and that you didn't care if it cost you a season, and fuck, did I love you even more for it." My shoulders dropped and my chest hollowed. "You decided to ride back to your parents' with Lina so you two

Variation

could game-plan how we should tell them." I blew out a slow breath. "Letting you get into that car is the biggest regret of my life."

She glanced at the ring, then back up at me. "My mother said the paramedics found me on the side of the road by myself."

I scoffed. "Your mother lied. She does that. A lot." I didn't bother masking my hatred. "She kicked me out of your hospital room and told me never to come back."

Her eyes flared. "And you *listened*?"

"No. I went back the day after, and she told me you'd woken up and didn't remember anything, and that if I persisted in my attempts to derail your life, she would tell you that I'd had plenty of time to save you both but had taken too long with you, leaving Lina to die, and you'd never forgive me for it." Remorse hit with the force of a battering ram, just like always.

She flinched. "And you left. That's the end of the story." She walked away again, and I followed just like I always did, halting only when she spun around once we reached the boathouse platform. "I deserved the truth!"

"You did." I nodded as the waves crashed beneath us. "I'm so sorry. I almost called you thousands of times, but once I got phone privileges at basic, I knew that ghosting you had already given you another reason to hate me. And as months and years went by, I'd dug a hole there was no prayer of ever recovering from, so I chose not to intrude on your life."

"You could have come back at any time and told me the truth." Her voice broke. "I left a seat open for you for a *decade*."

I felt the blood drain from my face, like it knew it needed to protect far more vital organs in danger of bleeding out. "Would you have forgiven me?" I stepped forward, and she retreated. "You told me the first day I met you that your sisters were the most important thing in the world to you, and I didn't give a shit that night. I chose my wants over your needs and didn't so much as hesitate. I make split-second decisions, always have, and usually they work out, but that one cost

407

the life of your sister. Could you ever have gotten past the fact that I pulled you out of that car instead of Lina? That I'm the reason you're alive and she isn't?"

She flinched.

"I'm right, aren't I?" I deflated. "Every time you look at me, you'll remember that I left her in that car. Or you'll wonder if I had just carried you a few less feet, taken just a little less time to stanch your wound, or hell, let you bleed for another minute, if Lina would be here too."

Her eyes flicked from side to side as she mulled it over.

"I wouldn't blame you for not getting past it, since I think about it every damned day. You are every person I go into the water for. There are hundreds of them, but they're all *you*. I'm so sorry I couldn't save Lina, too, Allie. You'll never know how sorry I am." I'd waited ten years to say those words, knowing they'd never be enough, and the pain of being right threatened to crush me.

She tugged the sleeves of her MBC hoodie over her hands. "You just let me live with the guilt of thinking I saved myself and left her there for a decade. Even if I could understand why you did all of that ten years ago, why didn't you tell me when I came back this summer? Why would you let me fall for you when you knew this would . . ." She shook her head and looked away.

Fall for you. That did it. My heart twisted, then flat-out broke at what I'd lost by holding on to the secret for too long. "I fucked up. At first, I didn't want Juniper caught in the crosshairs of you hating me, and then I didn't know if you could take another blow, and then you told me we couldn't last past the summer and not to tell you anything that wouldn't affect these five weeks." It sounded like bullshit, even to my ears. "But really, there's no excuse other than my own selfishness. I had you back and I was terrified of losing you again."

There it was. All of it.

"But you chose New York." She tilted her head at me. "Were you ever going to tell me? Or did you think it would never come out?"

"I was going to tell you after the Classic, but then everything happened," I promised her. "I was going to tell you and confront your mother so she knew she couldn't run me off again. Honestly, I was surprised she didn't tell you the second you informed her we were together."

"You thought my mother would spill your secret?" Allie laughed, but it came out on a cry. "It would have killed her leverage on me. God, Hudson, do you know how many hours I've spent with therapists trying to remember what happened? Asking why I would have left Lina there when I swore she went *back* to the car? You've known *all* this time! If you'd told me at seventeen, maybe I would have struggled because you chose to save me over Lina, but I wouldn't have despised you. Not like this." She shook her head. "And I understand keeping things private. I'm a master of it. But knowing this truth would have changed my life. Maybe our lives. And now, I don't know how to trust you. Or how to trust that *this* is the truth. And yet . . . you saved me."

"Allie . . . it's all true." The word *despise* took what was left of my heart and smashed it into sand.

"Thank you, Hudson." She looked off into the water as a wave broke against the shore.

I held my breath.

"I should have said that first. Thank you. If not for you, I would have died in that car with Lina. Though, if not for *us*, we wouldn't have been in the car in the first place, I suppose."

"Stop finding ways to blame yourself."

Her weary gaze found mine. "I really do wish you nothing but the best."

"No. Don't break us up." That's exactly what was happening here, and every part of me screamed to hold on this time, even as my heart bled out on the pier. "We can get through this."

"No, we can't. You can't build something when there's no trust." She looked my way. "The irony, truly, is that I've never learned to be completely open with anyone, but I got close with you. And maybe if

409

I had just let you in, if you knew the things my family . . ." She shook her head. "Well, maybe you would have made different choices, and we wouldn't be here. That part of the blame is on me." Her back straightened and I watched, horrified, as she put up piece after piece of her armor and rebuilt her walls.

"What does that mean?" My brow furrowed.

"Nothing that matters anymore. And this isn't a breakup. It was foolish to even entertain the thought that we could be anything more, not when we want such drastically different things for our lives. We've always had an expiration date, and we've simply reached it." She plastered on that fake-ass smile. "But it was good for a summer, right?"

Whatever was left of my heart stopped beating.

"Goodbye, Hudson."

This time when she walked away, I didn't follow.

CHAPTER
THIRTY-SIX

Allie

MelChelBarre: Anyone else refreshing the MBC website to see if the cast sheet changes?

I stormed into the house, replaying Hudson's confession in my mind and completely overwhelmed with the enormity of what he'd revealed while somehow simultaneously wishing he'd never told me.

Maybe we would have had a shot at being happy.

He saved your life. And he'd carried the guilt of it ever since.

But he'd also lied . . . at least by omission.

Anger was the easiest emotion to deal with, so I clung to it like a security blanket as I walked through the house and into the kitchen. Sadie wagged her tail and went back to massacring her latest squeaky toy.

Eva, Kenna, and Anne sat at the island, eating a late breakfast in front of a stack of manila envelopes, and all three of them fell silent and stared as I went to the refrigerator.

"You ready to start handling paperwork?" Anne asked. "You don't have to decide which company—"

Fuck it. It wasn't like I needed to plan my life around Hudson anymore. "I'll sign with MBC. I need *something* normal in my life."

Eva's shoulders dipped with relief.

"Make Vasily wait a week or two," Eloise suggested, peeling her orange. "Let him sweat it out."

"Good idea." I took a bottle of water from the refrigerator.

"Didn't see you when we got home after the reception," Kenna noted, her gaze leery. "Or at all this morning."

"Nope." I twisted the top and drank half of it down. How was I supposed to explain any of this to them when I didn't even know for certain that what Hudson told me was true . . .

"Okay, did you want to run the papers over to Caroline?" Anne asked. *Anne.* She'd been put in charge of the family paperwork.

I leaned back against the counter next to the sink. "Anne, did you see Hudson with Lina the morning of the Classic?"

Eva's eyebrows hit the ceiling, and Kenna and Eloise both shifted their attention to Anne.

She cleared her throat and set her spoon down in her bowl of oatmeal. "Yes."

"And they looked all secretive, like they were up to something?" I took another drink.

"Yes." She nodded slowly. "And I told him if he did something to hurt you that I'd tell you. I wouldn't keep my mouth shut this time."

"This time?" I sputtered a wry laugh. "God, if any of you had told me the truth the *first* time, none of this would be happening."

"Did he hurt you?" She stiffened.

"Did you read the accident report?" I ignored her question entirely. "From when Lina died?"

The entire room fell silent.

"Yes." She put her hands in her lap. "About a year ago. I found it in Dad's office."

412

"And when they found Lina's remains, was her seat belt still fastened?" I tilted my head. "Not the cloth—naturally that would have burned. Was the metal still connected?"

Anne glanced at Eva.

"Eyes here." I tapped my chest.

Anne gasped. "Is that Lina's ring?"

"Yes. Was her seat belt still fastened?" I had to know.

"Yes," Anne answered, looking me in the eye.

My chest constricted. Lina had never gotten out of the car. Hudson had told the truth. "And my door was open."

"Yes." She shifted her weight. "It wasn't your fault, Allie. I know what Mom says, but that's just grief talking. The detectives noted that the frame was mangled. It was a miracle you were able to force your own door open. Had to have been adrenaline, because none of them could figure out how you did it in your state."

Anger. Hold on to the anger.

"Simple. I didn't."

Anne's brows rose in silent question.

"We need to see Mom. Right fucking now."

"Her advisory team met this morning, and it's just not a good day," Rachel warned me as I strode down the hallway toward Mom's suite, Anne scurrying to keep up while Eva took her time.

"It never is," I replied. The doors didn't do much to muffle the sound of Tchaikovsky.

"You sure you don't want to talk about whatever's bothering you?" Anne asked in a rush. "You were silent the whole way here."

"Nope. Saving it all for Mom."

"If you're sure . . ." Rachel turned the handle and hurried in ahead of me. "Mrs. Rousseau, your daughters are here."

I walked in behind her, then stared.

Mom was dancing in a black leotard and pale-pink skirt, her left side in perfect alignment, but her right leg wasn't quite as steady. The incoming weather must have been wreaking havoc on her knee again. But there was no mistaking her grace and elegance as she moved through the choreography. She was still a beautiful dancer.

"*Swan Lake*," Anne whispered as she reached my side.

I nodded, watching Mom's arms, admiring the clean lines, the delicate splay of her fingers, which had never come naturally to me.

"She's still on demi-pointe," Eva noted with a touch of wonder.

"You sure you want to interrupt her? She usually uses this time as a reset before her afternoon sessions." Rachel's fingers hovered over the stereo system on my left. "One of the staff quit yesterday and she bit off two girls' heads earlier, screaming in French when they were late to a session. Even I'm only getting one-word answers out of her, and her day is booked." She clutched the clipboard in her right arm.

"One-word answers work fine for me." I walked forward, and Mom met my gaze in the mirror.

"Fifth," she ordered, halting her own dance with a sigh of frustration.

"No." I stood my ground once I was a few feet away from her.

The music died.

"Fifth!" she shouted.

"Hudson pulled me out of the car that night, didn't he?" There was no point mincing words.

Anne gasped for the second time that morning.

"Oh my God," Eva whispered.

Mom's arms fell to her sides, and her eyes flashed with anger.

"Yeah, the secret is out. I'll make this easy on you," I offered. "Let's stick to yes or no answers. I'm not interested in your excuses, anyway."

"Allie," Anne whispered, but I kept my eyes on our mother.

"He pulled me out of that car. He stayed with me. And you knew." I folded my arms.

"Rachel, if you wouldn't mind giving us a moment?" Anne asked, and the door clicked shortly after.

Lines bracketed Mom's lips as she pursed her mouth.

"You knew!" I snapped at Mom. "All the years you told me I left Lina for dead. All the times you told me that I owed her because I saved myself. You knew!"

"Yes." Mom looked out the window. "I chose—"

"Yes or no only, Mom," I interrupted, my blood rising to a boil. She'd kept me tethered to her wants, her dreams, for *decades*, binding me with little ropes she'd declared were love. But now I knew they were guilt, shaping me into someone I hardly recognized anymore, and I'd let her.

"Oh, Mom," Anne whispered. "How could you?"

Eva sat on the arm of the couch toward my right.

"He came with me to the hospital soaked in my blood from trying to stop the bleeding, and you threw him out." Each truth snapped one of those ropes, the rebound stinging my soul.

"Yes," she answered, almost bored as she folded her arms.

"He came back, too, didn't he?" My fingernails dug little half moons into my palms. "And you told him that I'd never forgive him for not saving us both, so he should go. That if he didn't, you'd tell me he'd had ample time to save us both but had left her there to die."

"You didn't." Anne sagged to my right, landing on the edge of the couch next to Eva.

"Holy shit." Eva's gaze darted between Mom and me.

Mom lifted her chin, her eyes focusing somewhere beyond the window as rope after rope splintered and broke.

"But really, you meant that *you'd* never forgive him. I mean, how could you know if I wouldn't if you never told me?" My voice rose and I didn't care. I clung to that anger like a life raft.

She swallowed and reached for a water bottle, then started chugging. Ironic that we handled our panic attacks the same way.

"Maybe she doesn't understand," Eva whispered.

"Allie, talking about Lina has always been hard on—" Anne started.

"I don't care." Rage colored my vision. "Why, Mom? Because you saw him—saw my feelings for him—as a threat? Realized that I had a year before I turned eighteen, and then you wouldn't have control anymore, that Hudson would give me the strength to be who I was instead of who you wanted?" I stepped forward, but kept watch on the bottle in case she decided to throw it. "Or did you punish him—punish *us*—because he saved the wrong daughter?"

"Yes." She swung her gaze to mine and crushed my heart in a one-word fist.

"Yes to which?" I demanded.

"He . . . Lina . . ." She shook her head. The muscles in her neck flexed, and she glanced beside me, to the picture on the wall. "Just. Left. My. Daughter."

"I'm your daughter!" I shouted, slamming my hand over my chest. She flinched.

"Anne"—I gestured to the couch—"is your daughter! Eva is your daughter! You had *four* daughters, Mom, not just one. Losing Lina did not give you the right to break us down so you could try to pour our pieces into her mold." *Snap. Snap. Snap.* Ropes broke and others frayed.

"No."

"Oh, right." I nodded. "It was never her mold. It was yours. You wanted us to live out your dream, and you never once asked us what ours were. Did you even ask Lina if she wanted to keep Juniper? Offer her support? Or was that relationship just another casualty of your relentless selfishness?"

"Lina." She swallowed. "Wanted." She shook her head like the thought was ludicrous. "Baby."

My stomach lurched. "And you made her give her up?"

"You could have told us," Anne said. "We would have helped her."

"Too weak . . . to do . . ." She struggled for the words. "I. Made. Lina. Principal." She lifted her left hand and jabbed it my direction. "And you."

"You made me a guilt-stricken mess who only finds joy in dancing when I'm *not* with your precious company. These last few weeks have been the first time I've enjoyed it in *years*." I seethed. "I never wanted the Company. I wanted *out*, to dance freelance all over the world, and you told me I owed it to Lina. You twisted my guilt for your purposes and told me I had to take the MBC contract, that it was my fault Lina had been out that night at all, and MBC wouldn't be MBC without a Rousseau onstage." The truth of that last sentence bit into me until I bled. "You twisted *all* of us. Lina kept her pregnancy a secret while you bribed Everett to make it easier to leave Juniper. Anne's a damned lawyer who uses her degree to plan Company events because we all know if you aren't dancing, you should support the ones who do, right? And Eva . . ." I laughed. "Eva stabbed me in the back and stole the role that had been created for me!"

Mom recoiled, her gaze flying toward Eva.

"I said I was sorry," Eva muttered, picking at her cuticles. "And Vasily gave it back."

"I'm sure she doesn't care." I cocked my head to the side at my mother. "After all, we're interchangeable parts in her little machine, right? Who cares which one of us is up there, as long as her last name is Rousseau."

"Allie," Anne warned as Mom's water bottle crunched in her grip.

"You. Are. *Rousseaus*," Mom said slowly.

"She's gotten so much worse," Eva whispered.

"It's happening quickly," Anne replied.

Mom shot them a look that dripped malice, but it was the edge of confusion that made me want to *scream*. Why couldn't all this have come out last year, when we could have had real answers?

"I'm starting to hate that name." I hated that I couldn't tell if she really understood, hated myself for being unable to stop. For the first time, I could tell her exactly how I felt without fearing the repercussions. But without the ropes binding me to her model of perfection, my emotions whipped out with a cutting, dangerous sense of freedom that I couldn't begin to fathom, let alone regulate.

Betrayal. Shame. Pride. Hope. Loss. Grief. Anger. They all warred for supremacy, but it was the ache in my chest that overruled them all.

"*Rousseau* made you."

"You didn't *make* me, Mom. You ruined me." My eyes watered and my nose burned. "And maybe I could forgive you for that, if you even cared. But you ruined Hudson. You put him in an impossible situation and decimated any chance we ever had at happiness!"

"His . . . choice." She had the fucking nerve to shrug.

"Mom," Anne chided.

"His choice!" she shouted, and the water bottle flew, hitting the mirror to my left.

"*He* had no choice!" My voice broke. "He was an eighteen-year-old kid, and you were supposed to be an adult, supposed to be *my* mom. You convinced him I'd never forgive him. That I'd blame him the rest of our lives for Lina's death." That was what had played in my mind over and over on the drive, after I'd left him standing on the beach, looking as shattered as I'd felt. "In his mind, he'd already lost me. Of course he left. He was my best friend, Mom, and I loved him! I loved him before I understood what that word really meant."

"Orange." She shook her head. "No." Her fists clenched. "Crush. River boy is crush."

"Not a crush." That ache swelled until my ribs strained under the pressure and my vision grew blurry. I didn't need to remember my response to his declaration on that beach to know with the utmost certainty what it had been. And now? He fiercely protected his family, protected strangers every time he jumped into the water, protected me time and again. He showed up even when I didn't realize it, tugged me out of my comfort zone without breaking my boundaries, declared his intentions without forcing me into an ultimatum. He told me exactly what he wanted from me—from us—and never demanded the same, giving me the space to figure it out instead of forcing me into another mask, another role, to fit into his idea of perfection. His smile melted my common sense, and his touch set me on fire, but it was the way he listened that broke through every wall I'd built. "I love him." I said the words out loud and the last rope snapped, setting me completely free and terrifyingly adrift. "I'm in love with him."

She scoffed.

"Maybe you can't comprehend the emotion, but it's when you would give up *everything* for that person's happiness. When their smile is essential to your heartbeat. When you know the gnarled, darkest, ugliest parts of each other, and you don't turn away." I glanced at my sisters and found Eva's hand firmly ensconced by Anne's.

My heart twinged. I hadn't given Hudson the same grace I always gave my sisters. He'd offered me truth, and I'd shut him out. But there were some wounds that even love couldn't heal.

"Lina!" she argued, her eyes bulging.

"What is she trying to say?" Eva whispered.

"I'm not sure," Anne answered. "Mom, what about Lina?"

"Wrong." Mom glanced at the ceiling, then breathed deep. "Choice."

"Lina knew about my choice!" I held up my right hand, and her gaze darted to the ring like a magnet. "She gave the ring to Hudson for me as a message to you that I wouldn't let you twist me like you did her, that I could make my own path, that I could *follow my heart* and choose love."

"His choice." Her eyes bulged. "Wrong. Girl."

"Mom!" Eva surged to her feet. "Allie, she doesn't know what she's saying."

"Sure she does," I answered. "Her memory's just fine, and it's not the first time she's made her feelings known." Without her tethers, her words fell into the ragged space between us, harsh and ugly, but unable to touch me. I took a single step toward Mom. "I'm done trying to prove myself to you, pushing myself until I break, tearing my body to shreds, done trying to win your approval like it's some kind of game where you keep moving the goalposts. I'm done." My hand fell. "I have loved you, worshipped you, idolized you my entire life, but I no longer *want* your approval. Whatever I do from here on out is for me."

I took one last look at her, then turned my back and headed for the door.

"Fifth!" she shouted.

"Bye, Mom." Anne stood, then came to my side.

"I'll come up more often," Eva promised, then hurried our direction.

"Fifth!" A painted canvas hit the wall to our right.

I slowly turned. "Oh, and Lina's daughter dances. She's beautiful and smart and tenacious . . . and talented. Eloise and I teach her, and it gives me so much hope for her future knowing you never will." Anne took my left hand, and I held on to her for dear life as we walked away from our mother, Eva following close behind so we'd fit through the door.

"Sloppy feet!" Mom screamed.

"Sloppy parenting," Anne retorted over her shoulder.

I took my first full breath as Eva shut the doors behind us. Anne made our apologies to Rachel for agitating Mom as Dr. Wakefield approached, and I concentrated on breathing in through my nose and out through my mouth so I didn't vomit after letting all that out.

Eva rubbed my back. "Hey, Doc. Nice bun."

"Thanks." Dr. Wakefield patted her glossy black hair. "Sometimes it just makes it easier to meet your mother wherever she is."

"She's worse than she was even a few weeks ago, and miles from where she had been in January," Anne noted. "It's taking her longer to find words. Her sentences—when she has them—are choppy too."

Dr. Wakefield nodded. "Unfortunately, her scan shows significant progression in that cortex. Lucky for us, neither her memory nor her mobility seems to be impacted yet, though we're seeing more frequent outbursts of violence. We're doing what we can to keep her safe and active in physical therapy sessions, art classes, everything we talked about."

"Writing? Reading?" Anne asked, and Eva tensed.

"We haven't gotten her to cooperate in months, so I'm not sure if she's incapable or stubborn," Dr. Wakefield responded, then glanced at us each in turn. "At this stage . . ." She sighed. "I can't estimate how much longer she'll be herself. You girls have done everything she asked to physically prepare, but it's progressing quickly."

We thanked her, then slowly made our way past other patients' rooms and down the wide staircase.

"Have to give it to Mom," Eva said as we reached the first floor. "She picked the bougiest assisted living facility known to man."

"It's not known," Anne replied with a sad smile. "That's why she chose it."

We walked over the Brookesfield Institute crest, and walked out into the August humidity.

"Feel better?" Anne asked, digging the keys out of her purse.

"No." I shook my head. "That wasn't exactly a fair fight."

"She's never been a fair parent," she countered.

"Hudson really pulled you out that night?" Eva tucked her thumbs in her front pockets.

"Apparently," I said softly. "Only three people really know, right? Lina's gone. Mom isn't reliable, and Hudson . . ." My throat tried to close. "I guess I have to trust his version of the events or make peace with never really knowing. He kept it from me all these years, and I don't know if he ever would have told me if it hadn't been for Gavin." Or maybe he would if I'd simply told him the truth about Mom.

"You love him," Eva reminded me gently.

"That doesn't mean we're right for each other." We stepped from pavement to blacktop.

"You could forgive him." Anne hooked her arm through mine.

"I just need some time to think about everything." The secrets, and the guilt, and the fact that his love had determined who lived that night. If Gavin had been the one behind us, Lina would have lived.

"You? Taking the time to overanalyze every possible outcome before picking the one that feels safest?" Eva snorted and made her way to the back passenger seat. "Imagine that."

"Take all the time you need." Anne shot our sister a look. "The same goes for the contracts. Screw the deadlines. Every company in this world will wait if you're not sure. There are plenty of them, but only one Alessandra Rousseau. Just have to decide what you want."

"That goes for you too," I reminded her.

She nodded, then patted my arm and headed for the driver's side.

For the first time in my life, I felt truly free, and yet I had no idea what to do with that freedom. I knew what I wanted. I just couldn't have him. Eva was right. I'd choose whatever felt safest, which meant sticking with the decision that made the most sense.

I was going back to New York.

CHAPTER THIRTY-SEVEN

Hudson

NYFouette92: You need to check out Bway11te new video. Cast sheet changed back to Alessandra Rousseau.

Tutucutex20: I saw that, too! No posts from RousseauSisters4, though.

A cab driver honked his horn at a pedestrian as I walked out of the coffee shop across from the Metropolitan Ballet Company's building. The sidewalks were as crowded as the roads, but at least the people moved faster than the gridlocked cars.

It was hard to imagine living here among the noise and millions of people, but if that's what it took to be near Allie, I'd adapt. Besides, the job stayed the same. It might not be Alaska, but ocean was ocean. And I'd have another shot at requesting Sitka in three years.

Three years was nothing in comparison to how long I'd loved Allie.

I checked my watch and sipped my overpriced cup of coffee, stepping out of the way so other customers could exit the shop behind me. Seven thirty meant I had ten minutes to make it the two blocks to Allie's place before she left for rehearsal. It also meant I hadn't slept in about twenty-four hours. Whatever. Sleep was overrated. I breathed in anxiety and exhaled determination.

My phone buzzed in the back pocket of my jeans, and my pulse jumped just like it always did, but it wasn't her.

GAVIN: Win her back yet?

HUDSON: Haven't seen her yet.

I slipped my phone back into my pocket and stepped out into the sea of nameless faces, heading east toward Allie's apartment.

The last five days had been torture. The Rousseau house had been emptied of all but one occupant. Allie had said goodbye to Juniper. To Caroline. She'd even stopped in at the bar to bid farewell to Gavin. Guess she felt our words at the beach were a sufficient end to whatever we'd become.

I didn't.

The flow of traffic slowed near the corner, and I stopped with the others walking their daily commute, waiting for the signal to clear us to cross.

I pounded the caffeine, then rolled my neck. It was a long-ass drive down from Haven Cove, but it would be worth it. What Allie and I had wasn't just rare, it was extraordinary. It had been from the moment we'd met. Soulmate. Love of my life. Whatever terminology there was still didn't adequately describe the connection.

She existed, and I was hers.

And if it meant moving to New York and begging her forgiveness until my knees were raw, then that's what I would do. I didn't have a lot of experience in the groveling department, but I'd be its fucking CEO for as long as it took. She'd loved me at seventeen—

She never said she still loved you.

But she did. I knew it with the same certainty I felt every time I left the aircraft, knowing that I'd make it back in. I understood her like I did the ocean, and its rhythms and waves, its tides and swells. Allie loved me. She said it with her smiles and her laughter. She screamed it with her body. She whispered it in the middle of the night when she covered me with a blanket and kissed my temple. She revealed her fear of it every time she tried to pick an unnecessary fight. She'd spent every spare minute she could with me in that last month, and I hadn't complained once, because while it may have only been four percent of her day, it was a hundred percent of what she had to give.

Now I was giving her the same.

My phone buzzed.

GAVIN: Your speed is less than impressive.

GAVIN: I have it handled here at home. Go get your dream.

I finished off my coffee and tossed it in the bin, then lifted my phone to type out a response as the light changed and people rushed forward to cross.

A dog barked across the intersection, and I looked up.

And froze on the edge of the curb.

Sadie trotted at Allie's side in a hot-pink harness and matching leash, her tail wagging as they crossed the opposite side of the street.

Allie. My heart started pounding erratically and it had nothing to do with the caffeine.

I immediately pivoted, fighting against the flow of people to keep her in my line of sight.

Her oversize sunglasses hid her eyes, but she was dressed in a close-fitted blue T-shirt, leggings, and tennis shoes, and her hair was already tucked neatly into a high bun—headed to rehearsal.

Fuck, I had her schedule wrong.

Allie adjusted the huge tote on her shoulder, and Eva stepped into view on her other side. Fine, if I had to grovel in front of her sister, I'd manage.

"Excuse me," I said, narrowly missing some guy in a three-piece suit as I walked against the current, desperate to keep my eyes on Allie. "Allie!" I called out, but she didn't hear me.

Eva talked nonstop, but whatever she said made Allie smile as they approached the studio doors, and I paused at the edge of the curb, estimating my chances of crossing traffic unscathed.

"Allie!" I tried again, only to be lost in a chorus of honking cars.

Everett came through the door and threw his arms around Allie, hugging her tight and lifting her off her feet. Allie grinned as he spun her around, wrapping Sadie's leash around them both, and Eva chased the pink nylon and grabbed hold so they didn't go tumbling.

Fine. Everett could hear me beg too. I didn't mind a bigger audience.

Allie laughed as Everett set her down, and the ache in my chest swelled. I didn't have to hear it—just the sight of her happiness started welding the pieces of my broken heart back into shape.

Reagan came through the doors next, holding a giant bouquet of pink and white balloons, then swept Allie into another grin-inducing embrace.

My pocket buzzed, and I absentmindedly reached for my phone as the group disappeared into the MBC building.

Allie was home, healthy, happy, and living out her dream.

What right did I have to fuck with that? To throw her life into upheaval when she'd fought so hard to get it back? Doubt crept in, and determination shoved it back in its place. There was no one on the planet who could love Allie as well as I could.

I glanced down at my phone, expecting to see Gavin's name, and instead receiving the reply I'd waited days for.

NIELSON: What's this I hear about you wanting out of Cape Cod?

My thumbs hovered over the keyboard. Coming here had been impetuous, but there wasn't a lot of room in Allie's life for that, as evidenced by her coming to practice even earlier than she said she normally did. Whatever move I made next had to keep *her* best interests in mind. Not just mine.

I had to fully commit, be the man she not only loved, but deserved. And the man she deserved would be just as driven as she was, just as passionate, just as considerate. We were connected, bound by fate, or luck, and that would never change. No matter how much time passed, or even if she never forgave me holding on to my secrets, I would love Allie Rousseau until the day I died.

Like she'd said, waves came in sets. She was happy here, and I had no choice but to match her energy. I was a dreamer who'd fallen in love with a dreamer, and it was time to stop dreaming and act.

ELLIS: I need to call in that favor.

"You're really not going to tell her?" Gavin sat in the leather armchair of my office four weeks later, spectating as I finished packing yet another box.

"Nope." Allie's absence drained the colors from the sky, the taste from my food, the peace from a hot shower . . . every cliché in the book applied. I'd lost them all, and it was time to go. "The show opens in less than a month, and she needs to stay focused."

"You're just going to . . . move." He reached for the display base-ball on the bookshelf beside him. "Pack up your whole life without so much as talking to her about it? Don't get me wrong, I'm all for you getting the fuck out of here. Chase that dream. Yay, dreams. But you do know her forgiving you requires actually talking to her, right? You have a plan?"

"Right now, my plan is to pick up the phone if she calls—"

"Since when are you the waiting guy?" Gavin sat back in the chair. "Fucking call *her*. Better yet, show up at her door and actually speak to her this time."

I shook my head. "That's what *I* need. Allie needs time to think things through—"

"She's had a month," he interrupted.

"Yeah, well . . . I pulled her out of a burning car and left her sister in it, then didn't tell her because I was too chickenshit to lose her." I put the last book in the box and grabbed the tape roll. "It might take more than a month—or even a year or two—for her to think of me without that particular fact involved." I couldn't fault her for it. "She might never forgive me. Why do you think I pulled that favor?"

"If I did, she can too." He threw the ball up and caught it. "Not that I'm saying you needed forgiveness. You acted like you always do, and because of it, Allie's alive. If you'd gotten there a minute later?"

I closed my eyes against the agonizing imagery that brought up.

"Time was the enemy, Hudson. Not you." He tossed the ball again.

"You didn't speak to me for weeks," I reminded him.

"Weeks, not months, and eventually I did." He repeated the motion, catching the ball every time it came down.

"Sure, after you came to the conclusion that if it had been you, Lina would have lived." Another reality I refused to accept, even for Juniper's sake.

He nodded. "Lina would have lived."

The tape squealed as I sealed the box.

"But as much as I loved that girl," he continued, "it was nothing compared to watching you and Allie." The ball went up and came back down. "And I told her that. Told her to let you hold on to her." He rubbed the bridge of his nose. "I'm sorry, by the way. Not sure I ever said that. I didn't mean to let it slip about the hospital."

"Thanks." I labeled the box with a black marker and set it aside. "I should have told her. I had a million opportunities and chose not to. That's on me. Not you. I'm the one who lost her." My phone vibrated, dancing across the desk, and I caught it before it fell over the edge.

BEACHMAN: Grizzly tonight?

I typed out a quick reply.

ELLIS: Done deal. But not too late. Movers are here in the a.m.

BEACHMAN: Fine, Cinderella. Midnight it is.

"I know you're not used to begging forgiveness, but it requires actually *doing* something," he lectured. "Sacrificing your pride, or your ego—"

"Giving her the space she needs *is* the fucking sacrifice!" I snapped. "She's happy, Gavin. Maybe for the first time in her life. She's back on top of her game. You think I don't want to show up at her door? Barge into her life and throw myself at her mercy? You think it was easy to walk away from her on that street? That *any* of this is about to be easy? I will have to fight my selfish need for her every single day. I will be this close"—I pinched my fingers, leaving an inch of space between them—"to having everything I've dreamed of, and yet so fucking far that I may as well just stay here."

"You're absolutely not staying here." He shook his head.

I gestured to the boxes. "Hence the moving. Allie puts everyone else's needs first, always has, and she's not going to put *mine* first.

If that means I have to watch from a distance as she lives her life without me, then it fucking sucks, but so be it. I love her enough to let her go."

"The if-you-love-something-set-it-free thing is overrated." He set the baseball down. "I still think you should have snatched her off the street four weeks ago, thrown her in the truck, and driven straight to Sitka. Off and gone, happily ever after. Dream place? Check. Dream girl? Check. You could have worked your shit out on the road trip."

"Kidnapping aside," I said slowly, reaching for another box, "you wanted me to drive her to Sitka, where there is no Metropolitan Ballet Company for her to be the badass she is? That's like taking the best quarterback in the NFL to live in Hawaii."

"There are no NFL teams in Hawaii." He looked at me like I'd sprouted wings.

"Exactly. I would never do that to her. She belongs in New York." I dragged the tape across the bottom of the cardboard. "Can we please change the damned subject?"

The door swung open, and I looked over my shoulder as Juniper walked in, Caroline close on her heels, carrying a casserole dish. "Honey, take this to the kitchen, would you please?"

"Yep." Juniper waved, then ran off with the glassware.

"Okay, I brought lasagna." Caroline hung her purse on the coat-tree. "Just need to pop it in around four—" She gawked at Gavin. "Please tell me that you're actually helping him pack and not just sitting there like our brother isn't moving the day after tomorrow."

Gavin shrugged. "It's not like the military isn't sending movers."

"Get up!" Caroline snapped. "Now. Get a box and get packing."

"So bossy," he whined, hefting himself out of the chair.

I didn't fight my grin. This right here was what I was going to miss. The bickering and the laughter. Watching Juniper grow and trying to figure out what she was going to scheme up next so I could get a step ahead of her. I was going to miss my family. They'd only be a visit away, but it wouldn't be the same.

I glanced up at the framed map of Alaska above my desk. Some dreams required action, but others had to wait, so that's what I was going to do. Wait.

Opening the desk drawer, I found the picture of Allie and me that Juniper had pilfered from storage earlier in the summer. My chest cracked open—at least that's what it felt like.

How the hell could I love her like this, need her like air, and not be with her? How did a love like that go to complete and utter waste? She loved me and I loved her, and it still wasn't enough. Time was my only hope of ever getting her back.

I slipped the picture into my back pocket and packed the rest of the drawer's contents in the box.

"I can't believe you're leaving," Caroline muttered, packing books at a speed that made me second-guess my own work ethic. "I mean, I can. I'm happy for you. You deserve everything good there is to have. Tape." She held out her hand.

Stunned and a little frightened, I handed it over. I glanced down at my phone. She'd be here any minute. Perfect timing.

"And we'll be fine." She sealed the box and pushed it over to Gavin. "Make yourself useful and label that. And no, writing *porn* is not a funny way to get back at him."

"You ruin all the fun." Gavin smirked and then absolutely wrote PORN on the side of the box.

"I think Tanner is ready for me to hand over the evening shifts at the café." She built another box, and I busied myself with the next drawer so I didn't get yelled at too. "Which means Juniper won't need a babysitter after school."

"Or I can stay by myself!" Juniper called out from the living room.

"Oh, that's *definitely* not happening." Caroline shook her head.

"Or you could accept some help," I suggested, spotting her car pull up outside. One thing about that woman? She was punctual as fuck.

"I'm not dragging Mom and Dad back here." She pointed the tape gun at Gavin. "And I'm not giving up the café. It's a love-hate relationship, but it's mine—and did you *seriously* put that on the box when I specifically told you not to?"

"I'm not saying you need to bring Mom and Dad back. And I'm definitely not saying you should depend on that one." I gestured at Gavin.

"Rude," he muttered.

"Facts," I retorted, backing out of the office slowly. "I'm saying that there's room in your life, in Juniper's life, for more people to love and support you, if you'll let them. Chances are you'll discover you're doing them a favor too." I reached for the door handle.

"And who would you like me to depend on, Hudson?" Caroline asked, leaning into the doorway.

I opened the door. "You have no idea how perfect your timing is." Or how much it hurt to see her. But this was the right thing for everyone, and she'd promised not to tell Allie what I was doing.

"I do try," she said, tucking a curl behind her ears and balancing a box of packing supplies on her hip as she walked in. She set the box down on the floor and headed straight for Caroline, holding out her hand. "Hi, Caroline. It's been a while."

Caroline glanced at me, then took her hand cautiously. "Hi, Anne. I thought you'd gone back to New York with your sisters."

"Actually, I decided to stay and get my very small, very rusty legal practice off the ground right here."

"Aunt Anne!" Juniper came flying out of the living room, raced right by me, and slammed into Anne's side.

"Hi, Juniper." Anne hugged her right back. "Ugh, I've missed you."

Juniper immediately launched into telling Anne all about her first week at Madeline's and how she wasn't sure her new teacher could ever compare to Eloise but she'd give her a shot, and I hung back and watched as Caroline laughed.

Yeah, they were going to be all right, and that was all that mattered.

CHAPTER THIRTY-EIGHT

Allie

ReeseOnToe: OMG. You look divine! I can't wait to see the show in two weeks!

"Good morning, Allie!" Jennifer, one of the new corps members, waved happily as she passed me in the hallway. "Hi, Sadie!"

"Good morning, Jennifer," I replied, wrapping Sadie's leash over my wrist, then pulling the frayed edges of my worn black hoodie over my hand as I pushed against the current of dancers headed to class.

I should already be in there, warming up, leading from the front as Vasily expected, but his one condition for Sadie's presence was that she remain in Kenna's office when I was in the studio, which worked out fine because Kenna loved her.

"Don't be late," Everett said, darting a kiss on my cheek as he rushed past.

"She's always fucking late," Charlotte muttered, shooting me a glare as she followed, a gaggle of her gossiping minions trailing after. "Doesn't matter when you're a Rousseau, I guess."

I stiffened my shoulders, but presented a pleasing smile, as Vasily would expect one of the leading members of his company to do. Being back was easy, normal, and I fell into the routine as easily as I fell into the masks I'd left here nearly five months ago. In fact, I'd been back six weeks and it felt like I'd never left at all.

Which was part of the problem.

It was the same, but I wasn't. Where I'd once seen perfection and excellence, now all I saw was dirt and deceit. This place was plated gold, and now that I'd scratched its pristine surface and seen what really lay beneath, it had lost its shine.

Or maybe nothing shone quite as bright without Hudson flashing his grin every now and again. I breathed through the immediate sting of pain that came whenever I thought about him, which was about every minute or so unless I was dancing. I'd spent more hours in the studio trying to hide from my heartbreak than I had training to get back here.

Eva appeared next, darting out of the corps dressing room as I approached. Worry immediately lined her forehead. "Do you want me to take Sadie to Kenna so you can go?"

"No." I shook my head and smiled at my sister, but I could tell it didn't reach my eyes. "I get there when I get there."

Her worry lines deepened. "Right."

I squeezed her hand in reassurance, then sent her on her way. I simply didn't care if I was late. It would be frowned upon, but no one was going to do anything. If Eva was late, well, the consequences weren't worth risking it.

The dancers sped by, all doing their best to beat the clock and get into the studio before Eloise arrived.

The hallway cleared as Sadie and I passed the last of the dressing rooms, then entered the stairwell and descended to the third floor. We popped out near the strength training center, and Sadie wagged her tail as we approached the entrance to Kenna's office.

"Oh, Alessandra," Maxim called out from the end of the hall, lifting his hand.

So close. I'd been so close to not having to deal with him, or his father, this morning. Every time I saw them, I thought of Juniper, and my anger nearly burned through my faux civility. "What can I do for you?" I asked, my hand on Kenna's doorknob.

"Sienna is looking for you." He arched a brow just like his father. "You need to sign your contract."

"I'll see if I can find time to stop by her office before leaving." I smiled and gave the same response I did every day since returning. It wasn't like I needed the money.

"See that you do. Not being on contract makes you a liability." He narrowed his eyes and moved to step between me and Kenna's door, only to retreat when he spotted Sadie already there. "We're two weeks away from performance, and my father may make allowances for you, given his fondness for your mother, but your refusal to sign has become as circumspect as the offers still pouring into this office on your behalf."

"Noted." My smile didn't slip even an inch. "Now, if you'll excuse me, I'm going to be late to take class."

He huffed a sigh of annoyance, then turned on his heel and headed for the elevators.

I knocked on Kenna's door twice, then walked in after she said to.

"Good morning, Sadie-kins." She leaned down and ruffled Sadie's ears, then looked me over with the same appraisal that had become her custom in the last six weeks. "Did you get *any* sleep last night?"

"A few hours." I let Sadie's leash go, and she immediately trotted to the bed Kenna kept under her window. "You?"

"Matthias was home, so I managed a couple." A smile curved her mouth, and she walked over to her desk, then picked up a stack of envelopes. "I grabbed these off Sienna's desk before Vasily could see them. Offers from"—she tilted her head and read the return addresses—"Atlanta, Sydney, Paris, Vancouver, and yet again . . . San Francisco." She tested the weight of the envelopes. "And they don't feel like contracts."

"They're offers to come for specific roles." I walked forward, then sat on the edge of her desk.

"Freelance," Kenna noted. "All of the fun, none of the politics. Dance in, dance out." She handed me the stack. "I'm starting to wonder if you *want* Vasily to see them."

I stared at the envelopes. Word had spread that I wasn't signing, and whatever offers weren't on paper were flooding my email. Misery surged through me, sitting on my chest and making it hard to draw breath. "I hate it here," I whispered.

"I know." Kenna sat back on the desk next to me.

"I miss him, and I hate it here." My thumbs pressed into the stack, denting the envelopes. "Yes, he kept the truth from me, but I kept it from Caroline. We were all doing the wrong things for what we thought were the right reasons, but he's the only one who got punished."

"You're doing a good job of punishing yourself," Kenna said. "You could stop the self-flagellation and just call the man."

"After six weeks of silence?" I shook my head. "He probably hates me for the way I walked out on him."

"You called him out on his bullshit and broke off a relationship on its predetermined date. You didn't fuck his best friend, Allie." Kenna drummed her fingers on the desk's edge. "That man is in love with you. If a decade apart didn't kill it, then six weeks hasn't come close to even wounding it."

I looked over at her wall of diplomas and accolades, then through one of her windows into the training area, where two members of the corps were working out. It was all part of the vicious cycle of dance, injure, recover, return.

And I was stuck in it.

"What good would calling him do?" I shrugged. "One of the reasons I walked away is because he'd hate it here." I wasn't even sure that going home to Hudson at night would make this place better, but at least I'd be happy for ten hours a day, even if eight of them were sleeping.

"So do you," Kenna countered. "You're not exactly *living*, Allie. You're just . . . breathing. And I love you, but I don't have time for you to wallow in my office, especially when the solution is a call, a drive, or a flight away. You could be happy in the next ten minutes if you walked back to the dressing room, picked up your phone, and dialed his number. But you insist on suffering, and making the rest of us watch. It's . . . disappointing. Why are you brave for everyone but yourself?"

My eyebrows rose. "I mean, tell me how you really feel."

"I feel like there's a reason you haven't signed a contract, and until you're ready to actually talk about that, the rest of this is just whining." She reached back over her desk for a clipboard. "And I'm happy to listen to you whine over margaritas, but my mother is going to kick your ass for being late again, so either go . . ." She looked me in the eye. "Or *go*."

Yes. That. My stomach tensed.

"I have my own role," I blurted. "It's the dream. You don't walk away from the dream." But she was right. There was a reason I wouldn't sign. I'd worked so hard to get back here, and now all I wanted . . . was to go. I wanted Hudson. Being scared to admit it wasn't going to change the fact that I was happier with him than I'd ever been on a stage.

"You do if the dream changes." Kenna tucked the clipboard under her arm. "Dreams aren't stagnant, Allie. They grow. They shift."

My heart started to pound. "Vasily would kill me for walking away two weeks before a show."

"Fuck him." Kenna shrugged.

"Eva needs—"

"To grow up." She backed away toward the gym door in her office.

"But you . . ." I shook my head.

"I am *glorious*. I have a career I love, a man I can't get enough of, a world-class brain, and an enviable designer handbag collection. You need to stop hiding behind what everyone else wants, because you're the only one responsible for your happiness. You may have told your mother off, but you're sure living the life she chose for you."

I clutched the envelopes. "I still love to dance."

"That stack you're holding says you don't have to be here to do that. Allie, you can have *everything* you want if you'd just get out of your own way." She reached for the handle beneath the glass panel of the door, then took a deep breath and gave me a sad smile. "I'm going to do the job that I adore"—she twisted the handle—"and I hope you do the same. I don't want to find you in this office when I return. Go, Allie. Be happy."

Eight and a half hours later, I stood on Hudson's front porch with Sadie and knocked.

Again.

I breathed through the nausea churning in my stomach, clutched Sadie's leash, and rang the bell.

She whined.

"He's probably just at work," I told her, scratching the top of her head and walking toward the closest window. This was *not* how the big grand gesture was supposed to work. I'd rented a car, driven all the way here with an obscene amount of luggage, and he wasn't even home.

I cupped my hands along the glass, then leaned in to see inside the house. My stomach pitched. It was empty. No bookshelves. No soft leather armchair. No framed map. Just hardwood and pristine walls.

Oh my God.

Panic kicked in as I backed away. Where could he possibly be? He wouldn't have moved in with Caroline—

Caroline. She'd know where he was. I got Sadie into the back seat of the rented SUV, then drove straight to the café and ignored the side-eye from a few year-rounders when I walked in with a dog. I spotted Caroline behind the counter immediately.

"Where is he?" I asked, walking straight through the center of the café.

Caroline looked up, as did the young man at her side, who she appeared to be teaching. Her blue eyes flared wide. "Allie?"

"Where is he?" I stopped on the far side of the fifties-style counter. "Because I packed all of my things, and I walked away from my company, and I rented a car and drove all the way here, and his house is empty." My throat started to close, and I arched my neck.

"I wondered when you'd show up," Caroline said. "Tanner, why don't you grab Allie a glass of lemonade."

"Sure thing." The young man grabbed a glass from beneath the counter, and within thirty seconds, I was chugging to save my life.

"Thank you," I said once half the glass was gone. "How's Juniper?"

Caroline softened. "She's great. She'd probably love to see you since she's at your house with Anne right now. You know you could have called."

"I know." I nodded and gripped the glass a little harder. "I just thought it would be so much more poignant to show up and surprise him, then launch into the myriad of reasons we shouldn't be together, but then I'd bring it back to the only reason we should, which is that we belong . . . together." I winced. "It sounded way better in my head. Look, I know you hate me for sneaking into Juniper's life, and you can't stand my family, or our last name, but I really can't either. Every time someone says it, I just think of my mother now. And I'm sure you can think of a million other people you'd rather see Hudson with—"

"Do you love my brother?" she asked, interrupting my ramble.

I startled, and my gaze snapped to Tanner, who was staring like I needed medical attention. That's when I realized the entirety of the café was listening to me. Awesome. "I think that's something Hudson should hear first."

Caroline nodded. "I don't hate you, Allie. Even when I was furious with all of you for sneaking around my back with Juniper, I never hated you. I'm just sorry you came all this way."

My stomach pitched and I scrambled to school my expression, to hold on to any vestige of dignity, but I'd left all my masks in New York, and now there was just . . . me. "It's too late, isn't it? I waited too long and blew my chance." My eyes prickled, but I *refused* to cry. Even if I had to sweep the remnants of my heart off this linoleum floor, I wasn't crying in front of Caroline.

"Oh, Allie." She came around the counter and squeezed my hand, leash and all. "You could be ninety years old, and it would never be too late for Hudson. I'm so dang glad one of you has come to your senses. Of course I'll tell you where he is. I just meant that it's a shame you came all this way, because you drove the wrong direction."

I nearly dropped the glass. "I what?"

CHAPTER THIRTY-NINE

Hudson

NYFouette92: I'd check the website because it looks like the cast sheet has changed again. MBC needs to get their shit together.

Three and a half weeks after unpacking the last box, I thought about Allie as I drove past Swan Lake on my way to what was now my home.

Not that I only thought about her around the lake. No, I thought about her while I unpacked, while I hiked the trailheads behind my house, when I woke up, while I was at work, and every second I lay in bed before falling asleep. The only time I didn't think about Allie was when I was in the water, which made me volunteer for every possible duty.

I'd only been here twenty-seven days and already had a reputation of being reckless, but that note had probably transferred with my file.

Every muscle ached as I pulled into the long driveway that I'd probably curse myself for choosing every time I had to snowplow in the coming months, but I loved the privacy of my house in the woods. For the first time in years, my life felt like . . . mine again.

My brow furrowed at the sight of a new red SUV parked dead center in front of my two-car garage. Temp plates were registered in Massachusetts.

I groaned as I put my car in park behind it. As much as I missed Juniper and Caroline, I was not up for a surprise visit, nor did I feel like sharing my space with Gavin or showing Mom and Dad around a town I wasn't quite familiar with yet. Not to mention I was supposed to be on an airplane tomorrow morning.

"For fuck's sake, do none of them know how to use a phone?" I muttered.

Every muscle in my body ached as I got out of the truck, protesting the hours I'd spent in a rather angry ocean, but I pocketed my keys and trudged up the steps to the red wraparound porch that had made me fall for this place hook, line, and sinker. No one was waiting at the front door, so I made my way around to the back.

And then I ceased to breathe, and blinked my eyes to be sure I wasn't hallucinating.

"Good girl." Allie's back was to me as she took the ball from Sadie's mouth and hurled it into the backyard. The little golden raced down the deck steps and scrambled after her target.

My heart jolted at the sound of her voice, then pounded when I recognized the faded, raggedy hoodie she was currently wearing.

"Allie?" I asked quietly, like she was a specter that would vanish if I said it too loudly.

She jumped and turned toward me with her hand splayed over the Rip Curl logo on her chest. "Damn, Hudson, you scared me!"

"Scared you? I live here." My gaze raked over her, taking in every detail I'd missed over the last two months. There were no noticeable changes other than the fact that somehow she looked even better. Healthier. Her cheeks were flushed from the cold, the circles under her eyes had disappeared, and her eyes were bright, but she twisted Lina's ring around her finger nervously as she looked me over too. Hurt to say it, but leaving me looked really good on her.

"Well, yeah." She pulled her hair over one shoulder as Sadie ran up the stairs, wagging her tail. Allie grabbed the ball and threw it again, earning the same result. "But I've been here a couple of hours, so you startled me, that's all."

"Hours?" What the hell was going on? "Are you okay? Is everything okay at home?"

"I'm fine," she assured me with a shaky smile. "And I think everyone's doing the same as they were when I left a week ago. Hope you don't mind that Caroline gave me your address." She twisted Lina's ring and took a deep breath. "Hudson, my mother isn't teaching at some exclusive boarding school."

"She isn't?" The subject change gave me whiplash, but she had my full attention.

Allie shook her head. "No. She has frontotemporal dementia with primary progressive aphasia. She's been in the assisted living facility she chose for about two years, and Anne has been in control of all her affairs. No one knows. Just Anne, and Eva, and Eloise, and Kenna, and Caroline . . . I told her so that she could have Juniper tested for the gene. The three of us are clear, but Lina never knew to get tested. And now you know. Anyway, the last time she left was for the *Giselle* performance, and she's gone downhill pretty fast since then."

"Holy shit, Allie." My heart broke for her. She'd been dealing with that the entire time? "I'm so sorry."

"Thank you." She twisted the ring again. "It's fine. I mean, it's not fine, but it's just a fact of my life at this point, and I figured telling you was the first step to letting you in. All the way."

"All the way," I repeated, my brain spinning to wrap itself around the concept that she was here, that she was telling me things I didn't have to pry out of her.

"Did you realize it took a week to drive here?" she asked.

"Yes," I said slowly. "Why did you drive all the way from Massachusetts?"

"Because that's where I bought the car," she said equally slowly. "Did you notice? It's the first car I've ever bought. It's red." Her smile widened.

"Yeah, I noticed." I walked two steps closer, then shoved my hands in my pockets to keep from reaching for her. "But why did you drive here? And what are you going to do with a car in Manhattan?"

Her smile slipped. "I didn't want to put Sadie on a plane." She looked down at her hands. "And because I was afraid if I called, you would tell me not to come. So, I bought a car, and we drove. And took a ferry."

This time when Sadie ran back, I threw the ball for her after a quick scratch behind her ears. "The chances of me telling you not to come are zero, and less than zero if you picked up the phone."

"So, I should have called," she said softly. "Look, if you're busy, or if there's someone you're expecting—"

"Someone I'm expecting? Like I've just moved on in the past couple months? Like there's anyone on the fucking planet who could possibly take your place?" I tipped her chin up so I could look in her eyes. "Is that what you did? Went back to New York and tried to replace me?"

"Of course not." Her eyes narrowed, and she jerked her chin out of my grasp. "I just *drove* here from the East Coast. I hardly think that's conducive to having a boyfriend."

"Oh, for fuck." I ripped my cover off my head and folded the blue cap, sticking it into the back pocket of my pants. "You have to help me out and tell me what you're doing here, love, because I'm thirty seconds from carrying you into my room and making good on that little plan to keep you in my bed."

"That sounds great." She nodded.

I backed up a step. "Don't screw with me."

"Do you think I'd drive all the way here to *not* screw with you?" A corner of her mouth rose, and I was a goner.

Three steps later, I had her back against the wall, my hands in her hair and my tongue in her mouth. I kissed her like I'd been thinking about her every second since she'd left, using every ounce of skill I had to steal her breath.

She pulled me closer and pushed up into the kiss, slanting her head in that little way she had of telling me to deepen it, so I did. She tasted like lemonade and the beach, hot summer days with hotter nights, and I groaned at the feeling of finally being home. I wanted her bare skin under my hands, her soft thighs locked around my hips—

I ripped my mouth away from hers and backed across the deck to put some much-needed space between us, noting that Sadie had given up on us entirely and was now happily curled up near the door.

"Why did you stop?" Allie pushed off the wall.

"Nope." I held out my hand. "You stay there until you tell me why you're here."

"Right." She slid her hands into the back pockets of her curve-hugging jeans, and my resolve unraveled to a single thread. "I'm here because I want you."

I gripped the deck railing and begged my body to obey the order to stay. "You're going to have to be a little more specific than that, because it seems like a really long trip for a few orgasms." I refused to get my hopes up, not when losing her destroyed me every time she walked away. If this was just a visit, I needed to know.

"How much more detail do you need when my car is packed to the brim with everything I own, Hudson?"

Yes. And *boom*, my mouth was on hers again. Need barreled down my spine like a freight train as I kissed her over and over, nipping her bottom lip, then sucking on it before licking back into her mouth to retrace every curve. God, I'd missed her. I needed her. I loved her. She wasn't the wave or the pylon; she was the entire ocean, as beautiful as she was impossible to fathom. But damn if I didn't want to spend the rest of my life figuring her out.

Fuck. I broke the kiss and backed off again, but there wasn't enough room on this deck—hell, in this whole world—to keep me away from her when she said things like that. "You're supposed to be in New York, rehearsing for a ballet created *for* you, that's supposed to open tomorrow night."

"Correct." She nodded, dropping her gaze to my mouth. "But I'm not, because I want to be here with you."

"Yeah, no." I shook my head. "That doesn't check out. You don't walk away from ballets created for you. I have a plane ticket for tomorrow and everything."

Her smile stopped my heart. "You were coming to see me?"

"Of course I was coming to see you. I wasn't going to miss your opening night. The opening night you're *missing*. And stop looking at me like that."

"Like what?" She stepped closer. "Like I want you and finally did something about it? Like I picked up my life and moved it to *Alaska*?"

"Yep. All of that." I could have her in bed in under twenty seconds if I had my keys ready.

"Have to say, it's pretty sexy that you finally went for it." She looked out over the backyard. "I mean, Sitka." That damned smile was going to be the death of me. "You got your dream, Hudson." She took a step my direction.

"Yes and no. *You're* my dream, and I put an entire continent between us in order to give you space and time." I pointed toward Sadie. "So you stand over there and explain why you just walked away from everything you worked your ass off for."

She arched an eyebrow at me. "Fine, we'll do it your way. I went back to New York and tried like hell to not think about you, which I failed at, miserably. I went into the Company and . . ." Silence reigned as she looked out over the forest and fought for words. "And felt like I had to be a million different things to a million different people, none of which were actually me. I sat there in the locker room as the other dancers buzzed around me, and all I could think was that I only feel like I'm truly myself, no pretenses or armor, when I'm with you. I hated being there." Her entire body moved with the breath she took. "So, I left without signing my contract. I don't care who dances in *Equinox*, because what does any of it matter if I'm miserable?"

"You are too good to hide out here with me." It killed me to say it. "The nearest professional company is something like six hundred miles away, Allie."

"I'm not hiding, Hudson, I'm living. Hopefully with you, though I'm starting to wonder if I overestimated your take-you-however-I-can-get-you mantra." She folded her arms.

"You can't quit. Not over me. I refuse to let that happen. Balance, yes. Quit? No."

She blinked. "Oh, I'm not quitting. I have offers from just about every company I could ever want to dance at."

"None of which are here." Holy shit, was I actually trying to talk the love of my life *out* of being with me?

"Of course not. I'll be gone for about three weeks at a time for up to three to four times a year, depending on what roles I'm interested in. I'm not signing with a company. I'm officially freelance." She shrugged. "You get to live your dream, and I get to live mine. Best part is we can do it together. I just need some practice space and to order some equipment. If you're okay with me living here. If not, I can find a place nearby and we can take it slow."

"Slow?" I shook my head. "Allie, I've loved you for eleven years. Anything less than me waking up next to you every morning would feel fucking glacial."

Her smile lit up her whole face. "Then wake up to me every morning."

There had to be a catch. "What about Eva?"

"She needs to find her own sunlight, and you know Anne decided to stay at the cape to be near Juniper." She tilted her head. "Any other reservations?"

"Besides the obvious?"

"Lina," she whispered.

I nodded, silently preparing to have my heart ripped out.

"I don't despise you," she admitted softly. "Obviously, because I'm here. I'm sorry I said that. It took about three hours for me to realize that my mother put you in a no-win situation and we both suffered for it. And I, of all people, understand what it's like to get caught up in a lie." She started twisting Lina's ring again. "I thought about it, really sat with what it would be like to look at you every day—other than the obvious appeal—and asked myself if the fact that you played a role in one of my tragedies overruled the simple, unshakable truth that I love you, and it doesn't. It's not your fault that Lina died, Hudson. You just happened to be there. And because you were, I'm alive."

My whole body tensed. "Say it again."

"It's not your—"

"Not that part." I closed the distance between us.

"Oh." She smiled and wrapped her arms around my neck. "I love you. I'm always going to love you. This is me holding on. I don't want five minutes—I want a lifetime."

"Every day. Every night. You and me." I lowered my forehead to hers and let the perfection of it slide through me and settle deep in my bones. "No one walks away. Not ever."

"That's what I'm asking." She brushed her lips against mine. "Can you do that?"

"Yeah. I can do that." I lifted her into my arms, and she locked her ankles behind my back. "I was born to do exactly that."

EPILOGUE

Allie

Five years later

The Metropolitan Opera House buzzed with palpable excitement as we made our way to our seats. I glanced up at the family box, which was no longer our family's, and smiled at the bright-eyed boy looking down at the orchestra pit with eager anticipation.

"Homesick?" Hudson asked as he led me down the back row, straight toward the center, his fingers laced with mine.

"No," I replied.

"Don't lie," Kenna lectured from behind us. "You know you can't find those bagels you love in Washington, or wherever it is you two live right now."

"You know damn well where we live," I retorted as we approached the center seat where Caroline sat with Gavin and Anne. Hudson had been stationed at Cape Disappointment for the last two years, and it was our favorite so far. Though I often missed our house in Alaska too.

"This is us, baby." Kenna pointed to their seats, then did a double take at her husband. "I know you are not texting work right now. Tell them I don't care who needs to be cut open—you are *mine* for the evening, Matthias."

"Just checking in with the sitter, Ken." He tucked his phone in the pocket of his suit coat, unbuttoned the top button, and sat. "He's fine, by the way."

"I know that because I texted her from the lobby." Kenna took the seat next to him, and I left one empty before sitting beside Hudson. "She probably thinks we're insane."

"Or just overprotective parents," I countered.

"No date?" Hudson leaned forward and looked past Caroline and Anne to Gavin.

"Eh." He shrugged. "Mind if I borrow yours?"

"Yes." Hudson sat back and slipped his hand onto my thigh. "Where are Miles and Tyler?"

A teenage girl with red hair startled in front of us as she saw me, then quickly turned around and took her seat.

"Ty's backstage with the girls," Caroline answered. "They're all nervous." She looked my way. "Did you get to slip backstage?"

I nodded with a grin. "She looks fantastic, and super calm."

"Miles has a deposition in Boston." Anne smiled and color rose in her cheeks. "But he'll be home tomorrow. You guys want your room, right, Allie? Because that's the one I made up."

"Absolutely." I nodded. Tomorrow kicked off the one week we'd all cleared in our schedules to spend at the beach house. Mom had passed over almost four years ago, but we still kept her rules.

I glanced at the empty seat next to me.

"She'll be here." Hudson brushed his lips over my temple.

"Punctuality is not her strong suit," Kenna reminded me, then arched her neck to look behind us. "But look who made it!"

"As if we'd miss it." Everett leaned over and smacked a kiss on my cheek. "Give us a second and we'll make our way around." His wedding ring flashed under the lights as he reached for Michael's hand, and they walked toward the end of the aisle.

"Not even a twinge of homesickness?" Hudson asked, his fingers stroking the top of my thigh.

"I performed here last year," I reminded him, turning my head so I could steal a quick kiss. "And you're my home. Best of both worlds."

He leaned in and deepened the kiss a step beyond what would be considered appropriate for the Met, and I reveled in every second of it. I would never get tired of kissing this man.

"Ugh. You two are nauseating." Eva slipped past Kenna and sank into her seat, the plastic wrap surrounding her bouquet crackling.

"And you were almost late." Peace settled in my soul, the same way it always did when we managed to get ourselves under one roof.

"It hasn't started yet, and therefore I am still on time," Eva argued. "Did everyone bring flowers? How many bouquets does one girl need?"

"I've counted six so far," Gavin answered.

"Sounds right." Hudson adjusted the roses in his lap to protect the blooms. "Caroline, are you okay? You look like you're going to puke."

"I'm fine." Caroline nodded, drumming her fingertips on the armrest between them. "Just nervous for her. It's not every day a little local studio gets invited to perform at the Met."

"She'll do great," I promised Caroline.

"Relax, it's in her genes," Eva added, then turned to me. "Want the latest Company gossip? We soloists hear it all. Oh, and did anyone grab a program?"

Kenna sighed and set an extra program in Eva's lap.

"No on the gossip." I shook my head. "But I'm glad you're entertained."

The young woman ahead of us turned in her seat, then stared at me for three awkward seconds before clearing her throat. "I'm so sorry to bug you, but you look like Alessandra Rousseau."

I smiled. "Alessandra Ellis, actually, but yes. That's me."

Hudson's hand flexed on my thigh, and I caught a glimpse of his dimple popping from the corner of my eye.

"Oh my God. I love you. I watch your performances all the time," the teen gushed.

"That's very kind of you. Thank you. What's your name?" I asked.

"Celine." Her face lit up, and her gaze caught on Eva. "And you're Eva! I follow you, and I'm absolutely in love with the series you did on the differences between all the different brands of pointe shoes."

"Thanks." Eva flashed a grin.

"It's lovely to meet you, Celine," I said. "I hope you enjoy the performance."

"You guys are legends," she whispered, then turned around.

Hudson leaned in and brushed his lips over my ear. "I fucking love when you say your name almost as much as when you say mine."

Heat immediately flushed my skin. "Behave. It's the Met." It had taken me all of three seconds to decide to take his name when we got married two years ago. I was simply done being a Rousseau.

"I don't recall you saying anything about propriety when we were in the dressing room last year," he whispered, his fingers sliding toward the hem of my short black dress. "In fact, I remember a lot of you asking for more, and harder, and *faster* at one point."

"I love you." And now I kind of wanted to tug him backstage for a repeat performance.

"I love you more. You're perfect, Allie. You know that, right?" Sea green eyes locked with mine, and I lost track of my thoughts.

"Awh, look!" Eva rustled the program. "Haven Cove Contemporary Dance, and there's her name!"

The lights went down, and Caroline started rocking in her seat.

Anne took her left hand.

I reached over Hudson's lap and took her right.

The curtain rose, and excitement bubbled through my chest like I was the one about to take the stage. My smile widened to impossible proportions as Juniper appeared with the rest of her class.

She was *flawless.*

ABOUT THE AUTHOR

Photo © 2022 Katie Marie Seniors

Rebecca Yarros is the #1 *New York Times*, *USA Today*, and *Wall Street Journal* bestselling author of over twenty novels including *Fourth Wing* and *In the Likely Event*, with multiple starred *Publishers Weekly* reviews and a *Kirkus* Best Book of the Year. She loves military heroes and has been blissfully married to hers for over twenty years. She's the mother of six children, and is currently surviving the teenage years with two of her four hockey-playing sons. When she's not writing, you can find her at the hockey rink or sneaking in some guitar time while guzzling coffee. She and her family live in Colorado with their stubborn English bulldogs, two feisty chinchillas, and a Maine coon cat named Artemis, who rules them all.

Having fostered then adopted their youngest daughter, Rebecca is passionate about helping children in the foster system through her nonprofit, One October.

To catch up on Rebecca's latest releases and upcoming novels, visit www.RebeccaYarros.com.